To Joe –
Best wishes
5/6/04

A Man of War

By

David R. Lusk

PublishAmerica
Baltimore

First printing

ISBN: 1-59129-558-0
PUBLISHED BY PUBLISHAMERICA BOOK PUBLISHERS
www.publishamerica.com
Baltimore

Printed in the United States of America

To my children Kindy and Vilay—
I hope that you're half as proud of me as I am of you.

Acknowledgments

A special acknowledgment must be given to my brother, Louis Lusk, for the countless hours he too put into this book. Anytime I needed an idea, an anecdote, or advice on physics, he provided it, even going so far as writing the initial drafts for several entire chapters. Without his editing, researching, proof-reading and general cheerleading, this book would never be.

Prologue

Navanh Mental Hospital
Vientiane, Asia
Terra
Sons of Terra Occupied Zone

December 15, 2661

I truly am glad they let me come back to Earth. I'm also glad that I can use that term again. Those of us who grow up here all call it that, but most others in the Charted Territories would look down on that term as provincial and uneducated. We know better though; we know that Terra is but a label for one planet among millions in this galaxy while Earth is the birthplace of humanity. It's also my home. I started here and I'll end here, thank you. Likely sooner than later at that.

Most others in the Charted Territories would also say that the planet is under the control of a lunatic breakaway group; rabid fanatics dedicated to restoring a way of life lost centuries ago. Perhaps they are wrong about that as well, I will no longer sit in judgment on such things.

In most ways, things haven't changed from the way they were when I was growing up. Sons of Terra or Terran Dominion; it seems to make very little difference to the general population. Funny how little most people really care about who claims to have power over them. All across the Charted Territories there are planets that have changed political hands literally dozens of times in the last few decades, yet the people there just go on living; ignoring this grand game of crowns that is played out around them. It's as though life has a momentum all its own, one that cannot be quickly redirected or altered by something so insignificant and trivial as a change in planetary government.

It's hard to know where to start this thing, really. It seems almost pointless. Somehow the doctors think that by writing my story down I'll be able to put it all in perspective and cure myself. They assure me that not only are they interested in knowing my whole story, but also that in revealing it to them

I'll reveal my own way out of this nightmare. Dispensing such brilliance as that, I see now why they must take so many years of schooling. Perhaps they don't realize exactly how well I know my past, myself, and my current state of mind. They don't understand how well I remember things. Indeed, how can most people understand what it's like?

A memory such as mine is both blessing and curse. To be able to look back over the many years and events of one's life and pick out all but the most minuscule of details; it's something by and large considered a gift of deity. In fact, Jonny used to say he was jealous that I could always review every move and mistake that I made in training so quickly and accurately. He said that was what really helped me learn combat applications and strategies so much faster than he ever could. He said a lot of things that might have been true.

I've told God how much I miss him; I wonder if He's heard.

Memory's a funny thing, though. I'm still apt to forget people's names, important anniversaries, the grocery list, which girl I was supposed to meet at seven and which at nine, and the myriad other minutia that impact us from day to day. I had average grades in primary and secondary school (which struck me then, and now, as a total bore and a complete waste of time), and I do not remember every word that I read.

The experiences, however, the things I do, the things I am a part of, my kinesthetic sensations; those I cannot forget. Of a certainty, I can, at any time, pick out the happiest moments and memories from my life and relive them in detail, complete with vibrant colors, background noises, and the emotions of the moment. Don't get me wrong either, there were happy moments; but just as certain as I can recall the good times, I can never quite force myself to forget the times of pain, of sorrow, of hurt and anguish. Though I can recall with crystal clarity the excitement and adventure of my first kiss, I can also, in unguarded moments, feel all the loneliness and pain, the heart-rending emptiness and loss I felt the day that I, alone and without any source of familial support, sat by my mother's bed and watched her take one last breath and die.

I find that the two memories fail to balance out.

Perhaps if I had lived differently, I would be more willing to thank God for this boon. I do not find any such thanks forthcoming. A man of war for too long, I pray each day that he takes this cup from me. I beg for some divine form of amnesia every night before I sleep. Those nights that I actually have slept, I have awoken to find my prayers unanswered still. Maybe, as my priest is wont to say, it's just that the answer is simply "no." In any event, I question God as to what purpose is served by this torture. He has yet to respond in any fashion that I find acceptable.

My doctor assures me that I am not alone—not by a long shot—in returning from Gottenheim with waking nightmares. Post-traumatic stress disorders abound after any war. Fortunately for most others, more traditional therapies have generally been successful, and they are finding their much deserved relief. Someday soon, I'm repeatedly told, our psychiatrists will perfect the means of accurately controlling the peptides and neurotransmitters responsible for memories. Supposedly this will give them the ability to treat this malicious, subconscious reliving of traumatic events in a new and effective manner; a great boon to all suffering from disorders such as mine. Personally, I don't trust a word they say anymore, and I'll believe it when I see it. When they can hand me something far more concrete than words; when they can let me sleep without the self-loathing and the images, the faces and the voices; then I'll trust them more. Until then, I must strive to remain content with the less effective, rather addictive, alternatives provided by the resident pharmacist.

I suppose I must also submit to doing other forms of therapy, like writing this. I'm not actually certain why I decided to try this. Perhaps some part of me still believes that once the whole story is told, a design or purpose will be found that will make sense of the incomprehensible, and see a divine pattern in the seemingly capricious events of life.

Truthfully, things were not always as they are now, and likely there is some point in looking back at all of it and putting it into some form of perspective. Maybe I'm prejudicing my own memories, insisting that there were more bad times than good, and that they were of greater magnitude. There was, in fact, a time when I dreamt of glory, when I believed I was destined for greatness.

The intense memories of the happy days of childhood, at least, are not denied me as they are to so many others. Numerous things become skewed when looking back with more educated, adult eyes, but it's a simple thing, really, to return to that time when the future was bright, the universe kind, and life just one grand adventure that needed to be lived!

Chapter One

North Vancouver, North America
Terra
Terran Dominion

July 1, 2632

I was five years old the day I first saw a Man O'War. Given how things turned out, I would have to say it was a bit of a defining moment in my life. I've been all over a good portion of this galaxy since then, and God alone knows all that's happened out there, yet still, in all that time, nothing has ever truly overshadowed my memory of that astonishing moment. I think nothing ever shall, and, in any event, I doubt I would welcome anything that possibly could.

As I recall, the sun was shining brightly, gleaming off of battle finished metal; a slight breeze was stirring the leaves on the nearby and heavily laden apple tree. A hint of fresh oil wafted my way, and I could smell the fresh bread my mother was baking. I watched intently as a Diablo crashed to the ground, the dust that was kicked up from the soft sand that cushioned its fall swirling up in whirlpool eddies all around it. Thunder rolled in the distance, which I thought was a nice touch given how the mighty machine had fallen, cut down by artificial lightning and all. Looking back with a greater experience I'd immediately know it to be a bit odd for a clear summer day. Nevertheless, at that young age, it increased the grand drama of the whole situation immensely, filling me with a vicarious sense of total victory.

The triumphant Battle Hammer, having just felled the other mighty Man O'War, slowly circled its dispatched opponent. Squeaks and creeks reverberated with each step the Battle Hammer took, itself sporting the wounds of many such deadly encounters. In fact, of the two machines, the conquered one looked to be in far better condition than the conqueror. Nevertheless, it was the Battle Hammer standing triumphant. It stopped near the head of the other Man O'War and ponderously raised a metal foot. In that brief moment, massive limb poised to crush the Diablo's head, the pilot had a change of heart. Instead of squashing the Diablo's cockpit into a metallic Rorschach inkblot test, the Battle Hammer reared back its mighty leg and began kicking sand on the unmoving form of its foe. Also spitting on it.

"Stop it!" Jonny yelled as he pushed me toward the edge of the sandbox. Shocked fury lent his muscles strength beyond their five years. "You'll get sand in the gears!" He snatched up his precious Diablo and frantically began rubbing off the surface dirt, horrendously scratching the formerly pristine paint job, and trying to shake out any granules that may have worked their way inside. Thunder rolled again, louder and closer. "I'm gonna tell Mom what you did!"

"Wait," I begged, "I'm sorry."

Of course, I wasn't really sorry, what five year old ever is? It's not like it mattered anyway. As soon as the dog got a hold of Jonny's new Diablo, it'd have a lot worse than sand in it—just like my teddy bear. Having Mom give me another one of her little "talks" about playing nice, however, was a fate worth lying to avoid, and lying was something I excelled at.

It wasn't that I wanted to deceive my parents as often as I did, but most parents just act like they know everything. At least, they do until the moment you start asking them important questions about where babies come from, or why they always lock the bedroom door when cartoons come on. Then they're suddenly stupid. It wasn't as if I hadn't already learned all about sex the same way everyone else does, on the street.

I watched Jonny cradle his toy Man O'War to his chest and walk toward the house, pouting the whole way. He was always a gentler soul than I, and he treated his possessions with far more respect, even at that age, than I ever would. That would probably explain why, after receiving them only two days before, his Man O'War still had both arms attached and mine looked like a special edition Picasso rendition.

Anyway, left to play alone, I felt bad that I was now going to have to use my green infantry men to fight against the Battle Hammer. One at a time they posed no threat, so I'd have to use the whole bucket's worth and arm them with caps or firecrackers to give them a chance. I already knew how effective Man O'War weapons could be on infantry, one of the reasons I had a magnifying glass and a lighter stashed nearby in a place Mom would never look. Somewhat later in life I would learn just how accurate my budding imagination was, and how very painfully real those images of burning soldiers could be.

I began placing the evil infantrymen in positions where they could best surprise, and perhaps kneecap, the gloriously heroic Battle Hammer. The whole world shook and it sounded as if, by some strange twist of cosmic justice, the proverbial chicken's warnings were true and the sky really was falling. Mom had assured me that it was but a child's story and could never happen, but things appeared otherwise at the time.

I was knocked off balance and fell face-first into the sandbox, discovering one of Spice's buried, sand-encrusted treasures. I've never much cared for dogs since, the filthy creatures, and perhaps that event had some small part in it. Shaking my head and spitting, I levered myself up onto my elbows and knees, ready to cry for Mom once all the faecal matter cleared from my airway, only to stop short at the wondrous sight before my eyes.

A gigantic metallic foot had crashed its way right through the fence of our backyard, smashing Mom's little crab apple tree. Splinters had blown away from the trunk, flung like shrapnel in all directions, scratching my face and arms, but I could not yet feel the sting. I blinked my eyes rapidly a few times to clear the sand, poop, and dismay from my senses. Yes, that was definitely a metal foot with the shattered remains of an apple tree scraping up against it. Craning my head up a couple score degrees I saw before me an Archangel. A real live Man O'War, if such a term can be used.

It rested on one foot and one knee, a result of the poor jump its pilot had made. The barely controlled descent had resulted in a significant impact, and not just for me and Jonny. From rather uncomfortable personal experience, I can now attest to the degree of pain involved in cushioning a poor jump with one's own spine, having it compressed harshly into a cramped jump seat. It causes a unique sensation that can only be simulated properly by entering an elevator on the third floor and having some accomplice sever the cables. To this day, I still swear that the machine, mirroring what its pilot was undoubtedly doing, actually shook its head and shrugged its shoulders to clear out the cobwebs and the kinks. I will continue to swear to that, no matter how unlikely the techs tell me my story is.

The incredibly real monstrosity regained its footing, rising up to its full ten plus meter height, towering over all the neighborhood houses and gleaming like a recruitment poster as it posed against a pure blue sky lightly streaked with gauzy clouds.

The machine was just like the storybooks, only more so! It was painted in crisp urban camouflage colors and sported a beautifully rendered Home Guard sigil on the front of its left torso. Other unit markings also graced the surface of the Man O'War, but I had no idea what they were, and they barely registered in any event. My stare was firmly locked on the steely gaze of that metal visage, and I felt I stared deep into the face of destiny. I could almost make out the pilot's form through the cockpit's reflective tinting. I saw myself there in his eyes, years older and eager for adventure, piloting an appallingly expensive piece of equipment into combat against the enemies of Truth and Righteousness. Those reflections echoed through my being, seeming to speak to me of ages to come, and those few fractions of a second felt like an eternity as I gazed down the endless hallways of the future.

Then the Archangel pivoted quickly, firing off a salvo from its large-bore cannon. I realized in a very maturing way that the distant thunder had come much, much closer, and I ran screaming (shrieking like a girl, really) for the shelter I instinctively thought our home would provide. Jonny, almost to the porch, had also been rooted to the spot when the Man O'War first appeared, but was now fleeing headlong for the backdoor of the house. His Diablo toy lay arched and twisted, forgotten on the ground. With a roar and a flash of silver-blue flame from its jump jets, the Archangel bounded off again.

Jonny and I crashed into Mom as she came running out of the house to check on us. Our nanny, Ruth, was right behind her, holding the baby. We sobbed and cried while Mom held us close and rubbed our backs, whispering soft words of comfort through her own ever so tangible fear. I looked over Mom's shoulder, wiped away tears, and saw Ruth, pale enough to do any ghost proud, gently bouncing the baby, who was, predictably, sleeping peacefully through all the commotion.

The Man O'War and its combat action retreated as quickly as the thunder had, and we calmed down almost as quickly. A growing sense of excitement and wonder replaced my fear. I glanced over my shoulder, but could no longer see any sign of that frightening, incredible machine. As we finished our last sobs, Mom released us and turned to herd us inside the inadequate shelter of our home. Without thought or plan, I dashed away from her, through the brand new hole in our fence. As fast as my stout little legs could carry me, I was down the back alley and off up the street before Mom even cleared the fence. Having shaken my own pursuit, I made my way up the hill we lived on, hoping I would be able to see more from the crest.

As I continued my mad dash up the hill, a burning sensation manifested itself in my legs and I began to feel the sting of all the cuts I'd received from the demise of Mom's apple tree. None of it mattered. Abrasions and lactic acid buildup were of no importance when compared to the need to see that Man O'War again!

I crested the hill to see a stunning display of what happens when giant robots of destruction go rampaging after one another in a residential zone. Fences, trees, cars, even several houses lay wrecked and burning in a path extending for what I thought must have been dozens of kilometers. In retrospect it was likely less than a single kilometer, but that didn't un-burn the houses or un-smash the cars. At the end of that path of destruction my Archangel and several other Man O'Wars seemed to be fighting a running battle.

I glanced up at a noise and saw a helicopter flying overhead, a woman's voice blasted out of the large speakers mounted astride the vehicle. She proclaimed herself to be a part of something called the Emergency Broadcast System, and assured everyone that the situation was under control and that no one should panic, but that we should all seek shelter in the corners of our basements. As if, somehow, such a flimsy structure as a house's cement foundation would keep the full weight of a Man O'War from making you very, very short indeed. This particular bit of wisdom must come from the same people who decided that school children, when threatened by a bomb scare, would be better off staying in their classrooms when what they really should be doing is pulling the fire alarm and running like hell.

Far from finding a corner or hole to crawl into and hiding, I climbed a big tree nearby, and perched on a branch. I didn't understand the whos, whats, or whys of the whole situation before me, but I was totally mesmerized by the things I could understand. Even a young child dumb enough to chase a firefight understands laser and missile battles between the greatest toys man ever invented!

As near as I could tell, the Archangel was being helped by a Sniper and a Diablo, though the Sniper lacked its massive gun. The three of them seemed to be hunting a Flak, which was busy smashing its way through a heavily developed part of North Vancouver much the way I was always wont to kick my way through Jonny's artfully and carefully crafted sandcastles and snow forts.

The pursuing Man O'Wars occasionally traded fire with the Flak as they hounded it. They weren't causing much less damage than it was, though. Despite the limited distances separating them, none of the Man O'Wars were able to get in a good, clean shot at the Flak because of all the multi-story buildings in the way. It was an interesting display of the difficulties these ultimate weapons of war face in urban settings. The Flak pilot was doing a wonderful job of using the twists and turns of the streets to his advantage, occasionally laying down some suppressing fire with his own multiple cannons and chain guns.

The pursuing Man O'Wars did all they could to box their prey in, but they were having a rough time of it, as their limited numbers would always miss an alley or back road which the Flak would then unerringly find its way down. Likely the pilot watched the broadcasts being sent out by the multitude of news choppers now circling the area and thus gained enormous amounts of intelligence from the media's generosity.

I watched intently as the Flak stepped around an apartment complex and fired a salvo into the Diablo's right torso. A puff of bluish-green smoke told of the destruction of a heat exchanger. It wasn't an immediately crippling blow, but the older Diablo design runs so hot with its poorly insulated high energy particle cannon that the pilot would almost certainly be feeling the loss the next time he fired. He (or perhaps she) must have been unaware of the damage, or just didn't care, because the Diablo replied with the HEPC and both laser cannons. One shot, emitted by the right arm HEPC, grazed the side of the building the Flak was now retreating behind. Such a miss is actually quite common in close-range urban combat environments when pilots fail to compensate for the angles at which they are shooting.

The missed shot had the effect one would expect, shredding several balconies, breaking dozens of windows, and scorching the fire-retardant surfacing. The other bolts of light, emanating from the Diablo's two torso mounted cannons and unseen to my naked eye despite the searing pain they caused, struck the Flak's right arm. Armor boiled off and both the cannon and the chain gun barrels melted before the lower half of the limb dropped to the pavement below.

The Flak was then behind the building, and with a few quick steps the Diablo charged after. Such recklessness cost him as the Flak had not continued its flight, but instead had aligned for the savage kick that now shuddered the Daiblo's right knee joint just as the Man O'War's weight was coming down on it. The Diablo trembled violently, then toppled to the ground, its leg twisted at a severe and unlikely angle.

This brief victory was about all the Flak pilot could really hope for and he had to have realized that. The Sniper and Archangel both jumped over lower buildings, trying to catch the Flak between them. Before either Man O'War could complete their landing and fully regain their balance, the Sniper was already being knocked flat and trampled by the much heavier Flak. The Sniper must have been piloted by the bravest warrior around. To dive into a situation like that armed only with a relatively small Man O'War designed for stealthy, long range operations takes cajones of the largest caliber. It was no surprise that the Flak chose to engage the significantly lighter machine rather than taking a chance with the Archangel's large cannon at such close range.

Even as it went down, the Sniper launched a volley of rockets into the pelvic region of the Flak. Explosions blossomed as the warheads' shaped charges detonated all around the Flak's legs. The light armor there chipped away and some internal actuator or structural damage was apparent in the way the Man O'War attempted to limp away, but the blow had not been completely crippling.

With a clear shot at the back of his fleeing opponent, the Archangel took careful aim. Time seemed to slow again and I remember clearly the way fire spurted out of the right arm-mounted barrel, as though some unlikely, angry dragon had taken up residence there, and its flames been harnessed to the weapon's destructive power. Bright flashes of light accompanied the beast's deafening roar, which was produced by a half-dozen high-yield, hundred millimeter cannon shells being explosively launched to several times faster than the speed of sound. Those shells flew out of the barrel and toward their target, dragging behind them a plume that disproved the theory of smokeless ammunition. At fifty meters, and with a carefully aligned shot on the Flak's head, the one shot kill was all but guaranteed. Hot death raced across the space between Man O'Wars in a fraction of a second. Impossibly, death missed.

It took me a moment to realize that the Flak hadn't actually lost its head and that the Archangel had missed an easy shot. In that moment, however, those large, explosive rounds had to go somewhere, and they went right into the fourth story of a fifty story government complex just down the block. Just as they were designed to do, the shells penetrated deep past the walls, windows, and insulation right into the reinforced superstructure where they exploded, completely eating away one side of the towering structure. A properly constructed building wouldn't have done much more than shudder, anything built in an area as prone to earthquakes as Vancouver has to be built to take a beating of a far greater magnitude than even Man O'Wars can dish out. My parents still talked about the Big One of 2619 when the seismographs had topped out at 9.0 on the Richter Scale. While it's readily conceivable that the facade, walls, and even floors could be damaged and completely destroyed by such a shock as those cannon shells dished out, the internal structure should have barely bounced. This one bounced and a whole lot more.

Years later, with the wreckage long since cleaned up, they would tell us all about how the general contractor had been arrested and tried for his fraudulence and deceit in constructing a building nowhere close to zoning code just to save a little money on a project gone way over budget. They would also mention, in passing, the inspector he had bribed. They would go on to assure us publicly that they had traced the Archangel's targeting problem to some sort of terrible mechanical failure and blame it all on a poor tech who would then hang himself after being dishonorably discharged. We would also be informed that the pilots in the Archangel, Diablo, and Sniper had been ordered to cease their pursuit through the city, and that it was their disregard of orders that cost so many lives, including their own. Years later, I would know better than to simply accept and believe everything I am told.

For now, the whole building came tumbling down. It was, as I remember it, much like a waterfall only not made out of water and it wasn't anywhere near a cliff. Perhaps not the best analogy but it made more sense when I was five. I watched as hundreds and thousands of tons of concrete, steel, glass, and people rained down into the street as hard and fast as a meteor bombardment. The Flak, the Archangel, and the other Man O'Wars disappeared immediately, and the whole scene was quickly obscured by the dust cloud kicked up.

My view blocked, I looked to the sky where I could see dozens of emergency vehicles, news helicopters, and military and police aircraft vectoring in on the area, circling on the wind like vultures waiting for some large animal to finish dying beneath a harsh desert sun. Shortly this animal did die, the smoke blowing away in the breeze and the dust settling to the ground. Behind that hazy curtain, an unbelievable sight waited to greet my eyes.

Everything for several blocks to the east of the hit building was in ruins, felled or crushed by the impact or shockwave. A mountain of rubble lay strewn and toppled where once, just moments before, an Archangel had had a clear shot at a Flak's unprotected back. It wasn't at all like in the vids, where they would have us believe that a Man O'War buried in tons of debris, be it from a fallen structure, rockslide, or avalanche, would simply dig its way free. Oh, certainly, there would be a few scratches on the paint job, and the pilot always had that obligatory cut on the forehead from smashing into something during the bouncing and jostling, but the great propaganda machine would have us believe that only a nuclear weapon or another augmented armor unit could possibly harm a full blown Man O'War.

The stark truth greeted my young eyes, and I gained a slightly better, if intuitive, understanding of the physics I would later be forced to study. A lot of mass and velocity make for a lot of kinetic energy and no Man O'War weighing a hundred tons or less, to say nothing of the warrior inside, is ever going to be able to survive the damage inflicted by that much material falling on it or him. A few thousand tons of feathers falling from over a hundred meters up will pound anything flat. Make those feathers out of steel, duraglass and ferrocrete and all you get is a debris strewn death-scape. Nothing stirred where those giants had last been seen, save what was induced by settling rubble, helicopter blades, and the wind.

I must have perched on that branch like a pole-axed cow, if pole-axed cattle could perch on branches, that is. Rescues teams, security guards, police units, fire crews, electrical workers, military units, medical personnel and just about everyone else and their dog converged on the area. Their response time spoke well of their training, especially considering the level of security one grows used to when living on Terra. I've no idea of just how long I clung to my seat watching the tumult, but eventually some instinct said the show was over, it was time to go.

Moving numbly, I climbed back down the tree. My mind seemed to be simultaneously in a state of shock yet racing a thousand kilometers per hour. My feet knew the way home, though, and without conscious direction from my brain, they mechanically took me there. It wasn't until I approached our humble abode and its recently re-landscaped yard that I began to feel the fear course through my veins. Mom was going to kill me!

Ruth was running out the front door with tears streaming down her face as I approached from the street, a strange sort of choking sob escaping her as she ran past me. Actually, now that I think of it, that was the last time I ever saw her. When I was fourteen Dad told me what he knew of her life story. I had no way of understanding, until now, how such a thing happening so far away (over a kilometer!) could so affect a person and her delicate emotional balance. She didn't know any of those people and, after that initial brief incident, she wasn't ever in any real danger. I didn't know then what she must have lived through during the Agamemnon War, or what had caused her to move to Earth. Even if I had, I couldn't have related to the stress this incident caused her; how it must have brought back the very real waking nightmares of the war. Now I can begin to relate somewhat better. Since Gottenheim I...well, I'll get to that part soon enough.

Mom sat on the couch holding the baby, rocking gently. She looked at me with a strangely tired face as I crossed the threshold. She blinked slowly, then just told me to go play in my room with Jonny. I noticed she had the holovision turned on, and they were showing the rescue efforts live interspersed with replays of the entire incident. She must have watched the whole thing as it happened, perhaps with a better view than the one I had commanded.

I kicked off my shoes in the entryway and trudged upstairs. For some strange reason I remember paying close attention to the way the carpet fibers felt as they stuck up between my toes. It was as if I were a Man O'War and these small woven creatures mere buildings to be crushed underfoot.

Jonny was waiting for me in our room, and he suggested we go play in the rumpus room. We dragged our other toy Man O'Wars along, forgetting the ones laying discarded in the backyard, and wondering how these pathetic, plastic creatures could ever compare to the awful majesty and splendor of what we had just witnessed. The awesome reality and imposing might of a Man O'War dwarfed all of our expectations and childhood fantasies, inspiring such reverent feelings of respect so as to almost preclude us from the hubris of pretending we were them.

Then we built buildings out of toy wooden blocks and reenacted everything we had just witnessed in person and on the newscasts respectively. We even added in a few toy soldiers to stand in as pedestrians getting smashed flat by falling debris.

It was probably a good two hours before we tired of repeatedly tumbling objects down on our Man O'Wars and civilians, laughing outrageously as little green army men were often catapulted across the room by falling rubble. Jonny didn't even mind that some of his toys got all scratched up. We were all smiles and giggles as we packed our toys none too neatly in the toy box, too cheerful to even grumble at the task Mom always insisted we perform.

By the time we were done thrashing our mighty machines Mom was preparing supper. The smell of liver pervaded the house and we were too young to know better when she assured us that she was preparing steak. Spice was asleep so we went over and gently slapped at him until he woke up and ran off. Then we had to chase him down and jump on him for a while. His mock little whimpers, whines, and nips did nothing to dissuade us. That poor mutt, the way we treated him it's no wonder he was dead a few years later.

I've killed a lot more than a dog over the years, yet I still feel a disproportionate amount of guilt over the way we treated Spice. Strange what irrelevant things the mind will hold onto and make us feel guilty for, even years later.

It wasn't long before Dad returned home from his mystical job as an actuary (something about using numbers to predict the future or something, which he didn't seem able to explain to my satisfaction). Later that evening, he gathered Jonny and I together in the living room. We had already enjoyed supper (well, Mom and Dad had enjoyed supper, we had just eaten as little as we could get away with), and Mom had made us bathe while she treated all my scratches, including one long, nasty one I'd gotten on the inside of my left thigh while climbing the tree. I hadn't noticed when I'd gotten it, but it stung like anything when Mom cleaned it. All that time we'd not been allowed to talk about what had happened earlier. Now Dad had a big hug for each of us, like he always did, and he finally asked us to tell him about our day.

"We saw a Man O'War!" Jonny blurted out, wide-eyed.

I nodded. "It broke Mom's tree, and Spice pooped in the sandbox, and Ruth was crying, and I climbed a tree to watch the fight, and we played with our toys, and it was loud." I knew that wasn't the best summary of the days events, nor did it present my adventures in the light I felt they deserved, but somehow, in all my excitement, the eloquent speech I had intended to give got all jumbled up somewhere between my brain and my mouth.

Dad just smiled at me and drew us both in for another big hug there on the couch. "I'm just glad you're all safe, that's what's really important." We nodded, still a bit too naive about life to truly appreciate the importance of a strong, stable family. For as long as they would last, those days would be the happiest ones of my life.

The dog started pawing Dad's leg, so Dad gave him a bit of a shove with his foot, sending him across the pseudo-hardwood tiles. Laughing, Jonny and I quickly sprang to our feet and gave chase. We pursued that canine around the house, shoving him along not-too-roughly using similar foot techniques. Dad always said we should have had a pit bull so that we wouldn't have gotten away with treating Spice so badly. We were five, though, and we didn't know any better.

Mom and Dad sat cuddling on the couch. They started discussing what they knew about the Man O'War incident, using nothing more complicated than rumor, prejudice, and innuendo to conclude somehow that the entire incident had all been the work of one of the Holdings in the Badlands. I had no idea how that made any sort of sense, and even with wiser eyes can only shake my head at the prejudice to which even my parents occasionally fell prey.

The evening concluded, as it so often did, with a few holovids, but we also got to play with Dad for a change. I didn't really have any understanding of just what it was he did all day in his office downtown, beyond knowing it was some sort of number magic, and it was nice to actually be able to spend some time with him during a weekday. I guess he was worried about us after all we'd been through, but young minds bounce back quickly. Soon enough it was off to sleep, and I had the most fantastic dreams of being a warrior that any little boy could ever have.

In school the next day the teacher brought in a special lady; a psychologist. The lady said that she had been sent because Tommy, who wasn't even in class that day, had lost some relatives in yesterday's happenings. Apparently he got to stay home because of that. She said that she would be talking to a few of us individually and asking us about what had happened, because those horrible machines had smashed right through our neighborhood and she wanted to make certain we were all okay. Of course, she went alphabetically, and that meant she started with me.

I was really nervous when she took me into a little room just beside the principal's office with the words Evaluation Center written on the door. I had been in there once before at the beginning of the school term, and had had to sit in the dark and push buttons when different lights flashed or different sounds blared out of speakers along the walls. It wasn't the most calming of experiences, and I could remember it perfectly. Granted, it also didn't help much that my classmates kept telling me that it was run by the Dominion to weed out the bad kids and the ones who weren't smart enough. It was even said that a couple of kids hadn't passed parts of their evaluations and they hadn't come back to class or school since. If I had known then that those children were actually put into schools specially designed to help them learn at the rate and in the style they were comfortable with, I might not have peed my pants when the special lady stopped to slowly push the door open.

The psychologist lady ignored my little accident and sat me down in the big, padded chair. Pity the kid who had to sit there next. She had me tell her everything I could remember about the incident with the Archangel and the Flak. Then she had me tell it again. And again. Each time she would look at me intently and occasionally scribble something down on her notepad. After the third time she told me that I had a remarkable memory, and asked me if I had any questions about what had happened.

I asked the first things that came to my mind. "Why did that Flak go off like that? How come the Archangel missed? That warrior was stupid. And why'd Tommy's relatives have to die?"

"Those are very good questions, Chase," she said with a startled little smile. "I'll try to answer as best I can." She paused, probably trying to decide how best to explain such things to a small child. "Now, I don't want you to tell anyone about this, okay? It's just our little secret?" I nodded, and she began a speech that I can now see had been well rehearsed. At the time, I had no way of understanding what all the big words the lady used really meant. It sounded like something about a security breach at the psychopathic personality using a stolen Man O'War for terrorist extreme party activities under the influence of a militant cult mannerism, or something like that. Basically, even after her answer, I still had no idea what had happened.

Many years after, shortly after being commissioned, I attempted to use my brand spanking new security clearance to find out the truth behind this pivotal incident in my young life. I found that the Flak had been stolen by its assigned pilot, an apparently loyal Terran Dominion citizen who had been participating in even more highly classified psychological warfare experiments. That was all I could ever find. Had he been a traitor, or perhaps a spy? Maybe he was just another poor mental patient. I couldn't find out, but he had been amok with a Man O'War and I guess that meant he had to be killed for everyone else's safety. Not a satisfying answer, but one we should be able to live with.

The psychologist lady continued to answer my second question by explaining about S.L.A. Marshall's findings so long ago during the World Wars: that humans simply do not want to kill other humans even during war. She explained that one of the reasons Man O'Wars are so effective is because they depersonalize combat to the point that you believe that you are killing a machine rather than a person; at least most of the time. She told me that this pilot was inexperienced and had likely choked at the last instant, when he realized he would be killing another human being with that point blank head shot. Rather than do that, he had instinctively tried to posture or frighten the enemy by firing a warning shot rather than a killing blow, oblivious to his surroundings. Armed with Man O'War weapons of mass destruction and standing in a large city, the results were predictably catastrophic. The phenomenon of posturing rather than killing had been studied in depth for the last half thousand years, but there was still no guaranteed way to avoid it.

"Do you understand?" she asked.

I nodded my head and she began to smile again. "Uh, no."

Her smile froze and her eyebrows dropped together. "And I cannot tell you why Tommy's family had to die. That's more a question for your religious leaders."

"Oh."

She shook her head and told me that I should go back to class and change my clothes. As I got up to leave, she spoke the rather cryptic words that, once I gained enough years and painful experience, would haunt me to this day. "Try not to judge that poor pilot too harshly, Chase. Someday, perhaps you'll be the one in a terrible, perhaps impossible position where innocent lives are at stake. Though I do hope you'll make a more appropriate choice than he did."

Chapter Two

Juneau, North America
Terra
Terran Dominion

October 14, 2644

It would be more than twelve years before I saw a Man O'War again. I don't wish to gloss over the other happy memories of childhood, nor downplay the other significant events that happened in those, my formative years, but I lack the patience to engage in such long-winded story telling. Besides, I'm unsure of exactly who would possess the voyeuristic desire to read of my first playground fight, my first date, and my first, almost accidental kiss. Those who do likely do not deserve the temptation of reading such material, and should, in all fairness, be confined to an institution similar to this one.

Perhaps that is the whole reason the doctors are here, inmates like the rest of us, seeking their own escape from life through the problems of others.

It was in the fall, as much as the North American West Coast knows of that season, anyway. Clouds had seized the skies and held them hostage for almost a week, and the gloomy threat of rain was upon us. In other words, it was most definitely a good day to stay inside, even if it meant attending school. This day, though, promised to be a little better than the monotonous tedium of most secondary school days. I was in my senior year, and we had been subjected to the horror of a career week in order to help all of us restless, goal-less teenagers decide which pigeon hole we wished to carbon copy ourselves into for the rest of our lives. Even after almost two decades I've still not lost the cynicism toward secondary schooling ingrained in me during those long years.

This day, however, unlike the previous days in career week, did not involve wandering around an auditorium filled with tables that were staffed by very bored looking people handing out pamphlets and proclaiming their transportation management company to be the most dynamic, fulfilling, and exciting place in which one could even conceive of working. Instead, as required by government mandate, we were taking a tour of the nearest Terran Home Guard facility. Today we would be guided around a military base—likely staffed by very bored looking people handing out pamphlets and proclaiming the transportation management branch the most dynamic, fulfilling, and exciting place in which one could even conceive of working. There would, however, also be the infantry, armor, cavalry, artillery, aviation, naval, space and interstellar warfare, and command and intelligence branches. All that, of course, and the augmented armor branch, the Man O'Wars. Somewhere in the back of my head, destiny's bell still pealed whenever I thought of those giants.

The likelihood of earthquakes now precluded the building of a base anywhere too close to Greater Vancouver, and was the stated reason that Fort Aurora, the base that had provided that memorable first Man O'War incident, had been closed down six years earlier. That meant we all got to ride on military transport choppers up to Juneau and Fort McMasters, where they also had a risk of earthquakes, but apparently an acceptable one. Like so many other things, military bases are political pawns, and, in most instances, decisions are rationalized after the fact.

As soon as an opportunity presented itself, I ducked out on the teacher escorting my group, and hooked up with Jonny's group. They were only being chaperoned by a young cavalry captain, who couldn't have been more than twenty-six, and they had no teachers with them, which promised to be much more interesting. From the war stories and bawdy jokes the captain shared with us as we waited for our ride, I knew I had made the right choice. While we took our turn standing around preparing to load into our helicopter, Captain Murray instructed us on the finer points of everything from fighting a war from the back of a rapid assault vehicle while dressed in light power armor to the best ways of finding the friendliest and cheapest women in any city. I was in tears from laughter by the time he let us know that it was our turn and we should be going.

The ride up to Alaska was uneventful, though still exciting for a young man who had never flown before. There was a majestic beauty to those huge, twin bladed Clydesdale helicopters we rode that stirred even my shallow, teenaged soul. Watching something about the size of most middle-class houses gently, and even relatively quietly, floating through the air and touching the ground as tenderly as a mother lifting her newborn child is enough to move even jaded, worldly teens such as those produced in a modern metropolis like Vancouver. Flying inside one as it performs those delicate maneuvers is immensely entertaining, but even more moving and inspiring. To me, it was as though God himself had granted us the use of angels' wings, and we soared through the sky all bedecked in righteous glory.

I grinned from the moment those marvelous Clydesdales landed on the football field behind our school to the moment we climbed out onto the tarmac at Fort McMasters. I was so thrilled by this wondrous new experience that I swore to myself then and there that if I was unable to become a warrior, then I was going to be an aviator, and that second choice, still fueled by the fresh memory of flight, was not far behind my first. Preferably, if given the chance, I'd become a combat pilot riding a bullet to glory, but if not, an aviator regardless. I thought it really wouldn't matter to me if I was piloting a fighter, a transport, or a scout, as long as I was able to touch the sky and continue to fly like a seraph. I had been that impressed with my first taste of flight. I was full of impetuous youth and optimism to be sure, but perhaps there is a wisdom in that impetuousness that we lose as we become adults more inoculated to having our dreams dashed to tiny pieces before our eyes.

After we de-helicoptered (yes, I made up that word), we were led inside the hangar where we hooked up with the other dozen or so groups of students. They came not only from our school, but also from other schools within the Pacific Northwest. All told we numbered about three hundred. Our captain had disappeared, as had a number of the other military chaperons, but I assumed they would be back, someone had to hold our hands. We all stood in a loose group, just milling around in that big, echoing hangar. Noise levels rose until our teachers and remaining military escorts quietly informed us that we were about to be addressed by the small man coming this way, the one accompanied by Captain Murray and the other officers who had disappeared.

He stopped right in front of the group, dead center and ramrod straight, then obviously put forth an effort to relax his stance and shoulders to assume a less intimidating posture. He wore a uniform decorated with the crown and three stars of a lieutenant general, and was no doubt used to being in command. I thought it spoke well of the man that he made an endeavor to put himself, and us, at ease regardless of how unnatural it felt for him. He looked good in the solid black, that's for certain, and cut a very authoritative presence.

The general's salad board of ribbons and awards covered his entire left shoulder, and not a few decorated his right. He had obviously earned the right to be in the position he held. Militaries throughout history and across the stars have always been so fond of decorating their soldiers with all the bells and whistles that can be designed and awarded. Perhaps it is only right that those that have earned the accolades be given visible reminders of them to wear proudly for all to see. Like pretty much everyone else outside the military, I had no idea then what they all stood for, but they gained my respect, and a little envy, immediately.

I no longer harbor any such envious dreams, having earned all the medals I could ever want, and quite a few that I despise vehemently. I would trade them all in a heartbeat for just one more minute with my mother, or a chance to do things differently with Rachael. Hell, some days I think I should just hand them out to the poor kids on the streets so they can play with them. Such is the transient value of awards of any kind.

The general used no microphone or podium as he addressed us there in that open and noisy hangar, but I could make out every word clearly. He projected his voice as well as he projected his presence. Somehow, it seemed all the more impressive coming from a small man. The fact is, General Gough was just an impressive man all around.

"Welcome to Fort McMasters," he said. "I'm General Gough, commander of the Fourteenth Cavalry Division of the Terran Home Guard, and this beautiful location in the mountains is our home. I hope you all enjoyed your trip up here, and I apologize that our weather is no better than what you were suffering from in Vancouver."

Most of the students kind of rolled their eyes and a lot shuffled their feet at this attempt at humor. I felt a little awkward with that, even though I also thought it had been a weak attempt. For some reason, though, I didn't want the general thinking that I wasn't appreciative of his efforts to humanize himself for me. For some strange reason, I wanted this man's approval.

I glanced around to ascertain the group's overall feel and was surprised to realize that most of them simply didn't want to be here. They had only come because the Dominion said they had to. It seemed that only a few of us, including me, Jonny, most of the others who had flown in our Clydesdale, and the scattered individual here and there were actually interested in what the military had to offer as a career and a way of life.

Perhaps I could understand why some would not care to be soldiers, but why anyone wouldn't want to visit a place where they kept things that blew up other things and destroyed large objects with ease made no sense at all. Even a teenager cannot fathom the minds of other teenagers.

"Today," Gough continued, removing his hat and tucking it under his left arm, "you are going to see what it is like to serve your nation. You will see some few of the millions of men and women who are willing to give their efforts, and even their very lives, in defense of our beliefs, our values, and our way of life." He looked around and could tell that only a handful of us were listening, really listening, to what he said. A lot of feet were shuffling, most heads were downcast, most eyes were looking away. It seemed to be no more than he had expected, though he did appear a bit disappointed.

"Whatever you think of the presentations you see today, when you go home tonight, go home knowing that there are many, many fine soldiers who are willing to do whatever it takes to protect that which is most important to you. Whether or not that is a sacrifice you would make yourself, understand that they have the courage and the dedication to take upon themselves the responsibility of defending your rights and your well-being. If you get nothing else out of your visit, at least recognize how important our ideals must truly be if the price for them is eternal vigilance, payable only in the legal tender of human sacrifice." He looked us over, and only a half dozen of us even bothered to make eye contact. It seemed to me that he nodded almost imperceptibly at me and those few others.

"So enjoy your tour, ask any questions you might have, but realize what this is really all about. And for the few of you who think that you too have what it takes to be among the best blood of your generation, to stand between the freedom and security of the Terran Dominion and the chaotic forces that besiege us from without, think about what we have, what we do. Then, when the time is right, come join us. Talk to your school counselor or a local recruiter." A lot more feet shuffling, and the echoes of a few throats clearing. Someone popped their gum.

"Before I let you go for the tour, are there any questions or comments?" Gough asked.

More of the same bored, uncomfortable noises from the group. Then one hand shot up toward the middle of the group. Gough nodded toward the raised arm. "Yes?"

"No offence, General, sir, but I think I'd rather get a real job." Laughter greeted that comment.

I think I have more compassion on them now, realizing how much they were products of their parents and peers. This smart ass wasn't trying to be tough for himself, his disrespect and rudeness stemmed from the way his parents had raised him and the pressures he felt from the group to show his superiority. At the time, however, I know my lip curled up in a sneer at the realization that someone would have the audacity to even say such a thing. My parents raised me to be more respectful to those in authority, and rightly so. Whether you actually agree with what they do or not, enlightened self-interest alone should prevent you from making such a stupid remark to a general, especially a general on his own base.

For his part, Gough just donned his hat again and calmly marched through the assembled students, who quickly made way, until he was almost chest to chest with the wise-cracker. Gone were all attempts to appear more human and less intimidating. Instead, the general looked like Mars himself come down from Olympus, ready to administer a well deserved beating.

The wise-cracker was a male student, actually quite large, probably a rugby player. He was able to look down at Gough, and he did so with a smirk plastered all over his face, nodding around at his friends. The general just locked his stare on the kid's face and glared at him with eyes that could have bored a hole right out the back of the kid's skull. For a moment, the boy held that stare, but only for a moment. Then he had to look away from the intensity of that gaze. That action opened the flood gates of hell itself.

"Son," Gough started, not yelling, but still making certain we could all hear every word. "When I was fifteen, I watched terrorist raiders destroy the town my parents lived in on Kittyhawk. My uncle was killed in that attack, as was his son, only four years younger than I. I promised my mother that I'd never let anyone else lose a sibling if I could do anything about it.

"By the time I was your age, I had already lied about my age and enlisted in the Home Guard as an infantryman, just to get off planet and where I thought the action was. On my first duty station on Omar, Tomiki Irregulars overran most of the entire planet. In the two short weeks that I fought with the resistance, before Home Guard evac'ed me, I watched mass executions and gang rapes of Dominion men and women on a regular basis. I watched as they rounded up everyone under the age of eight to hold as hostages of goodwill. I saw them execute a few of those hostages to prove their intent.

"Omar was where I killed the first man to die by my hands. He was just a kid like me, but he was a Tomiki soldier and he'd had a few too many drinks one night. I stuck a knife in his ribs in a back alley. He cried and asked for his mother with his last breaths and I puked all over the alley before I could stumble away."

Even Gough's *ears* were turning an angry red as he talked. I wondered if he would physically lash out at this idiot who had been trying to show how tough he was. That's one of the things that I've never understood about tough guys. Sure, most people will back down when you push them to the edge, but when you find one who won't, you're in for a butt whooping, so why take that risk and always push the limit? For his part, this kid without the IQ was starting to sweat visibly, and he kept wiping his palms against his thighs in nervousness. He was looking around for support, but, as is typical for tough guys, his friends who had so appreciated his humor before were abandoning him now, and Gough wasn't done yet.

"Once I got off planet, I was immediately transferred to the fighting that had broken out along the Krupp Hegemony border. I saw young women and children used to carry explosives into camps, forcing good men, far more valuable than you'll ever be, to agonize over the decision to shoot a child or risk having their friends blown up. I had to see what happens to men who make the decision to shoot and how hard it is for them to live with themselves afterwards." He paused for emphasis. "The ones who didn't shoot just died."

Gough thumped his right index finger against the kid's chest.

"I've suffered through harsh winters on distant worlds, and fought in humid jungles on alien continents. I've watched good friends die for no other reason than because they opened their armor to take a breath of fresh air that was contaminated with nerve toxins, on a planet that had nothing to offer any cause except that there were people there to convert. Ever see someone's skin boil off of their face? Have you ever held your best friend as he bled to death after taking a flechette through the kidney?"

Gough took a step forward, thumped his index finger again, harder this time, and the kid stumbled back.

"Can you say that you have given your blood, sweat, and tears to make the galaxy a better place? Can you say that you've ever saved lives, often a score at a time? Can you say that you have laid friends and loved ones on that sacrificial altar of freedom? Can you say that you have ever done anything of value in your entire life other than suck up the money you begged from mommy and daddy?" Gough was trembling with anger now. "Can you?"

The kid was trembling too, but in obvious fear. "I'm sorry," he mumbled. He had dark spots on his shirt beneath his armpits and a trickle of sweat was rolling off of his forehead.

"You're sorry? Son, I've watched an untold number of innocent Dominion subjects tortured and killed because other nations want what we have, because they crave our freedom or despise it. I've buried a great many friends who joined me in trying to keep that from happening, because they believed that what we were doing would give people like you the chance to have the future they chose for themselves, not one imposed by some foreign dictatorship. I've fought halfway across this galaxy and killed more men than I can count, men whose only crime was answering the call to service given by a nation that doesn't care about its citizens, all to give you a chance to live your pathetic little life, and you're just 'sorry' about it?"

The kid whined and made small noises. It was an almost comical site. In fact, if I hadn't been so certain that I was about to watch an execution, whether by hand or by weapon, I think I would have laughed. It was almost surreal, though, almost like I was watching it happen to someone else, which of course I was. What I mean is that it was hard to believe that I was actually there witnessing this little man who, without his armor, was probably no stronger than I, reduce this lumbering ox of muscle-bound rugby player to a moaning heap.

"Get off my base," Gough said. "And while you're enjoying your long, land trip home, for which your parents will be billed, try to remember that until you get command sign off on your attendance to a military orientation day, you can't graduate from high school." With that Gough bid the rest of us enjoy our tour and left.

Now, I later found out for a fact that Gough had let the kid come into his office, apologize sincerely, and go home in the gunner's seat of an assault helicopter. Inside, Gough was a total softy, but he wanted that confrontation to be remembered as a lesson. It was one I personally took to heart: don't ever mess with generals who have seen combat and paid dues with their own blood (and maybe a little something about sacrifice and respect too).

I think I can skip the exact details of the majority of the tour itself. Suffice it to say that, like any tour of any facility, civilian or otherwise, this one was obviously a fairly glossy overview of what goes on on a military base. The presentations given by the different branches and the services they provided were all canned, and generally presented by an officer trained in public relations skills. I can't say that there was nothing of value in the tour or the speeches we heard, in truth many of the points that I heard that day piqued my interest and certainly caught my attention, but it wasn't quite the grand adventure that I thought it would be. I was still interested in all the things that blew other things up, but I was more inspired by what Gough had said about service than I was by listening to the vital role played by the paymaster corps in helping our fighting men and women wage modern war.

Most assuredly, there were interesting things, like examining a tank up close, counting how many tubes there are on a multiple launch rocket system artillery piece, and taking a turn crushing bricks with the gauntlet from an infantry power suit. At one point, one kid even tried crawling down the barrel of a Big Cat howitzer, but he got stuck and the medics had to be called in to grease his big butt out of there. All in all, though, I wasn't too enthralled by explanations of what military accountants or nurses or lawyers do. In fact, I wasn't even too concerned over what the military police and field engineers do, and the presentations given by the combat arms spokespersons failed to paint the picture of endless heroism and immortal glory that I had expected, especially after the stories told to us by our cavalry captain. They almost convinced me that nothing a soldier did could be exciting.

The day dragged on, and we wearied of all the speeches that seemed so similar. I loved what I was seeing around me, usually held at a distance, but the sell job they were doing on military life and its glory basically sucked. Gough's impromptu encounter had been much more electrifying. By this time I no longer cared whether or not surface ships or submarines had the most to offer in terms of combat support and firepower during naval conflicts, nor did I do much more than yawn when we were informed of how painfully boring the job of an intelligence analyst really is. The entertainment industry really has failed to capture the true tedium of that job.

After an eternity, or so it seemed, we were led to the corner of the base complex that housed the aviation and space and interstellar warfare branches. I was tired and beat by the endless parade of military vocations being presented, the vast majority of which seemed no different than their counterparts in the civilian world, but I was starting to find some energy at the prospect of learning more about flight. The launch gantries that could be seen towering in the distance, many occupied by the most gigantic classes of dropships, were far more impressive than anything else we had seen thus far.

As our journey progressed, we passed by several busy runways where aircraft of all types could be seen taking off and landing. Atmospheric fighters raced away with the deft rolls and maneuvers that are impossible for any other flying vehicle to perform. Trans-atmospheric vessels, like dropfighters and some of the smaller classes of dropships, lumbered in on their oddly shaped wings, landing gently nevertheless. Helicopters dotted the sky all around, and I was very shocked to see just how slowly a cargo plane actually takes to the air. One would expect that giant form to stall and come crashing to the ground at any moment. Now this was more what I wanted, this was what being in the military was all about: action! I was anxious and bouncing all over, suddenly full of energy, impatient to get inside the presentation area and find out what was required to become an aviator.

I left completely depressed. Did you know that for the government to give you the honor of flying one of their painfully expensive death traps you have to be in the top two percent of your class from kindergarten through university? Did you know that they genetically test everyone for the physical requirements of the position and that women are fifty times more likely to have what it takes? I can't for the life of me figure out why anyone would want to strap themselves onto the front end of a bullet and launch themselves into combat, anyway. Seems like suicide.

I was just bitter at learning how hopeless my chances of being an aviator were. Like the proverbial fox, I spent a few minutes convincing myself that the grapes would have been sour, that flying wouldn't have been that much fun. I got over it quickly enough, though. After all, aviation had been my *second* choice.

As a grand finale, we toured the Man O'War hangars, the pride and joy of the modern universe's multiple militaries. I glanced around at the various models and types in restrained awe while listening to yet another canned presentation, this one about the importance of augmented armor in combat, but I had no feeling of destined inspiration; nothing at all like what I had experienced twelve years before. In fact, looking up at all those lifeless machines just slouching in their bays, I do not think I even considered what I had felt so long before, not right then. It was just a five-year-old's memory, after all, and I wanted more than this tour of frozen statues.

As everyone was filing out of the Man O'War hangar and toward our transportation home, most of them eager just to return to their couches and begin vegetating again, Jonny pulled me to the back of the herd. He waited until only a few stragglers were still making their way out.

"Chase," he said, "what's with you? You've been waiting your whole life for a chance to be this close to a Man O'War again, and you're not even the least bit excited."

I shrugged and gestured to the lifeless things around us. "I don't know, Jonny. Do these look like the inspiring visions we expected? They aren't even letting us look at them closely or anything, not even a demonstration. Frankly, the infantry presentation was way better."

"So let's go," he said, and started off toward a nearby gantry.

"What are you doing?" I raced to catch up with him.

"I'm going to have a look at what's inside one of these things, and so are you." With that he caught the first rung of the ladder and went up it like a squirrel after a nut. I hurriedly looked around to ensure there were no immediate witnesses and followed. I wasn't even thinking about how stupid this was, or how much trouble we could get in, I just followed the lead of my twin. Jonny later confessed that he did the whole thing because he figured I needed it, and that he was scared spitless the whole time. Things were always like that with him, willing to put himself in any precarious situation if only it would make his brother laugh.

If I could only have him back for just one day. But I cannot, can I?

We reached the top of the gantry, arms ready to drop off from exhaustion. It is so hard to climb that many rungs on a ladder that I only did it when I couldn't use a lift. I never did care for that part of being a warrior.

Jonny and I found ourselves standing next to the left shoulder of an Arson, a light, maneuverable Man O'War equipped with two extremely powerful flamethrowers. Usually employed in forests or urban settings, the Arson is a staple design found all across the Charted Territories, often employed in less populated areas and used as a deterrent to insurgent movements. Before I could utter so much as a squeak in protest, Jonny was climbing up beside the small rocket launcher located next to the Arson's head. I followed him again, and found that, for all their size, there just isn't much room to stand on a Man O'War.

We tottered there on our precarious perches for a moment, before belatedly realizing that the pilot access hatch was open. Jonny tossed his head in that direction, indicating that I should proceed to the penultimate conclusion of our little adventure. I shook my head vehemently, starting to think of just what kind of trouble we would be in if caught. For all I knew, it could be a capital offense. Jonny sneered and shoved me toward the opening. I damn near fell the full ten meters to the ground then, and once I'd managed to balance myself against the cockpit hatch, I turned to Jonny to let him know where he could go, where he could relocate his stupid plan once he got there, and offer to provide him a mallet to help with the insertion.

Before I could begin my eloquent tirade, though, there came the sound of someone climbing the ladder. Jonny's eyes widened all the way up to his hairline, and mine no doubt did the same. He jumped back onto the gantry and started away from the ladder.

"Where are you going?" I whispered as loudly as I dared.

He didn't tell me. Instead, he paused a moment, and then took off down the platform and away from the ladder. "Hide," he urged me.

I gave that universally recognized one finger salute to his fleeing back, then ducked into the only cover available to me: the open hatch.

One serious advantage of a Man O'War over a fighter plane is the amount of room in the cockpit. A plane has to worry about any and all excess weight, so they make the pilots wedge into their tiny little cockpits, another reason women are better at it, being smaller and lighter. Man O'Wars, thankfully, are usually not so limited.

I found just enough room to actually squeeze in behind the pilot's jump chair and crouch in the one meter space, my back pressed firmly against a short locker. A fan vent was to my left and a somewhat dusty tool chest took up most of the area to my right. Around the pilot's chair I could see lots of buttons, switches, levers, pedals, and other controls. I was surprised to see how complicated the cockpit was, as if I had ever stopped to think about what would be required to make such a huge machine move so fluidly and life-like.

The footsteps on the rung stopped and I held my breath, waiting for the tech I hoped it was to proceed on down the gantry walkway. I almost cried out when the footsteps proceeded right onto the Arson's shoulder. I resigned myself to discovery and punishment, and began to rise from my crouch as a male form silhouetted itself against the hatch opening. Then I realized that he was actually backing into the cockpit. For some reason, I hesitated to call attention to myself, probably an instinctive knowledge that surprising someone from behind is not the best way to gain leniency for one's crimes.

The man, now obviously a warrior and not the tech I had hoped for, sat in the chair and slapped his hand down on a button to his right. The entire Man O'War shuddered as power from the engine brought it fully upright and ready for action, imbuing it with an animation and life that had been so noticeably lacking before. As the pilot pulled his helmet down from the hook above his chair, he also elbowed the switch that closed the hatch. My sphincter tightened right up at about that time, puckering everything up real good, which is probably the only thing that prevented me from another trouser messing episode, one even more embarrassing than the one I'd had when I was five. I was sealed off from any escape and was in deep, deep trouble. The pilot adjusted the pickup on his helmet to rest in the proper place, and spoke into it as his hands rapidly ran through what I would later learn to be the always essential systems check.

"Prime, this is Omega One One," he said. "All systems give me the green and I am ready to clear the gantry and exit at North Two on your okay." Any response he received was in his earphones only, for he only nodded and eased his throttle control forward. The Man O'War took a step. A chill and a thrill raced up and down my spine, setting every hair on end. I was in a real, live Man O'War

This beautiful machine moved so gracefully that I couldn't believe it was walking and not hovering. The Clydesdales were quickly forgotten, relegated to the ranks of mere transportation. A Man O'War is an incomparable ride.

The pilot tapped a control stick to one side and the Arson smoothly pivoted to our right, and continued to march along with incredibly long strides. It was exhilarating in the extreme. Even though I wasn't in control, I still felt much as the legendary Titans must have, walking amidst mortal man. That's a feeling that never goes away when you're a warrior.

I'm sure my jaw dropped open at the view I could glimpse around the sides of the pilot's chair. Everything was so tiny from up here. I could see people in the distance, no more significant than ants, and the cranes and supply trucks that had seemed large from the ground were merely knee high obstacles to the Arson.

The giant doors that I had noticed before and thought so enormous were open and awaiting our egress, but seemed far too small for us to actually pass through. The warrior, however, did not seem at all concerned. Insanely, I thought, he actually pushed his throttle a little farther forward and adjusted his tack slightly with the pedals. The view of the gantry fled behind us, and the doorway raced toward us, too tight for us to actually fit through. I scrambled back, trying to brace for the impact that I thought was coming, and my foot kicked the pilot's chair.

"What the hell?" I heard him say as his head spun around to catch me with his gaze. He also turned his torso just slightly, inadvertently adjusting our course too far to one side. The open door rushed up to catch the Arson square in the left breast, and I flew forward.

The resultant head injury spares me to this day any memory of what Jonny had to go through after that. My only knowledge of it comes from descriptions provided after the fact. Apparently, I was taken to the Fort's hospital and treated for a fairly serious concussion, while Jonny was interrogated by the military police for a few hours. They talked to me too, until they realized that I could only babble out the names of different barnyard animals and the noises they make. The medics sprayed something in my ears that controlled the effects of my closed head injury, but it didn't make me coherent until suppertime.

Eventually, our captors concluded that we were just a couple of stupid kids who had gotten themselves into a bad situation and through plenty of dumb luck, and even more stupidity, had made it worse. Fortunately, a Man O'War is built tough for the rigors of the battlefield, so there was no real damage done save to my head and the pilot's ego, whose teammates had already nicknamed him "Stowaway" in my honor. The final assessment was that repair costs were minor enough not to be charged to Dad, and Jonny and I were sent home by special courier. We even received a note of commendation from General Gough, citing our willingness to take risks and our interest in the military. It seemed high praise to me.

Mom, however, was a little less understanding. She was so upset, once we'd reported on our activities of the day, that she could barely speak. Dad of course, just about fell over laughing. He was literally rubbing his hands with anticipation at being able to tell this story to the guys at work the next day. Predictably, this just made Mom even more upset. I guess pissed off would be a more accurate term. We all had to fend for our own dinner that night. Thankfully, my skull smashing had limited my hunger, and I wasn't forced to partake of whatever that foul concoction was that Dad put together.

Jonny was a bit shaken up by his interrogation ordeal, and felt extremely guilty over almost getting me killed, but he was obviously going to be okay. He even smiled and laughed as he described to Dad for the umpteenth time how the Arson had staggered back from the door and fallen over like a drunkard. He too could hardly wait for the morrow and the opportunity to share the story again and again.

As for me, I felt a bit giddy from the medical treatment and recent brain damage. I felt no worries over what I'd done, thankfully, nor did I have even any lingering doubts or fears from my injury, though I'd develop enough of those later in life. What I did feel was the trailing awareness of the awesome power resident within a Man O'War and the godlike feeling of being at one's controls. I knew then, as I had known in my heart since I was five, that I was destined to obtain that coveted Man O'War pilot title: warrior.

Chapter Three

Hell's Gate Annual Field Training Exercise
Hell's Gate National Park, North America
Terra
Terran Dominion

October 14, 2645

I almost missed out on my goal, for several reasons, right at the beginning. I think that only ended up making me even more committed to achieving it, though—it made me truly committed to the only way of life I have ever really known. It committed me to walking the road that one day led me to this institution and all the losses that necessitated my being here. Perhaps it is all a result of fate's fell tide, but perhaps I should have recognized a better way.

In any case, it was exactly one year after I crashed the Arson. How strange that I should put it like that, as if I had been the warrior at the controls. Nevertheless, that is how I envisioned it. Already I was bending my interpretation of events to suit the needs of my teenaged ego.

Around about the time that I was looking at which universities I would apply to, I had firmly decided that I would be joining the Collegiate Officer Training Corps. My hope was that this would get me commissioned and in the pilot's seat of a Man O'War, not an easy task or without competition. I had already ruled out the other two options I had found for becoming a warrior. Enlisting and competing for officer training after a few years, as General Gough had, seemed chancy at best. Competition from within the ranks is fierce and still requires that an undergraduate degree be completed. Besides, to be eligible to go that route you have to be an infantry combat veteran and I have never wanted to be a bullet-stopper in the Poor Bloody Infantry.

The other alternative I had was to try and get a senator or local house member to sponsor me to go to West Point. Since my grades in high school were only decent, quite far from the outstanding they would be looking for, that also seemed fairly unlikely. Besides, West Point is a contractual obligation where you are stuck for four years, with an eight year term of service after that whether you like it or not. Free room and board, true, but once you sign on the dotted line you had better hope that military life really is for you, and I wasn't that confident in either myself or my goal.

No, for this young man, COTC was the only way to go. With diligence and effort, I could still become a warrior after having given military life an honest try, without ever becoming a PBI, signing a binding contract, or experiencing the hardships of being a "real" soldier, or so I hoped.

Mom, predictably, did not approve. She didn't want me going anywhere near the military. She said she was afraid that her little boy was going to get killed on some godforsaken little rock hundreds of light-years away without her ever knowing about it. The number of times that that almost did happen makes me appreciate even more how smart my mother really was. At the time, though, I figured she was just being a typical mother, worrying over her little boy. What really caught me off guard was when she actually forbade me from joining up.

My mother was ever an authoritative woman, used to getting her way, never backing down from taking a stand. Even, or perhaps especially, during our plethora of late-night discussions and debates I'd always known exactly where she stood on every issue, whether I wanted to or not. Not surprising for a teenager and his mother, we were, as often as not, in complete disagreement on the many issues we argued and debated over. Never, in all my years, though, had she even once outright forbidden me to do anything. There were rules, and there were punishments that accompanied the breaking of those rules, but everything was left to me to decided as I saw fit. Nothing was truly forbidden.

I appealed to Dad to try to get her to see reason, but he informed me that it was no use. Admittedly, I'd have been a bit more satisfied with his response if he had actually tried. I told Mom that because she was my best friend (which she really was, though I didn't truly realize it at the time) I'd accede to her wishes. The look of relief that I saw on her face then was almost enough to make me turn that lie into truth, almost enough to deflect me from my race into infamous glory. Almost.

That September, I went off to Burke University in Portland to study neuro-linguistics with my parents' blessing. As soon as I arrived on campus, within the hour, actually, I found the COTC offices and signed myself in as a brand new cadet. I couldn't give up on my dream without giving it a bona fide shot.

Call it homesickness, call it just plain guilt, but a few weeks later, during a phone conversation with my parents, I let it slip that I had joined up despite Mom's admonitions to the contrary. She actually hung up on me. Dad said he understood and wished me luck, but Mom's indictment of my choice hurt somewhere deep inside for reasons that I couldn't quite put a name to. Still, I was a teenager, well used to fighting with my parents and restless to prove my independence, whatever the cost might be.

I called Jonny at Harvard (he received *really* good grades in school) and let him know what had happened. He said he was going to go join COTC too, the very next day, and then Mom would just have to accept it. It was wishful thinking on his part, since it only succeeded in making her furious at the both of us.

Just like old times, Jonny.

It was with that background that in mid-October I found myself on my very first field training exercise. FTX's are a unique experience that I highly recommend to anyone, regardless of whether or not they're actually interested in being in the military. Nothing will develop character, humility, and self insight quite the way being hungry, exhausted, cold, muddy, and yelled at will. And what the hell, you'll get to shoot automatic weapons and throw grenades at things.

All of us COTC cadets, years one through three, had bundled ourselves into our camouflage uniforms, packed up a rucksack with extra boots, rations, shelter, shovel, and clothing, and ridden off in a bunch of transports that delivered us to Hell's Gate Canyon National Park. Here the cadre, and the fourth year cadets who assisted them, had prepared a lovely and entertaining evening of yelling and shooting blanks at us, then knocking our bivouac down in the dark. Each time the Fours would insult us, throw mud at us, or otherwise belittle us as we attempted to fix whatever made up problem they claimed existed with the shelters. We got maybe three hours of sleep that night, and that on cold, hard, lumpy ground without padding of any kind. The cruddy food and the pouring rain didn't help with my morale much either.

Actually, now that I think about it, I wouldn't honestly recommend an FTX to anyone, military or otherwise. If you want to suffer, just listen to some classic twentieth century "rap" music while beating your genitals with the claw end of a hammer. Likely, you'll feel better and recover faster than the average participant in one of these character building field exercises.

By mid-morning of day two, I was not a happy camper at all. This wasn't Mom's hugs and kisses while being tucked-in to warm blankets, it was about as close to that as quasars are to Earth. Put bluntly, I wasn't having a good time anymore, to the point where I no longer cared about a Man O'War or all of the power it bestowed upon a warrior, I just wanted to quit and go home. I had never before been subjected to such harsh conditions and the stress, the humiliation, and the degradation wasn't something I could handle. Not much seemed to be stopping me from just getting up and taking a nice leisurely stroll down washout lane. It was a thought that kept pressing on my mind.

It was only ten o'clock in the morning, we'd already been up since six, and now we were practicing techniques for moving while under fire. I tried to tell myself it was only another day, only one more day.

"Get your head down!" Cadet Captain Ducell shouted. "Mud washes off, bullets don't! And it tastes a hell of a lot better than hot lead too!" The low *budda-budda-budda* of machine gun fire punctuated his statement.

Strung out in two single file lines behind Cadet Francis and me, our entire class was practicing how to do a proper low crawl. Mostly, it involves laying flat and pulling yourself along with one hand and one knee while digging a trench with your helmet. I'm not certain that it actually has any practical battlefield application, especially on a modern battlefield dominated by power armor, Man O'Wars, and orbital bombardments. However, militaries throughout history have been fond of doing things that make little sense and have no real purpose, excused by the flimsy logic that it's either traditional or a good form of discipline and team building. Thus, if three thousand years ago some Roman General Maximus Flavius found that you can polish all the paving stones in the street quite nicely by having your soldiers crawl along them in this manner, we now do the same exercise because it is, after all, tradition.

Practice was usually less uncomfortable than what we were currently facing, but that had been in a small arboretum or sometimes even a gymnasium. Instead of that relative comfort, our loving Cadet Captain had somehow managed to find a clearing in this forest that was full of fresh mud to practice in—no mean feet when it hadn't rained in this part of the park in days. To ice the cake, he had us going uphill with our rucks on while a very real machine gun fired blanks over us. My left arm and my right leg felt like they were about to fall off even though less than a quarter of the course had been completed.

I turned my head sideways so that I'd be able to breathe while I pushed my helmet and ear farther into the soft, warm muck. I could see Charlie doing a similar maneuver off to my left. He saw me looking at him and gave me a thumbs up. Charlie was in his second year, a Two, and he knew what this game was all about; he knew how to let it all roll, like water on a duck, off his back without taking it personally. I'd watched him go through all the things I had so far and just shrug and let it pass. I wished I knew how he did it, I didn't know how much more I could take.

I tried to smile my thanks for his support, but I don't know if he could make it out under all the mud and camouflage makeup I was wearing. The fact that he cared didn't matter much though, when it seemed like all the officers and other cadre members didn't give two whits about me or the abuse I was being forced to suffer through. I can look back now and say that it was nothing compared to what came later, but at the time I was coming from the ease of a home and family that supported me in every way, thrust callously into a brutal way of life that I couldn't justify.

Unfortunately for us all, Ducell was a sadistic fourth year moron, and he was trying to impress the cadre with his hard-nosed attitude hoping he'd get posted to a high profile Operations position. He was convinced that he was the greatest leader the Dominion had seen since the fall of the original Terran Alliance, on par with the legendary Marshal Hayes himself. Ducell was, truthfully, a legend in his own mind.

"Is that a smile I see on your face, Aarons? Are you enjoying this?" So much for trying to thank Charlie with a smile. Ducell's mouth was right in my ear and it was fragrantly obvious that he hadn't brushed in some time. "Do you see that fallen tree up there? That's a machine gun nest and it is trying to put a few dozen holes in you! Or have you somehow failed to notice exactly what is making all that racket that sounds suspiciously like machine gun fire? Now stay serious and do this for real or I'll have you doing pushups right here in the mud; ruck, weapon, and all! Do you understand me?"

"Yes, sir," I mumbled as best I could through the mud. It didn't come out very well, because Ducell shoved my head into the soggy ground at the same time. Ducell was a born phallus. He'd personally ridden my backside the entire evening before while we bivouacked, kicking down my shelter three times before I had it exactly the way he wanted it, though even then he berated me for being incompetent. At least the other Fours had been more indiscriminate with their abuse.

The idea of quitting once again sprang to my mind. It was almost a constant temptation, playing through my thoughts every five minutes or so. It grew stronger each time the entire loop of humiliation played through my mind, probably because each time the litany of abuses grew longer.

I had joined COTC because I was attracted to military life: disciplined, respected, and possessed of lots of really cool toys. Mostly it was the toys; it always would be. Anyway, I had a dream, a dream that I wanted to live up to. It was my destiny to be a great warrior, and I could feel it in my bones, but all that seems so far away when you're cold, tired, hungry, and being abused physically and mentally by some self-righteous schmuck named Ducell.

"I can't hear you, Cadet!"

Before we came out to Hell's Gate, Dad had tried to warn me by relating some of the stories he'd heard from his prior service colleagues. He told several anecdotes of the most belittling and abusive environments imaginable. Despite the fact that it violated every known principle of effective training and teaching, Dad claimed that this kind of behavior still persisted within the military. I had had a hard time believing him. Now I knew far better, and it was something I would encounter throughout my career. No scientific research into motivation or skill development has ever suggested that this kind of activity has ever helped anyone learn anything, but so often individuals, happy on their own power and unhappy with themselves, really don't care. Again, it's a tradition held over from days long past when some erroneously believed that abuse made soldiers tougher rather than simply scarred.

"Yes, sir!" I tried to scream into the mud, barely able to even breathe, much less enunciate every word perfectly.

I had no intention of putting myself through this kind of pointless degradation. I knew that I didn't have to take it from anyone. I was a volunteer, only here to play the fun games with the cool toys, not to be run through a meat grinder and put down. There were other career options available. Neurolinguists are in high demand and fairly well respected throughout the Charted Territories, so I could probably make significantly more money by *not* joining the military, which would certainly make Mom happy. A more extreme option, but still an option, involved running off to join the Republic's foreign legion, where I could still try to become a warrior. In fact, there were dozens of small nations in the badlands and periphery states that would probably be more than willing to take me on. Or mercenary units, there were plenty of those scattered throughout the Charted Territories as well. Or....

"I don't believe you!" Ducell suggested. He released his pressure from the back of my head. "Get your butt off my lane and give me thirty in the grass over there! Then start again at the back of the line!"

I dragged myself up, exhausted, sweaty, and caked in mud. My twenty kilo ruck felt like a hundred, and the assault rifle in my hands dragged me down even more. I wiped some of the mud away from my right eye with a gloved hand and stared Ducell down.

"Yes, sir," I said, with just enough respect to keep from sounding insubordinate to a casual observer. Ducell, though, would know exactly how much respect I had for him, and, just in case he wasn't too observant when it came to aural cues, I curled my upper lip into a sneer. Well, I tried to, but I found that it had already assumed that position without any conscious commands from me.

I took a few steps clear of the muddy path, escorted by the cadet captain, who slapped me in the back of the head when he thought I wasn't moving quickly enough. I dropped to the ground and assumed the proper position. With my assault rifle balanced across the backs of my hands I began doing the pushups I'd been ordered to perform. I shouted out the repetition number each time I reached the top position, fantasizing all the while about inserting my rifle into a predetermined orifice on Ducell's body and firing off a magazine on full-auto. I almost burst out laughing on the eleventh rep when my fantasy Ducell thanked me for helping him dislodge that annoying stick that had been lodged there for some time. I had to stop thinking and just concentrate on performing my punishment.

The repeated contact with the wet grass washed much of the mud from my tunic, and it almost felt good to cause *both* of my arms to hurt for a change. Blame it on my upbringing, but my thoughts waxed philosophical and religious as I tried to distract myself from my discomfort. I guess I was just trying to remind myself that life is made by God, not man, and thus follows his mysterious ways. He put me here, so there was something I needed to learn or do that would help me achieve my destiny, or help someone else achieve his. For now, that meant that life's energies should be focused on my goals and my abilities, not on any asinine runt with short-man syndrome.

Despite the energy I was using to perform my punishment, I actually felt better, more focused. I'd like to think it was that brief contact with the true nature of my soul, but it may have been as petty as my entertaining little fantasy about helping Ducell with his plumbing. Either way, I was now determined to stick things out and achieve the goals that I wanted to achieve. Nothing anyone did could really affect me, it wasn't like they were really beating me or causing lasting physical harm, and I figured I could put up with anything for a few more days. Then I could rest and re-evaluate before

I had to do anything like this again. I didn't understand how truly thin and brittle this layer of calm was.

"Sir! Cadet Aarons requesting permission to recover! Sir!" I barked as I finished the last pushup.

"Are you sure, Aarons?" he shouted, wafting the nauseating aroma of his pie-hole my way once again. I was reminded of dead dog for some reason.

"Completely certain, sir!" Fleetingly, I thought about how easy it would be to simply roll over and scissor the fool down. Then a quick butt stroke to the face and I'd feel so much better about life while he tried to put his unbrushed teeth back where they had originated. Granted, I'd likely spend twenty years getting gang raped in prison after that, but at the moment it seemed almost worth it.

"Recover, Aarons," Ducell said with a pat on my back, as though he were my best friend doing me some grand favor. Then it was right back to being an exit orifice. "Now get back there and do things right this time, Cadet! Unless you're as pathetic as I think you are and you still need your mommy to help you?"

I shrugged it off. I was committed to my ideal and my dream. Ducell would not, could not, stand in my way. I would be better than him.

"Perhaps you'd prefer to ask your daddy. Too bad not even your mother is certain who that is exactly."

There exist in this world people who have to make you angry. It doesn't matter to them that this makes their lives much harder, or that they can easily get themselves severely dead by acting in this manner. For whatever reason, they, like the previously mentioned tough guys, seem to get off on making you blow your lid. As my self-control and my temper boiled to the bursting point, I came to the vague realization that I'd just pegged exactly which kind of battery powered tool Ducell was.

When my restraint and patience went, I literally felt something snap. I could almost hear the noise it made as it broke.

"Go to hell," I yelled. No, it didn't take much time or effort on Ducell's part to make me forget all about my commitment of a few moments before. Something inside said that it was time to adjust how things stood between us, and the consequences be damned.

Cadet Captain Ducell's eyebrows shot up out of sight beneath his cap, his nostrils flared, and his jaw clenched. For a moment he was shocked into a gasping, dying fish sort of silence. I took advantage of that.

"I suppose that may have sounded slightly insubordinate, you stupid get.

I'll rephrase it so that it sounds completely insubordinate!" I shouted with a snarling expression that might almost have been mistaken for a smile, if seen from a distance. "You are the stupidest, smelliest, most incompetent individual I have ever met in my life! I can't wait for the day that I hear you died in combat, likely from your own men shooting you in the back! I want nothing to do with you, or any organization that would allow you to be a part of it! I quit!"

He was livid. From forehead to neckline, Ducell seemed to glow a bright red. "Don't you ever talk to me like that, Cadet!" he shouted. There are also people in this world who seem to believe that if you say something louder, it somehow becomes less stupid and more respectable, maybe even approaching right. They are, of course, wrong, but apparently Ducell was more talented, and even more of a moron, than I had thought. He could fit into two categories of idiot. "Drop and start cracking out pushups until I get tired! Now!"

"Weren't you listening?" I inquired, giving him a significant shove backward with both hands. "I said I quit, you fool. I'm a civilian, and that means I'm here voluntarily. This isn't a basic training boot camp out of some movie, you stupid gonad, and you're no drill sergeant. I don't have to take this. Have a nice life, dumbass." I threw my rifle at his feet and pulled the quick release straps on my ruck sack. Both hit the ground with satisfying splashes of mud.

Every cadet had been watching this exchange, many with smiles and nods. When I pivoted and walked away from the lane, several broke into applause. Ducell rounded on them and vented all of his frustration with me on those that remained. As I entered the trees beside the clearing, I could hear him ranting and raving at the other cadets to put their heads back down and move like their lives depended on it or he was going to do something suitably horrendous to their favorite pets or some such nonsense.

After walking out into the forest in no particular direction for about five minutes, I paused against one tree to begin scraping mud from my boots with the help of a convenient stick. I knew I had just thrown away my future and probably my destiny. A tear trailed down my cheek and I began to sniffle as the realization of my failure sank in. I knew Mom would just be glad that I was out and Dad would be proud of the way I'd told off Ducell, but Jonny would go ape at me for quitting what he insisted was my only true role in life and leaving him to do my job of being an officer.

I knew that Jonny was the right one, that I should have toughed it out, even for just another five minutes. I shivered and wept as it sank in that I was not, not ever, going to be a warrior. I had thrown it all away over a petty insult. I dropped my stick and just slumped there beside the tree, hugging my knees to my chest. Now what would I do?

I heard someone approaching. I didn't think Ducell had the backbone to actually follow me and try a fist fight, but after what I'd said to him in front of witnesses, anything was possible. I rose from my crouch, wiped a sleeve across my teary eyes and runny nose, and turned to face whomever was approaching.

"That was a silver-tongued little speech you gave there, Chase," Major Kay said. Kay was the cadre officer in charge of second year cadets, and he was an amazing officer, instructor, and leader. He was a career infantry officer; Ranger and Special Ops qualified; airborne, pathfinder, sniper and scuba certified. He'd been a part of the legendary Ranger assaults on Gottenheim back in 2630, when the Dominion had held the Krupp Hegemony at bay while our erstwhile allies, the Federated Earth Republic, had gobbled up a quarter of the systems belonging to the Confederated Empire. He never addressed anyone by first name. I was unsure whether the fact that he was doing so now was a good sign or a bad one.

Kay's slight frame waded through the short grass that grew between the trees. He stopped a few paces shy of my asserted position. In the movies, he would be played by some chemically and genetically enhanced freak who couldn't last two minutes on a real battlefield. Real world combat is so much different, and I have found that, unlike cops where the opposite is true, it is the small infantrymen who are the most dangerous, and Kay epitomized dangerous the way Ducell epitomized remedial.

I respected Major Kay a whole lot, and now I was aware enough of the world outside my own problems to be a bit concerned, especially as I realized there were no witnesses around. Kay was nothing if not dedicated to proper respect and order within the ranks, and I didn't know how he would react to my performance.

"What's the problem?" was all he said. I blinked a few times before answering, waiting for him to finish tearing my head off.

"No problem, sir. I just don't think this is for me." I dropped my gaze to the forest floor and toed a clump of quack grass.

When I looked up, Kay was just studying me with raised eyebrows. His head tilted to one side as he considered me, reminding me of the way Spice used to study me so long ago. I began breaking eye contact repeatedly to try and provoke a response, but whenever I looked up again he just kept looking at me, as though he was reading the blueprints of my soul.

Finally he said, "Why'd you join in the first place, kid?"

That was an encouraging sign, I'd been demoted from first name to kid. Major Kay had always had a way of seeming like he actually cared and was trying to help, though, and I hoped he was trying to help now.

"I wanted to do something that made a difference, sir, not just spend my life marketing the latest flavor of colored sugar water with the latest linguistic breakthroughs. I thought I might be interested in Counter-Krupp Intelligence." I had never confessed to anyone, save Jonny, what I thought I had known of my destiny. I was reluctant to let that secret out even now, especially after I had just left my chances back there in the mud next to my assault rifle. Kay nodded a few times, probably not believing everything I said, so I went on. "But, sir, I can't take this kind of lunatic abuse. Ducell is a complete idiot, and those kinds of insults about my family and...."

Kay shook his head violently, interrupting me. "You're wrong, Chase. Not about Ducell, he is unquestionably a complete idiot. But you can take this abuse, and it isn't lunatic. Without a doubt we need good officers like you. Ducell will be shipped off to spend the rest of his career counting hex wing nuts for the left side armrest of light tank driver seats. He'll be a footnote in the annals of the Dominion, probably listed with all the other fools who managed to strangle themselves trying to pull a shirt on first thing in the morning. Men like you though, they make history, but only if you can get over the obstacles in the way."

That was amazing. Kay actually thought that I would be a good officer, high praise indeed. I wonder if he knew, as I thought I did, what lay in store.

"But, sir, if you want to get qualified people, you need to treat them better than this," I protested. I called upon some of the human relations classes I was taking. "How can you attract good officers if they know they can sell their skills elsewhere without nearly this much fuss?"

"What makes you think a good officer is interested in selling his skills at all?" Kay countered. "In my mind, that doesn't fit with the concept of a good officer. We want men and women who have a desire to be here, men and women who know they could make more money and be more comfortable elsewhere, but still want to be here anyway. We need soldiers who are dedicated to their nation, and who know how to give orders, or take orders, or even buck orders, without just quitting the fight.

"We need to know that you will jump out of a dropship fifty thousand feet above a planetary surface, watch your best friend die from triple A guns, break a leg on landing, suffer privations and danger more extreme than you've ever imagined, fail in every mission and lose at every turn, and *still* not turn around and go home." He was pacing back and forth now, warming to his subject.

It seems to me that there are two universal truths about good leaders. The first is that they love to give speeches about their ideals. Gough gave a hell of a good one in Juneau, and now Kay was doing it here. I've never figured out what the second one is, but I'm sure it's just as important.

"Do I approve of what Ducell does?" Kay went on as he pivoted and continued his pacing. "Not in the least. I wouldn't let that man, and I use the term 'man' quite loosely, wash my toilet seat for me. But I tolerate his actions because he serves a purpose, even though he doesn't know what it is."

I sank to my haunches and leaned back against the rough bark of the tree. With all of his high praise, I had somehow thought he was going to back me up. Now that didn't seem to be the case.

Kay pursed his lips, narrowed his eyes, and crossed his arms over his chest. "Chase, why did you join? And don't give me that crap about Counter-Krupp Intelligence or any other nonsense."

I took a deep breath. It shuddered slightly, a sign that I was still close to bawling my eyes out. The truth then, I decided, holding nothing back. "Because I want to be the best Man O'War pilot ever, sir. I want to be a warrior and leave a mark on history that no one can erase. I want to be as famous a warrior as Heimdall or Musashi. Maybe a legendary general like Sun Tzu or Hayes. Because I have a feeling in my soul that this is what I need to do, what I will be good at, where I can make a difference."

I waited for him to laugh, but he didn't. He actually nodded.

"And you will. If you get off your butt, and get back on that lane." He stared hard at me. "You're not the only man I've ever met who felt that way, and every one of them went on to greatness. If that truly is what you want, then that is what you must do."

It was what I wanted. No, what I needed. I felt that being a warrior was a preordained requirement for my life, something God or fate had intended from before I was born. I had no choice.

"What about Ducell?" I asked

"Tough him out, prove him wrong, let him be forgotten by history while you make it. Make your mother proud of you. Make *me* proud of you."

That almost embarrassed me. Actually, it turned the skin beneath my camo paint a rosy color that, thankfully, only I could notice, and then only by the heat I felt in my face. "Not that, sir. I mean, what about what I said to him, what I called him, that I told him I quit."

He mulled that over for a moment, pacing a few steps forward to lean against my tree. I stood upright so that he didn't have to look down at me and I wouldn't be staring at his crotch, but then he ended up having to look up at me. Sometimes, there is no right action.

Perhaps, though, there are sometimes better ones. So often there must have been better ones.

"Do you think that Ducell will apologize to you? I doubt that very much. Why should you even pretend it happened? Of course he'll be rougher on you, but you'll take it as penance for your insubordination and be proud that you take it as part of a second chance that most people never get. As for the other, did you tell a cadre member you quit? Are you aware of any regulation saying you can't join back up anyway, even if you had told a cadre member?" He raised an eyebrow in question. I shook my head.

"Then get back on that movement lane double time, Cadet!" I snapped to attention and gave my best salute, waiting for him to return it before I ran back to reclaim my ruck, my rifle, and my destiny.

Kay was right, Ducell was much rougher on me after that, but the realization that others actually believed in me and felt that I belonged here made it simpler to ignore him, and I began to accept the abuse and punishment as badges of honor, challenges presented only to the strong to find if they are wanting. It also didn't hurt that I was now a hero in the eyes of every cadet present.

In fact, those cadets formed a human wall between me and Ducell. Every time he approached, someone made certain that they intruded upon him with a question or a concern, a request for enlightenment or some other such distracting tactic. I had half a dozen people help me clean the mud from the assault rifle that I had pitched to the ground, a sacrilegious act for the PBI, and when I was ordered to clean all of the latrines with a toothbrush, the whole platoon managed to be there with sponges and mops to ensure that there wasn't much to clean. I actually enjoyed my five hours of sleep that night.

On the final day we ran tactical infantry exercises with simulation equipment. Finally a chance to show what I had, to show my aptitude for combat, with nothing taken away by Ducell and his petty way of being. In this grande finale exercise, my squad was assigned to defend a small ravine against the rest of the platoon who would be acting as our Opposing Forces. The OPFORs had greater numbers than we did, they could call upon artillery support, and their platoon and squad leaders were all third year cadets with plenty of experience at this sort of thing. The theory ran that the Threes would gain experience, preparing them for their summer camp, and the presumed victory would give them confidence in themselves. No one, however, had counted on Marcel Williamson, an underestimated second year cadet who had been assigned to lead our squad. Truly, someone's confidence was about to be bolstered, but the cadre had neglected to tell Marcel that he was supposed to lose.

Cadet Steveson, himself a One, and I were assigned to lay concertina wire and tangle foot out within the ravine to create killing lanes for our heavy weapons. We also placed command detonated mines in the appropriate places. All of this was exactly as the textbooks have taught it for hundreds of years. Then something not in the textbooks happened. Cadet Williamson ordered us to abandon our post. As Steveson and I returned to the command post to reclaim our rucks, we could hear Francis questioning Williamson's orders.

"Uh, Mark," he said, "I don't think we're supposed to leave the ravine."

Williamson smirked. "Of course not. They want us to just sit here as good cannon fodder for the Threes. That's just too bad, because I don't like losing. Our express orders only said that we were to defend the crest of the ridge by preventing any forces from moving up this draw. Correct?"

Francis nodded his agreement. "So we can't leave," he protested.

"Wrong." There was no malice in his comment, simply correction. "You're still thinking inside the box, Charlie. If it isn't expressly forbidden, it is therefore permitted. Now, let's give the Threes a bit of a wake-up call, huh?" He grinned like a cat and clapped Francis on the shoulder.

Thus it was that when the OPFOR platoon approached the bottom of the draw they halted and spread out, all on line, in preparation for their assault. From my position I was so close I could actually hear what Rob Marsh, the Three acting as platoon leader, said in conference with his platoon sergeant and squad leaders.

"Damn, this kid Williamson is good. I can't spot even a single entrenchment up there. Too bad he left his wire in such a visible pattern, but he'll learn by next year, before he gets to camp." I smiled to myself at that.

Boy, were they in for a surprise. I couldn't make out what they said after that, as their voices dropped in conspiratorial whispers, fine tuning their battle plan.

Just as Williamson had predicted, Marsh called for a reconnaissance by heavy artillery fire to soften up our position. He ordered his whole platoon down as the telltale whistles of incoming fire began. Simulated explosions, basically flash lasers to activate exposed targets and a stick of dynamite for sound and smoke, began blooming all over the draw at the end of the ravine.

For almost a full three minutes these explosive devices rained down while the OPFOR platoon hunkered down on themselves. When they stopped, Marsh jumped to his feet, ever the poster boy glory hound.

"Follow me!" he shouted with a forward wave of his arm. He took off running up the slope, yelling at the top of his lungs and firing his weapon at randomly selected targets. It took him longer than I had expected to realize what was going on, and that meant I had to actually get up and run after him. I didn't appreciate the extra exercise, but I had to be up close and personal for this to have the effect I wanted it to have. When Marsh finally stopped to turn and look around, an extremely puzzled look graced his features.

He could hear no weapons fire of any kind, neither friendly nor enemy, and he could only see one soldier following him up the draw. Once he realized I wasn't a member of his own unit, his eyes widened and he tried to raise his weapon toward me. I smiled and nodded a greeting as I fired a burst that took him in the stomach and chest. He dropped like a rock when his muscular inhibitors went off, activated by my laser.

It seems that when artillery is falling that heavy for that long, and all of your people are hunkered down covering their heads, it's very difficult to tell when someone, or some squad, is using small arms fire to methodically take out every soldier in your platoon. I don't know what kind of ESP powers Williamson possessed, but he had arrayed us in exactly the right positions to cover the precise area where Marsh had stopped his platoon. It was simple really. The only thing that went wrong was that the soldier assigned to snipe the platoon leader had instead made an ass out of the poor Three by letting him charge up a hill all alone and then shooting him with a smile. At the time I thought nothing of this act of simulated cruelty, it was but a lark with a good laugh by all at the end, even Williamson. In hindsight I can see that it foreshadowed some of the things I would later find myself capable of, but there was no sign of that at the time.

Personally, I had rediscovered the joys I'd had when I was a child playing soldier with Jonny and some friends on the playground. Here it was once again, the adventure and action of running through the trees and shooting people with toy guns. Individual combat, pretend of course, unadulterated by the taint of Ducell or anyone else. Here I discovered what Charlie had been trying to teach me from the beginning: you can put up with an incredible heap of dung if it means you get to shoot people and blow things up afterwards.

I remained a cadet. I discovered a motivation to roll with the punches and keep going, and I found out at least one way to win the loyalty of your comrades, by insulting or humiliating your superiors. Life still had reasons to be lived.

Chapter Four

COTC Strategic Command Simulation Facilities
Burke University
Portland, North America
Terra
Terran Dominion

January 10, 2647

It's amazing how much information the human brain can assimilate and process in a single year when given the proper circumstances.

"We have multiple contacts in Alpha Nine. Eighty-six percent probability of Philadelphia defense profile. Concentration patterns of fire suggest high probability of single polar defense. I don't think they've held anything in reserve, Chase."

Think of what it's like for an infant, born without knowledge of the world around him. Within a single year that child will learn how to move, how to recognize sights and sounds, and understand many, many communication signals.

"Good. Launch orbital fighters and dropfighters. Send Angel and Babel wings to engage orbital resistance, watch out for those heavy platforms. Move in a few of the gunship class dropships too, but hold some in reserve, we'll need their air support later on. Vector the landing vessels and the rest of the defensive air cap south. We'll slingshot around their defenses."

Combat training for any soldier is similar to the experience of a newborn. When I joined COTC, I knew nothing about fighting a war beyond what we'd fantasized about as children. Within a year I'd learned the basics of unit movement, recognizing enemy movements and deployments, and proper communication strategies. Like an infant, one has little choice but to learn when thrust full force into a situation. As I'd almost done, a few cadets did fall by the wayside, realizing that COTC wasn't for them. Personally, my dedication to the program grew stronger every day.

"What about our naval resources?"

Simulation is one of the absolute best ways to learn quickly and the military uses it extensively. Whether it is through simulated infantry combat in an FTX or exercises like this one in the holo-tank, nothing makes you learn quicker than having to actually do it in real time combat. Even worse is this sort of faster-than-real-time combat.

"Leave the *Sierra* midway to the jump point. The *Shasta* and the *Olympus* can have open engagement orders on the orbital defenses. Bring the *MacKenzie* and the *Saint Helen's* in to provide support for the landing forces. Make certain that air cap takes out every satellite they can find: communication, entertainment, or otherwise. I want no planetary communication abilities left on Thule."

Then there was this girl. She had long brown hair that framed the kind of face used in advertisements for skin care products. Her soft, delicate features were a siren's call to the male anatomy. Her body was perfect, and looked outstanding in a uniform. She got straight A's in all courses and had all the Threes quaking in terror that they'd have to face her in an upcoming FTX. I doubt she even knew I existed, the way she was so focused on being the best Two in our unit. Make no mistake, she was good, very good. In the last bout of simulator exercises, she had gone head to head with Williamson, who had only been willing to participate in the Second Year Cadet Annual Strategic Simulation Assessments because he expected little threat from a Two. She had left the poor man wondering what had happened. He didn't seem to have any great appreciation for the taste of his own medicine.

"We have suborbital contact in the southern hemisphere. Minimal resistance."

Her name was Rachel; Rachel Evans. Every single male cadet had a crush on her, but no one had even come close to getting so much as a date out of her. She wasn't unapproachable, in fact working with her was easy because she was soft on the eyes *and* easy to talk to. She just seemed so far above the rest of us. She was one of those girls that is incredibly beautiful, but seems so unaware of it. She never flaunted her sexuality or used it to her advantage, as far too many good looking girls do, and thus became all the more alluring because of it.

"Launch air fighters as soon as possible. Begin attack runs with the gunships and attack craft. If the dropfighters aren't needed, give them weapons free status on targets of opportunity, energy weapons only. Let's conserve expendables until our re-supply abilities are confirmed."

I think I was really in love. Everyone assumes they are, that first time, but no one is ever certain. I only knew that I really wanted to get to know her better. Yeah, me and the entire male population of Earth! I should have picked a more likely target, one within my range, but the way she smiled when she won an engagement, the way she walked up the stairs to our classrooms, even the way she saluted the officers as if she considered herself an equal rather than a subordinate, it all attracted me to her.

"The first dropship has made a successful landing. Deployment of infantry and armor security forces has begun. Air cap reports no further contact above the drop zone. Requests permission to seek and destroy."

At a base level I could analyze my feelings as pure animal attraction, more lust than love. Rachel possessed the kind of feminine aura that could constrict cerebral blood flow from a hundred paces. Her aloofness and unconquerable spirit awoke that desire within in every male to climb the unclimbed mountain and tame the tiger found there. Take that as you will, but I believed then that I loved her.

"Negative on that. Concentrate on deploying the rest of the landing forces as soon as possible. Restrict attack runs to the Amber Reaction Area. Get our artillery support set up, that's top priority."

So, with the defeat of Williamson, the entire pride of the male COTC Twos (and, unofficially, the Threes) rested in my untried hands as I met Rachel in simulated battle. No one held out much hope for my success, especially after we drew lots and I ended up with the Parisian forces. I can't blame them for their lack of faith. In the classroom, my abilities on paper were above average, but not outstanding. I wasn't the pride and joy of the school in that respect, but then, thinking and theorizing about something aren't the same as actually doing it, and this was my first real chance to lead. I hoped to surprise them all with a few things I knew I was capable of.

"Orbital engagement is costing us heavily. They have greater numbers and superior fire support with those platforms. Suggest break off to conserve resources."

That was Marsh, younger brother to the now-Lieutenant Marsh whom I had shot at point blank range some fifteen months earlier. He had transferred in from Santiago State University and appeared to have all the charisma and leadership ability that his brother had possessed. I had asked him to be my executive officer because of his ability to accept orders and relay suggestions without any grave concern over following proper procedures or rules. He hunched over the holo-table, reading updates as they came in from the field at an accelerated rate.

Historically, when the Parisians had invaded Thule fifty years ago, it had taken ten hours to get this far. Since these recreated historical simulations were strategic in nature, we sped them up quite a bit (and removed a considerable amount of detail) to give us a better feel for high-level command.

I considered Marsh's suggestion for only a split second. At these accelerated speeds there was no time for lengthy deliberations. A great side effect of this sort of practice is an increased ability to make decisive choices while under serious time constraints. I combed my fingers through my hair and said, "Negative. I want nothing left at my back. That's how the Parisians lost last time. Release all dropfighters and orbit capable gunships to support. Have them break off planetary runs if needed."

Marsh didn't take the time to acknowledge that command, he simple began speaking softly into his mouth mike and adjusting various buttons, knobs, and slides on the holo-table control interface. He kept a cool demeanor in whatever situation he found himself, but damp spots were still starting to appear at his armpits and temples as he dealt with the stress of being an XO.

With a glance I tried to take in everything that was happening. Holographic displays set around the room showed different aspects of the conflict we were waging. Our surface forces were spreading out from the drop zone according to plan. They were handling the sparse resistance perfectly, taking prisoners where possible and leveling everything they came across. Unfortunately, the orbital fight was not going nearly so well. The *Olympus* was a fountain of flame; all hands had already abandoned ship. The *Shasta* would be suffering the same fate quickly enough if the tide didn't turn soon.

One of the main problems in any planetary assault has always been the difficulty in transporting enough forces far enough and fast enough to overcome an entire planet's worth of defenses. Popular fiction authors often write about mere scores of units, usually Man O'War units because they're the sexiest, taking entire planets, occasionally backed up by a few obligatory dropfighters but otherwise unsupported. How little they know of real combat. Fully half of my transports weren't even fully combat capable, stuffed to the gills with supplies and munitions. Also, my attack force was huge by necessity, which made command and coordination a nightmare. Even so, I didn't have a tenth of the forces defending the planet. Thus the saying: amateurs talk tactics, professionals talk logistics.

Even worse than the numbers needed for a successful assault is the way these amateur authors try to make it seem like an entire planet can only muster a few regiments for defense. Sometimes they make it seem as though an entire nation can only scrape together a few score regiments from their dozens of subject planets. Ludicrous. Even in early Earth history small countries of only a few million citizens could put together multiple armies worth of soldiers. Then again, many popular writers aren't especially educated and perhaps it doesn't make for as good a story to admit that it literally takes millions of soldiers, combat and support spread across many systems, to actually secure an entire planet.

It isn't quick, either. Usually, a planet only falls once the means to wage war have been totally destroyed, which usually takes months, even when done quickly. Too bad real life isn't like in the movies and books where a whole planet falls in mere hours, maybe days if the invaders must besiege. No one can take a planet that quickly, not unless they have some surprises tucked away like I did.

"Bring the *Sierra* in from the jump point. If a battlecarrier can't turn this around, we may as well surrender now," I told Marsh. He nodded again and made the necessary adjustments, clacking away on his keyboard and speaking a few brief commands into his mike. Within the display, the monolithic warship broke away from the point at which our forces had entered the Thule system and began its run.

"ETA is forty-five seconds," Marsh reported without glancing up from the displays.

We continued to watch as the *Sierra* bore down on the conflagration. I didn't really think even a battlecarrier was capable of fighting against the kind of firepower Rachel had on those orbital platforms. In fact, it would be a far easier target to hit than the fighter craft currently engaged were, and they were getting slaughtered.

One very harrowing thing about interstellar combat is the knowledge that the attacking force only has one advantage: picking the assault point. Beyond that, the defending planet has all the advantages until you make landfall, when it starts to even up a little bit. Until then, the defenders have plenty of warning that an attack is imminent because an attacker has to enter the system well away from any gravitational field. This means jumping in at least several hours transit time from the planet. Thus, no chance for surprise. More, the planet has plenty of dedicated orbital fighters and platforms, while the attacking armada, due to space limitations, must balance the number of orbital fighters it carries with the number of atmospheric fighters and trans-atmospheric dropfighters. Also, unlike what the aforementioned authors would have us believe, a dropfighter is far less effective in either medium than its dedicated counterparts, but dedicated fighters cannot protect the dropships from launch to landing and back up to recovery the way dropfighters can, thus the dilemma and the need to include them.

We were fighting a recreated battle, so, while we were free to use our own strategies and tactics, we were limited to using the same equipment that had been possessed historically. Lucky for me, the Parisians had picked a fairly even, and therefore flexible, balance in all of their equipment lists. I was quite confident that I knew how to use it all to its best advantage. Everything.

"Ground command reports all-clear. Armor, infantry, and augmented armor units are beginning deployment. We are secured at landing zone Bravo. That puts us close to where the historical Thule military had their six division Man O'War build up, the one that cleaned up after the orbital bombardment."

The holo-displays showed dozens of Man O'Wars, tanks, and power suited infantry pouring out of their massive dropships. The ten meter tall, humanoid machines moved rapidly across the terrain, closely followed by their shorter, heavier armor brethren. The infantry all but disappeared from view, lethally lying in wait. Naturally I was drawn to the Man O'Wars. For a moment I was lost in thought, fantasizing about how it would be to be down there inside one, pulse pounding in anticipation of imminent combat, senses heightened to pick up any sign of danger. It felt good just thinking about it, but I could only afford a moment.

"Outstanding. Tell air cap I want a recon flight confirmation of that area right now. Then we'll see how things could have been on Thule." A smile ghosted across Marsh's face at that, he thought he knew what my plan would be. Then he returned all of his concentration to the task at hand.

I watched the displays again. Huge artillery pieces were being set up within the drop zone, affording us an umbrella zone of heavy fire protection for our ground units. Triple A units spread out as well, ready to live up to their motto of "what flies dies." Military police were securing civilian and military personnel who had been in the wrong place when we landed or had since surrendered. Field hospitals were going up, along with chow tents and barracks. Surveillance and reconnaissance planes were mapping out the area in even greater detail than the satellites we had launched could. Advance warning and control craft circled high above the area, combining their own data with the information coming in from the air and land recon units and the satellites we'd left in orbit. The seconds were ticking down until the *Sierra* would be in range. I momentarily wondered just how complicated things got in real life.

"*Sierra* preparing for combat run on platforms. Launching all remaining orbital fighters and...what the hell is that?" Marsh actually looked away from the table to stare and point at one display. All I could see depicted there were the two moons, swiftly moving Thor and massive Odin, that orbited Thule.

"What?" I asked as intelligently as one can ask that question in that situation, which is to say rather stupidly.

"This!" Marsh almost shouted. A tiny little rectangle appeared just next to Odin, and the screen zoomed in on it. Now I could easily see what the excitement was. Two battleships coming out from behind the moon's dark side. Nothing special, just possibly the end of all of our carefully laid plans. Probably the end of our sortie too. Rachel was going to win. Maybe I'd have to adjust my plan to include surrender. Maybe not.

"What the hell is that?" I asked Marsh back. "Equipment tables in the historicals never listed Thule as ever having any warships bigger than a corvette on station, much less two friggin' battleships. They were supposed to all be at Lodoth."

Marsh had regained his normal demeanor and was again busy at his console. "Looks like two *Yreka* class battleships, that means Sons of Terra. Either there was information available somewhere that we weren't privy to, or else Kay's up in the god-room granting Evans her every wish. Any new strategies to pull out of your ass, Chase, or do you just want to kiss it goodbye?" That made sense. The god-room comment, I mean, not the ass kissing one. From the god-room, everything was controllable from weather to civil uprisings. Kay could have allowed Rachel to make a treaty with the Sons of Terra, whom we know had been interested in certain mining rights at the time, or else there was information missing from our briefing, which could also be possible given the secret information I had.

"Maybe you can kiss my ass goodbye," I retorted none too eloquently.

Marsh just smiled. "Someone's going to have to, the *Sierra* has just come within range of the orbital platforms. Also, night's falling on the DZ and air cap reports they've leveled everything bigger than a farmhouse in a two hundred klick radius, but no sign of any Man O'War build up."

"Damn it, we have to find it. How long can the *Sierra* hold without additional back up?" I asked.

"Maybe two or three minutes, tops. Then those *Yreka* classes will be on her and it's all over." The display showed the truth of his words. Fire from the remaining orbital platforms was lighting the *Sierra* up like a Christmas tree. I made my decision.

"Broadcast a wide band demand for surrender to Evans."

Marsh raised his eyebrows. He was already carrying out his orders despite his skepticism; an excellent follower and leader. "Any particular reason she should give up now, oh fearless one? She's kind of winning, if you haven't noticed."

I just smiled. "Give her a chance to reply."

Red lights flashed across the DZ displays and a quiet alarm began sounding. Marsh slid his chair down the holo-table to get a better look at what was happening. "I'd guess this should be interpreted as a negative response on her part. Scouts estimate nigh on three thousand Man O'Wars plus armor and infantry escort are closing on the DZ. Estimated time of arrival is two minutes."

I clenched my fist in victory. She was playing right into my hands.

"Tell the *Saint Helen's* to target the Man O'Wars, the *Yreka* battleships, and Reykjavik with Novas. Fire immediately upon solution, full spread."

Marsh shrugged again as he relayed a command that could not make any sense to him. He had not been privy to every bit of information I received in my command level briefing, and he knew that, so he just did as he was ordered. Missiles leapt from the *Saint Helen's* launch tubes and streaked across the distances separating her from her targets.

The battleships were the first to go. Their anti-missile systems knocked out two thirds of the incoming missiles. Even one getting through to each would have been sufficient, though.

In the original battle for Thule, the *Saint Helen's* had never left its position at the jump point. When orbital platform bombardment had reduced much of the assault forces to ash and smoking craters just waiting for the Man O'Wars to overrun their position, the *Saint Helen's* captain had jumped her out of the system. No one had known why any missile frigate that could have severely damaged Thule's orbital defenses had fled the battle without firing a shot, but most had presumed cowardice and nervousness on the part of her untried captain. What wasn't public knowledge, or so I had been assured during my briefing, was that Dominion intelligence was convinced she had been loaded to the gills with what I had codenamed Novas: nuclear weapons.

That made sense, the Parisians must have had something in reserve that would make them confident enough to launch an offensive with such a small force. Either the captain or the sortie commander had lacked the determination to use them, though. Me, I had no such compunctions in this simulation.

With an average yield of one hundred and ten megatons per warhead, the *Yreka* classes were gone in a series of brilliant flashes which lasted only for a second on the holo-displays. Shortly after that, thousands of Man O'Wars, along with Thule's capital, suffered a similar fate. A few of my own units had been lost in the detonations, but only a fraction of the losses the original Parisians had suffered. In my mind, that justified the sacrifice.

It would be much harder to justify it on Madrigal, but that would come later.

Marsh swallowed hard, but offered no verbal criticism. His tone of voice told a different story, however, one not openly expressed in words. I watched his face go blank and his jaw tighten. He obviously did not approve of my strategy, even though he tried to control himself. "Thule planetary command is broadcasting on all channels in the clear, no effort at encryption whatsoever. Orbital systems are powering down their weapons. They've surrendered. You've won, commander."

So I had.

We immediately proceeded to our debriefing. Me and my XO, Rachel and her XO (a competent Two name Maurice Hughes), and Captain Kay met in the main observation room. Kay had sat us down and asked for first impressions. They hadn't held back.

"Anyone can nuke a planet into submission," Marsh was jumping all over me. "Where's the skill in that? Where's the respect for life? The opportunity for your enemy to go down fighting if they so choose? And a civilian target?"

We were seated around the holo-table. I ran my hands across its smooth surface, rubbing imaginary dust between my fingers, secure in the knowledge that I had won, regardless of what they thought of my methods. The table was dark now, just a black surface, reflecting my own face back at me when I looked down at it. The main overhead lights were on also, making the room appear larger than the one we had been in for the simulation. It was an optical illusion; I knew they were the same size, but without the additional holographic displays that had cluttered the area and the background darkness that had removed the walls it seemed much bigger.

"I followed my orders to take the planet at all costs, without harming the northern continents' vast manufacturing resources," I defended myself. I personally thought that Marsh was just upset that he hadn't thought of this solution. Whose side was he on, anyway? We had won!

Hughes protested right over top of me. "The Taurus Accords have prevented the use of nuclear weapons for over three hundred years! You cheated!"

That offended me.

"New Paris never ratified the accords," I explained. "It's not my fault you didn't consider this possibility. You should have done more research."

I had counted on the fact that nukes hadn't been used in centuries to catch them by surprise. Mom was always fond of saying that most people get so set in what has always been that they suppose it will always be. She also said that most people don't care for being proven wrong. Mom was right about so many things.

Hughes slapped his hands down on the table as he leapt up from his chair. His bulbous nose was reddening, as were his ears and forehead. He gritted his teeth and leaned toward me over the table. "Are you saying I'm stupid because I thought you had more brains than to plunge the entire Charted Territories back into the Dark Ages of nuclear warfare?"

"No," I replied soothingly without moving from my seat, but making solid eye contact. "I'm saying you're stupid for entirely different reasons."

Kay was on his feet now, which didn't make him much taller than when he'd been seated, but that motion gained everyone's attention. He cleared his throat and asked if everyone would like to be seated again. Hughes grudgingly complied, though both he and Kay shot me warning looks that promised dire consequences if I didn't watch my smart-ass mouth a bit more closely.

"Cadet Evans," Kay said, turning toward Rachel, "what's your interpretation of these events?"

She had already been in her seat when I'd arrived for the debrief, and had not said a single word the whole time. She had just sat there looking around the table at each of us in turn as we had argued over my little surprise. Now she turned to look directly at Kay.

"I lost, sir," she admitted simply, with a slight shrug of her delicate, lithe little shoulders. "As Cadet Aarons suggests, I failed to consider the possibility of thermo-nuclear weapons being unleashed on Thule. It would be unfair to criticize him for using every advantage he could when I did not hesitate to do the same. I mean, I sent two *Yreka* class battleships into a battle I was already winning. I admit that I would never have considered using nukes if our positions had been reversed, but then I would have lost if our positions had been reversed."

She said it all as if it were merely a concession that she'd lost a game of chess. Obviously, she didn't take these assessments nearly as seriously as Hughes and Marsh did, or as seriously as I took them, for that matter. I gained some insight into her character then, and one of the advantages she held over the rest of us Twos. Rachel was looking to learn and improve herself, while we were all looking to win. She had learned to separate her ego from her position, allowing her to lose without damaging her self-esteem, so she could take risks that others could not. It was something I would consider more later.

For now, I was just admiring the perfect, smooth lines of her face. Her soft cheek bones and pert nose drew attention to her most amazing green eyes. Her dark brunette hair was pulled back in a perfectly coiffed braid—without so much as a strand hanging loose—that hung over her left shoulder and down across her chest. I jolted myself away from admiring her chest too obviously and tried to focus on the conversation, though I still stole glances at that nicely filled shirt.

"Cadet Hughes? Succinctly if you will." Kay nodded to Hughes.

Hughes took a moment to organize his thoughts. "We never considered the possibility that anyone would unleash nukes on military targets both naval and ground, sir, much less on a civilian target causing millions of casualties. It is something we should always be aware of, I suppose, but I must admit I've lost some respect for Cadet Aarons knowing that he believes this is an acceptable way to win a war, even a simulated one."

Kay just accepted that, which surprised me somewhat since I thought, of all people, he would understand my reasoning. Then he turned to Marsh, and gestured with a raised hand that he too should provide some feedback.

"I'm appalled that anyone would ever use nukes on a civilian target. It doesn't matter what role we were assigned for historical purposes, for this mission we were supposed to be acting on our own decisions and conscience, not in the character of someone else. I don't like it, sir. It makes me wonder."

"Cadet Aarons, your thoughts? Other than patting yourself on the back?" Kay asked me finally.

"I accomplished the objective without losing more than twenty percent of my force, which was otherwise far too small to accomplish a mission of this magnitude anyway. I thought outside the box and was successful. Attacking a civilian target was the only thing brutal enough to ensure that my opponent knew I wouldn't hold anything back and enable a swift victory." That summed it up pretty well, I thought. Let them eat their hearts out, I knew they were just jealous.

"Then you are dismissed," Kay said simply as he stood. I rose and followed the others toward the door, a little uncertain of what I was supposed to have gained from that debriefing. "Chase, a word please." Kay was using my first name again, warning bells went off in my head.

"Sir?" I asked. He shut the door behind the other cadets and motioned for me to return to my seat.

I removed the service cap which I had begun to place on my head, then perched on the edge of my chair. My palms were sweating with anticipation at this unfamiliar development. I told myself it was just a biological reaction, a readying of the fight or flight reflexes in an unknown situation. It wasn't as if I'd done anything wrong, I tried to convince myself, but my body didn't listen nearly as well as my brain talked.

As I sat there trying to convince the various parts of my body, especially my bladder, that I wasn't going to be shot on the spot and that I couldn't be in any real trouble, Kay paced back and forth. He had that expression on his face that many fathers get when they have to have the "talk" with their sons, or have to teach them how to wipe. It was a look that said he was building himself up to talk about something that "normal" adults took for granted and never discussed in public. Finally he sat down, running a hand over his head.

"Chase, do you know why Hughes and Marsh are so mad at you?" He asked it as if he believed that I really didn't know the answer.

"Yes, sir," I replied confidently, if unsure where this whole thing was headed. "They think I cheated because I thought of a solution that they didn't. It's jealousy." I trailed off because he was already shaking his head.

"I don't doubt that that plays a part, at least with Hughes, but there's more to it than that." He looked at his fingers, steepled together on the tabletop before him. "Some things cannot be explained adequately with words. Social norms and mores fall into that category." He glanced up and saw that, despite my ongoing education in neuro-linguistics, I had no idea whatsoever what he was talking about. He breathed in deeply, then let it all out in a sigh.

He tried again. "Every nation in the Charted Territories has honored the Taurus Accords limiting the damage done to civilian targets and collateral for two hundred years, whether they ratified it or not. Even Gaul. Hell, even the Sons of Terra, as fanatically insane as they seem to be most of the time. We've been following the accords so long we've adopted them as a way of life, Chase. Along with that comes the assumption that no one will ever break them. That's part of being a Dominion citizen, a commitment to preventing the Dark Ages from coming again." He fidgeted after saying this, as though he couldn't believe he was being forced to explain something so personal.

"But," I protested, "there are two differences here. First," I ticked off the point on a finger, "accepting a truism only makes it accepted, it doesn't indeed make it true. Someday, somewhere, someone will take advantage of that assumption and use it against us." How truly I prophesied. Oh, the wisdom of youth. I ticked off another finger. "Second, I didn't actually nuke an entire city. It was all in the simulators, it was all about the game." I blinked, then hastily added, "Sir."

Kay sighed deeply again. Apparently he wasn't getting his message, whatever it was, across to me effectively. "First," he said, "you have a point, but I'll be damned if it's ever going to be the Dominion that uses the excuse of opportunity to break the Accords. We don't work like that. And second, you did nuke an entire city full of people. You know these simulations aren't games. They're not about winning, they're about learning and I'm not sure I like the lesson you think you learned today."

"I don't understand, sir." Can't make it any more obvious than that, just blurt it right out and admit you're brain damaged.

I could almost see Kay saying the words to himself. One more try. "You lost almost ten percent of your forces in your own nuclear blast. You sacrificed how many lives from your own nation just to accomplish the goal? Is that the way you believe in fighting a battle, Chase?"

My temper flared slightly. I tried to make him see reason. "In the original invasion of Thule, the Parisians lost over forty percent of their forces to orbital bombardment alone before they surrendered, sir. My losses were far less. My actions actually saved lives."

Kay seemed to slump in defeat. He stood up and was obviously readying himself to leave, adjusting his cap in his hands preparatory to donning it. "I'm not comfortable with that line of thinking. You boil it all down to numbers, willing to sacrifice your own men to your own guns if it accomplishes your goal a little sooner. And maybe that does save a few more lives on paper, but it does something to the morale and even the souls of each and every soldier that has any part in it. Most especially the one that orders it. Is that better than a few more clean deaths? Think it over." With that he slipped on his cap and simply left.

I slammed a fist down hard onto the table, frustrated and angry. What kind of way was that to run a war? I was trying to *save* lives for heaven's sake! What was there to think about? This wasn't a dishonorable action, it was like the American bombing of Japan long ago in the first use of atomic weapons. Yes they had been used against civilians in violation of traditional rules of war, but by all estimates it saved lives on both sides!

If only I'd known then. Why, God, do we have always have to learn too late? Why are prophecies only recognized as true after they've been fulfilled? But at that moment, I had no inkling of what was to come, no perspective beyond the fact that I was going to be a warrior, a great leader, and a name in the history books. Vision without understanding, that was my gift. Now, after having made a definite mark in the history books, I've all the understanding but no vision. Life turns a full circle.

I shook my head as I stood and assumed my own cap. I adjusted it squarely on my head, then carefully pushed my chair back to its proper resting position. Captain Kay was my mentor in so many ways, not just my teacher, so why couldn't he see what I was doing? It was just a simulation anyway. If he was so disturbed by my actions, why hadn't he just told me I was wrong and that I should never do anything of that sort again? Why the lecture on social norms? Questions bounced around in my head at light speed for the brief moments it took me to cross the room, fling the door open hard enough to scratch the paint where it collided with the door stop, and sulk down the stairs outside.

"Aarons?"

All of my thoughts fled from my head. They probably followed the flow of blood to other, more important organs when I turned and saw Rachel standing there. I ogled her for a long moment before I mentally regained my balance, or some modicum of it anyway.

"Hi, Evans. I thought you'd be off studying for your next class by now like you always are." I mentally winced at my verbal ineptitude. Yep, that was me, ever the smooth talker with the ladies. Then it dawned on me and, like a total tool, I just threw it right out in the open to produce yet another awkward speed bump in our dialogue. "Were you waiting for me?"

She smiled at that. We've already established that my kinesthetic memory is superb. Well, this is what I remember when she smiled: someone struck a large bell right above my head, flashed an extremely bright light in my eyes, and then kicked me in the stomach. I never got a good look at the bastard who did it, but he probably wore a diaper and wings and carried a bow. It was hopeless, she was as beyond me as being an aviator was, but I was helplessly in love.

"I wanted to talk to you about our simulation. You raised some interesting points that I'd like to explore further." She was so perfect. She didn't think of herself as better than me after all, she was just so focused on her goals that she came across that way. She was actually human, with human interests, human failings, and human ambition. I realized I was staring.

"Which raised point of mine did you want to explore further?" I asked. Good Lord, I still cannot believe I said that. But she just laughed as if it was the cleverest thing she'd ever heard. I tried again. "Why don't we go up to the cafeteria and talk over some lunch, I'm starving." Finally, something smoother than twenty grit sandpaper.

She even said yes.

Chapter Five

COTC Evaluation and Placement Camp
Fort Lundquist
Baja California, North America
Terra
Terran Dominion

Summer 2648

It's funny how quickly three years can pass. When every day something new is learned, and every weekend holds the promise of adventure, life passes by at a phenomenal rate, but it is a very satisfying life, one where you can say you made a difference, you lived the adventure, you were striving to be all that you could possibly be. That sent me off to Third Year Evaluation and Placement Encampment.

E and P Camp, now there's a disjointed memory. Ten weeks of hell in between a cadet's third and fourth years. It's a career breaker if not taken seriously enough; evaluations at camp determine if cadets get placed in the units of their choosing, if they go active duty or reserve, or if they even get commissioned at all.

The whole idea is to simulate ten weeks of the difficulties and stresses of combat duty. During those weeks a cadet can expect to be wet, tired, cold, hungry, scared, and, as often as not, bored stiff. Communication with the outside world is sporadic at best. Even in my precise memory the whole experience tends to blend together into one blurred whole. It has been compared, fairly accurately I'm assured, to having an extremely high fever, complete with hallucinations, physical privations, and only the occasional lucid moment, and that is how I remember it.

It was week one and we were moving into the barracks that would be home, more or less, for the duration of our stay. France, the guy from England, had the bunk above mine, and we were assigned as battle buddies. Luckily, we hit it off right from the start, and I knew we'd become fast friends.

The cadre assigned to work with us, teach us, and evaluate us had actually guided us here, introduced themselves, and helped us settle in a bit. I wasn't fooled, I knew not let my nervousness trick me into getting comfortable with the cadre. Williamson had warned me that they would try to get close to make the stress and trauma even more disturbing when the bad things started happening. Which was exactly 2 AM.

Drill Sergeant Thayne went through our rack of bunks with a machine gun and a full belt of blanks. He would randomly stop at the foot of some bunk and fire a dozen rounds toward the ceiling. Anyone who tried to ask what was going on was told to shut up and be quiet. When he left after fifteen minutes of raw fear, no one was certain whether this was part of camp or if Thayne had just gone insane. Not many went back to sleep afterward.

At five o'clock we were told to report to formation on the dirt quad in front of the barracks. As we were forming up, cadre members were soaking the ground with fire hoses. We all balked at lining up where the hoses were spraying, and received a complete dressing down from Thayne and his megaphone until we rushed forward, slipping and sliding on the mud. Half the formation was being sprayed with the cold water, but we began our physical training exercises anyway. We did pushups so that our chests splashed mud, we did sit-ups so that we were laying in the mud, and then we sat and stretched so that everyone was soaked thoroughly and covered in mud from head to toe. I cannot recall exactly when they turned off the fire hoses.

Drill Sergeant Thayne then had us form up once again, just as the sun was peeking over the horizon. He paced down our ranks, his massive yet still lean frame blocking the light from our eyes for long seconds, staring at our muddy, shivering forms with a sneer on his face.

"It has only been fourteen hours since you arrived at my camp, and most of you already want to quit," he announced in that universally recognized drill sergeant voice. A quick glance at the faces around me told me he was right. I mentally blessed Ducell for having driven me to that edge once already, and Kay as well for all he'd done. I knew what to focus on for my motivation. "You look like the kind of warmed over crap that my wife's pathetic poodle would bury in the backyard," Thayne continued, bolstering our self-confidence. "It seems to me that the Dominion has wasted an awful lot of money bringing you all here just so that you can fail. Well, by damn, I am going to see that any of you who last the whole ten weeks will have learned how to be good soldiers. If that means I have to kill every one of you, I will. Do you understand?" he shouted.

"Yes, sir!" the formation shouted back. Not loudly enough, though.

"Apparently you do not! But I guarantee you will," he assured us. "Training Sergeant Murphy!" A lithe dark man presented himself confidently to us. Thayne faded back to stand with the rest of the cadre off to one side.

"Drill Sergeant Thayne is convinced that you are not fit to live in his army. I have argued on your behalf that I think at least a few of you have the potential we need. So you are going to prove me correct. Starting right now. Ten kay run! Follow me!" With that, he took off, bounding away and across the field like a startled deer. I didn't even hesitate to follow. As cold and dirty as I was, I knew lagging behind would just make things worse. I glanced back and saw that at least three cadets from our group of fifty had stayed back in formation. When we finally returned, their lockers and bunks were empty. They were only the first to go.

Sometime during the second week we were running an obstacle course. I was boosting France up onto one of the walls. Something hit me behind the knee, and I sprawled down into yet more of the ever present mud. France scrambled up to the top of the wall despite the loss of his support. I looked up to see Thayne and his thrice damned megaphone staring down at me.

"What in the name of all of Dante's circles do you think you are doing, Cadet?" He roared loud enough without the megaphone, with it I could hear him in my colon. "Were you told to help other cadets?"

"No, sir!" I shouted up, scrambling to my feet and attention. "Nor was I ordered not to, sir!"

"Carry on, Cadet!"

This surprised me enough that I actually turned my head to look at him. A mistake. He jammed his megaphone right in my nose.

"Do you have problems following orders, Cadet? You were told to carry on, were you not?"

"No sir! Yes sir!"

"I want your skinny ass over that wall yesterday, Cadet! So why the hell are you still standing here staring at my pretty face?" I turned to attack the wall again, but I wasn't quick enough. Thayne had heard France's snicker.

Thayne looked up in time to see a pair of hands disappear from the top of the wall. He stomped himself around to the other side and confronted the Englishman. "Exactly what is it about my face that you find so humorous, Cadet?" I pulled myself to the top of the wall and observed that it was now France's turn to have his nose stuck in the megaphone. "You will finish this obstacle course in record breaking time, or you will repeat the entire course again. Both of you. Do you understand?"

"Yes sir!" we both shouted as I dropped to stand beside France.

"Then why are you still here?" Thayne shouted. We ran.

"Guide it onto the road," Bushel said. That was a bad move. Training Sergeant Murphy immediately spun on him and got right up in his face.

"What kind of an imprecise order is that?" he shouted. "You expect this whole column to somehow simply follow the winding of this twisted trail without constant guidance from its leader?"

Bushel should have known better by now. Every cadet that had led a formation march thus far in camp had been chewed up for the exact same mistake. Now he was just glancing nervously over Murphy's shoulder as the formation continued its march, totally bereft of his guidance, straight across the trail and headed for a fence. I was far enough back in formation to have a clear view of the dressing down and the imminent collision of bodies and prefab fencing.

"Do you realize that I am talking to you, Cadet?" Murphy asked. "Why are you looking over there?"

Bushel snapped his eyes back to the sergeant. "Yes, sir. Nothing sir." He was trying to play the game perfectly to get away from Murphy before disaster struck. Murphy knew that of course, and was not about to be beaten so easily.

"Nothing? So you think that's more important than paying attention to the words coming out of my mouth? Do you?"

"No, sir," Bushel knew what was going to happen.

I saw the formation ahead begin to buckle and fall apart as the front ranks ran out of room to march and the ones behind plowed into them. Bushel closed his eyes momentarily, knowing what was going to come next.

"Cadet Bushel!" Thayne's bullhorn shouted close behind me. The drill sergeant strode past me to put his megaphone right in Bushel's face. "Exactly what kind of ate up mess is this you are running? Is this how you think you'll impress a review board sufficiently to be made an officer? This is the stupidest thing I've seen in my entire career of dealing with stupid cadets!"

Murphy was also shouting at the poor guy. "Quit, Bushel, quit! If you can't even hack this simple a task, get out right now. Go home where it's safe and you don't have any responsibilities!"

Bushel was quivering. "No, sir! I will not quit, I will not give up!"

The formation continued to fall apart as we, in the absence of orders to the contrary, continued to march into the fence, rank upon rank. It was a horrible snarl that Bushel was going to have to disentangle.

"Then why are you standing here talking to us when you should be fixing the problem you created in the first place?" Murphy bellowed while Thayne glared. "Why are you allowing your formation to get even worse than it already was?"

Bushel turned away from them and quickly began the arduous task of sorting out the mess.

It was the middle of the night again, I had lost track of which week we were in. Instead of sleeping the normal four or five hours we were usually allowed, we were out heaving around huge logs and doing pushups by the squad. This was the fourth night in a row we'd done this. Again, we were being hosed down with cold water. Someone was lighting off landmine simulators at random, and occasionally firing flares into the air. I could hear other units doing similar things at locations not too distant from ours.

My vision blurred as my squad hoisted our log off the ground and up to rest on our right shoulders. My knees buckled somewhat as we pressed it over our heads yet again, but I forced myself to stabilize it. As we were lowering it to the left, someone slipped in the mud. The whole squad crashed down and I felt a good portion of the log's weight bounce off of my chest. The agony was intense, but the disorientation we were already suffering from actually helped me by making me unable to truly focus on the pain. I just laid in the mud, under the log, tempted to simply let myself go to sleep, despite the pain in my chest and the screams that I could hear nearby.

Then the log was gone and I was being hauled to my feet and flashlights were shining in at me from several directions. Thayne was nose to nose with me reading the life in my eyes. "Do you need a medic, Cadet?" he asked. His tone suggested that I should be dead before he would accept a positive response. "Answer me, Cadet!" he barked.

"Chest hurts bad, sir," I mumbled, then winced when he shook me. He ran his eyes down my frame then pulled my shirt open. His eyes narrowed and his brow tightened up at whatever he saw there.

"Aarons," he began in a tone quite different from his normal one. If I hadn't known better I might have called it caring. "You have a choice here. You can call a medic and get out of here right now, tonight, but you'll have to start E and P all over again, from day one. Most cadets who medivac this late in the program never come back to finish. But it looks to me like mostly bruising and maybe some sprained rib joints, nothing too serious. Pushups will hurt like a witch's hemorrhoids on her broomstick, but you'll be okay." Then he returned his voice to its more familiar cadence and tone, "So do you need a medic, Cadet?"

I couldn't think at that point, I was on autopilot. Perhaps if I had been able to think clearly, I would have called a medic just to be safe with my health. Likely, I too would not have returned to take my place at E and P, and would have ruined my career.

From where I sit now, that doesn't seem like such a bad alternative.

"No, sir," I tried to bark. It hurt, but I was adjusting to it like an overly hot bath. Maybe it wasn't as bad as it had felt at first.

"Then attend to your injured squad mates, Cadet!" Thayne shouted.

I turned to see who was injured and how badly. France had gone down at the very end of the log, and avoided all injury. Most of the others were generally unscathed, if perhaps scraped and bruised. Two cadets had obviously fractured ribs and one had sprained his wrist, but one poor soul, probably the one who had slipped, had an open fracture on each shin. She was sobbing hysterically as our squad put together makeshift splints and a stretcher. We helped all of our injured off the exercise field, and left them in the care of the medics there. Then we were broken up and told to go join the other squads who had continued hoisting their own logs without interruption.

At least three or four times a week we would receive orders for combat missions. On one of those days during one of those weeks I was running up a hill, trying to get back to the rest of the platoon. I had been the forward observer, ordered to await contact with the enemy, set off our command detonated mines, and then beat feet back to let command know they were coming. When I had set off the mines, the OPFORs had all hit the dirt, so I was making good on my getaway.

I passed the sentries on the run, calling out the password long before I was challenged. They relayed back to command that the FO was back in, and that the OPFORs were coming. I was already scrambling into the large foxhole that France had dug us.

"Hey, you made it back, buddy," France said. "I just won two grenades from Min."

I looked over at Sook-Yin Min where she hunkered down behind a tree talking softly with her battle buddy. I smacked her helmet with a tossed clump of dirt to catch her attention. "You bet against me making it back?" I inquired.

She smiled and shrugged. "You're fast on your feet, man, but only in the thinking department."

I gave her the finger, then heard the machine guns start up. Artillery began falling down on both sides of the combatants. Most of the rounds were simulated high-explosive or anti-personnel, but some of the rounds were smoke, turning our battlefield into a multi-hued hazy blur. I brought my rifle to the ready and thumbed the selector switch to four round burst.

Soon enough the artillery barrages stopped and I could hear the OPFORs approaching, yelling back and forth and shooting in our general direction. I saw a shape approaching through the man-made fog and fired two bursts. The silhouette dropped, but I was unsure whether it was from activated muscular inhibitors or from a dive for cover. It didn't matter, as there were plenty more shapes moving around out there.

France and I started shooting in alternating patterns, only pausing long enough to switch magazines or occasionally toss a grenade. Regardless of our efforts, or the similar efforts of Min and the others around us, more and more OPFORs were getting closer and closer to our position. It was only a matter of minutes before we were completely overrun.

"Fall back!"

The command rang out from the platoon leader and was passed along by every voice in succession. The machine guns and assistant gunners fell quiet as they were the first to pick up and begin retreating up the hill. Then the rest of us fell back by bounds, laying down cover fire for each other.

When we reached the top of the hill, we were quickly split into one heavy fire group that would lay down suppression fire and one assault group that would be going back to take out our attackers. I was assigned to the fire support group but, when no one was looking, I stepped over to the assault group where the real action would be.

With no more thought or planning than that, we were plunging back down the hill, far enough over to be approaching the OPFORs at a right angle. The first we realized that they had had time to dig in was when the majority of our group got dropped by a machine gun nest.

I hit the ground with the rest of them, and rolled behind a tree stump. A quick glance around told me that only two others remained mobile some ways down the hill. They both popped up and were quickly dispatched by the machine gun.

I risked enough of a glance around my stump to confirm the location of the machine gunner, then ducked back down to ready myself. I took a deep breath, then cleared the stump with a smooth bound, shouting out a battle cry worthy of any ancient barbarian.

I had taken the machine gunner by complete surprise. He desperately tried to get his heavy barrel pointed back in my direction before I could finish my attack. With a smile I lined him up in my sights and squeezed the trigger. Nothing happened, and a quick glance confirmed that after my last shot my rifle had double fed, forcing two rounds into the firing chamber and jamming the mechanism. The last thing I remember before my muscular inhibitors knocked me down and out was the look of pleased surprise on the gunner's ugly mug.

Everything looks different when you're ten stories up, standing at the rail of a catwalk and expected to jump off. For one thing, the ground looks a lot harder. For another, the people belaying your rope don't look nearly as competent as you'd thought moments before when they were helping others rappel down. It was my turn to go though, so I let them hook me up. Two ropes through my snap-link and I was set to safely descend to the waiting earth below. At least, that was the plan.

I backed up until only the toes of my boots were left on the edge of the catwalk to still support my weight. Then I sat back until my legs were ninety degrees to the wall and my body formed that perfect L-shape. I took a small jump away from the wall and pulled my right hand away from the small of my back to allow the rope to play through the snap-link and my left hand. After descending a few feet, I replaced my right hand and swung back in towards the wall.

Thayne's familiar, if disliked, features peered down at me from the catwalk above. "What the hell are you still doing on my rope, Cadet? If you don't get your skinny ass down there faster than Sisyphus' Boulder rolls down hill, I will be cutting this line!"

I bent my legs and once again pushed off from the wall. Before I could move my hand at all, I heard a sharp pinging noise, and then I was in free fall. My head went back and I arched over like a diver off the high platform. I didn't even have time to scream before I came to a sudden halt still about six stories up in the air, dangling upside down, my still healing ribs twinging in protest of this abuse. Min was still on belay, but she had been joined by two other cadets in an attempt to put enough tension on the rope to keep me from falling. My cap came free of my head and fell to the ground below. It took a disturbingly long time to hit.

"Aarons," France called down to me, "check your snap-link!"

I regained my grip on the rope with both hands, noticing in a detached sort of passing that the friction of the line had burned right through my left glove and left angry red burn marks on my palm. I didn't feel the pain until later.

A bit of a pull with my arms and a big sit-up and I could inspect the snap-link at my waist. The whole thing was twisted up like a pretzel, and the only reason my fall had stopped was because the warped shape had entangled the rope quite securely. With the belay team sitting on the other end of the line, I wasn't going to fall anymore. Probably.

"Drill Sergeant." I tried to yell but it came out in squeaks and rasps. "I can't fix this, sir. It's bent up too badly."

"Sit tight, Cadet!" Thayne yelled down to me, as if he did indeed seriously believe that I might do something else. It seemed like forever that the cadre and other cadets huddled together trying to decide what to do about my situation. With each passing moment, it became increasingly difficult to fight down the giddiness that was bubbling up inside me. I closed my eyes and just held on for dear life, praying some of the most heartfelt prayers of my life.

I thought I had been hanging there for at least an hour, though objectively it was probably no more than fifteen minutes, when I was ready to burst with the fear and panic.

"Help me!" I shouted up, down, and to God. "I don't want to die here." I prayed the last part a little more quietly. A small voice in my head asked me where I wanted to die instead, but I had no answer for that question back then.

"Control yourself, Cadet!" Thayne barked at me. Now he was below me, despite the fact that I had not seen him go down either the other rope or the ladder. Maybe teleportation is one of the skills they teach in Drill Instructor School. I know all those with military experience share my suspicion. "You are going to cut yourself free and drop down on to this net! Do you understand me, Cadet?"

I arched back again, trying not to release my death grip on the rope. A safety net like those used by circus performers had been set up below me. My head told me that I was safe now and that there would be no problem with falling a few stories onto one of those contraptions. My heart, stomach, kidneys, bladder, and every single muscle fiber in my body told me that there was no way in hell that was ever going to happen.

"I can't, sir!" I cried out.

"Horse shit! Cadet France, you will cut that line now!" Thayne shouted up with his megaphone. France had obviously been waiting for that very command, because I hadn't even finished puckering my butt before I was falling ass over elbows into the net below. Ten stories worth of rope also fell with me, entangling me quite thoroughly within the mesh of the net.

When I was finally untangled and pulled free by the other cadets, I was still thanking God for watching over me. I tried to take a step away from the net and my knees buckled, dropping me to the ground where I gratefully kissed the earth. My limbs were shaking as if I were palsied, but I knew it was just adrenaline and would stop in a few minutes.

"Exactly how long do you expect to be sprawled there on the ground shaking like a sweat bead in a fitness bunny's thong, Cadet?" Thayne wasn't using his megaphone, nor was he shouting, but he was projecting for all he was worth.

"Give me five minutes, sir," I replied, trying to salvage some modicum of dignity. I figured a cocksure lie would sound better than the truth. "I'll be fine."

"Outstanding, Cadet!" His megaphone was back on and right by my ear. "Because in five minutes you will be up on that catwalk and you will rappel down like everyone else had to! No one gets to just jump into a net in my unit! Do you understand me, Cadet?"

I did, and five minutes later I tried again.

Once again we were running around at two o'clock in the morning when we should have been sleeping. You tend to want to be asleep at that time of night, especially after weeks of not getting nearly enough shuteye, but instead of enjoying sweet dreams of fresh bread and apple pie served up by mermaids, I had joined the rest of my platoon in climbing into a flight of helicopters and using our newly gained rappelling skills to perform an air assault on a target set up way out in the forest.

After hitting a few OPFOR sites, we made ready to spend the night out under the stars with our ancient canvas shelters. Part of any proper bivouac included posting patrols and setting up proper facilities to handle POWs just in case the cadre or any OPFORs decide to try and slip inside our area of operation. They were sneaky about it, too. In our first week, we'd all been dressed down because a major general had been allowed to just walk right into our AO without being challenged. What cadet would have thought to challenge a general? Now we knew better. We'd seen impersonations of boy scout leaders, lost motorists, even a soccer mom with two little kids, and every time we'd been right to challenge them, even arrest them when necessary.

France and I were quietly walking the length of our perimeter. We were doing our absolute best to remain quiet and unseen, yet observant for any sign of intruders. As we approached the old dirt road that formed one edge of our perimeter, we could see headlights approaching in the distance. Obviously, a vehicle was going to try and penetrate our AO's perimeter.

The two of us took a quick huddle and sketched out a rather hasty plan. France called in for backup while I dragged a fairly hefty tree branch across the road to form a makeshift barricade. Then it was just a matter of taking positions on either side of the road and waiting.

When the ground-car came a bit closer we could see that it was made up like a state police cruiser. I smiled. The cadre had really gone to a lot of effort to create this fake, or maybe they had just borrowed a real one from the local force. Either way, they were going to be stopped. I'd learned my personal lesson on the main part of the base when I'd gone easy on the drunk high school students who had gotten lost on the way back to the officers' housing area where their parents lived. Thayne had not been pleased.

As the car stopped at the barricade, France and I made our quiet approach. Two men, dressed in full state trooper outfits, got out of the vehicle and looked at our barricade. Both were of medium height and build, obviously infantryman, not cops. I pumped my fist twice at France telling him to take the lead.

"Freeze!" France shouted as he brought his assault rifle to bear on the two OPFORs. They quickly turned and drew their sidearms, but France was faster. He fired two bursts that sent them both diving for cover behind their vehicle.

"Throw out your weapons and come out slowly with your hands raised!" France ordered them. They made no immediate response.

"You will do as you are ordered now or I will perforate your forms!" I instructed them. They wheeled around, though they had no way of seeing me in the darkness. "Throw out your weapons now and come out to the front of the vehicle with your hands raised! If you do not move immediately I will be forced to eliminate the threat that you represent!"

The two OPFORs looked at each other. Then the one who had been driving shouted back at me. "This is Officer Merd and Officer Richless of the State Patrol! We have backup en route! I recommend that you throw down your weapons and give yourselves up right now! It'll be easier on you!"

I couldn't help but snicker, their lines were so pathetic. They sounded like the only thing they knew about cops was what they watched on holo-vision. I decided to play along and shouted back, "This is Cadet Aarons of the Terran Dominion Armed Forces! I have a grenade that is about to be en route to your pie-hole! Now come out immediately as instructed or make a widow out of your wife!"

The OPFORs looked at each other and appeared to be conferring. France had worked his way around to the point where he could cover them. He now fired a burst over their heads to add impetus to our commands. Each OPFOR quickly raised his hands and placed his sidearm on the roof of the car, then they pushed both sidearms over to the other side of the vehicle. They stood up slowly and made their way over to the front of the car where they were blinded by the vehicle's headlights.

"Each of you put your hands behind your head and kneel down facing the vehicle," France commanded them from where he had moved behind them. I was working my way down the hill and taking the appropriate position to support him.

"Look, kid," the one who had identified himself as Merd said, "we've obviously interrupted your little pretend game, so why don't you just go get your officer and no one will have to get in trouble, okay?" He began to turn to face us.

France kicked him square in the kidney, dropping him writhing to the ground. I shouldered my rifle and when the second one made to help his partner, I grabbed him at collar and belt and slammed him in to the radiator of the car. "You will do as you are told or we will shoot you where you are!" France bellowed.

He moved to the side of the vehicle and retrieved their firearms. He was just in time, too, because the one he'd sent down was back on his feet and rushing him with murder in his eyes. This time France put him down for good with a boot to the balls and a spinning hook kick that he'd learned in his kickboxing days. When my prisoner began to struggle I used a little less finesse and just smashed his face down on the hood twice. On the second one his head bounced up higher than I'd expected and when I loosened my grip he crumpled to the ground.

Eventually, our backup arrived, complete with two cadre officers and a team of medics. The medics treated our two OPFORs for their injuries, and then the cadre officers debriefed all of us separately. By the time we finished being debriefed and were told to stand down a ways away from the car, another state patrol vehicle had arrived. This one carried a ranking patrol officer. At about that time it dawned on me that we had just beat the crap out of two real police officers, but from what we could hear of the conversation between the cops and our own officers, it was the police who were in trouble. It seems they should have known we were in this area and once they had entered our AO they should have respected our authority.

When Thayne showed up to drag us back to camp, berating us the whole way for anything he could think of, we were feeling pretty smug. He fixed that problem quickly enough, but as he dragged us off, we caught glimpses of two very sore state troopers receiving a very thorough dressing down from their own superior and two very angry cadre officers.

It was in the middle of the day, and we were baking out on the parade ground as we practiced our marching and formation drills in dress uniform. I was officer-of-the-day, so it fell to me to ensure that everyone was pulling their weight and staying in step. We were working on a counter-column march, a maneuver that allows a formation to reverse itself and change direction quickly without losing cohesion.

"Cadet Aarons, you will report yourself to my inbox immediately," a familiar voice called out over the PA system.

I turned command of the formation over to Min with a quick salute, then double-timed it across the parade ground and skidded to a halt at the door to Thayne's office. I knocked on the door and was bid to enter, which I did. I took three precise steps into the room, then halted at attention and saluted.

"Cadet Aarons, reporting to Drill Sergeant Thayne as ordered, sir!" I barked.

"At ease, Cadet," Thayne told me. I dropped to a more casual stance and made eye contact with the drill sergeant. Something seemed changed about him. The way he sat comfortably and not like he had a bayonet up his arse, the way he was speaking in the tone of voice that the cadre at Burke had used, even the way he returned my salute as if he really did respect me was so different from what I was used to receiving from him on a daily basis. It was eerie, as if he were trying to become human.

"Chase," he began. Warning bells again went off in my head. It is never a good sign when cadre use a familiar form of address, never. "You have been granted permission to call home. Take it through that door, in the Drill Sergeants' Lounge." I hesitated, somewhat puzzled that I would be granted a call home when no one else had. Thayne motioned for me to go, so I did, bemused as I was.

That lounge was nice! It was laid out in circular fashion around a wet bar. About a hundred well-padded, leather chairs surrounded tables of various shapes and sizes. I admired the plushness of it all (especially as compared to the sparse quarters we cadets were living in) as I made my way to the phone I had spotted on the bar. I keyed in the number for home and waited for the contact to be made.

"Hello?" Jonny's voice answered. The screen remained blank.

"Jonny, it's me," I said. The screen sprang to life, and Jonny's features appeared on the screen. We weren't identical twins, but we had enough similarities that no one ever mistook us for anything but brothers. We both had the same jaw line, the same dark eyes, and the same flat ears that we had inherited from our father.

"Chase! How's camp going?" He must have been genuinely interested, because he was scheduled to ship off for his own camp session the week I got home.

"It's hard, but you'll make it," I said with a shrug. "Jonny, what's up? They don't let us contact anyone outside unless it's for an extremely important reason." I was looking for some pieces to help me put this puzzle together.

Jonny sighed heavily. "Dad's dead," he said.

I was shocked into momentary silence. "Wha...what...how?" I stumbled out at last.

"He had a massive heart attack during a coffee break at work. He was gone instantly."

I sat dumbfounded. Dad was gone. "When's the funeral? I'm coming home. I can pack up here and be on the next transport."

"Chase," Jonny cut me off, shaking his head, "Dad died two weeks ago. The funeral is long over. We put in a request for compassionate leave for you, but we were told that it was in the military's best interest, and yours, to keep you unaware until it was too late for you to leave. They want to make sure you finish up there."

I was stunned. My father had passed away and command had kept it from me. Tears began welling up in my eyes. "How's Mom? Can I talk to her?"

Jonny looked down for a second before looking back up. "Mom doesn't want to talk to you. She blames you and your desire to be a warrior for your being unable to attend Dad's funeral, for not being here when she needed you the most."

That hurt, a lot. The tears sprang forth and quickly started streaming down my cheeks in twin rivulets. Jonny saw that. "She's just really distraught at losing him like this. She'll be okay in a while, but you have to give her some time," he said.

"But, can't I leave her a message?" I sniffled through the tears. Even that was denied me as Jonny shook his head again.

"Give her time." He looked aside. "I have to go, a bunch of the relatives are over, and I need to get back."

I nodded my understanding. I sniffed and wiped at my eyes. "Just tell everyone I love them, okay?"

Jonny smiled and nodded, then hung up. For several long moments I just sat there staring at the blank screen. Eventually, I became aware that Thayne was standing off to one side of me. I don't know how long he had been there, but he was just standing quietly. When I looked over toward him with tears cascading down my face, he broke eye contact, tossed his cap on a table to one side, and slipped behind the bar.

Two glasses clanked down on the bar-top surface. They were quickly filled with ice and an amber liquid. I took one and swirled it in my hand. "Drink it down," Thayne suggested. We each tossed off a glass and Thayne immediately began refilling them. We finished three more before he brought a bottle of whiskey out and sat beside me so we could nurse a few more glasses.

"My father's dead," I said stupidly. Obviously Thayne would know by now why I had been granted leave to call home.

"I know," he said quietly, "they told me this morning. For the record, I object most strenuously to command's decision to deny compassionate leave. Not for any logical reasons, or intelligent rebuttals, but because I've been there. I know." He paused and took a sip of the whiskey. "My father and my mother were killed in a car accident when I was in Ranger school. I didn't know until I got home. I lost a child to lymphatic citrial while I was on Gottenheim and they didn't tell me until we were pulling out." Another pause and a bigger gulp. "I know."

He must have known, because he said just enough to let me know that he shared my loss, but nothing to annoy me. No platitudes about Dad going to a better place, because that didn't matter when he wasn't here with me anymore.

No advice to focus on what I still had, because I couldn't, I'd lost something irreplaceable. No assurances that the pain would pass, because right now I was so hurt I was beyond feeling.

We just sat there for long hours, sharing stories of the loved ones we'd lost and drinking ourselves out of our sorrows.

There were other events that I can pull out of that fog: memories of artillery simulators thrown carelessly by cadre that almost took off my leg; memories of climbing cliffs hundreds of feet high, cliffs that were so unstable that if you stepped wrong they would crumble underneath even the slightest pressure; even memories of a couple of female cadets that wanted more companionship than I was willing to give and still be able to feel loyal to Rachel.

But above that all is the memory of losing my father, long after he had already passed on. That isn't a memory I want to relive any more than I already have, so I think I'll end it here.

Chapter Six

Commissioning Hall, Burke University
Portland, North America
Terra
Terran Dominion

May 31, 2649

My commissioning ceremony was only slightly marred by the fact that the university president refused to attend. It was her first year as president of Burke University, and she believed that it was necessary for her to show resolve and commitment to her pacifistic ideals. She sent the COTC cadre a signed, binding notice saying that she, unlike her spineless predecessors, would not support the evils promoted by the military in any way, especially not by legitimizing the corruption of bright, young people like us poor cadets. She, for one, was taking a stand against the perpetuation of a warlike culture and all that it stood for.

Unfortunately for her, Burke was a land-grant university, funded by Dominion taxes. She would have done well to examine the duties required of a president of a public university a bit more closely. Law enforcement officers found her at home enjoying dinner with her family when she should have been attending the commissioning ceremony and giving speeches about the duty we fulfilled to the Dominion. Much to her surprise, she was actually arrested for second degree sedition—public refusal to attend to the civic duties required of a public official. I don't know what the outcome of her trial was, nor do I truly care as she brought it upon her own self. Perhaps today I have more sympathy for her ideals, but at the time I was deeply offended by her insulting behaviour.

Was I truly that excited about dashing off across the galaxy ending lives and risking my own? For what? A few lines drawn across a three-dimensional map, that's what. So many lives ended, so many lives ruined, everything from homes to families broken and destroyed.

That aside, most of us Fours were eagerly awaiting the ceremony where we would become full-fledged officers in the Terran Dominion Armed Forces. It was the culmination of four years of hard work and study, and the fulfilment of another step in my lifelong dream of glory. It also held a sharp edge of anticipation, as tonight would be the night we would find out which branch we were to be assigned to and whether we would be active duty or reserve.

Rachel found me pacing outside the commissioning hall, trying to burn off some of the nervous energy I had built up so I wouldn't make a fool of myself during the ceremony. She looked stunning in her tapered officer's uniform, lacking only the gold diamond-and-sword pips that would mark her an officer. I glanced down at the matching grey and white uniform I wore, then smiled at her. Her return smile was pure brilliance and took away what breath my excitement had left me.

"I thought you'd be in there mingling with the parents like everyone else," she said, inspecting me closely. "You look good as an officer," she added. Naturally, she immediately started straightening every little wrinkle she could find on my uniform. Typical perfectionist.

I pulled her hands away from fixing my collar, but retained my grip on her wrists to pull her close. My smile became a leer as I said, "You look pretty good yourself, babe." I tried to kiss her but she flattened her hands on my chest and pushed herself away from my amorous lunge with a giggle.

"That's conduct unbecoming," she waggled a finger in my face. "Forcing your unwanted advances on a poor, defenceless young girl like myself. For shame!" We both laughed and then she hugged me tight and I did get my kiss. I felt both of our bodies trembling slightly. It could have been from the closeness we shared, but it was likely just the anticipation we shared about the coming future, both near and far.

"So, come on," she urged me after we stopped to inhale. She disengaged from my embrace and started pulling my hand toward the doors. "I want you to meet my family, then you can introduce me to yours."

I pulled up short so fast that I think I may have hurt her arm. She whipped around and, I imagine, saw that my expression had changed dramatically. I hadn't meant to be so abrupt, but what she had said hurt more than I had would have thought, especially for such a casual comment I had known was likely coming.

"I'd rather wait until the dinner and dance afterwards, if you don't mind too much." I turned from her and tried to walk off down the hall. Unfortunately,

Rachel had never been so easy to manipulate or encourage. Or coerce. In fact, she couldn't even take a hint, but I loved her for that as much as for anything else.

And I did love her, never doubt that.

She hurried around to put herself back in front of me and took my head between her hands to force me to make eye contact with her. "Chase," she said in that tone that meant I would tell her everything or suffer long for my impudence. "What's wrong?" She tucked her chin and looked up at me from under her perfectly coiffed eyebrows. She was so beautiful.

I sighed deeply, then took her hands and guided her to sit with me on one of the white couches that dotted the foyer. I patted her hand and stared at it as I tried to collect my thoughts. Finally, I worked up the courage to look her in the eyes, afraid that I would find pity there. "My mom's not coming," I said simply. Then it all burst out in a flood. "She went to Jonny's commissioning last week and pinned his rank on like your parents are going to do today, but Jonny told me she won't be coming here. I thought maybe by now, and for this one night, she'd forgive me, but...I guess I'll have to have you and Major Kay do it."

I blinked away the tears that were forming, then I waited to see what emotions her face would show. Thankfully not pity, but sympathy, even understanding were there. She hugged me and brushed away the tears that were threatening to drop despite my best efforts. "I'm sorry. We can wait until the dinner if you think that's better."

I nodded and she retrieved her hand from my grasp, then put both of her palms on my knee. "Do you want me to wait out here with you until we form up?" Her eyebrows raised as she asked the question, and I knew she meant it. She would actually have abandoned her family for me. Love is a powerful thing, stronger than family or friends.

I shook my head. "I'll be okay alone," I said. "Go spend time with your family, they're proud of you." My voice broke on the last part, but I regained control before any more tears fell. Rachel understood, perhaps even better than I did. She gave me one last hug, then stood and left me alone on the couch. Once she left, I cried quite thoroughly. Again.

Self-pity only lasts so long though, especially when you're standing on the brink of forever, and I was able to remind myself that I was being commissioned today. I went and splashed some cold water on my face and once more inspected my pressed and polished uniform in the mirror. Rachel was right, I did look good as an officer, and I wasn't being purely narcissistic. I had no medals or ribbons to adorn my salad board, but I expected those to come with time. Even the epaulets on my shoulders were bare, awaiting the rank pins that would be placed there later. I noticed that, annoyingly, some of Rachel's lipstick had smudged onto the collar where my branch insignia would go. They can send a man across a good portion of this here galaxy, but they can't make a lipstick that won't smudge. Technology. I spent a few concerned moments carefully wiping the brilliant red mark off with some splashed water and a towel.

I returned to the foyer where all the other Fours had arrived and were beginning to form up in one of those universal constants: alphabetical order. Oddly enough, I already knew where my spot would be. Only the Twos bearing the Dominion and University flags, and the Threes in the colour guard with their rifles, stood in front of me. Rachel smiled and squeezed my hand once as we brushed past each other, then she took her place farther down the line.

I took my place at the front of our group, took a slow breath, and squared my shoulders. I was proud to be worthy of becoming a sub-lieutenant, and I was excited to see if I would be granted my dream of being assigned to the augmented armor branch. I was still alive, and long ago I had told myself that, by damn, I'd make a difference in the universe even if I had to walk through hell itself. I smiled at my own audacity, not understanding just how truthfully I had, once again, prophesied.

The national anthem began playing, its martial tones trumpeting throughout the hall. The color guard captain signaled a forward march and, in perfect unison, we all stepped off on our left and marched through the heavy hardwood doors into the hall proper.

I had refrained from entering the hall before because I wasn't sure I could handle seeing everyone else with their families, so I had been unprepared for just how much pomp and circumstance had been put into decorating it. Pennants of the various units that had contributed to our cadre stood proudly at the right of the stage, just in front of the cadre's seating area. In the positions of honor, the stooping eagle of Major Kay's 141st Rangers hung proudly next to the chess king silhouette of Colonel Fuller's 5th Heavy Guard.

To the left of the stage, banners containing the names of every Burke University Collegiate Officer Training Corps graduate who had fallen in defense of the Dominion covered an entire wall. I had once spent an afternoon reading some of the names and deeds listed there, looking for possible ancestors or relatives. Two in particular still stick in my mind. Captain Jason Aaronson, commissioned to armor May 15, 2557 had died on Trafalgar rescuing his childhood friend from an Aphesian ambush. Sub-lieutenant Carolyn Aarons-Jeh, commissioned to the infantry May 23, 2562 had also died on Trafalgar, killed by friendly fire.

The stage itself was bare, awaiting the flags, but the sigil of the Dominion Armed Forces, an eagle snapping a sword in its beak while clutching an arrow in its talons, dominated the entire back wall. Beneath scrolled the phrase *For Right, For Truth, For Freedom Above All.*

Even though I kept my eyes forward and focused on the flag that I would swear to protect this day, I could still see the proud smiles and happy tears on the faces of all the parents and family members who were assembled in the hall as I marched past them. It tugged at my heart strings, knowing that I was here alone on this very important day, but I tucked that all away. I promised myself time to feel the pain later, but for now, I would accept the hand fate dealt and just be happy that Rachel had her family here to support her, and I would be happy that today I joined the ranks of the few and proud who would defend our nation from foreign threats.

The color guard broke off to set the flags in their rightful places slightly to the left and right of center on the raised stage. I led the Fours to stand in front of our proper seats at the very front of the hall where we would be the center of attention. Once the flags had been placed and the color guard retreated, we stood at perfect attention awaiting the end of the anthem. When the last note finally faded I executed the role that I had been assigned by virtue of having a surname starting with two A's.

"Attention to the national flag!" I bellowed in my best bass command voice. "Present arms!"

In unison with all the other military personnel present, and a good number of the civilians I'm sure, I raised my hand to my brow in a perfect knife edge salute. I made everyone hold that pose for a good ten count, allowing us to reflect on the meaning of that piece of cloth decorated simply by a blue-green planet, two olive branches beneath, on a field of stars. More importantly I wanted everyone to reflect on the lives that had gone into it.

"Order arms!" I bellowed, snapping my arm back down to my side. "Take seats!" I concluded. This allowed all of us to be seated in the red, padded auditorium seats, the designs for which have probably been in use since the Babylonians first built bleachers. I sat back with a bit of pride. As Major Kay was known to say, if you can't get a salute to the flag right, one of our most cherished gestures of patriotism, then you can never even hope to be a good officer. I believed Dad would have agreed and been proud. I think he would have been proud of everything I'd done.

Perhaps, even now, he'd still be proud of all I've done. Only God knows that, though, and there is no pride left within me.

As everyone shifted to get comfortable, Colonel Fuller marched up onto the stage from the cadre's seating area on the right. His grey and whites practically snapped with their crispness, while his crown, sword, and circle pips blazed with reflected light, as did the golden crossed arrows that denoted his artillery branch assignment. He approached the center of the stage, then made a precise left turn and faced the audience in a parade rest stance, hands clasped behind his back as the PA announced his position as head professor of military science for Burke University.

"I'd like to thank all of you for coming here today. Your presence is very much appreciated by all of us, but especially by those close to you who will be participating," he began. His voice carried clearly and easily, projected with the calm confidence that comes with many long years of leading and training soldiers. "You are all here today for a very special purpose. Some of you will be participants as cadets or parents, and some of you will simply be observers. Regardless, we will all be witnesses to one of the most solemn and exciting events that ever takes place within the Dominion. Today we will ensure that the continuing defense of our nation, and all of the myriad freedoms and rights that we enjoy, is made possible by placing the rights, responsibilities, and duties of a commissioned officer into the hands of these worthies present."

Fuller looked around slowly, his serious demeanor driving home for all present the true import of his words. "It is not a drawn out ceremony, and one that is oft mocked, by those who do not understand, as being far too simple to be of real importance. Yet it is in simplicity that we see truth. Let no one present this day ever forget that today these men and women take upon themselves the mountainous burden of defending the lives of every Dominion citizen and resident. It is a duty that may ask them to forsake friends and family, to endure crippling hardships, or to lay their lives down upon what we often call the altar of freedom. And that is why they are deserving of the respect, privileges, and salutes that we will offer them from this day forth." He smiled down at us cadets.

"You cadets have all worked very hard to earn the right to be here this day, and many of you have sacrificed a lot in doing so. For the work you have done and for all that you have given already in the pursuit of safeguarding our nation, all of us are in your debt. But make no mistake, you will be called upon to make even greater sacrifices in protecting this great nation. Some of you will lose friends and families, some of you will give up the wealth and fame that you could find in the civilian realm, and some of you will be asked to choose between the lives of your wards and that most precious of all possessions, your own life. After knowing you for these last years, I believe all of you will make the right decision as these choices come to you.

"Never shirk these responsibilities, and never allow them to crush you. Bear up under this burden, and win for yourselves a place in the history books by keeping our nation great. May God bless you and watch over you."

Fuller drew himself to attention. "Fours, on you feet!" he commanded.

With the others, I jumped to attention, my chair snapping back up behind me. The colonel looked us over and nodded in approval. "The Dominion has judged you hard these past four years, and has not found you wanting. You are to now be officially offered the opportunity to take your oath of commission and step forward as officers of the Terran Dominion Armed Forces. If any of you have any reservations, any whatsoever, you may leave now. No one will question your decision." That I found hard to believe. We'd all question the decision of anyone who backed out this late in the process, but tradition required it, though the public pressure made it extremely unlikely.

Fuller waited a moment, as the ceremony demanded, to see if anyone really would back out at the last instance. No one did. He nodded in approval again.

"Then I will now administer the oath of commissioning. It is a powerful statement, one that reveals the Truths upon which this great nation is built. Now, each of you raise your right hand to the square, the ancient symbol of truth and accuracy, and repeat after me," he ordered. We each lifted our right arm to the position he had dictated, and then repeated every word as he said, "I hereby accept the duties and responsibilities of an officer in the Terran Dominion Armed Forces. I will never disgrace this sacred duty nor desert my companions in the ranks. I will fight for my nation, her flag, her constitution, and her citizens, both alone and with many, defending them against all enemies both foreign and domestic. I will obey and uphold the lawful and correct commands of my superiors, the laws of my nation, and the freedoms of my fellow citizens. If any person, group, or nation should seek to set these things at naught, I will do all in my power to prevent it. This I swear to do, forsaking all else to this end, even my own life if it be necessary. So help me God, and uphold me in this sacred duty as an officer of the Terran Dominion Armed Forces."

I felt a tingle run up and down my spine as I took the oath. I knew I was not alone, especially when the cadet next to me, Pete Antine, couldn't suppress his shiver. "You may be seated," Fuller told us as the auditorium erupted with applause. We smiled at each other as we sat down, Pete and I even shook hands in congratulations.

The colonel relaxed to an at ease posture. "Now, as our custom dictates, those who have been asked by our cadets to honor them by pinning their rank pips on will do so. Traditionally, it falls to cadre to pin on a new officer's branch insignia and to parents or friends of high position to pin on the officer's rank insignia. So, cadets, and this is the last time you will ever be addressed as cadets, please come forward when your selected cadre member is in position and the announcer calls your name. For those family members and honored guests who will be attending our cadets, please assemble to the left of the stage and approach when your names are announced." Colonel Fuller left the stage to retake his position with the rest of the cadre.

There was a bit of rustling around as parents and a few other close friends and notables left their seats and congregated to the left of the stage, preparing to share this wonderful day with their children or friends. On the right, the cadre also formed up to perform their part. I had to pad my heart again, knowing that I was the only one without parents and other loved ones present. Later, I reminded myself, later I could cry.

Once everyone was in position a silence fell across the gathering, awaiting the announcement of our names. "Chase Aarons, approach the stage," the disembodied voice called.

As I rose from my seat, I frowned and glanced around for Major Kay who was supposed to be center stage right now, but he was still standing with the other cadre members. I raised an eyebrow and he just motioned me to mount the stage as we'd been instructed. Confused and wondering what was happening, I ascended the steps at the right of the stage. From the rear left side of the stage, another man approached. He wore the black dress uniform of a general.

"General on the deck!" our newest cadre member, Master Sergeant Kit Randleman, bellowed out. Everyone shot to their feet and I snapped to attention once again.

"As you were," General Gough said. Recognition of the general dawned in my mind somewhere beneath the strong currents of dismay. He hadn't changed from when I saw him in high school, save that he now wore a fourth star and possibly a few more ribbons. He clapped me on the shoulder, leaned in toward me, and quietly said, "Did you think I'd let anyone else pin a branch assignment on the kid who crashed one of my Man O'Wars long before he was allowed to pilot one?" He smiled broadly at me and I found myself returning the expression.

"No, sir," I said as he turned to address the assembly. "I should have guessed, though."

He spared a glance back at me, winked, then spoke to everyone in the hall, just as I started to figure out the full meaning of what he had just said about my branch assignment. "For outstanding performance at Evaluation and Placement Encampment, for exceptionally high scores on the requisite aptitude tests, for having gained straight one hundred percents in all COTC classes, and for having a slightly better than mediocre GPA in all other courses," Gough paused to let everyone laugh at that part, "it is my singular honor to announce Chase Aarons' assignment to an active duty position within the augmented armor branch, the Man O'Wars!" Everyone applauded as the general held up the Man O'War *silhouette en guard* insignia of my new branch. My knees almost buckled at the announcement. I had hoped and prayed for this assignment, and I had worked hard, but until now I had not known for sure what would happen. Jonny had fantastic grades at Harvard, and he had applied for the augmented armored reserves. Instead of his first choice, he'd been sent to the infantry reserves, his second choice, so, despite everything I'd done, at no point was I ever certain that I'd get what I wanted.

As the applause died down Gough smiled at me, pinned the insignia on my collar, and then shook my hand firmly with an even bigger grin. Then he continued his surprises as the announcer said, "As Sub-lieutenant Aarons has requested, his rank will be pinned on by his brother, Sub-lieutenant Jonny Aarons, and his mother Anna Aarons."

I ignored all proper military decorum and protocol I'd ever learned and turned to gape slack jawed at the two people approaching from my right. One was a sharp looking young infantry officer and the other was a shorter, middle-aged woman. Jonny was all smiles and laughter as he came closer. Mom was smiling widely too, but she was crying her eyes out. My eyes also filled at the sight of them. I could see Rachel clasping her hands to her mouth in delight where she sat.

Jonny and Mom each took a rank pip and pinned it on an epaulette, officially concluding my commissioning. General Gough shook my hand again, then Jonny tried to break bones with his handshake and rib crushing embrace. Then Mom gave me a big hug and, through her quiet sobs, whispered that she was proud of me and that she knew Dad was proud of me too, up where he was. I wept openly and didn't care who could see, then.

The dinner after the ceremony was extremely formal, and fancy as can be imagined. We stuffed ourselves on the catered meal and got tipsy on the fine wine. A live orchestra serenaded us, and I think Rachel found the whole thing terribly romantic. I personally would never publicly admit to such a thing, though in theory it is possible that I felt the same. After all, the whole pomp and martial air of the day made it easy to see ourselves as newly-dubbed knights of old, escorted by our ladies. That many of those knights were female and their escorts male did not mar the simile in my mind.

During a break in the dinner, while Mom was refreshing herself with the hundred other women who flocked *en masse* to the washrooms, Jonny explained to me that General Gough had shown up at Harvard to pin his rank on too.

"Bastard just showed right up without telling anyone ahead of time. I almost swallowed my gonads," Jonny told me. "He gave an entire speech about the high school kid who had talked his younger brother into crashing one of his Arsons, and how said student had spent a long time with the MPs trying to explain that he was neither a spy nor a saboteur. Then he pinned my branch insignia on and shook my hand. It was pretty surreal."

I sipped from my crystal wine flute. It was a deep red that almost had a thick, rich texture when I swirled it. Much like blood, but that might be only in hindsight. "How did you convince Mom to come here?"

Jonny smiled and held up his hands. "I don't know all the details about that." He shrugged and grinned even more widely. "All I know is that Gough asked Mom to sit and talk with him for a while at the dance. They talked for almost two hours. After that, Mom just told me that she was coming to pin her other son's rank on too. I figured if she was going to do it, we should keep it secret like the general's surprise visit and make you look like a total prat by bawling in front of everyone." He smiled again and took a sip of his own drink as I gave him the finger.

I never found out what words finally unlocked the wall that Mom had put up between her heart and her son, but they changed everything in our relationship. For that, I will be eternally grateful to General Gough. When I told him that very thing, he just said it was a leader's duty, part of the oath we'd taken today, and that I would do something similar one day. At the time it seemed like the best thing that ever happened to me. After everything that has happened since then, it *still* seems like the best thing that ever happened to me.

After the meal, there was dancing and socializing in a much less formal fashion. I finally got to meet Rachel's family and, surprisingly, she actually got to meet mine. Mom loved her instantly, and the two of them went off to a table in the corner to talk. Jonny and I found ourselves face to face and more or less alone for the first time in almost four years.

"So, brother," I said to him. "How does it feel to be a mighty bullet-stopper officer?"

He laughed. "Ah, it was my second choice. I just wasn't good enough at perspective spatial analysis to be a God of War like you. It's alright. You should see what a powered armor suit can do."

He also swirled his wine, then took another drink of it. "I'm off to OBT next week. That's about two months long, and then I'll be heading off planet to Lomthen for a training seminar at LDT's expense. We need to hang out a bit over the next week. You know, let me get to know your girlfriend a bit better."

"Are you glad that you went reserves?" I asked to switch the subject away from Rachel. For some reason I felt uncomfortable with the idea of Rachel mixing with my family. Maybe I was just uncomfortable with her spending too much time around Jonny. He had built up quite the reputation, after all.

"Yeah, I'm not in it for the glory like you." He shrugged. "I just want to do my part, but I enjoy being an accountant too. And the paycheck I'll be bringing home from LDT every month will turn you green."

"I'm not heading out for OBT until after you go off world. Do you think Mom's okay now? I mean, will it be all right if I go home for a few months?"

He glanced across the room toward where Mom was chatting amiably with Rachel and her family. "I'd guess she'd welcome it. She'd probably like to have Rachel come, too, especially since Liz is taking off for her advanced baccalaureate studies. I think she'd like having another girl in the house. I already discussed this a bit with her."

I nodded at that. "I hope so. It's been a hard year."

Jonny nodded and glanced down, studying his hands intently as they lay folded in his lap. "I know. I tried to talk to Mom so many times and she was always so closed minded and angry about the whole situation. I was so frustrated and I didn't know what to do. I'm glad that General Gough finally got through to her."

"Yeah, me too."

Rachel found me after that and hauled me out on the dance floor. She was at her most beautiful that night. Her smile was pure joy, and her movements were smooth and free. Somehow, she managed to make the light sparkle from her branch insignia with every turn and bob, the delta wings of a dropfighter marking her as bound for aviator school.

She laughed at my attempts to dance in my slightly inebriated state, deftly avoiding my clumsy feet as they stomped toward hers, but she would not let me retreat to the safety of the tables. We stayed on the dance floor for several hours straight, breaking only for some more drinks and the occasional washroom trip. I loved her as much then as I ever have. Eventually a slow dance was called for and she draped herself happily across me, arms locked behind my neck.

"I'm coming to Vancouver," she told me. "Your mom says I can have your sister's room for a while and then keep her company when you go off to OBT."

"I'm glad to hear that," I said. "Did you find out when your class starts?"

She frowned slightly. "They haven't finalized the schedules yet. Orbital school starts in August and sub-orbital is four months after that. I don't know when the rest of it is going to happen."

I pouted at her. "When are you going to find time for me in there?"

"You don't even know where you're going, silly." She pushed playfully on my shoulder. "If you're still on world it will be easy. Otherwise, we'll have to link up for our month vacation. Are you worried that I'll leave you?" She placed her hands on her hips and tried to look stern, failing miserably.

"No, I'm just going to miss you," I corrected her. She replaced her arms around my neck and leaned her head against my chest. "You've been there everyday for most of three years now, I've grown somewhat attached."

Her head tilted back so she could look at me. "Sub-lieutenant Chase Aarons, are you trying to propose to me?" She wasn't as drunk as she seemed, I guess.

"Would you like me to?" I asked her honestly. I really was ready to, too. I'd been thinking about it for several weeks.

She pushed one finger against my lips, then kissed my neck. “Not yet,” she whispered in my ear. “Not quite yet.”

I held her there long after the music stopped, wondering what would happen to us once we parted ways for our separate careers. Then Mom and Jonny came over with Rachel’s family and I pushed those thoughts aside. After all, we still had several months together. That could be an eternity.

Chapter Seven

Officer Basic Training: Augmented Armor
Abu Dhabi, Arabian Peninsula
Terra
Terran Dominion

August 22, 2649

I fell into formation along with everyone else, excited to finally be attending the school that would make me a warrior, fully trained in the art and science of Man O'War combat. I wanted to immediately impress my instructors and let them understand how much of an asset I would be to the Dominion, so I elbowed my way to the front of the formation where I could not be missed. All of us freshly minted officers stood rigidly at attention there as the cruel rays of a harsh sun beat down on us, the kind of sun that can only be found in the Middle East.

A hard looking captain with a face that seemed filled with combat experience and lessons and an even harder looking colonel paced around our formation, examining us from all angles as if inspecting some novel substance they had just scraped from the bottom of their boots. Both wore numerous combat decorations including Medals of Honor, and neither one looked impressed by the latest crop of young sub-lieutenants sent to fill their shoes. I was a bit nonplussed, having thought that we would receive a warmer welcome than this. A bead of sweat already trickled down my nose, smelling salty and just plain hot. I could see thermal waves rising up off the ground in the distance, the air shimmering with heat. The air even tasted hot, thirty seven degrees and only nine o'clock in the morning.

As some of my mentors had taught me, I directed my thoughts away from my current discomfort and toward something more enjoyable, trying with all my might to ignore the way my black boots felt as though they were beginning to melt into my feet. Instead I thought about how I had spent the last few months at home in rainy Vancouver with Mom and Rachel. It had been pleasant to just idle away a few weeks with nothing to do. Even more pleasant had been rediscovering a solid relationship with my mother, a relationship I had feared gone forever.

During those weeks Rachel and I had explored many of my favorite childhood haunts and many of the area's tourist attractions. We were able to discuss our feelings for each other in ways we never had before, and look at our dreams of the future, no longer strictly as individuals, but as a couple. We talked about our greatest hopes and fears in combat, about the horribly impossible situations that commanders could sometimes find themselves in, and how we hoped to deal with them should we ever find ourselves in such a predicament.

I showed her the tree from which I had witnessed my first Man O'War battle, and the monument that had been raised near there to the memory of those who had died that day. I tried to communicate to her the kind of awe and inspiration I had felt that day, and how it had affected me. I really wanted her to know and understand the events that had led to my firm conviction in my destiny. She really hadn't been paying very close attention and just kept trying to kiss me. I admit, I didn't resist too hard or too long before I gave up on verbal communication and settled for a more primal form of information transfer. I smiled at the memory of it.

"Is there something happy happening here, Sub-lieutenant?" Somehow that hard captain had gotten nose-to-nose with me without my noticing. "Do you enjoy standing at attention under a hellishly hot sun in full combat fatigues and waiting for someone to tell you what you will be doing with the rest of your life?"

I killed my smile and met his gaze. "Yes, sir. I do, sir."

He looked down at the name tape sewn to my left breast. "And why is that, Aarons?"

I carefully looked him straight in the eye without blinking. "Because this is where I become a warrior, sir."

He nodded once, then backed up to address the formation. "This is indeed where you, all of you, will learn to become true officers and warriors. But none of you are yet worthy of that second lofty title. So, let us begin. I am Captain Perry Horn, but you will always address me as Captain Sir. Do you understand that?"

"Yes, sir, Captain Sir!" The formation barked in unison. At least that we knew how to do already.

"There is one ground rule you must understand right here and now. It is based upon the first law of combat, which is that you cannot ever fight alone if you want to win a war. Man O'Wars are not sneaky. Despite our best stealth technology they will eventually be found and then easily hunted down if found alone. Man O'Wars are not omniscient. Without military intelligence, spotters, orbital observation or satellite directions, they will become bogged down, lost, or uncoordinated and, again, easily eliminated. Man O'Wars are also not omnipotent, they do not come fully equipped with kitchens, plumbing, naval capabilities or air support. A Man O'War cut off from these things also will die easily. A warrior is only a small part of a team that starts with the lowest ranked janitor and finishes with the highest Field Marshals and not one of those links is optional. Should you ever think that you can treat your pit crew like dirt and not pay the price for it, stop and think again before you get yourself and a lot of others killed. Therefore, from this moment until the day I pronounce you fit to serve in my branch of the military you are all a team. You will act like a team. You will think like a team. The next two rules derive from this first one."

Captain Horn paced across the front of the formation, conspicuously not sweating anywhere near as heavily as I was. In fact, he looked almost comfortable in the stifling heat.

"The second rule is this: if any one of you, any single one, fails to complete any requirement of this course, that person will immediately be dropped from the augmented armor and reassigned to some branch that does not deal with dangerous weapons, a branch where they can perhaps make a difference without getting themselves killed. Not everyone is cut out for combat arms, there is no shame in that, though you should have realized that before you asked to pilot a Man O'War."

Horn paced down the side of the formation as he continued his speech. The colonel replaced him, examining us from the front.

"The third rule is that should any single one of you drop out or be dropped out, this entire unit will repeat training from day one. Never forget that you are a team and that teams must always, always work together to succeed. They do not succeed well if the members do not support each other at all times.

"Are these three rules understood?"

"Yes, sir, Captain Sir," the formation barked.

"Outstanding. Now drop down, knock out fifty good ones, and then report to the simulators."

No one questioned the order, we all just dropped and started doing pushups. Horn and the colonel got in the ground-car and zipped away while we were still counting. Once we recovered, we discovered rather quickly that none of us had any clue as to where we would find the simulators. Our only lead was the trail of dust being left by the rapidly retreating car. We sprinted after it. I suppose we could have simply walked, but it had long been ingrained into all of us that walking between training sites is a cardinal sin.

We didn't catch the car, but we managed to keep it in sight, and found the building, clearly marked in two meter high letters as the simulations center. A helpful young civilian clerk behind the desk in the lobby directed us to the main simulation room on the fifth floor.

The simulator room was simply a large gymnasium crammed wall to wall with little black pods about the same size as the head of a Man O'War. They were shaped like oblong pork buns, peaked on the top almost like tulip bulbs where thick clusters of cables attached. The room was, thankfully, well air conditioned, and already occupied by a dozen technicians, easily identified by the grey jumpsuits with the word "technician" clearly embroidered in white on the back. The techs had us draw numbered lots as we passed them, and told us to find and go stand by the pod with the matching number. With no other instructions, we did as soldiers do, as we were told.

Captain Horn entered the room then and, like every other drill instructor in the galaxy, without further ado began issuing instructions.

"For those among you who may be a bit slower than the rest, this is the main simulation room. This is where you will practice large group projects and learn the elements of large unit Man O'War combat." He paused in his slow, deliberate walk to place a hand on one of the few unassigned pods in the room.

"This is the Hewlett & Wesson XL-191E Man O'War Training Sled and Simulation Capsule. It is the latest, most state-of-the-art, brand spanking new technology to come out of H&W. It can fully simulate every conceivable battlefield reality and configure to simulate every Man O'War currently in use within the Dominion, as well as a few without. It will become your best friend over the course of the next few weeks. You will learn to love it, but you will do nothing in it without my express permission. Do you understand?"

"Yes, sir, Captain Sir," we shouted out.

"Good. Now follow my instructions exactly. Stand on the left hand side of your capsule. Hold both of your hands in front of you in fists, palms facing away from you. Extend you thumbs and index fingers. One hand now forms the letter L. This is your left hand. Drop your left hand to your side." While I did my best to follow his instructions to the letter, Horn rounded quickly on one poor girl who had dropped her right hand. "Do you have such a difficult time knowing your left from your right that you can't even do it properly when the difference is spoon fed to you, Edwards?"

"No, sir, Captain Sir!" Edwards barked back as she swapped the positions her hands. "Just checking to see if you were paying attention, Captain Sir."

"That's what I like to see in a warrior, spunk," Horn said with a nod. "But if you pull that kind of attitude on me again I will drum you out for insubordination, understood?" He didn't even wait for a response before bellowing out more commands.

"With your right hand, grasp the latch clearly labeled 'Pull' and swing the hatch clear. If and when you have successfully completed this daunting task, I want you to take a look inside. Before you, you will see a large, well-padded chair surrounded by just under a thousand controls and displays. You will…" he stopped in mid-phrase to stare hard across the room. He moved quickly with long strides to approach his next target. He stopped beside the open door of a pod and confronted the young man that was seated inside. "Did anyone tell you that you could sit in that chair, Priest?"

The subject of his attack, a young Australian, paled then bounced up to his feet stammering. "I just thought that you were going to say that right away, sir."

"You did not think at all, did you? Isn't that the problem? You were expressly ordered to not do anything without my instructions. Is that task too complicated for you, Priest? Do you need some remedial training in following military commands?"

"No, sir, Captain Sir!" Priest shouted. Wisely, he didn't attempt any kind of witty rejoinder like Edwards had. Once again, Horn just turned away and resumed his instructions where he had left off.

"You will seat your out-of-shape behinds on the padded chairs you have now observed. With the exceptions of Edwards and Priest, you have all now successfully completed the basics of entering the Hewlett & Wesson XL-191E Man O'War Training Sled and Simulation Capsule. Congratulations, you are that much closer to becoming true warriors. I believe I will allow myself the risk of giving slightly less detailed instructions in the hopes that we will have enough time to actually teach you something today. You had best not screw anything up if you want this more trusting form of communication to continue." He took a deep breath as if bracing himself for our inevitable disaster causing errors. "Close the hatch on your capsule."

The room echoed with clicks and slams as each trainee grabbed the inside handle and pulled the door of his or her module closed. I followed suit and then tried to relax in the command chair that was, after all, quite well padded. There was only a small amount of light within the confines of the pod, about the same level as a full moon produces, coming from an indeterminate source. I began to explore this small chamber in which I found myself, but no sooner had I reached a hand forth than Captain Sir Horn Sir's voice emanated from some speaker nearby.

"Don't any of you go touching anything without my permission, it is possible to mess it up. Show respect for this equipment and your own ignorance. Doing this now will save you time and potentially fatal injuries later." I quickly folded my hands into my lap where they could not accidentally stray and invoke the wrath of Horn.

"Today, you will all be blessed with the experience and opportunity of piloting a Battle Axe, one of our heavier Man O'Wars. The controls will mostly be run on standard settings, and the computer will compensate for just about everything you do save throttle and directionals. A few more advanced maneuvers take a bit more finesse and a better, more detailed understanding of your controls and the brainwave interface, but that will come later. Should you think this a 'weak' or a toned down version of the real thing, I will remind you this one time only that one or two very successful warriors have actually had to enter combat this same way. No, it is neither recommended nor ideal, and they did not do so voluntarily, but it is possible, and it is the way you will be doing most of your training in the first few weeks.

"Now, later on you may choose to customize your own settings and computer responsibilities, but until then, most everything else has been disabled in your cockpit. For the time being, remember this very important principle: just as a sword is not simply a big knife, so a Man O'War is not a big suit of power armor. It will not respond to your every movement no matter how much you wiggle around in your seat, and it is most definitely the computer that controls everything from target lock-ons to balance.

"So, if you have managed to stay awake through this very important, though admittedly dull lecture, locate the button that should be flashing near your right armrest, and tap it firmly but gently."

I looked to my right, but saw no flashing button. Just to be safe, I looked to my left and checked over there too. Nothing. I was puzzled for a moment, unsure of what I should do.

"Adjust your harness for snugness and comfort so it can hold you in without impeding your movements," Horn said. "Grasp the two grips that have presented themselves, and...Aarons, why exactly is it that you haven't activated your unit yet? Do we need to have Edwards come explain to you the difference between right and left? Or perhaps Priest can discuss the importance of following orders?"

I felt my face flush in deep embarrassment. Of course it would be me with the screw up. I rubbed my eyes with my palms and said, "No, sir, Captain Sir, it's just that there isn't a flashing light in my pod."

Horn's voice cut out but I heard some mumbled words exchanged, then punctuated by a fairly clear expletive describing the true value of these new simulators the Dominion had purchased. I probably wasn't supposed to hear that.

"Aarons," Horn said, "exit your capsule and try the one behind you." Another muffled, yet discernible, invective about the parentage of Hewlett and Wesson and their various acts of animal husbandry followed.

I just shook my head at my own bad luck and pushed the release lever to open the hatch. The hinges jammed less than a quarter of the way up, and I couldn't budge the hatch any farther in either direction. After a brief struggle, two sets of hands appeared from outside, yanking on the hatch with no greater success than I had had in trying to move it.

"Uh, Sub-lieutenant," a disembodied voice, probably one of the technicians, spoke from outside, "I think you're going to have to crawl out if you can. I don't think Colonel Hastings will approve of us delaying the whole schedule while we take this entire door off."

I sank back into my chair and rested my head back. This was going just swell. At least everyone else was locked in tight and what was bound to be a decidedly graceless exit would go unwitnessed. I figured I was skinny enough to get out, but not skinny enough to do it smoothly or without effort. I sighed and went to work getting my camel sized rear through the eye-of-a-needle sized opening.

It was a tight fit, for certain. My legs made it through just fine, and, once I unhooked my belt buckle from the lip of the hatch, so did my pelvis. It took a little sucking in to get my stomach through the gap though, and a big exhale for my chest. The rest was painful, I thought I was going to rip my ears off trying to get my head out, and once it did come out, it felt like I had left a couple of pieces of my scalp behind. I retrieved my cover, which had been knocked from my shoulder epaulette, from the pod and turned to see Captain Horn trying extremely hard not to laugh. His efforts contorted his face to the point where he looked as though he had attempted to swallow an incontinent rhesus monkey sideways. The group of techs nearby weren't even trying to hide their grins and snickers.

Horn didn't say anything, he just threw a thumb over his shoulder indicating that I should enter the next capsule back in line. Later I would be able to fully see the humor in the incident, but at the time I was so embarrassed that it made me furious. I wanted to throttle Horn and every tech in the room for laughing at me.

I stalked over to the next pod and yanked on the handle. The hatch smacked me smartly in the shins, causing me to let out a muffled cry and infuriating me all the more. Worse, the techs completely lost all control and just burst out laughing. Completely embarrassed, I hopped right inside, nearly braining myself on the hatch lip, and slammed the hatch shut with all my might. I took one look at that incessantly blinking button to my right, the square, green one marked as the ignition, and smashed my fist down on it.

A four-point harness seemed to spring out of the air and secured itself across my chest, pulling me firmly back into the command chair. At the same time, a portion of each armrest rotated to present gripped control sticks studded with still more controls. These grips slid back to stop at a perfect distance for me to hold comfortably.

"Grasp the two grips that have presented themselves and prepare to enter the world of Man O'War combat," Horn said once again. Perhaps it was just my imagination but I was certain I could now detect a note of levity in his voice, and perhaps snickering in the background. I vowed to get even this day by proving myself for all I was worth.

I reached forward to grasp the sticks and felt a slight tingle in my fingertips as the onboard computer checked my identification. Then the view screens around me came to life with a slight flicker and suddenly I was looking down and out the front window of a ten meter tall war machine. My embarrassment and anger fled like a pin-pricked soap bubble, leaving me feeling awed and excited. All around me I could see, in perfect detail, the busy hubbub of a vast Man O'War bay. Techs scurried around on their various duties; weapons and munitions were being loaded, damaged parts being fixed, and tune-ups being performed; everything seemed perfectly real, down to the last details of sight and sound.

Outside the simulated window to my right, I could see a gantry walkway and ladders for accessing the Man O'Wars. Beyond that was just a wall of corrugated sheet metal designed to protect from mild elements and little else.

To the left I could take in an incredible view of what seemed an endless line of Man O'Wars stretching into the distance. Straight in front of me lay a fifteen meter tall door which stood open on gently hilled, grassy terrain. Beyond that I could make out the beginnings of what looked to be a vast forest.

"Reach under your seat and withdraw the Bell 1H-51b Man O'War interface helmet you will find stored there. Place it upon your head such that the opening in the front aligns with your face and the wet orbs there that we colloquially refer to as eyes."

I groped down between my legs and found the thick helmet Horn was referring to. It was a lot lighter than I had expected it to be, but when I placed it on my head I found that it was also far too large for me.

"For those of you who are about to whine that it doesn't fit, shut up. Reach above and behind your head and locate the cable that should be dangling there. Attach it to the socket that you will eventually locate at the very top of your helmet. I understand that this particular maneuver is especially complicated, so for the sake of Edwards I will allow you ample time to perform this essential task. Take some comfort knowing that this is one of the few things you only have to do in simulators, not in the actual machines."

I didn't find it too difficult a task to locate the cable where it hung directly above me, but for the life of me I couldn't get it into the socket on my helmet by touch alone. I ended up just taking it off to make the connection and then putting my helmet back on.

"On your left armrest you will find a button labeled 'IntConnect.' For your ease of reference it will be flashing right now. Find it and press it."

Just beside the control stick on the left, a blue backlit button began flashing. It was, indeed, labeled "IntConnect" as we'd been so graciously informed, so I pushed it. I jumped a bit, slightly startled when a visor I hadn't suspected even existed quickly slipped shut over my face, and the helmet automatically adjusted to fit my skull perfectly. Now I could easily move my head around without having my helmet jiggle around or turn sideways on me.

"Right next to that button you will find a switch labeled 'Overlay.' Turn that switch on and look around a bit."

Again I manipulated my controls in the manner instructed, then began to look around out the cockpit windows. As I moved my head around I noticed that I was now seeing double in a way. I could still easily see all the controls around me and out through the cockpit windows, but I was now also seeing the overlay through my visor. When I looked out the window this overlay provided detailed ranging information and vectors, as well as geological and meteorological information that I had no idea how to understand.

Then I noticed something else that I thought really neat. If I looked at an opaque part of the cockpit, whether the floor, ceiling, or even the back, I could now, with the tactical overlay, see right through it. The computer rendered image was as detailed and real as the view out my window had been, such that when I looked down I could even see the feet of my Man O'War standing astride a small grease stain.

"Cool," I said to the air.

"No doubt a few of you at least have noticed one or two of the distinct advantages provided by our image and targeting system. In case you are wondering, and I'm certain at least the smartest of you is, you can indeed also receive whatever audio information the Man O'War picks up as well as the visual."

Horn went on to explain the basics of controlling the throttle and direction of a Man O'War, and how to use the tactical overlay for compass directions. He mentioned something about how to get the targeting computer to interface as well as fire control, but I wasn't really paying all that much attention. My mind was still going over all the opportunities before me, and I was just too excited about the possibilities presented by controlling a Man O'War.

"Now, enough gawking at the shiny toy and listening to my really interesting lectures. Let's see if the lot of you have even the slightest iota of talent when it comes to the art of warfare. Somewhere out there in that forested area, Colonel Hastings is piloting a Sniper. It is a smaller, faster Man O'War than the ones you are piloting, with far less armor. Go find him and kill him. There are forty of you and only one of him, so it should be simple enough. For your continued enlightenment, I will occasionally add one or two helpful comments, in the hope that maybe you will be able to learn something here."

With that instruction I could now hear, and visually confirm, that all of the gantry connections were disengaging from my Battle Axe. I didn't wait for anyone else, the door was open and my destiny awaited me. I eased the throttle up slowly, very cognizant of my last painful experience with trying to maneuver a Man O'War through a door. Surprisingly, the simulator managed to convey the exact types of feelings that I remembered experiencing when riding a Man O'War before. The vibrations from the engine were the same, the feel of its slow tread was identical, and even the kinesthetic sensation of motion was there. I slowed down a bit further, just in case these machines were also capable of fully simulating the shock of hitting a doorframe.

My tactical overlay showed that I was heading north as I exited the bay. All the way down the line thirty-nine other Battle Axes also stepped timidly through their exit doors. After some experimentation I decided that I couldn't communicate with anyone else, apparently our automatic computer settings didn't cover triple C. A little voice in my head told me that Hastings was not facing a unit of forty, but forty individual units all standing in the same area.

I faced something of a dilemma here. Horn's very first instructions had been to fight with the team and stick together, to always work as a team, yet as I watched all these other novice warriors stumbling around in their Man O'Wars I yearned to leave the pack and step out on my own. My instincts, and perhaps blood lust, cried out for me to throw off the shackles of conformity and prove to God and the world that I could stand alone, but Horn had not equivocated even one whit in his admonition, and probably thought himself a good proxy for the Almighty Himself.

Frustrating as it was, but definitely not wanting to be branded the lone wolf or the black sheep, I curbed my desires and stayed with the group. Instead of going off on my own, I expressed my individuality by playing with my speed and directional controls while most of the others merely milled about. I couldn't understand why they weren't doing anything, it wasn't that much different from the holo-games we've all played. If nothing else I expected them to experiment as I did.

While they all sort of shuffled around, I entertained myself by trying out my new ride's capabilities. I learned a lot in those few minutes, beginning to truly bond with my Man O'War, to become one with it. Together, man and machine, we walked, we ran, we turned, we almost did a forward roll tripping over a fallen tree trunk. For a few moments I was lost in the sheer thrill of pounding an eighty ton war machine across the plains at two hundred and fifty kilometers per hour and still turning almost, as it were, on a dime.

With a grin on my face and on an endorphin high, I brought my Battle Axe trotting back toward the herd. Somehow, without communication (assuming that it wasn't just another malfunction with my pod and that no one else had com abilities either), they had turned, more or less in unison, and arbitrarily set out heading due west. There was definitely a herd mentality at work here. In all likelihood someone had started to move, perhaps even inadvertently, and the rest had simply followed.

A few other warrior trainees had copied my example of experimenting alone, and we few, perhaps a half dozen, ranged out to the sides, front, and rear of the main body, which held to a steady, if leisurely, ninety kilometer per hour pace. One pilot, apparently dissatisfied with either our pace or our structure, struck out alone, heading southwest. Perhaps he or she expected us to follow such a bold move. Perhaps we would have, given a bit more time, for most everyone is willing to follow just about anyone who makes a decisive move. Unfortunately, just as our rogue's Man O'War crested the slight rise of a gentle hill, a kinetic penetration round of molten depleted uranium tore its head off.

"I believe I already mentioned the idea of never fighting alone," Horn's voice echoed in our ears. I was glad the I had made the decision to stick with the group, lest I be the one forever haunted by Horn's words of warning and branded as the first kill of the day. I had no doubt at all that there would be many, many others.

Like a flock of birds, our loose formation turned as one and headed for our fallen comrade, but some of us apparently had more desire for a straight-up fight than others. We broke all semblance of rank and order. About half of us, including me, charged up the hill at full throttle. The others held back, whether from a fear of failure or because of some other strategy I do not know, I only remember thinking at the time that I wished they would stick together. Just as we crested the hill, right beside the wreckage of the previous victim, another shot decapitated a second Man O'War.

"Were you not watching what happened to your fallen comrade? Never just go straight over a hill like that. You silhouette yourself perfectly against the sky, and you have no idea whatsoever what is on the other side."

Keenly aware of the risk that I could be next, I began feeling that nervous-excited feeling so familiar to all combat veterans. My tactical overlay was now showing all sorts of symbols that I didn't readily understand, though I did figure out that a couple included vector information on incoming fire and triangulation calculations. As of yet the computer couldn't find anything out there to lock onto, but Hastings had to be out there somewhere, and, if I was even close to reading my display correctly, he was over in the forest to the southeast a fairly good distance off.

I tried to throttle up again, despite the fact that I was already at full speed. I guess I was just happy to be moving the lever—a nervous drive to do something, anything, that might be productive since I wasn't actually shooting anything yet. My Battle Axe rocked with a nice rhythm as it raced across the clear area toward the trees. Another shot flashed, blowing off the leg of the machine next to mine.

"Do not be caught out in the open. It just makes you one big target. Or one big group of big targets."

The legless Battle Axe plowed face down into the earth, sliding headlong like a runner stealing second base, dirt spraying up from the furrow it incised in the virgin turf. I had no time to think of anything clever, I just turned my Man O'War sharply to the right. It was barely in time, as one more blob of superheated liquid glance off the armored shoulder of my Battle Axe.

I discovered a bit more of what the simulator pods could reproduce as I was hurled hard against my restraining straps. I remembered what happens to vehicular passengers that aren't strapped in when they are struck hard, and gained a new appreciation for why those lifesaving restraints are automatic. I also briefly wondered how anyone thought that a human could possibly be able to compensate for the severity of such a disorienting blow, dreaming up Man O'Wars that would be balanced by human, rather than by computer, abilities.

"The main weapon usually carried by a Sniper is an eighty millimeter kinetic penetration rifle. It is capable of firing a liquid depleted uranium round accurately over a half dozen kilometers. The entire Man O'War was built around this weapon and the superior targeting systems that go with it. When combined, they give the Sniper a deadly combination of accuracy and firepower." Horn again with his helpful statements of the obvious.

A low siren alarm was sounding in my ears, and a persistent blinking red light outlined a picture of a Battle Axe without a left arm. Fortunately, I still seemed able to maneuver properly and hadn't lost any speed, allowing me to reach the dubious shelter of the trees, only slightly off course from the rest of my companions.

Just in time, I remembered to throttle down, slowing my mount to a walk before I could carom off an oak. The idea seems laughable to anyone who hasn't been in a Man O'War, but at least three of our numbers clothes-lined themselves on low branches or smashed into thick tree trunks, sending their Man O'Wars crashing to the forest floor with comical sprawls and flips.

We spread out somewhat, each finding our own individual way through the thick woods. The tactical overlay was giving me mixed signals, one moment showing a confirmed fix in the direction it had before, the next skewing things off at least eighty degrees. I cursed at myself for not having studied up before coming to training, and wondered at what my excuse could possibly be. Then I remembered that my excuse was a girl named Rachel, and I smiled.

That almost got me killed.

I had been straying a bit from the group, trying to stay spread out and finding my way through the trees, still attempting to decipher exactly what all my readouts were trying to tell me. That and hoping, really, that my armless Man O'War, so reminiscent of the toy I'd had as a child, would be passed over by Colonel Hastings and his deadly accuracy. Of course, more likely, he'd want to finish the job he started. In any event, I wasn't paying nearly enough attention to where I was going, neither to the maps on my secondary screens nor to the cues I could observe visually with the aid of my sensory augmentation.

I had just walked between two trees when I was thinking of Rachel, and suddenly I was out in the open again, separated from the group I had gone chasing off with, but now reunited with the group that had stayed behind. I was right back where I'd started. Unfortunately, without communications, they didn't recognize me as a friend immediately, and I was greeted by the business end of at least two dozen weapons' barrels. A few of them fired, their hair triggers activated by the nervous pilots behind them. Luckily for me, their accuracy was as green as their judgment and all the shots went wide.

"Try to remember who is on your side, and who the enemy is," Horn said. Once again, I could detect some levity in his voice and hear laughter in the background. "I will give you a tip, though, look behind you."

Just as the last syllable of that so timely warning finished, someone's Battle Axe exploded as another deadly round burst out right through its torso. Everyone twisted in the direction that our overlays indicated, back-tracing the rounds. We all pulled the triggers for our main weapons, despite having no lock on whatsoever. I supposed blind luck might have allowed us to hit something, but that seemed unlikely.

In any case, the forearm mounted, high-powered pulse laser rifles with which we'd all been outfitted as our primary weapon, spat high energy death all over the place. Invisible to the naked eye, they showed brief flashes of blue and red through my active overlay; flashes that, like lightning, were seen more as afterimages burned on the retina than as actual images. The focused and directed energy released by our salvo exploded trees as their water content instantly vaporized, started flash fires, and mowed down a surprisingly large area of woodland, yet it all failed to hit anything resembling a Sniper. We halted our fire, allowing our Man O'Wars a chance to shunt away some of the heat built up in our weapons.

As we stood there gawking around, another Battle Axe went down, its entire pelvic region torn off by yet another round.

So it continued. We would run around, or stand in place; stick together or break into groups; hold our fire or level the countryside. It didn't matter. Never was there a sign of Colonel Hastings and his deadly Sniper save that there was always one more shot ringing out, one more Man O'War lying mangled and broken on the ground. Occasionally Captain Horn would add some snide bit of advice, always too late to help the latest victim. How I survived for as long as I did, I do not know. Call it intuition, call it innate skill, call it blind stinking luck, but once more I turned aside just in time to have a round swipe my side, leaving a fair amount of damage behind, if not disabling me.

Eventually, my luck and Hastings' other targets both ran out. I hadn't seen another trainee in quite some time, and I was a few score kilometers from where we had started when I stumbled my almost crippled Man O'War down a nearly dry riverbed. I felt hunted, like some poor deer, its haunches torn and bleeding, hounded by a wolf. Somewhere out in those shadows, somewhere that I couldn't see, someone very dangerous was hunting me. It wasn't a feeling I enjoyed much at all.

Gone was all thought of impressing my evaluators, gone was any belief that I had even the slightest chance of finishing my mission. All that remained was a desire to take one more step, to breathe one more breath. A part of me wanted to just give up and die, end the simulation; for that was all this truly was, a mere game. A stronger part, pride perhaps, forced me to continue running my Man O'War all over the place, between trees, down hills, around clearings, and now along a riverbed. Now all I wanted to do was prove I could survive as prey since I could not hunt as predator.

A glint of sunlight was my first warning, and then there was a horrendous crashing and I was pitched forward and to the left, almost going cockpit first into the mud. My damage board lit up once again, showing that I had lost another arm just above the elbow. As I regained some semblance of balance, I took in the full figure of that small, lithe yet deadly Sniper, standing full astride the trickle of water flowing in this drying river.

My targeting indicators confirmed a lock and I immediately tightened up on my triggers, firing off the only remaining weapon I had. Ten anti-armor rockets erupted from my Battle Axe's right breast, riding tails of flame straight into the Sniper. They crossed the distance in a heartbeat, sheathing one side of my enemy in explosions.

Colonel Hastings stumbled his Man O'War to its knees and I gawked in total surprise. On my first ever attempt at piloting a Man O'War, I had defeated a warrior as decorated and obviously skilled as Hastings. My mouth literally dropped open in dismay. I had won!

So I thought until Hastings righted his Sniper, the tattered remains of his shield dangling from the ruins of the left arm he'd had it mounted to. Even with only one remaining arm functioning, he still possessed the accuracy to send one last round straight through my cockpit window.

I cracked the hatch open on my simulator pod, as instructed by Captain Horn. The cool air that hit me was both a surprise and a welcome relief. I hadn't realized exactly how hot it had gotten inside the confines of my cockpit. My back was soaked with sweat, requiring me to pluck my shirt away from my skin while I welcomed the feel and taste of air that hadn't been re-circulated a hundred times.

I made a considerably more graceful and dignified exit from this pod. I straightened up and took a big stretch, then paused when I realized how many trainees were just standing alongside the wall. It looked like all of them, save me. My eyes quickly ran down the line, confirming my suspicion that no one was left. I stood there puzzled for a moment, then they started clapping.

Colonel Hastings strode up hastily from my right. He also looked hot and sweaty, but plastered on his face was a look far different than the one he'd worn on the parade ground. He actually looked pleased. I stayed where I was, my feet rooted to the floor, nonplussed as he shook my hand and clapped me on the shoulder while the applause of my classmates died out.

"Hell of a job out there, Aarons," he said with relish. "I haven't been led on that merry a chase by any class in years. And you came so close to taking me out there at the end, I'm impressed. We'll be certain to have another go, you and I, one on one, before you ship out." He grinned even more, obviously looking forward to slaughtering me again.

"Thank you, sir, we'll do that," was all I could come up with to say. It sounded lame, even at the time, but what else could I have said? Words were never my strongest weapon and I wield them clumsily, much like my first attempt at using a Man O'War in combat.

"I look forward to that," Hastings said. He nodded to me, then walked away. I stared after, confused, while my classmates once again broke into applause, whistles, and cheers.

"Don't just stand there with your mandible on the floor, Aarons, you've been given the highest complement I've ever heard the colonel give a raw trainee." I turned to see Captain Horn hovering just behind me. "But don't let it go to your head, you still suck like a punctured lung. There is, however, a possibility, if an admittedly small one, that, given the colonel's faith in you, you will be able to actually complete the majority of this course on your first try."

"Thank you, sir," I said. A mistake.

"That's Captain Sir!" Horn snapped into my face. He still wore a hint of a smile, though that could have been my imagination. "And I was not giving you a compliment, I was trying to help you understand that you will now be expected to work three times harder than anyone else in order to justify the colonel's faith! Do you understand me, Sub-lieutenant?"

I snapped to perfect attention, focusing my eyes on the wall behind Horn. "Yes, sir, Captain Sir!"

"And don't you forget that!" He rounded on the rest of the class. "Now, everyone of you other losers drop and give me forty for letting someone as pathetic as Aarons outperformed you! Aarons, you stand there and count the reps."

Chapter Eight

Fort Pyotr
Vladivostok, Asia
Terra
Terran Dominion

October 15, 2650

It was with a surprising amount of trepidation that I stepped off the plane that morning and out onto the windy Russian tarmac. My hands shook and felt clammy no matter how much I told myself that I was confident and cocky enough to handle this situation. It's a strange feeling, when you're king of the hill, to look behind you and find that there is a much larger hill that you hadn't seen looming over you.

I had reigned unchallenged at OBT, the hero of the group who could always be counted on to beat the cadre at their own game, and I had grown comfortable with my status as the best trainee in the class. Even my epic loss to Colonel Hastings during our rematch had built my reputation. If only I'd not gotten quite so cocky, maybe I would have lasted a bit longer than twenty minutes and finished off his Sniper. Tripping my Man O'War over that large rock hadn't exactly helped either. Now, instead of ruling over anything, I was just another scared kid pretending to be an officer and stepping off a plane at his first duty post.

I nervously switched my kit into my left hand as I descended the staircase to the pavement. I needed to free up my right in case I had to salute someone, but no one waited to greet me. I sort of milled around with the other disembarkees, trying to hide the fact that I didn't really know what I was doing or where I was going. I had really expected to be met by someone who could guide me to wherever it was that I was supposed to be.

Nevertheless, fully determined to make the most of things, I followed the movements of the rest of the group, all civilians, hoping they would know enough about how to get around the base that I might possibly find my new home. In hindsight, with far more maturity than I had back then, it's easy to say that I should have simply asked for directions, but there's a certain male pride that makes that option rather distasteful, especially for a male who is also a newly minted officer. Besides, my idea wasn't without merit, and the group did lead me to a base transit station very near where we'd landed.

I made certain that I was slow enough to not get on the transport with the others (I didn't want them to think I was following them around, even though I was) and waited for the next one to arrive. That took about thirty minutes, but I felt better doing that and appearing stupid than appearing weak and helpless.

That worked out all right, though, because the next transport was empty, and the transport driver was friendly enough. She was a young corporal who liked to talk, and once we started chatting, she told me she was just trying to save up enough money for school. I made the mistake of asking her then if she wanted to come back to the military after that, maybe as an officer, and she just laughed at me. I heard her mutter something under her breath about the ignorance and self-obsession of officers, thinking everyone should be like them, but I didn't catch the rest and I was awfully reluctant to call her on it.

The drive ended up being a fairly nice guided tour of the base. The corporal enjoyed showing me all the sites and pointed out the various attractions such as the theaters and swimming pools, a couple of mess halls, and the officer's club. She even told me a bit about the current state of affairs on the base, meaning she caught me up on all sorts of gossip regarding the resident general officers. I laughed at several of her tidbits, shaking my head at how widely known at least three or four generals' indiscretions were.

It was only about twenty minutes before we reached the Putin building, where the 88th was headquartered. Topping off a steep hill and commanding a spectacular view of the whole base, it was a beautiful building, done in the sweeping lines of classic Russian architecture, complete with flame shaped domes at the tops of wide towers.

"Here we are, sir," the corporal said opening the door. "Good luck."

"Thanks," I nodded to her as I retrieved my bag from the rack. I stepped out and looked the building over again while she pulled away. I had calmed a bit during the ride, but my nerves started up again as I walked up to the doors. With a focused determination I pulled my shoulders back to the square and strode on in, trying to appear confident. The lobby was empty, save for a lone security guard at the desk, apparently a sergeant if I was reading his rank correctly.

"May I help you, sir?" he asked politely enough.

"Please," I said. "I'm supposed to report to Captain Sierra."

"You new, sir?" I nodded. "May I see your orders?" He held out a hand expectantly.

I produced them from a pocket and he looked them over briefly. "Is there a problem?" I asked.

"No, sir, it's just that the 88th received a mobilization call up only an hour ago." He handed my papers back to me. "Everything appears in order, sir. Just take the lift up to the eighth floor. First set of glass doors on the right, that's where Captain Sierra's office is. Can't miss it, sir."

I smiled my appreciation for the help and nodded. "Thank you."

The lift was as old as the building's architecture, as in it would have been faster to just run up the stairs. At least there wasn't any annoying background music. As the floor indicator crept up it finally dawned on me what the guard had said. My nervousness and my focus on looking confident had kept it from sinking in, but the 88th had just been called up, and I was now, theoretically at least, a part of the 88th!

A ping announced my arrival at the proper level, cutting short any further reflection on the situation. I exited and found the door just where security had said. I took a deep breath, even as a chill washed over me, plastered a totally cheesy smile on my face and pushed my way inside.

Entering the main office area was much like stepping into a war zone, even though no enemy appeared to be present. The pace and activity level overwhelmed me and for a shocked moment I just stood there staring. Enlisted personnel were literally running everywhere, most of them yelling either at each other or into some form of communication device. Papers were being shuffled and flung around madly and computers were so busy you could almost hear them humming.

I rather timidly stepped fully into the room, completely disregarded by everyone. The doors swung shut behind me as I tried clearing my throat to draw some attention. Everyone continued to pointedly ignore me. I reached out and tapped a passing sergeant on the shoulder. "Excuse me, Sergeant, could you point me in the direction of Captain Sierra's office?"

"Look," he started saying before even turning to face me, "why don't you go f-," he flinched then as he turned far enough to catch sight of my officer rank insignia. He caught himself quickly, eyes widening slightly as he continued with only the slightest pause, "-ind him down the hall there, sir? Yes, sir, that hall right there, sir, that's the one you want for the captain, sir."

With a toss of his head indicating the direction I should go, he was off again, conspicuously holding a file folder over his name tag and keeping his face mostly averted from my gaze.

"Thanks," I said sarcastically to his retreating back even though he couldn't have heard it over all the noise. "Thanks a lot."

I walked down the indicated hallway, past several office doorways blazoned with the names of the company's full lieutenants. I tried to remember their names after I read them, but was too nervous to do so with much success. Each of these offices was empty, the doors opened wide and the lights extinguished.

The second to last door apparently belonged to the executive officer, but it was closed tight and I could hear a fair amount of yelling coming from inside. I assumed that he or she was in, but I didn't think I should interrupt, so I bravely choose to not try and introduce myself to the XO at that particular moment, especially given some of the words coming through the door that I could make out. Most of them seemed to consist of rather painful sounding suggestions, even for a contortionist. Besides, I reminded myself, tradition is that you don't officially meet anyone in the unit until you formally meet the commander in person.

At the very end of the hall, a hardwood door marked the captain's office. It stood slightly ajar, enough so that I could just peek in and make out some details. The captain sat behind his desk speaking animatedly with what looked like a pair of lieutenants and several enlisted personnel. I was about to knock on the door, more balls than brains, when they all stood up as if about to leave. I wisely decided to let them do so before I went in to make my presence known.

As the small group filed out of the office I was disappointed that not a single one of them so much as spared me a glance. Once they'd all passed me, I stepped into Captain Sierra's office and stood at attention until he looked up from the work at his desk to stare hard at me.

"And just who the hell are you and what the hell are you doing in my office?" Not the best way to start off an introduction, but it was too late for me to turn and run away, perhaps surviving to try again another day. I did seriously consider it though.

"Captain Sierra, Sub-lieutenant Chase Aarons reporting, sir." I saluted. When he roughly returned the salute I stepped forward and extended my papers and a hand to shake. Sierra accepted the transfer and assignment orders from me, then threw them into the disposal without giving them a second glance. The proffered hand he simply ignored. I was shocked, to say the least.

"Does it look like I have time to baby-sit you right now, Aarons?"

I stood there working my mouth the way a fish out of water does. No sound came out though.

"An hour and a half ago a seven point nine earthquake leveled a good portion of Yokohama. Colonel Glenn says that the 88th is going to be onsite three hours from now to help secure the area, and provide whatever aid we can. That takes priority over giving you an orientation, a facilities tour, and breaking a bottle of champagne over your first Man O'War. So fall in soldier, we're moving out."

"But, sir, I just got transferred in!"

"Aarons, we are a rapid response unit under a class four alert. Get the hell out of my office, get your ride, and be on the dropship in half an hour like everyone else or go get yourself a lawyer. Dismissed. And close the door on your way out." He pointed at the door rather rudely, driving his point home.

Confused I might have been, but I was fresh out of training and well indoctrinated. My heels clicked together with a snap and I stood at ramrod attention with a salute in place before I could even think over my actions. With a sardonic smile the captain tossed a return salute at me and I immediately spun on my heel and walked out the door, pulling it gently shut behind me. Then I leaned back against the latched door and blew out hard. That had not gone anywhere near as well as I'd hoped.

Still, Sierra hadn't been wrong about my where my duties lay, and I knew that I'd better be getting myself squared away with a Man O'War immediately, that would be top priority—even accommodations could wait until we returned from Yokohama. I paced back down the hall, shaking my head as I realized I didn't even know which patrol leader I was supposed to fall under. I couldn't ask any of them, their offices were all empty, as was the XO's now. I briefly considered returning to speak with the captain, but quickly discarded that avenue for gaining information. I'm somewhat ashamed to say that I ended up resorting to the lowest trick of all, bullying.

I went back down the hall to the main paper chasing area, which was still a mess and even more chaotic than before, and looked around until I found the lowest rank present. She looked to be about eighteen and a fresh PFC. Perfect.

I walked over to stand directly in front of her desk. "Private," I said sternly.

She looked up from her seat, no doubt wondering why I was talking to her. Maybe she guessed I was afraid that any NCO would just tell me off, but she lacked that confidence and her voice quavered when she said, "Sir?"

"I need to find a Man O'War to assign myself to. Where would I go to do that?"

"Oh, that's easy, sir," she said, grateful that my pathetic question was so obvious even the newest recruit could answer it. "You just go down to the basement and find room four, you can't miss the big sign that says 'The Dungeon.' Ask for Ted Much, our head quartermaster. He'll take care of you, sir."

I nodded my understanding. "This Much, he's a civilian?"

"Retired master sergeant, sir, but he doesn't care much for rank."

I nodded and said my thanks, which made her smile briefly before returning to her work. I briefly regretted having made her uncomfortable, but I figured my need was more pressing than her comfort, and I'd been nice enough about it.

I left the offices and once more I was back in the elevator before I remembered how slow it was. I sighed in frustration as I counted away far more time than it would have taken to simply run down to the basement. When the lift finally stopped, not that it felt like it was moving, the doors opened on a ludicrously darkened cement hallway. I felt my brow wrinkle in consternation, wondering why someone didn't just hang a lamp from the ceiling. That wasn't what I was here for though and, sure enough, about ten paces down the hall was Room 004. There weren't any other rooms around, so why it was the fourth I had no idea.

I opened the door and walked on in to see a truly fat man leaning back in a chair, his feet up on the most cluttered desk I have ever seen, a game demo running on the computer station behind him. He was laughing hard, his entire body jiggling like a gelatin dessert slapped by the Hand of God. A rather frustrated looking sub-lieutenant stood nearby.

"No way in hell that's going to happen," the fat man said between guffaws.

"But," the sub-lieutenant started.

"I said no already, Simons, I'm not going to change my mind and I don't care what your problem is," he said, still braying out his derisive laughter. "Now get out of here."

Simons turned away, murderous anger readily apparent on her face. As she stormed by I heard her muttering, "Stupid fat prejudiced bastard, son of a," the rest was lost to me as she kicked the door open. When she slammed it shut behind her a picture of some ancient general fell off the wall and struck the floor hard enough to crack both the frame and the covering.

"Ooh," the fat man chuckled toward me, as though I were some well known intimate in whom he could confide, "she's pissed. That's priceless!" Then he started laughing loudly again.

I was not impressed. I had no idea what had just gone on, but it definitely did not sit well with me, and left me with an unpleasant taste in my mouth. I took a couple of strides forward to be certain I'd have the fat bastard's undivided attention.

"Are you Much?" I asked.

He smiled up at me, still caught up in his own mirth. "Maybe, depends on who's asking. Who the hell are you?" I was getting really tired of hearing that.

"Sub-lieutenant Aarons, newly assigned to the 88th in Captain Sierra's company. I need to get set up."

The fat man looked me over, his double, maybe triple, chins wagging as his head wobbled from side to side. "You look sharp, Aarons, I think you'll do just fine." I raised an eyebrow, but did nothing more. "Unfortunately, I'm all out of Roughnecks right now, the two I have are dismantled and useless for another month or so." He paused to consider. "Think you can handle a Lodestone?"

I didn't want to say anything. I had a horribly bad first impression of this fat man who so delighted in making another angry, and I definitely didn't want to be his friend or accept gifts from him, yet here he was offering to put me in a specialized Man O'War on my first assignment when most warriors waited at least a year before earning that trust. I licked my lips, fighting the sneaking suspicion that I was being bought off.

"I'm rated for it," I said, nodding slowly.

"Good," Much said, still chuckling. He rose from his chair, which creaked slightly as it moved back toward its original shape, the one it had before being introduced to Mr. Much's weighty backside. He rooted around his desk for a moment, shuffling papers and reorganizing drawers, then came up with an access card which he flipped to me negligently. "Take this over to hangar two at the bottom of the hill here, there's a tube at the end of the hall out there that'll take you straight there."

I nodded my understanding. "Shouldn't I sign something or some such?"

Much waved that off. "You don't need it. I take care of good kids like you, Aarons. Whatever you need, you just come see Uncle Ted and he'll hook you up, even that hard to find stuff." He winked at me. Somehow, I realized, I had gotten on a different list than the one Simons was on, though I had no idea what I'd done to achieve that. Maybe Much was normally like this and she'd just brought it on herself. It was possible, though unlikely. I shrugged off the question, it was just another mystery that I wasn't going to figure out; at least not today.

I found the tube to the hangar easily enough, and was whisked away at a far more satisfactory rate of speed than the lift had provided.

There was no one in the hangar save for a single security guard, which wasn't surprising given that the hangar was just a scarp yard. The guard asked to see my pass and ID which she ran through the computer, then nodded me in and wished me luck as she gestured toward the only Man O'War in the hangar still on its feet. I picked my way carefully around the piles of scrap augmented armor parts to inspect my precious new Lodestone, worried that it might not be in much better shape than the scrap surrounding it.

I need not have been concerned. Despite a paint job that could stand to be touched up here and there (apparently it hadn't been scheduled for use just yet) it was perfect. I took the small elevator up to the cockpit level of the gantry feeling much like a teenager on his first date. I was full of boundless energy and couldn't have kept the smile off of my face if I'd tried. It was a beautiful sight. Ten meters tall and built like a linebacker, doubled up MLRS racks on each shoulder, heavy laser on chest and back, twin wrist cannons on each arm—after all of that the anti-infantry weapons at the hips seemed almost pointless. This beast just shouted beautiful killer and, with apologies to Rachel, I was in love with it at first sight.

I trotted over to the hatch and slipped on in. The access codes Much had provided worked to start it up, and I then replaced them with my own personalized ones. Everything came on line perfectly, the systems checked good to go, and I got a distinct rush realizing that I now had control of a fully operational Man O'War, with no one looking over my shoulder or evaluating my performance. It was heady.

I pulled my communications online, my computer promptly providing me with the needed call signs and protocols. "Eight Eight Prime, this is Epsilon Foxtrot Romeo," I said to control, just as I'd been taught at OBT. "All systems are green and am ready to exit hangar two. Request guide to my dropship."

"Romeo, this is Prime. Follow the way points I am giving on nav screen." This was all right, this was something I knew how to do. I adjusted everything I needed to in order to leave as control continued, "Be advised, boat leaves in ten minutes. Move out, Romeo."

That lit a fire under me. Ten minutes would barely be enough time to trot over to the launching area, assuming I could keep a good speed up all the way to the tarmac. I throttled up and moved forward, completely forgetting to check for umbilical connections, as are sometimes made when repairing augmented armor. Of course, they were there, still securely attached, and a good sized chunk of gantry pulled out behind me and fell to crash among some of the other junk on the hangar floor before I could sever the couplings. I looked back to see the extent of the damage I'd done, almost tripping over one of the parts piles. I pulled up short to see just how much damage I would probably be paying for.

It wasn't too bad, just a big portion of scaffolding torn away and a couple of smashed parts. Still, that equipment was worth more than I'd likely make in a very long time, but I'd have to worry about that when I got back. Maybe Much could help me out. The last thing I noticed as I turned to leave was a security guard doubled over, laughing so hard snot was coming out of her nose.

I did manage to get to the boat (that un-glorious label for dropships that has been around longer than I have) on time, if only barely. I had just enough time to confirm I was on the right one and lock myself in before we were blasting skyward in a suborbital arc across the Sea of Japan. I was also finally able to find out that I was supposed to be in Lieutenant Hobb's patrol, and I got an awful lot of questions about why I was running around in a Man O'War as expensive as a Lodestone while the majority of them, all with more experience, were getting bucked around in Roughnecks. I tried to sound aloof, as if I had contacts that they should respect, but someone suggested that I was merely Much's latest bitch, and that idea rapidly gained the consensus of the others in the patrol.

That prompted the questions and none-too-gentle ribbing about my qualifications to be driving a Man O'War at all, let alone one so valuable. The same joker that had labeled Much's attitude toward me speculated that I was such a newborn I'd probably forget to undo my gantry umbilical the first time I had one. I again chose to stay aloof and made no comment on that one. The flight wasn't over quickly enough for me, but we got there.

The scene on the ground in Yokohama, that was horrible. It was simply the worst thing I'd ever seen outside of a theater. We landed in the middle of a park, the only space open enough and large enough to handle our operation, and even it showed extensive signs of damage with its toppled trees and fallen playground equipment. I surveyed the scene in shock from my ten meter height advantage—higher actually, as I was at least another ten meters up standing at the top of the dropship ramp. For kilometers I could see toppled buildings, some still structurally sound enough to be leaning against other buildings, but most simply tumbled to the ground and broken. Fires blazed everywhere and the smoke nearly blotted out the sun, turning midday almost as dark as dusk. I shuddered.

"Move it, FNG!" Someone shoved me from behind, I guess he or she had not appreciated me stopping at the top of the ramp and gawking at everything around me like some tourist. I stumbled my Lodestone down the ramp, quickly catching up to the rest of the column as they trudged along ahead of me. Other 88th dropships were setting down all around and the infantry boys and girls has already gotten started on establishing a perimeter.

We weren't exactly prepared for this exact sort of mission, me in particular. This wasn't a war zone, it was a rescue mission. The city was still in the very early stages of response, and getting aid in was proving difficult with all the blocked access routes and fires. Our first job was going to be clearing the streets, providing some law and order, then locating and rescuing survivors whenever we could.

Lieutenant Hobb decided to take me under his wing, and, after he sent the rest of the patrol ranging out in pairs, the two of us began carefully picking our way south. Hobb was an all right kind of guy from a small town north of San Francisco. He wasn't pompous or standoffish at all, partly because he'd only recently been made a patrol leader and remembered how it was down in the trenches, and he was more than willing to hold my hand during these first baby steps. That and his ribald sense of humor guaranteed that we got along well.

"Watch your atmospheric readings," Hobb told me as I gingerly lead the way through the slightly burnt wreckage of another toppled office building. "They'll let you know if there are any poisonous or explosive gases in the area. Keep your audios turned up too, might hear a cry for help."

I stepped over a supportive beam over two meters thick, the kind used to support those massive skyscrapers. It had been twisted and snapped easily by the power of the earthquake. "You mean there could be gas pockets out here?" I ducked under another girder that had also been bent, though not all the way to the ground. It was slow going, the rubble was loose underfoot and sometimes we had to climb over things. We tried to clear workable paths as much as possible, but we weren't in construction equipment so our success was limited.

"Easily," Hobb said, following roughly in my footsteps. "Make a wrong step in one of those, maybe scrape something hard and send up a spark, and you could find yourself flying. Of course, that's not the problem, it's the landing part that hurts." He stopped his Crossbow short, motioning me to also stand still. "You hear that? I think it's coming from over here."

I listened closely and finally identified the faint, repeated ringing sound Hobb had noticed, perhaps the sound of someone hitting a pipe repeatedly. It could have been something as simple as water pressure or released heat from the fire of earlier pinging the pipes, but we had to check it out.

By slowly and carefully circling the immediate area, which took considerable time given the amount of debris around, we triangulated the approximate position of the source of the sounds, though how accurate that was we couldn't say. It looked impossible, though. The computer put the location at seven meters underneath the pile of rubble we were so carefully stepping around. Huge chunks of concrete and twisted masses of metal lay over everything. Our Man O'Wars just weren't designed for that sort of thing.

"There's nothing we can do with this mess," Hobb said. "Mark the location for priority, and upload it to higher." I knew he was right, but it still burned. Our first contact with someone who truly, desperately needed our help and we had to just walk away. It tasted a lot like defeat in my mouth.

It wasn't long though before we'd found a place where we could help. After about another half hour of carefully stepping around (we only covered a few blocks) a ground car lay partially crushed by a fallen overpass. At least two people inside were still alive, waving and shouting when they caught sight of us, but they couldn't get out, their doors all bent out of shape and blocked by rubble.

We approached fairly quickly and began clearing rubble from around the doors. As we did I reflected on how lucky the city had been that the quake had struck when commuter traffic had been at its lowest ebb. Otherwise there could have been hundreds of other vehicles out here crushed like this one.

The people trapped inside were obviously relieved at our arrival, visibly breaking down and crying. It moved me to realize that I could make that much difference in someone's life and I immediately redoubled my efforts. It wasn't an easy task, even with a Man O'War. Some of the wreckage weighed a lot and it was only with both of us working on it that we were able to move some of it at all. It was about fifteen minutes before we cleared the vehicle, then Hobb just reached down and pulled the one door right off the vehicle. The two people inside emerged, looking for the most part unscathed, if terribly frightened. We broadcast the prepared messages we'd been given in several different languages, instructing them how to find shelter and essentials. They bowed gratefully several times before they began picking their way back the way we'd come, careful to follow the safe markings we'd left.

"And that's why you and I are warriors," Hobb said after we watched them leave.

"Amen, Eltee." I'd done it. My first day on the job and I'd helped save a life. It was a good feeling, and it excited me. "Let's go find some more."

Hobb laughed at my exuberance, but I could tell from the tone that he felt the same thing. I had just enough time to see him fall over on his face before I was thrown flat backward. The whole earth was moving, though I don't recall it making a noise as I would have expected. I slid over onto my side, trying to do what I'd been taught in OBT and curled into a fetal position. There I stayed, curled up in a little ball, shaking back and forth insanely as the aftershock pummeled the already beaten city.

After only a second of shaking the pile of debris that the bridge had become lost all cohesion, it basically liquefied, and the rest of the structure, which had been somewhat supported by the collapsed portion, came tumbling down on us. I briefly wished I'd had time to pick up a shield, despite how useless such a thin piece of armor would be against a thousand ton chunk of concrete falling on it. A few large, heavy chunks fell near me, rolling against my armored form and bouncing me away.

Fortunately, the aftershock only lasted for a few seconds, maybe twenty or thirty, and I was able to regain my feet, uncertain if I could ever again trust the ground to support me. I ran through an essential systems check, but my indicators only showed superficial damage, including a fair sized armor breach in my back, but nothing that should matter in a non-hostile environment. I worked my way back to the overpass, surprised to see just how far I'd been bounced.

The vehicle had been totally crushed, we'd just saved those people in the nick of time. Assuming they'd been okay however far they'd made it afterward. "Eltee," I called out both on transmission and on external speakers, "you okay?"

"I'm fine," his response came back immediately, "but I think my Man O'War may have a slight problem."

I looked around, but couldn't see anything but more rubble where the computer said he should be. "Where are you?"

"Just a sec," he said with a grunt of effort. A fairly impressive explosion burst up to my left, pelting me with minor pieces of rubble. An arm and a portion of a Crossbow torso came up out of the hole created, but there wasn't much more movement than that. "That's just between you and me, right Chase?"

"Uh, yeah," I agreed, though I had no idea exactly what he was talking about. I moved over to stand next to him and visually inspected his Crossbow. Everything below the mid-torso appeared to be crushed by the remains of a large support pillar that had fallen down on the eltee.

"Looks like you got lucky, sir," I said, trying to put the best face on it. "That Crossbow of yours is history, but another couple of meters and you'd be flat."

"Yup," he agreed. "This is my lucky ride."

"Yes, sir, though it isn't much of a ride anymore."

He laughed. "All right, Aarons, give me minute to call higher and then I'll be begging you for a ride."

True to his word, only a couple of minutes passed before Hobb's Crossbow locked motionless (not that it had been moving a whole lot, anyway) and a small figure exited and threw up a hitchhikers thumb. I squatted down and allowed him to scramble up and squeeze into the space behind my seat, the space I remembered so well from not so long ago.

The trip back to the park was quick enough, for we'd not gone all that far. It had been slow going as we'd tried to mark and clear safe pathways and scout for survivors. In our patrol, however, we'd encountered almost no one, just a few dazed stragglers wandering about and the two people we'd saved at the overpass. It was different now, back at the park.

The whole perimeter of our operational HQ had been surrounded by crowds. We could hear them chanting and shouting in three or four different languages, and occasionally hurling bottles and stones. The computer translated some of the phrases as demands for food, shelter, and medical attention. Our infantry were holding them at bay, barricades had been set up all around and armed power armor manned each one.

"This is getting ugly," I said to Hobb.

"They're confused and injured, they don't know where to go but they expect the government to help. We're the government so they want us to do something."

"Well, let's do something," I said.

"We're trying to, but it takes time, and there are a lot of people that need help. Try to get past them."

I did as I was told, but when I moved toward the park gates, dozens of people ran forward to block my path, some of them linking arms, all of them shouting and shaking fists up at me.

"Why are they mad at me?" I asked.

"Ah, those would be our trouble makers," Hobb said. "The ones that think they should be given special treatment because they're too good for the rest of us. They're not really here to find necessities or get help, they're trying to make a political statement. Yokohama's always been a hotbed for civil unrest."

I nodded at that. "But how do we get past them?"

"Fire a burst at their feet, that'll scatter 'em."

"Excuse me, sir?" I said. "Did I hear that right?"

"Yes, Aarons, I want you to put a burst right next to them so that they will disperse. It's standard procedure for dealing with mobs in times of crises, especially politically motivated mobs."

I shrugged and pulled a trigger as I'd been ordered, sending out a stream of carefully aimed fifty caliber anti-armored personnel bullets. The burst of machine gun fire chewed up the pavement in front of the mob, flinging pieces of asphalt everywhere and sending them all running away and diving for cover, many screaming in pain and panic.

"What in the seven hells was that?!?" Hobb was standing as best he could, hunched over one side of my chair. I looked back and saw his eyes comically bulging out of his face.

"You said fire a burst, sir."

"I didn't say perforate them and spread their chaff to the wind! What kind of ammunition are you carrying?"

"Standard load, sir, that's what was loaded when I picked it up. Why?"

"Because you're supposed to have civil enforcement loads only! It's illegal to carry this stuff in a civilian zone! You'll have us both up in a court martial!"

I was confused. "But this is what I was given, sir. Besides, you had something active on yours, didn't you? Otherwise how did you blow up that girder you were under back there?"

His face drained of all color and he sank down. "I'm done. They'll pull up your logs in the inquiry, and then they'll check my Crossbow. When they find out I was carrying a live rocket, I'll be discharged at the least." He looked down at me. "But I only had the one, just how much are you carrying?"

"I've got a full load, sir," I confessed, "I thought I was supposed to." I was getting really nervous now. "What do we do?"

Hobb wiped a hand across his face and took a deep breath. "We go in, we turn ourselves in, hoping for leniency, and then we start looking for a new line of work."

I stood at perfect attention, frozen in place, willing every muscle to remain motionless as I stared at the wall behind Colonel Glenn, very careful not to make eye contact with him. Beside me, Captain Sierra and Lieutenant Hobb held almost identical poses. The three of us barely dared to breathe.

"Gentleman," Glenn said, glaring at us hard enough to cause physical pain, "I am not at all pleased with this." I could hear the battalion sergeant major snort from his position at the wall behind me, emphasizing the understatement. Glenn's attention momentarily flicked to him, then back to us. "I have reviewed the record, is there anything any of you wishes to say before I complete my recommendations?"

We sounded off in unison. "No, sir."

He nodded, expecting that traditional answer, then rose from his chair coming to stand directly in front of us. "Lieutenant Hobb, you stand accused of carrying battlefield weaponry into a non-hostile civilian zone, and of using the same, in breach of the Taurus Accords sections twenty-seven and thirty-one. You also stand accused of allowing a subordinate to do the same. In examining this incident, I find that your record indicates a history of casual indifference to regulations and proper procedure. That is intolerable, Lieutenant, and now you can see what dangers come of it.

"I believe your conduct to be both intentional and reckless, and your history makes me believe that this is very likely to continue. I have no choice but to recommend that you be held over for a full hearing before a court martial." Hobb swallowed loud enough for me to hear, but otherwise he made no move. "You are relieved of all duties, and confined to quarters here until such time as your preliminary hearing sets other conditions. Dismissed."

Reflexively, Hobb saluted. Glenn refused to return the salute, as tradition forbids saluting those awaiting criminal proceedings. Hobb pursed his lips as that drove home what he faced, and I think tears shone in his eyes. He about faced and strode from the room.

Glenn didn't wait even a second after that before he rounded on Sierra. "Captain Sierra, you stand accused of two counts of allowing subordinates to violate sections twenty-seven and thirty-one of the Taurus Accords. You were negligent in handling the assignment of Sub-lieutenant Aarons to your company, and in everything that happened after that." He took a deep breath, then blew it out in almost a sigh, sitting back against his desk. He looked down at his hands, clasping them before him, before continuing. "It should never have come to this, Gary. But you've had too many problems with new assignees. I've got a stack of complaints against you and that quartermaster of yours that is thicker than my hand is wide." He looked up directly at Sierra. "I'm giving you a chance to resign with some semblance of honor before I recommend you for a summary and dishonorable discharge. You have twenty-four hours before I file my recommendation, Gary, I suggest you do the right thing for everyone concerned. You're dismissed." Sierra also saluted, and this time the colonel returned it. Then Sierra too was gone and I face Glenn alone.

My career, brief as it was, flashed before my eyes when the Colonel turned to face me. Sweat, already soaking my armpits, leapt unbidden to my brow. A salty bead trickled down my face, tracing a saline trail across my cheek and down my neck.

The sergeant major moved over to stand right next to me. When he barked at me I nearly fainted. "Sub-lieutenant Aarons, sir, you also stand accused of breaches of sections twenty-seven and thirty-one of the Taurus Accords. You've seen what happened to both of your commanding officers over this, that should tell you just how seriously this incident is being taken. Now, I have just one question for you, were you trying to get civilians killed or were you just stupid, sir?"

My mouth was parched and it took three swallows before I could stammer out a shaky reply. "I was stupid, Sergeant Major. I didn't know any better, and no one told me what I was supposed to do."

Glenn folded his arms across his chest and studied me for a moment. "Aarons," he stopped then started again, taking much of the gruff edge out of his voice. "Chase, I understand this is your first day on the job. It doesn't seem like a very good way to start your new career, does it?"

"No, sir." I was certain they could see me shaking now, my knees almost buckling each time they knocked together.

Glenn nodded and smiled gently. "You may go, Sub-lieutenant."

I wasn't certain what that meant. Was I being discharged or just remanded into custody? It took a dozen heartbeats (not a very long time in my state of panic) for me to realize that his statement didn't really make any sense. "Sir?"

Glenn spread his hands. "I see no reason to believe that any of this was anything other than the result of a tragic comedy of errors. You personally were not to blame for any of it. The other two, they shoulder a lot of responsibility, for this and many other things, but you just showed up at the wrong time. I believe that this experience and an official reprimand in your record should suffice to prevent future difficulties. I don't believe a court martial is necessary." He looked next to me. "Sergeant Major?"

"Violations of the Taurus Accords are supposed to require a mandatory hearing, but in this case I concur, sir," the Sergeant Major said. "I doubt Sub-lieutenant Aarons will ever need to be in here again, will you, sir?"

"No, Sergeant Major," I said. "Definitely not."

Glenn smiled widely then. "Then you are welcome to the 88th, Chase. Dismissed."

Chapter Nine

North Vancouver, North America
Terra
Terran Dominion

June 14, 2651

The rain was pouring down, as it always does in Vancouver in the winter. I kicked my trench coat clear of the cab door as it closed, and wiped away the water that had already pooled on my hat's brim. The house didn't look any different from the outside, despite the dark and the damp, but everything felt older and more solemn. I didn't want to be here. I wanted to be twenty years away and curled up warm and safe in my mother's lap, held tight by the arms of her and my father.

I paid the driver mechanically, failing to tip him properly. He sneered at me through the window and then sped away with a steely eyed glare. I didn't even notice, not then. Instead I walked slowly up the front path and climbed the steps to the porch. The cracks in the sidewalk had grown a bit, and the lawn hadn't been edged properly this last year, but those minor details were about all that seemed to have changed from my last few homecomings, infrequent and brief as they had been.

My key still turned the lock without a problem and I quickly ducked across the threshold to get out of the rain. As I shook the clinging, cold drops from my coat and hat onto the convenient mat, a plump, middle aged woman approached from the direction of the kitchen. Barb and I had talked through several telecommunications, but had never met in person. The last time I had been here, she'd been away on a well-earned vacation, visiting her family in Johannesburg. She looked as matronly as the word itself and all but exuded apple pie and home with her presence.

"I was unsure if you would be okay in this weather," she said, taking my coat. She opened the finished walnut doors on the closet and placed the garment on a hanger to dry. I stepped out of my shoes and tossed my hat onto the shelf at the top of the closet. The water that spattered off of it turned the wood beneath a darker shade.

"This is normal weather for this time of year and this part of the world, Barb. You should see what February is like in Vladivostok. Fort Pyotr turns into one big skating rink. You ever see a Man O'War trying to figure skate?" I tried to smile. Almost, I may have succeeded. "But I don't think Liz will make it out of Boston with the ice storm. Power is down all along the East Coast and communications are unreliable." I ran a hand through my hair, rain-dampened despite the covering I'd used.

Barb didn't even try to smile. "I saw on the news. Two years in a row, I wonder how many people will die this time? But I am glad you made it to see her before the end." She choked off the last couple of words and I felt my own throat tighten up. *God*, I prayed, *give me strength*. "There's some warm food in the kitchen if you're hungry."

I shook my head. This woman was so much a nurse and caregiver that she couldn't break the habit, even tonight. Especially tonight. "I'd just like to talk to her first."

She shook her head. "She's resting now, and you need to take care of yourself first, Chase. I can see just by looking at you that you haven't eaten all day." That part was definitely true. Breakfast isn't a meal I normally eat, and I slept all the way on the flight over.

Barb took me by the arm and led me into the kitchen where I was greeted by the comforting smells of fresh bread, beef stew, and what was probably a peach pie baking in the oven. It's good to be home when home feels the way that kitchen did. It called up memories, triggered mostly by the smells, of long days playing hard in the backyard. On a whim, I crossed to the window and looked out to where it had all started. In the dim light I could just make out where the apple tree had been, though the stump had long since been removed just as the hole in the fence had been repaired.

Barb pulled out a chair and bade me sit, giving me little choice but to accede to her wishes. She placed a bowl and plate in front of me, quickly followed by the appropriate utensils. Her movements were practiced and efficient, but not at all cold. Obviously she was not going to tolerate any dissent on this point. She turned back to the counter and filled a mug from the kettle resting there.

"Here," she said, handing me the mug. "I crushed some retticate leaves into the mint tea. It will warm you up and give you a bit of energy."

I nodded my thanks and accepted the vessel. It warmed my hands quickly, and I had to set it on the table before it became painful to hold. Already Barb was ladling a hefty portion of beef stew into my bowl. Then she cut a thick slice of fresh bread, spread butter across it generously, and placed it on my plate.

"Eat up," she said.

I twirled my spoon through my stew, looking for answers that cannot possibly be found in any culinary creation, regardless of how plain or elaborate it may be. "I'm not really hungry."

"Posh," Barb said as she took another chair at the table. "Whatever you might think, your body's need for sustenance has not changed, and it still reacts the same way when hunger is confronted with food."

She was right, of course. The smells from the food were causing my mouth to water and my stomach to rumble. With a small sigh, I dug in and was cleaning my bowl with the bread in a surprisingly short period of time. I was honestly cognizant of no desire for food, but Barb also forced a small piece of the piping hot peach pie down my throat. I didn't struggle to resist very much.

"How is she?" I asked finally. I already knew the answer, but I didn't want to face it, and I hoped God had some miracle in store that would make this all a bad dream.

Barb sat across from me looking at her hands as they sat folded on the table and heaved a sigh. "She's a terribly strong woman. She won't give up, and she's made it far longer than anyone predicted, but this couldn't last forever. The woman you see tonight is...not even as good as the one you saw when you were here in October."

I nodded, not surprised but resenting that answer. "When will she be awake, do you think?"

"I'll go check on her," she offered. Before I could stand and just go myself, she was already out of her chair and on her feet. "You just stay here and sip some more tea, I'll be right back down."

She walked down the hall in her unique rolling gait, and then I could hear her climbing the stairs. I sighed again, and refilled my mug. I didn't recall emptying it, but I think it helped out. I don't know how long I just sat there reminiscing and thinking about everything, and thinking about nothing. The vast mysteries of the universe yawned up at me, but only questions sprang forth, no answers. Barb came back into the kitchen and found me just staring at my mug, trying to read divine will in my tea leaves.

"Anna's awake," Barb said gently. "She said to tell you that she's been waiting for you. She said that she knew that at least the favorite would make it in time." Her eyes sagged down into the dark bags beneath them. I hadn't noticed them before, so self-involved was I. Nevertheless, there they were, emphasized even more so by the deep lines embossed around her mouth. She had obviously grown very attached to my mother these last few months of living with her. In a less stressful time I'd have welcomed her warm, comforting aura. Instead, I can only notice it now, many years after the fact; much too late to appreciate it in full.

I nodded and again ran my hand through my hair, vaguely surprised at how wet it still was. I wiped my clammy hand dry against my trousers as I rose, then walked to the end of the hallway and began to climb the stairs. The carpet was no longer so plush as it had been when I was a child, but it was still a soothing sensation to feel it underfoot again.

Strange what memories will surface in times of stress or sorrow, but I suddenly recalled many happy days of childhood, running up and down these stairs, sliding down them on mattresses, throwing toy Man O'Wars headlong down them, and being always, inseparably, constantly side-by-side with Jonny. Always, Mom was there to scold us, to hug us, to give us treats, or to laugh and take pictures of our exploits.

Rounding the landing, I ran my hands along the walls, savoring the texture that my parents had painted into them before I had been born. I smiled almost bitterly at the painting of the bullfighter hanging by the upstairs hall closet. It had always been my favorite, capturing the ineffective attempts of the ever proud bull to catch its executioner. Before, I'd always loved the grace and fearless determination of the matador, but tonight I felt for the bull. Those swords sunk to the hilt in that proud back must have felt much like the ones buried deep in my heart. At least the bull could rage back at his tormentor, I was not so lucky. Regardless, neither one of us stood a chance, the odds were stacked completely against us both. Some battles, those like tonight's and the bull's, are impossible to win but necessary to fight. All you can really do is lose with honor.

I approached the door to my mother's room, and I could already hear the gentle hisses, whirrs, and beeps of the life support equipment that was doing the work of most of her failed organs. The door stood slightly ajar and I stopped to first peek through at the woman who had given me so much more than just life. She lay slightly propped up in the middle of the smaller bed she'd purchased after Dad died, tubes stuffed into her arms and nostrils. Only one dim light illuminated her from the left hand end table, where books rested in a neat pile next to several bottles and vials of different medications.

Her eyes were closed and she seemed to be sleeping.

My heart moved up to partially block my throat. For a moment I couldn't breathe, I could barely swallow. I didn't want to disturb her rest, so I decided to just head back to the kitchen, allowing my own cowardice to hold sway.

As soon as I even thought of going back, Mom's eyes opened slowly. Perhaps she sensed my presence through that still mysterious motherly instinct, or perhaps she was more alert than I had thought she could be given her condition and the medication she was on. She lifted one hand ever so slightly and gestured toward me weakly, as though it cost her everything she had to do so.

"Come in here, Chase," she called to me softly. She wheezed as she spoke and the pump at the head of the bed inflated slightly faster to compensate for her failing breath. I stepped carefully into her room and pushed the door almost closed again. "Is Elizabeth coming?"

I could already feel salty tears pooling in the corners of my eyes as I approached her bed and perched there at her right hand side. The bedspread was thick and soft, the dark red color that Mom was always so fond of. "I don't think so. They had a huge ice storm along the entire East Coast last night and everything is messed up again, just like last year was." One drop ran down my right cheek, dripping from my chin and landing on the front of my shirt which was already damp from the rain. I thought she would miss it but she never missed anything.

"Is it so hard?" she asked with that slightly tilted head she often used when she wanted to draw my attention to something I already knew. "We've known for many months now." She sucked in hard at that, another symptom of how bad things were.

I didn't want to make eye contact, knowing that I'd break down. Instead I focused my attention on the fluids pumping through their various tubes and into my mother's arms. I kept my eyes directed there until I could speak. Once I had regained a bit more control, I looked back down at her.

I smiled at her and more tears streamed down my face, despite whatever increased control I had believed I'd gained. I couldn't breathe, and finding my voice took several moments. In those moments, I looked at her closely. Once fine lines had deepened into creases all along her face. Her hair had grayed almost entirely, and thinned out considerably, much like her entire body. The irises of her eyes had dulled and they almost matched the color of her hair now. The lips that had once kissed a small child goodnight and produced the most beautiful lullabies had also thinned down to pencil thin lines on flat, flaccid flaps of skin. She was only forty-five.

"Knowing something and doing it," I began but could not finish. I hadn't been there when Dad died. I didn't know what Jonny, Elizabeth, and Mom had gone through; watching the doctors trying to revive him, waiting for the inevitable failure, and not having me around to share the pain and grief. For myself, I had thought my position had been the worst, but now I knew that it wasn't. When Dad passed away I never had any chance to fear it, to confront it, to lose that confrontation, or to retreat gracefully from it. Neither had I the chance to say goodbye, but I'd not been forced to feel so powerless. Grief after the fact and at a distance is so much easier than grief at the moment.

Another hard lesson learned too late, and at too great a cost.

One fat tear drop fell from the tip of my nose and landed on Mom's hand. I gently took that hand in my own and wiped away the teardrop. I think she fell back asleep at that point, because her breathing evened out and her eyes closed completely. How long she stayed that way I cannot say. I just sat there, holding her hand and looking at what remained of my mother. Gone was the strong, proud mien that had always adorned her face before; nowhere to be seen was that set to her neck that bespoke confidence and experience. Even the soft laugh lines that had accumulated around her eyes had changed into marks of pain and suffering. This empty shell was not at all the way I wanted my mother to live, not at all, and yet I was not ready to give her up forever.

As I sat there observing her, I remembered so many times we'd spent together. From throwing a beach ball back and forth in the park when I was five to kissing a knee I'd scraped falling off my bike when I was nine; from the time Mom watched while Jonny and I duct taped Dad's head to his pillow while he slept to that special party we'd thrown for her when we graduated from university. I remembered so many long discussions we'd had late into the night talking about morals and religion, about girls and dating, about the future and the past. I remembered the fights we'd had about girls and dating, about COTC and the military, about school and work. I remembered so many different things we'd done together as I grew up, and I knew that tonight they would all end. So many things sprang to mind that needed to be said; a whole lifetime of emotions and memories that begged to be discussed. Yet no words presented themselves to fill my mouth, nothing rolled easily off my tongue as the appropriate place to begin.

There was one thing though, not about any of that, that she had to know first. The most important news brought, news that I wanted to tell her before it was too late. I hoped she could hear me. When I saw her breathing slow even more, and heard the heart monitor take longer between beats, I begged God to give me this chance, to not take this away from me too.

"I'm getting married, Mom." I blurted out. If she couldn't be there to watch it happen, she at least needed to know that I was going to do it. "Rachel asked me when I called her at the airport before I left. She must have gotten tired of waiting for me to propose." It was all coming out in a babble. I managed a small laugh, even as more tears fell. "I know she talked to you last week, did you know this was going to happen?" Perhaps it was just the light, but a small smile seemed to curl the corners of her mouth, so I assumed she was able to hear what I was saying. "I know you've always liked her, the way you talk more to her than you do to me. She's going to look so beautiful in a wedding dress, isn't she?"

I stopped for a bit to keep from rambling too aimlessly. I couldn't prevent a vivid image of Rachel in a long white gown, smiling as she walked down the aisle, springing to mind. I knew Mom wouldn't be there to see it all and whatever semblance of a dam I had constructed around my emotions burst wide open; tears flooded my eyes and fell like rain, my breathing coming in ragged gasps and sobs.

How many of the important times in my life would she miss? Every promotion I earned, every child I had, every joy and every sorrow would be without this most remarkable woman. I cried for her not being there to once again pin on a pip and congratulate me. I cried for children I didn't have because they would not be blessed with having her as a grandmother. I cried for Jonny, who didn't even know yet that this was happening, or how quickly, because he was on the far side of the Charted Territories, attending a conference on Santonio. I cried for Liz, who did know, but couldn't make it off the East Coast or even get a call through to say goodbye. I cried in a way that I have never cried before or since.

I think I may have dozed at some point. Tears still ran from my eyes, and, emotionally, I felt like I was going into shock. I felt a hand weakly stroking my back. I blinked away enough tears to make eye contact with my mother. She smiled another weak smile and dropped her hand to her side. I clutched after it with both of my own. They trembled, but it didn't matter any more.

"Did you get promoted?" she asked.

I nodded, pained to see her like this. I had been warned that the medications would tend to make her forgetful and lead her to focus on the inconsequential. I had told her of my promotion months ago. "Yeah, they made me a full lieutenant and gave me command of a full patrol."

Her eyes fluttered closed again, but she still smiled. "That's good. You'll be a good leader. Just remember what your mom always taught you."

"Of course I will." What else could I say? Now I can wax eloquent about the poetry that her existence had brought into my life, I can grow loquacious on how much her strength of character had been the iron that brought purpose and resolve into my very being. Now I can even express all of the regrets I had for things I'd said when I shouldn't have, and for things I didn't say when I should have. It's easy to look back and put words in my mouth, words that would have expressed all that I truly longed to say in that moment, but it won't make it so. In the end, when confronted with that final goodbye, even being prepared months in advance, there was little I could do but mumble mindless dialogue with my mother and hope that beneath all of the drug induced mental fog she was able to read straight from the pages of my heart and know that I loved her.

"What are you piloting now?" she asked, almost as though she were genuinely interested.

"They gave me Crossbow, Mom," I told her.

"Do you like it?"

I nodded. "It suits my style more than the Lodestone did. Less ground and pound, more finesse."

She smiled slightly at that. She was probably remembering the little boy who would melt toy soldiers and tie firecrackers to toy Man O'Wars. Very little finesse there.

"And what does your command involve?"

I looked at her and could tell that she didn't find this the least bit interesting. She didn't care, she was just looking for a distraction.

"But that stuff isn't why I'm here, Mom," I said. "I'm here for you."

"Oh, Chase," she said, tears trickling from each eye, "it's the mommy that's always supposed to be there for her little boy, not the other way around."

That made me smile, even through my own tears. "Sometimes little boys grow up, and suddenly it's the mommy that's little."

I once read that life goes full circle, parents take care of children when they are young and helpless, then children must take care of their parents when they are old and helpless. That's all garbage. The truth is, we are all helpless, and that never goes away. Nothing I could do would take care of my mother in her state. I could only sit impotently by and bear witness to her pain and misery.

Now I can only sit and bear witness to my own.

More tears ran from the corners of Mom's eyes, watering the troughs and crevices that lined her face. "I'll miss you," she said simply, giving my hand a slight squeeze.

I didn't want to talk about that. Who wants to confront death so forthrightly? "I'm going to miss you, too, Mom. More than anything, even..." I had to trail off; I couldn't continue.

For another period of time we just sat there, silent and motionless. Was it cowardice that kept me from speaking, or was I truly, as I wanted to believe at the time, respecting her strength limitations? She *was* tired. I sat there studying her, wondering how I could say what I truly wanted to say.

Then Mom shuddered, her back arching high. Her eyes sprang wide open, showing huge amounts of white. She choked a bit, but before I could move to do anything at all other than feel the sudden thrust of panic and fear stab through me, she collapsed back to the bed, limp as a rag.

An alarm had sounded at the attack and Barb was quickly in the room. She checked Mom's vitals and consulted some readouts on the various pieces of equipment. She made some minor adjustments and Mom appeared to relax a bit more, even in her unconscious state. Barb beckoned me to follow her out of the room and into the hallway.

"Does this happen often?" I asked in a low, worried voice once we were safely out of earshot.

Barb nodded. "Quite frequently." She chewed her lower lip for a moment then blatantly made eye contact with me. "She cannot last much longer, maybe not even an hour."

I indicated that I understood, and thanked her. The thanks was as much reflex as anything truly meant at the time, though all that Barb had done was clearly deserving of thanks and more. I returned to Mom's bedside and once again took her hand in my own. She stirred and smiled again.

"Chase, I knew you'd make it in time. Did you get promoted?"

And so it went. Always continuing in a pattern, staying focused on the trivial and inconsequential, steering well clear of anything truly meaningful. The times we did wander toward the things I wanted to say, either Mom would collapse or I just couldn't say what needed to be said. Somewhere inside, there were barriers that couldn't be broken, not even now.

In the end, Barb was wrong, though I cannot blame her for that, Mom was always stronger than anyone thought. I sat there with her throughout the whole night. I watched her writhe in pain, her teeth ground tight and her back arched. I watched her collapse into unconsciousness and rouse again a few moments later to have the same conversation over and over. I doubt that she ever understood that Rachel and I were engaged. I don't think she really knew why Jonny and Elizabeth weren't there. At times, I think she even wondered why Dad wasn't sitting here with her, though maybe he really was right there the whole time, after all. One day, perhaps sooner than later, I'll know for certain.

Toward morning, just before dawn, Mom's eyes just snapped open and were clear, devoid of any drug influence. Suddenly she was totally lucid. Her face still betrayed the signs of extreme pain and suffering, but her mind was her own for that moment.

"Chase," she said with renewed purpose, "tell Jonny I love him. I love him very much and he has made me so very proud. And Elizabeth. Tell her the same thing. I won't get to tell them like I can tell you." She paused to take several breaths, as deeply as she was able. I could see how much the pain cost her in terms of will power, yet she struggled on. That she had been able to hold out this long was a testament to her strength and will. I suddenly realized that she really had been waiting for me, waiting for one last moment of clarity when she could get her message across.

Suddenly I was filled with panic. I knew what was coming and there was not a damn thing I could do to stop it. I grasped at any straw I could, hoping to prevent the inevitable.

"No, Mom," I began babbling. "Don't say it yet. I can't let you go. Don't leave me!" I was begging. With her, with God, with fate, with death, I was begging with anything and anyone to spare me this loss, but Mom had focused only on this moment, this last chance to say goodbye, and it was the only thing she had left.

She raised her hand to my cheek, where I pressed it hard. Another ghostly smile fell on her features. "I love you, Chase, you've made me so very proud. I know your father is proud too, and we'll be reunited soon. Tell Rachel I loved her, too, and I want you two to be happy." Her hand felt so very cold against my skin, even as she moved her fingers ever so slightly across my cheek. "I love you, Chase."

"No!" I cried out. I hugged her around her shoulders and drew her close to me, holding her in a crushing embrace. It was as if I hoped that I could pull her so close that my own delicate life energies could migrate across the gap and strengthen her own weakening ones. "No, no, no!" I shouted repeatedly. "Please, God, no, no, no. Don't do this! Not yet, I still need her! I can't face tomorrow without her support!"

Mom's eyes just closed gently with that slight smile still on her face as the pain that had so tormented her finally ceased its torture and let her be. The life support systems had been programmed to support and comfort, not to resuscitate. They simply stopped when there was no longer anything they could do, and, as the sun rose in the window behind us, Mom slipped away from me, pain free at long last, as the night slips away before the dawn.

I never did tell her that I love her.

Chapter Ten

Fort Pyotr
Vladivostok, Asia
Terra
Unified Terran Republic

March 3, 2652

The call that heralded the biggest change in my life found me in my studio apartment at three o'clock in the morning. Bleary eyed and barely coherent, I listened to Captain Yabe explain to me in short order that we were being called up for a general mobilization. It had only been a month since the Terran Dominion and the Free Terran Republic had concluded their negotiations with the historical merging of the two nations. On the surface nothing had changed, I wore the same uniform (albeit with a new insignia), was assigned to the same base, and used the same currency to pay my rent, but that was life here on Earth.

Across the Charted Territories war had erupted at the news, and not on the scale we were used to. In this galaxy, with hundreds of settled worlds, we've grown accustomed to always hearing about war on one or two planets, sometimes involving three or even four nations. Historically speaking, though, war by one nation across multiple worlds hasn't happened since the fall of the Terran Alliance. The logistics involved just make it all but impossible, or so we believed.

With the unification of two of the largest, most powerful nations in the Charted Territories, dozens of nations were suddenly battling us and each other, each trying to adjust to the new balance of power, carving out their own piece of the reformed pie or trying to shatter our piece. States were realigning themselves, usually by joining our allies or our enemies, though more than a few chose, perhaps wisely, to follow their own paths. Whatever the case, battle was joined on literally scores of planets. There were too many facets to keep track of it all, I could barely follow all the conflicts directly involving the Republic.

With all hell breaking loose and the possibility of us being called up for duty just about anywhere at anytime, I'd tried to keep my unit members on their toes, ready for anything. Captain Yabe had told me she expected us to be moving out very soon, and apparently she was right.

It took me a lot longer to get up and moving than it should have, considering just how much adrenaline my glands managed to squeeze into my blood stream at the thought of impending battle. I was scared in a way that I'd never felt before. In training I had faced simulated and even real life threatening situations, and I'd never been afraid like this. I had always believed that when the call went up, announcing the moment where I would meet and accept my destiny, I would step forward gladly, eager to rush in and live or die proving myself. I believed the adventure would excite me to levels which would top any mediocre rush caused by merely piloting a Man O'War.

The reality was something disconcertingly different. Even as I did all of the usual preparatory toiletries, and dressed in my best set of battle dress fatigues, I could notice a slight shake in my hands, and I could feel a cold grasp around my heart. I did not purposely delay, it was not cowardice I suffered from, but I could not bring myself to rush either. Perhaps some part of me, that part of each and every one of us that can feel the future and give us gut instincts, was warning me away from what would happen on Madrigal. I do not know, I only wish now that I had refused the order and accepted a dishonorable discharge and perhaps prison sentence. My life would have been so vastly different, and many others would still have theirs to live.

Jonny would still be here.

Once I was fully presentable, externally if not internally, I called a cab. I'd blown the transmission on my own vehicle two days earlier, and it was still being repaired. Waiting for the cab gave me a few moments to kill while I was waiting, moments I used to contact Jonny.

It was light in Cambridge, and Jonny picked up the line in his office immediately. He had the visual on and I could see that he was clad, as I, in battle dress. He grinned when he saw me.

"Morning, Chase," he said around his teeth. "Aren't you a bit overdressed for this time of day in Vladivostok?"

"Bite me," I said cordially. "Judging by your own business attire, I assume you recently received a call similar to the one I did?"

Jonny nodded agreement. "Everyone's mobilizing in the entire Terran

Guard. Active, reserve, listed reserve, everyone. I've got word that nearly all active and a whole bunch of the reserve are to be off planet within twenty. Including yours truly."

"That's tight, for listed," I said, though that would actually give me plenty of time to get my active patrol squared away properly. The reservists, though, would definitely be pushed to their utmost limit trying to locate everyone, get them back in uniform, and off world in less than a single day. "We're only leaving some reserve and the listed behind? This must be huge. You get word on where we're going?"

"This will be public in a few hours, but why take chances?" Jonny to looked down at the corner of the display, then he hit a control to send a secure encryption mark scrolling across the bottom of the viewing area. "Madrigal."

His one word answer sent chills up and down my spine, though it shouldn't have, not really. Again, it was just a gut reaction. I only vaguely knew for certain where Madrigal was, and it wasn't in any area currently threatened by combat. "Why Madrigal? And what does that mean? Sunnite opposition?"

That possibility was a little bit worrisome. Sunni has never ratified the Taurus Accords, and Sunnites reportedly do not respect POWs, feeling them without honor and thus eligible for human experimentation. That philosophy has occasionally been applied to conquered populations as well.

Jonny shook his head. "That's not what's on the scopes. The rumor that's going around in my circles says Confed. We have deep intelligence that says they'll be there soon, but by deep transit and completely and totally *incommunicado* while they are moving through Sunnite territory. So we're going to jump in just ahead of them, reinforce the locals, and be waiting when our friends arrive."

I didn't bother asking how he knew, Jonny always knew. His incredible network of business and political connections, along with his other contacts from Harvard, made him privy to far more knowledge than any reserve lieutenant had a fair right to make a claim on. Anytime anything controversial or top secret was rumored to be going around, Jonny always had advanced knowledge of it.

"It looks like we'll be going up against the Empire head on, bro."

I suppressed another shudder. "This isn't some small excursion if everyone and their dog is mobilizing. It sounds huge. What kind of opposition are we going to be facing?"

"Like you said, expect something huge. The lion's share of the Terran

Guard is being transplanted to supplement the Madrigal Guard. Analysts say that the Imperial plan is to hit nearly every major city simultaneously, so we have to defend everywhere. That would fit with their past performances, and it is severely troop intensive. Current thought is that they fully intend to set up shop and stay for a while, so no quick hit and run. It's going to be very ugly out there before this is all over." If only he had known what an understatement that would turn out to be.

I took a deep breath and blew it out. Something inside me didn't like this at all. I never thought I would suffer from cowardice, yet there I stood, afraid. "Are you ready?" I asked. Whether I spoke to Jonny or myself I wasn't certain.

"Of course," he said. "This is what we've looked for all of our lives. The grand adventure, the ultimate game, the stuff dreams and legends are made out of. Why? Aren't you?"

Before I could answer, before I had to choose between the truth and a lie, a horn sounded outside. "My cab's here, I better get on base. You'd likely do well to get moving too. I'll give you a shout in transit, if there's time. Keep your head down, Jonny." With that I cut the connection.

I quickly shrugged into a thick, warm parka to shelter my favorite body from the worst of the early morning weather and trotted downstairs. Through the window in the door I could see my cab waiting out in the street, steam blowing off of it in waves like smoke from a fanned fire. I stuffed my hands into my fur mitts, pulled up my hood and elbowed open the exit door. The blast of cold that greeted me took my breath away momentarily, and quickly froze the tears it drew from my eyes. I struggled through the freezing, cutting wind and dove into the waiting shelter of the cab.

The driver sped away as soon as I told him I was heading to the base. He apparently understood that there was a full scale mobilization going on, and that he was well-positioned to make some good money if he could hurry enough to catch a good number of the available fares.

I don't believe I've ever made the trip to Fort Pyotr faster than that. I thought we were going to die several times as we skidded through intersections and caromed over the curbs. Stop signals meant nothing as we blew past them one after another. All the while the driver kept prattling on about what a patriot he was and how he meant to do his part by getting our fighting men and women to their duty stations as quickly as possible. I assured him that we had plenty of time, but he waved down my objection and just told me to hold on as we accelerated onto the main thoroughfare.

By the time we arrived on base, my adrenal glands were empty, every last drop of adrenaline squeezed from them. We skidded to a stop more or less in front of the 141st Terran Heavy Guard's command building, me fully expecting to have a full blown heart attack and the driver cheerfully asking for his payment. I purposely stiffed him for his terrible driving, then dashed through the cold and inside the shelter of the building. I could still feel a pounding in my chest, though I tried not to think about it as I trotted down to the 10th Man O'War Company's arena.

I hurried through the maze of hallways and slipped into the command assembly room, trying not to draw attention to myself until I could better assess how everyone else seemed to be handling everything. The room was really a small theater, similar to the kinds you can find on any post-secondary campus. Only about half of the seats were occupied, and those mostly by support personnel. This was to be a briefing only for team leaders and higher. Of those, it looked like at least a third were still missing.

I stood in the shadows surveying the room for a minute. At the podium, surrounded by a half dozen communications and logistics personnel, the company's executive officer, Lieutenant Randstad, looked to be hard at work. Not wishing to disturb him (in truth, trying to avoid him and any assignments he might think to give me), I moved to a seat toward the back of the room between two of my three fellow patrol leaders. Those two were good friends, Thomasz Asoc and April Hansen, of our reconnaissance and primary assault patrols respectively.

They both looked bleary eyed and unfocused, almost sick. That made me smile, for I saw some humor in this pair of officers (who should most certainly have known better) getting totally bushwhacked when a call up was possible.

"You two feeling lively at this early hour?" I asked loudly. I wiggled their seats around a little bit, teasing them. I almost felt bad for that, especially seeing the look of anguish that passed over their faces. Even more so when I momentarily thought that Hansen was going to puke right in my lap, which I'm sure would have amused everyone in the room save me.

"Look, Aarons," Asoc said in that thick Polish accent of his, "I got a call a half hour after I stumbled in from the greatest party I've had all year. I'm still three quarters drunk, and totally in the dark. I have no idea what's going on, and some nitwit who thinks himself clever is trying to make me blow chunks all over the company arena. Do you think just maybe you could spare some pity for me and not make this any worse than it already has to be?"

I held my hands up in mock protest. "Sorry, Tom, I didn't realize you weren't feeling so well. You know I'd never do anything cruel on purpose."

I grinned.

"I already knew you were the cruelest man I'd ever met," Hansen groaned as she tried to retain her last meal, "but why would you demonstrate on your friends like this?"

I shrugged. "Because you're my friends."

Asoc tapped my arm and I looked over at him. "C'mon, Chase, you always know what's going down. Give us the dirt." Both of them leaned in toward me, awaiting my response and sharing their fragrant breath with me.

"You just wait and see," I responded cryptically. "But rest assured, it'll be Confed." I slouched back, putting my well-rehearsed, smug smirk in place.

"Bull," Hansen said with a surprising amount of animation. "My money is on something Kalamatran. Offensive. Hit them hard and take back a bit of what we lost or let them feel what it's like." She stood and made a powerful punching gesture as she spoke, which would have been far more impressive if she hadn't immediately turned three progressively lighter shades of pale and collapsed back into her seat.

Asoc disagreed with both of us. "It's Kaifan," he assured us. "There's no way they're going to let the Satrap break alliance and hit Krupp like that, it's risking everything we tried so hard to prevent. We're bound for the rim."

I shook my head. "You guys must have been smoking something at that party. Kalamata is moving too fast, never sticking still long enough for us to strike a decisive blow, and they're not allowing themselves to be bogged down in protracted combat. Unless we actually assault Kalamata itself, we'd be unsuccessful at doing any lasting hurt. While that would explain a general mobilization call, that doesn't really seem warranted at this point. And Kaifa is so close to being swallowed whole by Krupp that they had little choice but to break alliance. They also haven't caused us any pain, and, in any event, I'm quite certain that Krupp can take care of Krupp."

They both snorted at my eloquent little speech.

"Well, why don't you tell us why you think Confed, oh great soothsayer?" Hansen asked.

It was convenient that Captain Yabe chose that moment to make her entrance, because I didn't have a ready explanation. The only reason I believed we'd face the Confederate Empire was because of Jonny's tip, and I wasn't about to reveal my information source. If left to my own analysis, I probably would have suspected a Kalamatran target along with Hansen.

I noticed that the rest of the company leadership was now present, even as I scrambled to attention to watch Captain Yuri Yabe march down the aisle and straight to the podium. She had a hefty stack of papers and folders stuffed under one arm, her long black hair trailing behind her slight frame like the tail of some dark comet.

"You may be seated," she told us. We all complied readily. Once the shuffling and general noise died down again, Yabe dimmed the light with the controls on the podium. A spherical map of the Charted Territories sprang up in front of us, slowly rotating on its axis. In typical Captain Yabe fashion, who believed that it was called a *briefing* for a reason, she just jumped right into things, without preamble or other breath wasters.

"As you should have read in your classified communiqués these last three months, intelligence has been reporting a slow but massive troop build up in the Confederate system of Romesh. Initial indications were that this was meant as a stab at the heart of Sunni. We now have reason to believe that is not the case. At oh one hundred hours this morning intel resources confirmed their initial reports that this Imperial armada has jumped. Current analysis indicates that a Republic target is likely; another attempt to disrupt the reunification. Based on several highly placed sources of information and some good old fashioned people work, intelligence has narrowed the choices down to a single world."

Randstad adjusted some of the controls at his station and that map quickly zoomed in, almost to the center of the sphere. "This is Terra. A fairly diverse world with a population of about ten billion. Some of you may have heard of it." Despite the sarcasm, no one made a sound. Complete silence hung over the room as we understood that Earth was a target for invasion. Yabe scanned her audience, getting an accurate read on our reaction to this bit of news that not even Jonny had been aware of.

"Fortunately for us, even jumping max distances through the most isolated systems won't allow them to merely come out on top of us. For one, our warning systems would pick them up no matter where they went. Theoretically, of course, they could just jump through deep space, but we're all aware of the dangers inherent in that. More importantly, to take on a task as daunting as the assault on Terra, the Empire will need to have a secure supply system that we can't touch. That brings us to this, the reason why we believed they were going to attack a target in Sunni."

At a nod from Yabe, Randstad zoomed the view in to show a number of systems comprising a portion of the border between the Republic and Sunni, an area often referred to as the Bulge. One world stuck out farthest from the Republic side of the border, almost completely surrounded by Sunnite controlled worlds.

"We believed that because they are going to start their march on Terra with a target right next to Sunni. For those of you a bit weak on your national map, this is Madrigal. Population three point five billion, greatest extra-planetary trade is in software, and they generally vote Federalist during elections. Conquering Madrigal would give the Empire a strong, self-sufficient staging area for further strikes against the Republic, and Sunni as well. Ladies and gentlemen, we are not going to fight another war on Terra. The Confederate Empire will be stopped on Madrigal, and that means that a lot of people are going to die."

This was such a typical Yabe briefing, never beating around the bush or trying to sugar coat things. She killed the holographic display and brought the lights back up.

"Tactical and strategic briefings will be ongoing both here and in transit. Check the posting here at the podium for a schedule. For now, get your Man O'Wars, your units, and yourselves saddled up, squared away and ready to break ground at fourteen hundred hours. If you have any questions or problems between now and then, talk to the XO, he'll take care of you." She took a moment to look us over, all twenty-five of us. "Right now, are there any comments?"

No one said anything at all. I suppose we were all still in shock at how very real the war had suddenly become. We would no longer be off fighting for a world that was but a part of our nation, we'd be fighting for our very homes and families. The reality of that was overwhelming. The intense fear which I had felt earlier returned even stronger, and I hadn't even realized it was gone. I think many others present there felt as I did. We made for a somber, disheartened group until Hansen belched softly. A few nervous laughs went up, and even the captain smiled.

"Ladies and gentlemen," she said then, "this is what we have been trained to do. Most of you have never seen combat of any kind before. Now you are going to see it at its worst. Remember that however daunting this may seem to you, your warriors, some of them so green they're fluorescent, will be feeling it ten times worse. Take that into account when you deal with them. Now get going. Company dismissed."

With that she tucked her papers up tighter under her arm and left via the same route she had used to enter. Again we stood at attention. Well, most of us. Hansen wobbled a bit and then sat down with her head in her arms. As soon as the captain had left, the room burst into a fairly tumultuous racket.

Some warriors were talking to the XO, others were just talking to each other. All seemed to be postulating different theories on what our real mission would be, or what strategy we should take in the upcoming battles, or even some ideas that we were being purposely misled by our own leaders for security reasons.

Hansen's deathly ill expression turned to face me square on. "How's it that you knew this was coming down the pipe, Chase? You got a direct line to God?"

"Maybe he's sleeping with one of the officers in intel," Asoc offered.

My gut was still clenched tight with a fear I couldn't name. If I thought about it, I wasn't afraid to face combat, I wasn't even afraid of dying; no more so than anyone with a strong faith in a benevolent deity and an afterlife, anyway.

Nevertheless, I was afraid, and I didn't feel up to this verbal sparring. Instead I just offered a weak smile, hoping that in their present condition they'd mistake it for a knowing one instead. "That's only for me to know. But I was right and you were wrong, so you two owe me something big. Maybe another round of drinks?"

Both of them groaned at the thought of drinking anything more and I laughed maliciously.

"Get out of here, Aarons," Hansen growled. "You get your people together and on board their dropship faster than I can get mine, and you'll have that round."

"Fair enough. You in on this, Thomasz? Last one squared away buys the first round in transit?"

Asoc thought that over for a bit. I could almost hear the gears grinding in his head as he tried to calculate all the odds and variables that could affect his performance in this bet. Asoc was always a very meticulous soldier and officer, even drunk. Finally, he nodded. "I'll take that bet."

We shook hands and then were all turning to find our team leaders.

I was extremely blessed in that two of my team leaders, Zhon and Stewart, were prior service. Both had served as sergeants before they had gone on to officer training, Zhon with the Marines and Stewart in motor pool. They knew what needed to be done and had no problem taking care of it. I think they actually wanted me out of the way, convinced that they could do a far better job of assembling the people, machines, and various other logistical supplies that we'd need without me getting in the way. I sort of believed something along the same lines, so I didn't resist their efforts to get rid of me very hard. Instead, I lost myself in my office, ostensibly getting started on the requisite paperwork, but truthfully I was unable to find anything constructive to do. I called Rachel.

When she answered, the first thing that struck me was just how beautiful she looked. She also looked tired, completely drained like the way she'd look after going through a session of high G simulations, but still beautiful sitting at her desk. Over her shoulder I could see a window that looked down on the Earth. The crescent of blue-green light that reflected up was breathtakingly beautiful, but it only paled next to that face. She smiled, if weakly, when she saw me, and had the energy to comb her hair back over her ear with one hand. "And how are you doing, handsome?" she asked.

I smiled at that. "I wouldn't mind getting used to hearing that more often. We're pretty busy getting ready here, but my team leaders think they can handle things better than I can. They're probably right, so I'm just trying to stay out of their way. How are you doing? You look exhausted."

"I am pretty worn," she admitted. "I was just coming off of swing shift when the call up came, so I haven't had much sleep, and I'm supposed to be double checking all of the requisition orders for the entire wing." I winced at that. Rachel was always good with details so she was her commander's logical choice for the job, but it was a large load to pile on those delicate shoulders.

"Oh," I replied wittily. "Well, I don't want to interfere, but I'm not sure how much opportunity we'll have before transit, and I'm not sure what to expect from our trip, so I wanted to check up on you and wish you well." I shrugged.

Rachel smiled another tight smile. "I'm fine, just tired. I'll have to fly a few patrols once we're en route, but other than that I should have plenty of time to catch up on my zee time." She looked at me for a moment, during which I could think of nothing to say. Finally she sighed. "Chase, I'm fine. I'm a big girl, all growed up and fully trained for what we're going to be doing. I love you, and I appreciate that you're worried about me, I worry about you too. But I'm kind of busy here so if you don't mind too much, I need to get back to work." She raised her eyebrows at me, questioning.

Even though it didn't feel quite accurate, I assumed that she was right, that I had been worried about her and wanted to check up on her, as useless as that gesture would be in protecting her from harm. I raised my hands defensively before her stare, almost taking an inadvertent step back. "I just wanted to tell you to be careful and that I love you. Is that okay?"

"That's sweet. I'll talk to you soon. Don't worry, I can take care of myself. Bye." She had already turned back to her work before the connection was fully severed.

"Women," I muttered to myself, but in my head I was replaying what little she'd said. Rachel assumed that I was worried about her and wanted to contact her to assuage those worries. The truth, though, was that I really wanted her to calm my anxiety over something I couldn't name. I had called not to be a big brother and check up on her, but to be a small child. That led my thoughts back to my family.

The next person I tried calling was Liz. I had no idea where she was right then, probably in Cairo, so I called her mobile.

A sleepy voice answered, audio only. "Hello?"

"Liz, it's me. Did I wake you?" I don't know why we always ask that when the answer is obvious.

"It's okay," the groggy reply came back. "I had to get up anyway, the phone was ringing."

It was an old joke, one that I recall teaching her, but it had grown comfortably familiar between us.

"I won't keep you up long, I just wanted to let you know that we're shipping out. Jonny's coming too, so he'll probably call soon as well."

That woke her up. A light turned on and I realized the visual hadn't been turned off, it had just been dark in the room. "Where are you going? Why's Jonny going?"

I answered her second question first. "This is pretty big. A lot of reserve are coming along too, even the listed are being called up to replace all the active duty that's going. We're pretty swamped, so I wanted to call while I still had a chance."

"Where are you going?"

"Madrigal. We're expecting a defensive siege. It's a big push and we'll be there till the fat lady sings. Watch the news, I'm sure they'll cover everything."

Liz peered at me with her reddened eyes. "I'm scared for you guys. Promise me you'll be careful, okay?"

I almost laughed. "I'm scared too, and I don't even know why." I shook my head. "I can't place my finger on it, but it's like something awful is going to happen on Madrigal. I'm not scared for myself but...oh, I don't know. I can't really explain it."

Liz stifled a yawn. "Maybe you shouldn't go, you don't have to. Sometimes

God gives us hunches and feelings when he's trying to tell us something. You could stay behind."

Was she right, God? Were You really warning me, and I just didn't heed You? All of this because I didn't have the courage to believe?

Instead I shook my head. "I don't know. My duty is to go, and I can't throw away my entire career and all my goals on a feeling, can I? I have to do this."

She nodded her understanding. "I'll being praying for all of you. Have you talked to Rachel?"

"Only for a moment. She's really busy and didn't have the time or patience to listen to my baseless fears." A wry smile crossed my lips. "I should probably get back to work, too. Take care and wish me luck."

She did just that before I cut the connection.

I sat at my desk for some time, pretending to be working, though in truth I was just trying to figure out what was so wrong. Was it how I would react to combat? Would I be scared? Probably. Would I be angry? Somehow I didn't think so. Would I die?

Unwilling to dwell on *that* thought any longer, I pushed away from my desk and paced the small room for a bit. I still couldn't actually think of anything real to do. I called Jonny again.

He answered from a starport tarmac. I could see gantries and dropships over his shoulder, and the unmistakable sounds of huge engines boosting enormous payloads into orbit echoed over the audio. For his part, Jonny didn't look drained a bit, not at all like Rachel. In fact, he looked like he was having a good time playing soldier once again. His eyes flashed, his features were fully alive and animated, and he was smiling like he really meant it. This was Jonny at his best. Far better than most any other man I've ever known. Certainly better than me.

"Well," I said. "I'm impressed. Who'd have thought that a measly little reserve PBI could round up his weekend warriors so quickly? I must say I would have bet against it."

"Chase!" he exclaimed with an even bigger grin. "Don't you have anything better to do than keep calling me?"

I thought about that for a moment. "Well, no, actually. We active duty warriors are so on the ball all the time that something as minor as a planetary mobilization doesn't even phase us."

He laughed lightly at that. "Just give me half a sec." He turned away from the visual pickup, granting me a wonderful view of his boots as he marched along. I could still hear him, though. "Thorne, get the platoon squared away. Set up a schedule for drilling on the sim deck in transit. Bully us up some extra time from someone else, I want us making the regulars look pathetic. All of our boys are going to be coming home again."

I could sort of hear a reply in the affirmative, and then Jonny was back smiling at me. "Look at you, all enjoying yourself," I said. "What's the scoop on that? You'd think you were five all over again."

"I am," he said. "You think I get to have this much fun every day crunching numbers for some suit? Give me my power armor and I'll show you some accounting."

I laughed at his bravado. "How long do you think this will take?"

He shrugged. "Can't say for sure. If we've calculated this right, we'll have a distinct numerical superiority. I'd bet you we'll be home for Christmas."

We know how accurate *that* prediction turned out to be. Jonny was a good leader, an effective snoop, a knowledgeable businessman, and the best brother one could ever ask for, but he wasn't a soothsayer. If only; if only.

"Aren't you scared at all?"

Jonny raised his eyebrows. "Now where did that come from? We're about to embark on the greatest adventure of our lives, risking everything for glory, and basically getting our names firmly established in the history books. You are about to do what you have always been meant to do, become a true warrior. So why do you want to talk about emotions at a time like this? Especially one so distinctly unmanly as fear."

I didn't have a ready response. "I don't know. It's just that everyone else seems to be like you, either completely fine or even enjoying themselves."

"As they should," Jonny said with a nod. "This is what separates us from the sheep out there, the ability to look at danger as a challenge to be overcome. Why? Are you saying that you're not? Of all the people I wouldn't have thought would have this problem."

"I don't know," I repeated. "Somewhere deep down I feel like I've swallowed my own kidneys. I almost want to just run away." I felt like a coward just for saying it. "Aren't you even a little bit scared?" I persisted.

I got that look that Jonny inherited from Mom, the one that said not only had I asked a stupid question, but by insisting on an answer I was inviting a severe thrashing.

"Chase, I don't know what it's like in a Man O'War, but every day you put on a power suit, you run the risk of getting injured or killed. Sometimes they malfunction and there goes your ability to land a jump properly, or get feedback on your strength, or breathe underwater. It doesn't happen often, but every infantryman faces that possibility. Yet we still go out and do what we have to do. We do it because it makes a difference.

"Of all the combat branches of the military, the infantry is the biggest. That's because we are the only ones capable of finally taking and holding land. Even augmented armor can't do that. But that means we also soak up the most punishment, and we're the ones who receive the most casualties. We live with that knowledge full-time.

"So, yeah, I'm scared. I'm scared that my dropship will end up on the evening news as it crashes into the North Atlantic after blowing a booster on launch. I'm scared that my transit ship will mis-jump and hit a rock out there somewhere and I'll have just enough time to realize what's happening before I get blown out into space and expand into a vaguely lingering red mist. I'm scared that I'll have to do a HALO drop and my foil won't deploy properly and I'll end up being very short. I'm scared that while I'm off playing soldier, I'll lose my seniority at work, that I'll be behind and ruin my career. I'm scared that my son will be born without his father here and when I come home I'll be a stranger, maybe even to my own wife. I'm scared that I'll step on some booby trap and lose a limb or an eye. I'm scared that I'll die a very painful, drawn out death on a world that my son will never even care about, though he'll probably notice that he doesn't have a father. Frankly, I'm scared of just about everything you can think of. Does that make you feel better, Chase, now that you don't have to feel alone with your fears in your cramped, armored cockpit? I certainly hope so, because now I feel like crap. Goodbye."

Even after he cut me off I thought I could still hear him swearing loudly.

Chapter Eleven

Bravo Two One Area of Operation: Scion Forest
Thiona Province, Yang-tze
Madrigal
Unified Terran Republic

March 21, 2652

"Incoming!"

My audio interface picked up the whistling sounds of falling artillery shells and conveyed them straight to my ears. I dropped my Crossbow down to the earth, lying as flat as I possibly could, anticipating the impact. It came down in large multiples as an entire battery's salvo landed all too close to us. I was bounced in every direction conceivable, and maybe a few new ones. My restraints did an admirable job of holding me steady while the chair padding and shock absorber system spared me from the worst of the shockwave that rolled over us.

"Up!" I ordered. "Twelve o'clock. Five hundred meters. Go!"

My patrol pulled their Man O'Wars to their feet and we all sprinted five hundred meters straight ahead. That salvo had almost landed right on top of us and I wanted my unit moving around quickly now, making it tough for the arty gunners to get a fix on us.

"Zhon, status report," I requested once we'd covered the ground I wanted.

The reply came back quickly enough. "No losses, but Amori lost her left arm. My rifle is reporting intermittent errors as well. And we've lost contact with the rest of the company."

I nodded, though no one could see the gesture. The whole patrol was finding the best cover they could, crouching behind trees and rocks, squatting in depressions or just laying flat. I joined them in trying to make myself a smaller, more covered target. Then I switched to the operational frequency, which seemed to be the only one working beyond the range of our tactical grid. "Tac Sup One Zulu, this is Proximal Recon Niner. Request counter-battery fire in grid five six five niner. Over."

There was a slight pause filled with an annoying hissing that continued even once a reply was incoming. "Proximal Recon Niner, this is Tac Sup One Alpha. Zulu is gone. I say again Zulu is gone. Tac Sup Two Bravo will support. Will advise that last incoming was not from your Alpha Oscar and was hit by air support. Should be quiet now. Also be advised, counter-battery fire is not available at this time. Proximal Recon Niner is not primary support. Only Tango Romeo Papas will be targeted. Out."

"Shit." The invective slipped out before I thought to break communication, but I was in the middle of combat, so who cares? I called up my map and latest intelligence reports, conveniently displayed on my tactical interface. No more artillery seemed to be coming our way for the moment, so the fly-girls must have done a good job on them.

"Patrol," I called, switching back to tactical frequencies. "Be advised that our arty support has been suppressed. Only tactical reference points will be targeted, and we may have to wait for those, since we are temporarily down the list a ways. Team leaders, let's loosen things up a bit, diamond formation. Comsat info shows our target refinery five zero klicks ahead. Stay lively. Move out."

We started walking again, working our way through the thick woods. The giant trees of the Scion Forest were beautiful. Taller than a redwood, shaped like a giant olive tree, with red bark and bluish leaves, they'd been genetically engineered for no greater purpose than to impress, and impress they did. Two weeks ago they provided an excellent tourist destination. Now they provided excellent cover for our Man O'Wars as we sought out our Imperial adversaries.

This whole op had pretty much gone anything but according to plan. We'd jumped in system four days ago, after spending two weeks in transit. I'd enjoyed the off time with little to do other than run simulations and play games with my unit, but beneath it all had run a tangible current of fearful anticipation. I'd also found enough time to call Jonny and get back on better terms with him, and I'd spent many long hours tying up intrafleet communications just chatting with Rachel. She apologized for having been so short with me earlier and I, of course, forgave her easily.

When we made our final jump into the system, we had thought everything was in the bag. We had a bigger force than the Confeds, we were making an uncontested landing onto a planet whose military had already prepared much of the defensive work we'd be using, and we were expecting the Imperials while they were not expecting us. We were very wrong indeed.

To start with, Madrigal had been wracked with civil unrest and one or two fairly major uprisings. One of the severe disadvantages of our system of government is that we allow an amoral press too have to much freedom. The news of imminent invasion had been blown all out of proportion (so said our officials) and millions had rioted. Worse, Imperial backed partisan groups and dissidents had risen up in open violence against the local government. None of it was of a severe enough nature to preclude the successful defense of the planet, but it meant that valuable time and resources that should have gone into preparing for invasion had instead been used on an internal target.

Making things much worse, we did not have the head start we had expected. The fleet had only been in system for six hours when our Imperial friends arrived. We still had the advantage of numbers and (nominally) home turf, but that was about all that was left to us. As we hit the atmosphere, another fleet arrived flying Sunni colors and declaring the system occupied territory. That's when things really got interesting.

"Hold up," Johansson's voice came over the comnet. "Lieutenant Aarons, you'd better come forward, sir."

I moved away from my position in the middle of the patrol and carefully worked my way up to where Johansson was on point. Everyone else took a kneeling or prone posture, again seeking the best cover. All save Marshall, who joined me crouching near his team member.

"What is it?" I asked.

"Sir, over there." Johansson's Roughneck pointed one arm off through the trees. "It looks like at least two Man O'Wars. I range them at two hundred and five forty. Nothing on passive scan except a little lingering IR."

"Marshall," I ordered. "Check it out."

"Yes, sir," he said. He switched to his team frequency and then he, Johansson, and Xiong were carefully moving forward, their Man O'Wars stepping cautiously. They looked around for a few moments before I heard anything more.

"Sir," Marshall's voice was strained, and surprisingly, coming over a private channel. "You should get down here before the rest of the patrol. This first one is Lieutenant Asoc's Roughneck. His body's still inside."

A cold chill went down my spine and tightened up my sphincter. I'd never seen anyone die in combat before, it really bothered me that the first one would be a friend of mine. I brought my Crossbow back fully upright and worked my way over to the remains of Asoc's Man O'War. While I was doing that, I had Stewart bring the patrol up to put the diamond around us and secure the area. Then I looked down at the battered Roughneck.

Asoc had obviously taken some artillery shrapnel at some point before going down, his Roughneck's armor was shredded all along the right hand side, though it looked to be superficial damage only. That didn't surprise me, many of the spots we'd passed had shown the scars of artillery and even a few pieces of damaged augmented armor from friendly and enemy units alike. The killing shot, though, was the big hole to the left of the head mount, where a human's collarbone would be located.

"Looks like a HEPC, sir," Marshall stated the obvious. "Some of the discharge angled up to the cockpit and caught the Eltee. You can see from the burn patterns on the body."

I verbally supported Marshall's assessment with a grunt, but in truth I didn't even look. I recognized the Man O'War well enough to identify the pilot, enough unit insignia survived for a positive identification, but I had no desire to zoom in and look at the remains of my friend. What would I do, try to brave it out? Instead I turned away. Was that wrong of me? A weakness, that I couldn't look death in the face again? Even now, fully conscious of all my many faults as a warrior, I still don't think so.

"Whose is that other one?" I asked instead. We quickly moved over the three hundred and fifty or so meters between the two fallen giants.

"I'm not sure, sir, but it's one of ours."

I could see he was right, the left leg still bore the 141st insignia. I also knew why he was unsure of the exact identity. The Lodestone had been blasted and twisted in every direction. Holes gaped in it's armor, and large pieces were missing, some strewn nearby, others just gone. The head was missing as well, but that appeared to be more a case of the pilot ejecting successfully than anything else.

"Ammo cooked off," I mumbled, more or less to myself.

"Yes, sir," Marshall responded, unnecessarily. "Looks like someone got in a Dragon. Could be infantry still in the area. But whose Lodestone? No one has one in the recon patrol."

I didn't have the answer and instead just got us up and moving again. Zhon was still having intermittent weapons malfunctions which we couldn't fix, and he couldn't raise company command either. The good news that he did have to report was that our artillery status had been upgraded so, while we still couldn't count on immediate anti-battery suppression fire, we could now expect prompt delivery of TRPs and even some free fire support.

It was about noon, local time, when we finally rendezvoused with the remaining units in Asoc's recon patrol. Their senior team leader, Siddiqui, had assumed command of the unit and led them on to the hook up point. He informed me that they'd lost many along the way, victims of artillery, air strikes, and a couple of small skirmishes that had clashed and then broken away. Asoc had been the victim of a Saber that had strafed them on its way overhead.

It was so stupid. Asoc had died because of a freak, lucky shot from one of the gunners in a lumbering old cargo plane originally modified by guerillas to attack dropships. It seemed impossible. The odds said it was impossible. Nothing that inaccurate, flying that high, and that fast could even have a prayer of hitting a warrior, locked up tight in the cockpit of his Man O'War, through trees this tall and thick. Nevertheless, Thomasz Asoc was dead, and there was no time for mourning.

Typical of the confusion of combat, Siddiqui also had no idea of where the Lodestone had come from. Apparently it hadn't been there when they'd been going through the area. Another one of those questions of life that go unanswered.

Upset, confused, and still scared to death, I assumed control of both patrols, making myself the equivalent of an acting XO. Zhon got to play patrol leader, and one of his team members took over as team leader. Stewart took over the job of routine communications, and he quickly informed me that company command was now just barely available over all the jamming. I had no idea how long that might last, so I immediately pulled up the command frequency.

"Yankee Yankee this is Proximal Recon Niner. Have linked up with Distal Recon. Distal Recon Niner was Kilo India Alpha. We are ready for Op. Echo Tango Alpha on target is current plus one Hotel. Request current sit-rep. Over."

Instead of Yabe's voice, I thought I recognized Hansen's coming over the channel, interrupted by enough hissing and popping to assure me that the Confed attempts to jam us were proceeding apace. "Proximal Recon Niner this is Alpha Patrol Niner. Yankee Yankee is Kilo India Alpha. X-ray Oscar is Mike India Alpha. Do you copy, over?"

Captain Yabe was killed in action? Lieutenant Randstad missing? What had happened?

"Say again, over." She did, and even through the increasingly fuzzy transmission her message remained the same. Our company had been decapitated a hundred kilometers away from us.

"Copy, Niner. What is Alpha's current sit-rep, over?"

More hisses and pops were sounding on the channel. It was becoming very difficult to make anything out. "Alpha, Bravo, and…armor and infantry support has us pin…to be evac'ed…" Whatever she said next was completely drowned out by hissing, then, briefly, the signal was partially audible again. "…ray Oscar…Proximal…for relief…" The entire frequency peeled loudly in my ears before I could switch away.

"Scopes are dead!" Johansson yelled on tactical. "High-strength jamming!"

"Keep your heads up, boys and girls!" I ordered, even as I check on Johansson's report. He was right, everything was gone from radar to IR, and every channel beyond tactical grid was squealing like a stuck pig with a megaphone bolted inside its throat. I couldn't even access any intel satellites. Jamming of that strength is extremely difficult over anything more than a very short range, and is usually only done during ambushes and other surprise attacks where the risk of an enemy getting off a message is greater than the risk that some passing combat satellite or fly-girl will fire a self-guided missile down on you.

"We are not waiting here for them," I told the patrol. I really wanted to just turn us around and head back to support the firebase, but our training had been quite specific on how to handle a situation like this. First, our mission hadn't been changed, and that took priority. Second, our own safety required that we find out what threat was posed by whomever was doing the jamming. Third, and most painful, was the understanding that by the time we returned to the firebase, there would be nothing left for us to do. "Siddiqui, your patrol has lead. Wedge formation. Active scans on. The second that jamming weakens I want to know where every ant is in this forest. Let's go find them before they find us."

We found them all right, but they weren't actually looking for us. After traveling about three kilometers toward our objective, we could see smoke plumes rising above even these giant trees. Audio sensors started picking up the sounds of combat. Unmistakable were the explosions of high yield artillery and the diverse pitches of chatter emanating from automatic weapons of varying sizes.

"Patrol leaders, form up on line. Center on me."

As Zhon and Siddiqui organized the unit into a rough line abreast, I studied my maps. The combat seemed to be located right in the middle of our area of operations. I couldn't figure out which friendly units could possibly be in this area. It was conceivable that someone had strayed off course, like the pilot of that Lodestone, but since we were the only unit stationed at the only firebase this far forward, I felt it unlikely.

We moved forward cautiously, taking plenty of time to approach the combat area. What would have taken a few minutes at full speed, and not much longer at patrol speed, took nigh on to a half hour as we checked every rock and tree stump for signs of the battle that still lay ahead. I halted the unit at the base of a slight rise, and continued to the top with Siddiqui and Stewart in the hopes of gaining a visual understanding of the battle that still did not register on most passive or active scans. Toward the top of the rise, we placed our Man O'Wars in a prone position, and shuffled forward on elbows and knees to see what the forest beyond would reveal of our situation.

Halfway to the top it felt like we were struck by an extremely powerful earthquake. I had flashbacks to Yokohama as every Man O'War in the unit, whether crouched or prone, was thrown violently to the ground and then tossed around some more. Many of those giant trees came crashing down around us. Miraculously, none of our warriors were killed outright, but the comm channel was filled with cries of pain both minor and major. The moment the shaking stopped, I ordered Zhon to get me a status report on our people, while the three of us continued to the top of the rise. Our sensors were now working, but they showed nothing, and I immediately ordered everyone over to passive scans lest we give away our position.

At the crest, the forest didn't reveal anything, it ended. For kilometers in both directions, and at least five hundred meters straight across from us, the forest was gone. The landscape was littered in the shredded remains of giant trees and what looked like military machines. Craters pockmarked the land, some filling with water that seemed to be the remains of a small stream. A few small fires could be seen burning both on the killing field and around the edges of the remaining forest, but they were small and weak, robbed of their sustaining oxygen by the explosions that had given them life.

Siddiqui whistled. "Arc-light."

Again I nodded though no one could see. "Get a team down there to scout. You have five minutes before I want to be well on our way."

"Yes, sir." Siddiqui understood full well my desire to be gone. When an entire wing of heavy bombers flies over at forty thousand feet and drops thousands of five hundred pound bombs, no one with any glimmer of sanity wants to be anywhere close by if they decide to make a second pass.

I went back down the rise to receive Zhon's report. I could have done that simply by talking to him from where I was, but I wasn't thinking about it, and my natural instincts told me that I should be in close proximity to get a report. Throughout a warrior's training it is made abundantly clear that a Man O'War is not simply a big infantryman. Time and time again we are cautioned against acting as if they were. Nevertheless, almost every warrior will, at sometime, catch themselves moving about as if they really were simply in an overly large suit of power armor. This was one of those times where I made that mistake. Fortunately, it was one of the few mistakes I made that didn't hurt anyone.

"Status report," I demanded of Zhon, as I piloted my Man O'War right beside him.

"We lost two Man O'Wars from Proximal, Taya's and Parke's Roughnecks. Both have severe internal damage, but both pilots are okay. They've been assigned to ride double with their team leaders and help out with communications. Distal lost one Mercury, the leg's smashed. Unfortunately that warrior has a nasty closed head and neck injury. We're leaving her where she is for now, but I recommend that we call for her extraction as quickly as possible."

I agreed with that recommendation and detailed Stewart, who was already on the horn trying to find out what the hell was going on, to designate this area as TRP Theta and call in for a single med-evac ASAP. He said it went through, but we couldn't be certain of that. "Anything else?"

Zhon replied in the negative. "Just a whole bunch of scrapes and bruises on warriors and machines, but nothing serious. My rifle seems to be working fine now, though, so I guess there's good in all things."

I grinned slightly to myself. "Let's try to keep that positive outlook." I was about to say something more, but Stewart cut me off.

"Dust off is coming in twenty, Eltee. They're asking that we secure the area and be ready to move our injured party out into the open as soon as they arrive. ETA is twenty minutes."

I most seriously did not want to stick around for that long, but we had little enough choice. Whomever had dropped the arc-light had provided a perfect landing zone, one we weren't likely to duplicate anywhere nearby.

"It's a go. Pass the word," I said. "Siddiqui, what have we got out there?" This time I remembered that I didn't need to go walking all the way over just to talk to one of my people.

"Looks like the remains of a fairly heavy armor unit. Some infantry as well, even one or two Man O'Wars. Farther down that freshly swathed area are some scraps that look like Confed Man O'Wars. Best guess? I'd say that an Imperial unit stumbled across a very large Sunnite combined arms contingent. After they got the snot kicked out of them, someone decided to divert an arc-light over the area. That would explain the high level jamming. Probably an ECM plane flying low to cover the bombers higher up. Just as well, maybe, sir, or we might have been the ones stumbling over them."

It made sense, and was likely the best we had to go with at the moment. Stewart broke in again on a private channel. "Sir, reports and communication are sketchy at best but Firebase Monk has been overrun. Higher reports that casualties were pretty severe. The captain's gone, and about half of the others. But we are still on mission."

That did not make me feel better at all.

"We've found some pretty good tracks, sir," Siddiqui was saying, almost right on top of Stewart since he wasn't privy to the news. "I'd blame that Lodestone on some of the infantry that were probably running perimeter for the Sunnites. The direction looks about right. Maybe..."

He was rudely interrupted by startled shouts going up from the scouts. "Enemy units incoming! We've been spotted!"

I switched my sensors to active, and my board lit up with contacts coming straight at us from the other edge of the newly landscaped stream bed. I quickly mounted the rise to just behind the crest, yet again. There, close on the heels of our scouts, who were making all haste to get back to our lines, was a small combined arms unit. I estimated them at about equal our numbers, not counting infantry, but those tanks each had about twice the firepower and three times the armor of a Man O'War all tucked into a more compact, harder to hit target. The infantry riding on their backs were going to be able to cause problems too, and the augmented armor was heavy enough to be almost as of a much threat as the tanks. Apparently someone's reinforcements had arrived.

"Patrol leaders, bring us back on line. Ready for covering fire." I made a tough decision, one that I'd known might have to be made since my earliest days of COTC. "Call off the dust off." It was what I was taught to do, protect the evac, but it still felt wrong saying it.

We waited for the long seconds it took for the patrols to comply, seconds that dragged on for what seemed to be hours. It seemed that our scouts would actually be able return to the comparative safety of the tree line without difficulty when the tanks opened fire. Half the team went down with the impact of heavy cannon fire driving through them. We had no time to spare checking on them, nor did their teammates, those who remained mobile, pause to account for their fallen brethren.

"Weapons free," I heard my voice saying, though I'd not given it permission to speak. Apparently all the drills and training had done their job. "Fire when you have a lock." My own hands were guiding my firing controls to target the second tank to left of center. It appeared to have the most communications gear attached, and I hoped it was the commander's tank. "Snipers concentrate on the Man O'Wars, Crossbows take out the heavies, everyone else light 'em up as the opportunity presents itself."

My lock on tone sounded softly in my ears and the cross-hairs skewering my target gained a double box around them. I thumbed the firing stud atop my left stick and felt my whole Man O'War shudder as an M-77 Bolt anti-armor, self-guided missile launched free from its rack. Along our line other missiles loosed, and many rockets as well. The cannons from our enemies did not fall silent, but now their roar was also joined by our return fire.

Fireballs burst across the front of our opposition's advance, several tanks were destroyed in that first volley and much of the infantry was sent racing for what little cover they could find out there. I couldn't pinpoint the sounds of the Snipers firing, but I could see the effect they were having as enemy Man O'Wars suddenly lost heads or gained gaping holes in their torsos. Even as I got a second lock, I watched the Bolt I'd already fired tear through the front left corner of the targeted tank. Its tread broke and pieces flew through the air. The whole vehicle lurched sideways and then spun in place, coming to rest facing ninety degrees to its original line of travel.

The Roughneck immediately to my left exploded, taking a heavy tank cannon round right in the lower torso just as I was launching my second Bolt. I ducked back behind the tree I was using for cover, removing myself from the line of fire. That was the same moment that several proximity alarms went off. My maps and sensors, disturbingly, showed many new contacts quickly approaching our position from directly behind us. Without ever knowing the enemy was even there, we'd been outflanked. I felt like a fool.

In a moment the enemy tanks and their unstoppable firepower would be upon us. We had nowhere to retreat without moving back to engage whomever and whatever was behind us. I had to make a decision instantly, right or wrong, or everything would be lost. I didn't hesitate.

"Follow me!" I slammed my throttle to full, rolled around my wonderfully protective tree, and pounded my Crossbow across the ridge and down onto the rough, fresh scar on the land. It was quite a rush to be followed by two patrols worth of, in my oh so humble opinion, the most amazing war machines ever created by God or man. We burst over the ridge in a staggered line and my first taste of real hell broke loose.

If only it'd been my last.

Sunni, for we could positively make out their unit markings now, Marauder heavy-tanks, powered infantry, and at least a patrol of medium weight Man O'Wars bore straight down on us. I remember shouting a war cry, though I do not know what inspiring phrase I used. I'd like to think it was something suitably motivating like "Cry Havoc!" or "For Terra!" Just as likely, it was "Oh shit!" or perhaps some other expletive. Life is not like the movies and I'd never thought to rehearse my lines.

I got a solid lock almost immediately and launched one of my remaining Bolts at the nearest Marauder, less than a quarter klick downrange. The other Crossbows in our unit joined in, also firing their tank killing Bolts as lock-ons were achieved. The Roughnecks opened up with their god awfully loud autocannons, and our handful of Snipers continued the grim process of putting those huge bullets through people's heads, not an easy task when running full speed across a battlefield.

Our blind charge obviously caught the Sunni force slightly unprepared, as the return fire, while still heavy, was initially poorly aimed and had little effect. That only lasted for a split second. Then those tanks, with all their armor and firepower, were once again blasting into our midst as if they were trying to level a forest and we were the trees.

I remember telling my unit to break through their line, lose ourselves in the trees on the far side. My thought at the time was simply to use the same survival tactics of a cavalry rush, breaking through the enemy's line to prevent being bogged down and killed by infantry. It was a sound tactic, even if thrown off the cuff.

Combined arms units tend to be the most versatile there are, and generally the toughest, so we did not want to get stuck in a slugging match with them. Fortunately for us, those tanks that provide so much of their firepower and thrive in open terrain aren't really well suited to heavy forest, and the infantry alone are too slow. If we could gain the shelter of the trees again, we could use our Man O'Wars' vastly superior maneuverability to either escape or set up engagements of our own choosing in more appropriate settings. First though, we had to break through.

I plowed right into the center of their formation, heedless of the danger, certain only that to stop or turn away would be a guaranteed death sentence.

I'd like to claim that I wanted to lead by example, or that it was my courage and confidence that led me to run right down their throats, but it was really just the shortest distance between where I was and where I wanted to be. My limited supply of Bolts quickly ran out while my lock-on pinged constantly. I fired the last one into the side armor of another Marauder sporting extra communication and sensor gear. It exploded very satisfactorily, and hopefully robbed the Sunnites of some of their triple C abilities.

I had no time to stop and think about things. I sent a flight of rockets streaking into another Marauder, blowing off its main barrel and fusing the turret in place. With a slight hop I stepped my Crossbow up onto yet another tank and fired several rounds from both hand cannons straight down through its weak top armor. The holes that blew open produced a copious amount of thick, black smoke, so I assumed I had killed or crippled it. Another quick hop brought me down off the tank and onto at least one infantryman, compacting his suit. I fired at his companions with my antipersonnel chain guns, unaware of what effect they had, if any, and drove on.

A Scimitar raced toward me from my right, its HEPC seeking to remove me from the conflict. I turned sharply into the Sunnite Man O'War's approach vector to throw off his aim, then triggered a salvo of rockets. For added effect I fired both hand cannons twice into his torso. The rockets detonated all over him. I don't know if I actually destroyed the unit or not, but it fell down and that was enough.

A siren blared around me and glaring red warning lights flashing in several places informed me that somewhere out there, someone had gotten a positive lock on me. Again I turned sharply, ninety degrees to the left this time, and then hit my counter measures. I could hear the dispensers launching chaff and flares just behind the head unit of my Crossbow. Since I didn't die, I assumed I'd been successful.

Something flew right past my cockpit window and struck one of my Snipers just above the hip. It detonated, separating the Sniper's torso from its legs. I scanned the battlefield quickly, and saw that the Dragon crew was already being fired upon by a pair of Roughnecks as they ran past.

Before I knew it, I was out the other side, sprinting toward the tenuous safety of the trees beyond. My rocket supply was halfway depleted, my missiles were gone, and my cannon ammunition was already down a third. I sincerely hoped we wouldn't be doing anything like that again anytime soon.

"Regroup, one klick, my one o'clock," I ordered. "Stewart, you have rear guard."

We bound through the trees in a flight to escape the heavy fire that could shred trees and Man O'Wars with equal ease. However, I soon realized that we weren't receiving any more fire. Thanking God, I pulled the patrols up short, just inside the tree line where we could still see the enemy.

There was some background talk on the communications channel. Most of it was related to reorganizing the unit and taking stock of our losses and current levels of expendables. Some of it concerned me specifically, though, and that disturbed me.

"Did you see the Eltee? Charged right down the middle!"

"...got how many kills?"

"...jumped right up on that tank..."

"...saw him duck a Dragon in mid-flight!"

"I've never seen anything like that..."

"...so fast..."

"Cut the chatter," I said a bit too sharply. "Leaders, I want reports in five."

Our Sunnite adversaries hadn't turned to pursue us, in fact they still seemed to be engaged at our previous position. With the proper magnification I could still see Man O'Wars moving back in those trees. I hadn't left any of my people behind which meant it was another unit, but whose? My answer came almost immediately as one Man O'War lost its leg at the knee, and came rolling out into the clear. Before the Marauders blew it into very small pieces, my computer had identified it as a Gator, a purely Imperial design.

I immediately hit the operational comms, and found them to be choppy, but functioning. "Tac Sup Two Bravo, this is Proximal Recon Niner. Request heavy rain, Tango Romeo Papa Theta. Over."

The response was swift, if still fuzzy with all the jamming noise. "Niner this is Bravo. Heavy rain is on the way. Out."

It wasn't more than a few seconds before huge fire balls, exploding up so high into the sky that we could see them towering high above even the tops of these monstrous trees, drew a harsh line right across where my active scans said the Imperial forces were.

"Tac Sup Bravo, this is Proximal Recon Niner. Adjust fire plus one five zero mikes. Heavy rain. Over."

Again a confirmation was broadcast, and once again huge explosions ripped up the already ruined landscape. Many of the contacts on my sensors disappeared as well, this time among the Sunni force. I could see Man O'Wars and infantry that had thrown themselves flat to escape the worst of the blast's effect. Many of them began moving immediately after the salvo's impact, but many more did not move at all. The tanks were doing better at soaking up the punishment of shrapnel and shock wave, but even their casualties were high. I wanted to finish them off.

"Bravo, this in Niner. Repeat. Out." I figured since we had primary artillery support, we should use it. Again the explosions and casualties. Sensors showed many targets destroyed from both the Confederate force and from the Sunnite force. The rest seemed to be moving rapidly away from the engagement and heavy artillery fire, none of them in our direction.

Enemy air or artillery strikes on our position were almost guaranteed now, certainly imminent, so I formed up the patrols and started them moving farther down, paralleling the arc-light induced clearing. We resumed our passive scan procedures and prayed that anyone else looking for us would not find us as we moved at top speed away from the engagement area.

"Zhon, Siddiqui, status," I said.

"Zhon's gone, sir," Siddiqui said. "I saw him eject after that Confed Dragon hit him."

So that's whose Sniper it had been. Life's just not like the books at all. Who would believe that an infantryman could so easily kill a Man O'War?

"Who else?"

My team and patrol leaders took a few moments to confer. All the while I was guiding us farther away from the killing grounds, taking the point myself, as no good patrol leader ever should. Eventually, they reported that we'd lost eight Man O'Wars, with another ten sporting varying levels of damage. Amori had been all but vaporized, two others were confirmed killed in action. The others were missing, and we didn't have the option of going back to look for them.

I felt doubly sick in my soul as we trotted away from them. On the one hand I prayed that God did not think me a murderer, that He would forgive me for leaving behind my own people, though we had no choice.

On the other hand I prayed that He would guide my hand in the destruction of our enemies for, God forgive me, I had loved every moment of combat. I felt more alive than I'd ever felt in my life, and I longed to taste that sweet nectar once again.

Chapter Twelve

Bravo Two One Area of Operation: Huang-tsu Valley
Thiona Province, Yang-tze
Madrigal
Unified Terran Republic

July 16, 2652

"Fullerton, get your platoon up on top of that ridge and set up the Dragons. And see if you can't find somewhere fun to put those mines of yours," I said. "Not only do I want to knock a bunch of this rock loose to block the pass, but ideally I want it pounding down right in the middle of our armored column friends. That sort of thing tends to ruin most people's day. But keep an eye out for forward scouts."

"Yes, sir," Fullerton responded, his voice heavy with sarcasm. "Are there any other obvious things that I probably already know that you'd like to tell me, sir?"

"Just go, Lieutenant." I shook my head. Fullerton was so much like Jonny, I wondered if God didn't stamp all infantry officers from the same mold before he sent them down to this mortal realm to torment the rest of us sinners.

The war was going badly, very badly. No one could firmly predict who was eventually going to win possession of Madrigal, and it would be neither a quick nor a painless victory, but at this point it did seem pretty certain that the planet would not remain under Republic control. The Confederate and Sunnite forces had managed to push us back all over the planet, even whilst regularly pounding on each other. We'd tried to defend too many places at the same time and it had cost us. Here, on the Yang-tze continent, we were literally on the verge of being pushed into the ocean. Our initial defensive positions had all been lost and we were scrambling to keep our withdrawal from becoming a total rout. Strategically withdrew sounds so much better than "ran away with their tails between their legs."

All three nations had been steadily dropping reinforcements on Madrigal, and we got our share, but the Republic had other conflicts to concentrate on, many others, and supplies were coming from increasingly distant sources. Moreover, Field Marshal Hanton had decided long ago that Yang-tze wasn't our most crucial position. She had been focusing our forces mostly on the Parsis, convinced that the war would be truly won or lost there.

I hated being a captain.

"Siddiqui, set up your patrol here," I marked the point on my map and the computer reproduced it on his visual display. "I'll be right behind you with Russell and his patrol. We'll hit them hard and pull back, let the infantry cut them off, then box them in against the tanks." Siddiqui confirmed his understanding of the plan more eloquently and with far less attitude than Fullerton had used, for which I was duly grateful. It was a simple plan, hit and withdraw, cut off, then crush. Straight out of every textbook on ambushes.

Left unspoken were our convictions that we could not win here. Hell, we weren't *supposed* to win, just delay, but to speak of such things would be to openly admit the improbability of survival, and that's not something anyone wants to acknowledge.

As a sub-lieutenant, my job was simply to be a warrior, run around in a giant, two legged tank and shoot things—life at its absolute greatest for a young man. True, I was eventually made a team leader, but that's still just like being one of the boys. You go out and blow some things up, then you all go have a drink and tell stupid jokes. Too soon after that I'd been promoted to full lieutenant and patrol leader, and then the younger sub-lieutenants had started to keep some distance. Even as a patrol leader, though, you work so closely with your men that you have their support and camaraderie, it's still easy to socialize with them. You have friends.

"Prav, you win the prize. Set your big guns up right at the mouth there, and when they stampede around this corner down here, wipe them out." I could almost hear Sub-lieutenant Prav smiling as he acknowledged his orders. He and Lieutenant Russell were part of the batch of brand new officers who had just arrived on planet and were eager for their first taste of combat, still believing in the glory of righteous warfare.

I no longer harbor many delusions along those lines, but at the time I too was a victim of the same deluded dream. While I had experienced some of the worst that warfare had to offer, I'd also proven myself a warrior of great skill and determination, and a little part of me was very, very proud of that. The greatest sin of all, pride. How many dead because of it? But it did mean that I sympathized with how my new officers felt facing their first real battle,

I just hoped they'd live through it.

Now, with the loss of Hansen back in June, I had been bumped up to a full company commander, burdened with all the necessary and often frantic decisions required for all needed supplies, maintenance, personnel paperwork and medical attention—and still combat. I'd spent no time as an XO that I might apprentice to the company commander position, and hadn't ever really wanted to. To make it all very lonely indeed, a captain can have no comrades in the ranks, only peers of equal rank in other units, seen too infrequently to ever be called true friends. As if thrusting the knife deep into my stomach wasn't enough, due to officer shortages, command had arranged it such that I didn't even have an XO.

Jonny didn't have much sympathy for what I considered the loneliness of command. He said aviators and warriors are spoiled because everyone is an officer. In the infantry and armor, only the unit commanders are officers, surrounded by enlisted personnel. From their first day as a sub-lieutenant commanding a platoon, they all know what it's like to be alone.

"Russell," I called my green patrol leader, "let's go." I felt a lot of sympathy for him and his situation. Every single one of the sub-lieutenants under him had months more combat experience than he did. Yet he was taking everything in stride, keeping his ears open and his mouth shut, and listening to his team leaders' advice. He relayed my command to his patrol, which used to be Siddiqui's patrol before that worthy in turn took over my old one. We jogged along the bottom of the valley. "Set the Roughnecks up, there's lots of cover out here, but let the Mercury guys know that I want them available to jump up top to support the PBIs if it becomes necessary."

I hadn't even heard from Rachel in over two weeks. Our orbital and sub-orbital forces were fairing far better than our ground troops. That was the only reason we hadn't been overrun long ago. While our air and space superiority was far from complete, it was still a definite superiority. If we'd not been blessed with such phenomenal combat aviators knocking out sizeable portions of enemy reinforcements before they landed, and a good number more even once they deployed, the situation on Madrigal would have been much worse.

Rachel hadn't been promoted as quickly as I had, though, because her branch hadn't lost officers at the rate we had, but she had been given a lot of extra responsibilities. She'd been an ace not long after we made planetfall, knocking out seven orbital fighters and snapping off a successful shot at a high flying atmospheric ECM plane as well, all within a few days. Apparently such things mean a lot to fighter jocks, so they gave her more work to do. These added duties, and my own crowded schedule of administration and combat patrols, left us with little time to do much more than say a quick greeting and tell each other to be careful before we had to cut off.

I checked my timer again. It said we had no more than five minutes before we could expect a whole column of armor and augmented armor to be blasting right through this canyon in an attempt to secure the entire valley. Doing so would allow the Empire to strike at our retreating forces with impunity.

I wiped the sweat from my palms. Facing combat never seemed to get easier for me. I still felt scared and worried, I still felt excited and alive, I still felt wholly inadequate yet simultaneously glad for the chance to yet again exercise the tremendous skill I knew I had, and I didn't want to lose any more people in my command. Somewhere inside I still couldn't shake the feeling I'd gotten on Earth that something horrible was going to happen but, like most days, it still seemed distant. One part of me wanted to just be out once more in the glory and blood pumping excitement of combat. Another part told me that I really just wanted to go home and actually marry Rachel and have glorious adventures some other time.

"Captain, the FO's back in," Fullerton reported. "She says what we've got coming is one hundred percent pure Minutemen, and they're right on schedule."

I swore. The Minutemen were singularly the most successful Confederate force on the planet. In every major conflict that had resulted in us getting our asses handed to us in a sling — which is to say every single major conflict of the war thus far — the Minutemen had played a pivotal role in producing the Confederate victory. Against my small force, half of which were fresh out of training, they would be all but unstoppable.

But what choice had we? We needed to hold here for as long as possible, and that was simply the way it was. The rest of the division was pulling back and expected that a handful of companies like mine would hold the passes and buy them the invaluable time they needed to make it safely to our next line of defense. It would be our last try to bloody someone's nose before we would be forced to abandon the entire continent.

Deciding to send some troops out to die so that others may live and continue the war is a decision that is almost impossible for a commander, hell, for anyone, to make. Much has been made of the painful deliberations that precede such a decision, and the difficulties in choosing which units to sacrifice. They say it is hard to give such orders. They are right, but receiving such orders is much, much worse.

Every one of us knew how important this action was, as reticent to speak of it as we may have been, yet no major objective would be accomplished, no turning point reached. At best we would merely slow the inevitable, perhaps delaying someone else's death for a few more weeks. Still, we accepted our orders, our duty. We accepted the necessity of the mission even if we couldn't quite accept the necessity that it be us performing the killing and, all too likely, the dying.

"Pass the word, but don't let anyone get overly worked up over it," I told Fullerton. "Did your FO manage to pop any of them?" The more that went down now, the less we'd have to worry about later. I could certainly use some good news.

"That's a negative, sir." Of course, wouldn't want to give us any chance at all. "She called an air strike down on them but the results were less than stellar. These canyons just provide too much shelter from indirect fire. Anything less than an orbital bombardment or an arc-light just isn't going to do the trick." We both knew that neither one of those options would be coming our way in the near future.

"Then we do it the old fashioned way," I muttered, as much to myself as to Fullerton. *Like I already knew we'd have to.*

I suddenly found myself wishing that Jonny was there to watch my back. Fullerton was competent enough, very much so, but I didn't trust him with my life the way I knew I could trust Jonny. Not only was he my own flesh and blood, but his heavy weapons platoon had already earned a reputation as being the most able to accomplish any mission and still bring everyone back alive. I think he'd only lost two men by this point in the war, a phenomenal achievement when compared to the losses my unit was sustaining. He had succeeded in his goal of showing up the active duty units.

"All right, folks, listen up," I told the company. "We have two minutes to finish up whatever preparations we're working on, and then I want everyone in their hole and ready to go." I received a chorus of affirmative responses and everybody I could see, from a few of the rearguard infantry to the warriors and armor jocks, appeared to redouble their efforts to dig or build positions of cover, clear lanes of fire, or prep the few nasty surprises we had in store for our Imperial friends. Our time ran out quickly, as preparation time always does.

"That's it," I broadcast to the patrol and platoon leaders. "Get everybody in position and ready to go, right now." My bowels complained that they wanted to liquefy and paint my trousers a unique color of camouflage. I took a few deep breaths to help settle things down and said a quick prayer like I always tried to do, imploring the Almighty that He would watch over me and all of my little flock, grant us victory and glory, and spare any pain or suffering for those who fell today. It was a sincere prayer, and I actually believed it made a difference.

Maybe it did, maybe my prayers were more effective back then.

Prav confirmed that his tanks were in position, fully ready to support our withdrawal and lay down a serious wall of fire as only a platoon of Thumper heavy tanks can. Fullerton let me know that his infantry was good to go, Dragons locked and loaded, snipers in position, mines set, and retreat planned. On one of my displays, their armored forms were shown dotting the surrounding cliffs, ledges, and the occasional cave. I already knew that the Man O'Wars were ready, since I was right there with them, and I shortly received confirmation of this from both Russell and Siddiqui. Then came the waiting.

Waiting for the shooting to start is always excruciating. Knowing the nature of our mission this time and the dangers involved certainly did not make it easier. Those three minutes that I simply sat there doing nothing seemed like an eternity. I thought about all the things that I'd overlooked, and everything that could possibly go wrong. My mind drew forth images of every little thing that I could possibly have missed. My psyche, ever helpful, conjured up visions of ammo shortages, improper positioning, faulty intelligence reports and everything else you can possibly imagine. From rockslides to orbital bombardment, I worried over all of it. Potentialities that I had dismissed as ludicrously unlikely by the cold light of reason suddenly seemed almost inevitable when simply sitting waiting for someone to start trying to kill me.

These worries beat at me to the point where I was almost convinced of my own incompetence. It's enough to drive a very sane man crazy, and I wasn't very confident in the strength of my sanity either then or looking back at it now. I wanted to beat my kneecaps with a hammer or stab toothpicks in my eyes, maybe thread a string of concertina wire through the length of my colon making a sudden right angle turn at my prostate, anything to distract me from the nervousness and anxiety of just waiting. I was no different from everyone else who sat there, save perhaps I felt a greater burden of responsibility by being the one in charge. I really, really needed to take a piss.

Soon enough, objectively speaking, all of that passed from my awareness. I could now quite clearly hear missile fire as Fullerton's Dragons started smashing the front guard of the Minutemen column. The sounds of return anti-infantry fire and even the occasional rocket salvo were also quite audible, and getting closer very quickly. I could see dust and smoke plumes rising in the distance, and even make out some vague shapes on the valley floor. My palms were sweaty and I wiped them three times on my pants, nervous that they might slip from my controls at a critical moment and cost me everything.

It was almost immediately after that when I saw our powered infantry come bounding across the top of the canyon rim, ducking and weaving as they tried to avoid the enemy fire coming their way. They looked far less comical now that they'd discarded their spent Dragon launchers. Instead of looking like hunchbacks carrying telephone poles, as was the case when they tottered around under the mass of a Dragon, they now appeared more like the ancient samurai.

When they reached the lip, for whatever reason, a few slowed to try and pick their way down the wall as best they could, but most just jumped right off and deployed their airfoils to glide more or less gently to the valley floor. Two of them went down under enemy fire there. One was hit directly with large caliber machine gun fire, probably from a tank's coaxial weapon. The bullets punched holes right through one side of the armor suit and out the other, pulverizing any flesh that happened to be in between. A short flash of blood sprayed from the hole, but nothing like the fountains portrayed in the movies. It's odd that death can be so septic.

The second infantryman to get hit caught a clip to the airfoil, dropping him the entire distance to the canyon floor where he didn't move, not even to twitch, nor did he respond to any hails. There wasn't much we could have done for him under the circumstances anyway, even if he had somehow survived. In some ways I hoped he'd died quickly, rather than suffer in agony without any help available.

"We got their attention, Captain," Fullerton said. I could see his power armor zipping along the ridge to my left. He ducked just as a rocket flashed past him. "I'm heading for higher ground to get a good view so I know when to detonate those mines we left behind. The rest of the platoon is falling back to reload." With that he kicked in his jump jets and was out of my view.

As quickly as he said them, his words faded from my conscious thought. "I have incoming!" Johansson was shouting. "Make them to be mostly Hughes tanks and Blade Man O'Wars."

Siddiqui called him back from his forward position and had him find what cover he could behind the rocks. Then the opposite end of the canyon was filled with running Man O'Wars and thundering heavy tanks.

"Light them up!" I shouted. I still needed to work on a better battle cry, but so far I was managing to get the job done.

The first kills went to the Snipers, of course. They fired first and sent a half dozen Confederate Blades stumbling or crashing to the hard earth beneath us. Then the Bolts launched from our Crossbows streaked into their targets, rending metallic limbs from their bodies and blowing gaping holes in tanks. Finally the Roughnecks' cannons started tearing into the enemy formation, mincing up just about everything on the battlefield. As is common in successful ambush situations, the first few moments appeared to be a totally one sided massacre.

"We got 'em!" Russell was shouting. His excitement at seeing so many of the enemy wiped out so quickly got the better of his virgin battle reflexes. He stood his Roughneck up from behind his cover and began blasting away at anything he could still see.

"Get back down!" I shouted, too late. One of those Hughes out there found the easy target, and Russell's Roughneck disappeared from mid-chest down. There was no time to see how the warrior inside fared. Instead I dropped my cross-hairs over one of the few Flashpoint Man O'Wars being fielded against us. I didn't want to be dealing with those heavy flamethrowers if we came to close quarters in this tight canyon. My lock on sounded and I fired.

Preparing for a defensive mission, I'd abandoned the hand cannons I normally carried on my Crossbow in favor of a heavier, harder hitting bullpup rifle (though not as hard hitting as a Roughneck's rifle, not by a long shot) and a shield. I certainly wouldn't be able to move as quickly as before, but I thought the sacrifice worth it. The couple of extra Bolts were welcome additions too.

My rifle kicked and barked loudly as it fired a five round burst of forty-five millimeter shells. I saw the impact as some of the rounds hit a rocky outcropping next to my target. I didn't see if any of the rounds hit, but they certainly made the Flashpoint move out of sight in a hurry. I felt a welcome rush of excitement and confidence as the game truly began.

As if in direct response to my own strike, a flurry of rounds impacted the rock just in front of me, spraying chips into my chest plate. I turned my Man O'War's left shoulder into that vector as I crouched further down behind my rock, putting more boulder and shield between me and death. A moment later I popped back up and took a snap shot at the Blade that had been hoping to add my head to his count.

The full burst struck the Blade square in the chest. Just as they were designed, the bullets' armor piercing casings sheered off as they passed through his chest armor. This meant that, while they still had plenty of kinetic energy, they were unlikely to exit from the machine. Instead, much like their infantry counterparts, they were intended to bounce all over the innards of the Man O'War and wreak holy havoc on any mechanisms they might encounter there. These rounds were functioning perfectly, which is somewhat surprising considering they're made by the lowest bidder (with an even more surprising tolerance for defects), and the Confederate Blade folded in on itself as it fell back.

A Flashpoint, possibly the one I'd been shooting at before, went racing across my field of view. I took no chances and, when my lock sounded, sent a Bolt into its weaker back armor. I saw no more than that as I turned to snap off shots at other Man O'Wars that were trying to get closer to our position by scampering from rock to rock, one covering another. I managed to hit one in the kneecap with a lucky shot and it slammed into the ground when the damaged leg buckled under its own weight. Another burst through the head put it out of the fight.

"Captain, the bulk of the column is in the pass now," Fullerton said. "I suggest we bring the rock down on them." I honestly did not know why he was asking me. He'd never been indecisive before. Maybe it was the thought of crushing so many people, at least some of whom wouldn't die for days, and only then from lack of water, that was slowing him in pushing the button. Indecision of any sort gets your own people killed on the battlefield, though, and that made me mad. Not that I wasn't already a bit pissed that people were trying to kill me and everything. I would have smacked Fullerton if I'd been standing next to him.

"Blow it!" I screamed shrilly at him.

Fortunately, he didn't hesitate after that. I heard the explosions quite clearly, even over the closer, more imminent sounds of battle being waged. I could also hear, and feel, the low pitched rumble created by the tons of rock that were now pouring down into the pass.

"That looks like it'll slow them down a bit, Captain," Fullerton said. "But we got about a half battalion in here. It also looks like a few more might be able to make it over on jets." Fullerton had hesitated far too long in blowing the pass. We were outnumbered and outclassed.

To the credit of the Minutemen, which should come as no surprise given their formidable reputation, they *were* decisive, and very courageous. Suddenly cut off from their rear support and caught in the midst of an ambush by a foe of unknown size and ability, they still did not hesitate when their commander gave them the order to attack. They rushed us fast and hard. We cut down many of them, littering the landscape with broken Man O'Wars and burned out tanks. It wasn't enough, there were just too many of them.

"Fall back on the armor," I ordered. I held my ground as each Man O'War rushed past me in turn. I crouched there, hunkered down behind my rock and shield and snapping off shots whenever possible, wanting to simply flee for all I was worth, scared that those Hughes and Blades were about to rush right over top of me, pounding me flat. When the last Man O'War went by me, I too turned tail and ran as though the Devil himself were hot after me, trusting that the supporting fire laid down by my comrades would spare me from receiving any shots in the back.

I took the turn in the canyon at full speed, coming within a hair of crashing headlong into the canyon wall. I fought my controls and my Crossbow fought inertia and together we slid around the corner to temporary safety. There I took up position with the entirety of my all-too-small company to await the enemy. We didn't have to wait long, but once again things did not go as planned.

In hindsight, my vividly painful imagination was right, I should have prepared better. Of course no leader can predict everything, but I consider my mistake a stupid one, and it got my own people killed. It should have been obvious that the leadership of a unit as renowned as the Minutemen wasn't going to allow something as stupid as a headlong chase of a retreating enemy in a confined area that has already proven to be mined, and I should have changed my plans once their identity had been ascertained. Many things seem obvious now, things that no young soldier would even consider, all of it too late to be of any real value anymore.

We crouched there, a wall of guns, optimistically awaiting a blind rush around the narrow confines of the canyon corner. I could hear my own heavy breathing loud in my ears, even feel the pounding of my heart in my temples.

"Man O'Wars on the south ridge!" Fullerton, shouting from whatever nook he'd found to hide his reloads, gave me just enough time to realize and understand my blunder.

I spun to my left and reflexively triggered a burst toward the top of the wall. A Blade stumbled back from my fire before losing its balance and pitching forward, falling headlong and crashing in a heap within our ranks.

"Scatter!" I shouted just as enemy fire started raining down on us. "Get to cover! Mercury units to the north wall!"

Our few Mercuries lit off on their jump jets, bounding to the top of the canyon wall. One was hit midway up, probably by a Hughes judging from the damage done. It disintegrated from the hips up, apparently no piece larger than my head surviving intact. The shrapnel sprayed everywhere and the legs bounced off of the canyon wall, ricocheting back to crash against one of our tanks.

Those of us left at the bottom of the canyon scrambled to find any possible cover from the deadly hail that was unleashed on us from above. Our return fire was sporadic, uncoordinated, and ill aimed. Having effectively pinned us down, the Minutemen closed their trap. The rest of their units actually did come pouring around the canyon bend like the flood waters of a burst dam.

Our Mercuries were taking some of the pressure off of us, allowing us a bit more freedom to move and exchange fire with both those units above us and those bearing down on us at a hundred kilometers per hour, but it wouldn't be enough. Without the liberty to truly unleash the destructive firepower of Prav's tanks, we were going to be overrun.

"Hold on, cavalry's coming," Fullerton said. "We're almost on the far ridge."

I prayed Fullerton would be of some aid even as I fired off my last Bolt. I watched it streak up the canyon wall and take a Blade full in the head. The now headless and pilotless Man O'War fell backwards out of sight. That too was not enough. I watched as two more Roughnecks were rendered inoperable, one with a direct engine hit and one just crumpling to the ground and burning as a Flashpoint drizzled white hot fire down upon it.

Prav reported that only a third of his tanks had been able to stay close enough to the wall to be out of the direct line of fire, and the others were sustaining heavy losses. Those tankers fast and agile enough to find protection under the angle of the ledge weren't able to fire as a unit against the Minutemen bearing down on us, though, and the others were too busy worrying about countermeasures and staying mobile to concentrate their fire effectively.

An enormous flight of Dragon missiles arced out from just beside the canyon bend. Half exploded into the ranks of the onrushing forces, sending

Man O'Wars stumbling with pieces missing, and smashing tanks into scrap metal. The other half arced all the way across the canyon to impact against the enemy forces above us. I didn't know how much time, if any, we would have thanks to Fullerton's infantry's insane attack. They must have carried two or three Dragons each, an enormous load, and been so slowed down that the return fire they took decimated their ranks. I fully intended to make the most of what they'd done, though.

"Prav, you're on!" It was mad, it was insane, but I saw little choice. Despite Fullerton's best efforts, our opponents still had superior cohesion and greater momentum; if we didn't act now and act madly we stood no chance at all. They flanked us from above and in front, and Fullerton could not have any Dragons left after that. Once again I shouted, "Follow me!" Once again I took the lead and rushed forth into certain danger.

I've noted before that everything slows down during combat. It doesn't make any sense, because everything is happening all at once and so much is going on that no one can follow it all, yet that's always how it seems for me.

Before I even managed to fully clear the rocks I'd used for cover I had placed a burst square through the faceplate of an oncoming Blade. I cranked the throttle to full and put another burst through the side of a tank as I thundered up to full speed. Prav's tanks, finally allowed out of their protective yet confining spaces, fired in unison and the shockwave alone threatened to bowl me over. The salvo from those heavy tanks made the entire front rank of Minutemen disappear, but there were still more behind.

I jigged my Crossbow to the left as a Hughes fired right through where I had been. My return rocket fire opened it up from front to back. Our two lines rushed madly together at a combined speed of almost two hundred kilometers per hour. It was a stupid tactic brought about by the desperation of both units. Neither side could retreat, neither could expect reinforcements anytime soon. It was either fight things out tooth and nail or sit down and declare a truce. I was young and stupid at the time, full of a desire to be a hero and a legend despite my worries and fear. The idea of calling for a truce never consciously occurred to me.

An instant before our lines crashed together — tanks smashing through Man O'Wars, Man O'Wars dancing around tanks to fire through their weaker rear armor, and a few pesky, annoying, Godsend infantry doing what little more they could to mess things up — I dropped my Crossbow to its knees, skidding along the rock and what little dirt and dust had gathered there. I swung the reinforced edge of my shield out hard, scything through the leg of one Blade as it sprinted by, sending it to bounce and roll crippled along the ground. I fired a double burst into the belly of a second Blade and triggered off a full spread of rockets at the turret of a Hughes. Both exploded impressively as their ammunition cooked off.

I rolled to my right just in time to avoid being run down by another Hughes intent upon crushing me like the bug I appeared to be. Even as I rolled I shot a burst into its treads, causing it to skid sideways, almost overturning. One of the Roughnecks shredded it with its autocannon, but I was already regaining my footing and searching for new targets.

We were well and truly furballed now. So many units of varying types were moving around so fast, in so many directions, in such a confined area that the targeting computer was having fits. Lock-ons were gained and lost so rapidly that I totally ignored them. Instead I rushed right through the middle of the conflagration, physically laying about me with my shield, firing on instinct or at point blank ranges. I smashed one Blade upside the head with my shield, disorienting the warrior within, then fired a burst into its chest at point blank range. Another spin brought me around to shoulder check another Blade. One of our Snipers fired its big rifle right through the Blade's back, also from point blank, only to be cut down in turn by a Hughes. Some of Prav's gunners got the Hughes and I was just running again.

How much more detail can I add? I hacked with my shield and fired off the last of both rockets and rifle ammunition. When nothing was left I clubbed with the rifle itself. When the rifle broke I lashed out with armored fists and boots. I kicked at tank barrels and slashed Man O'War limbs with my shield. I dropped to the ground and tripped Blades and tried to crush the treads of Hughes. I killed and I killed and I killed again. I knew that I was out of ammunition, that my rifle was long ago destroyed and discarded, that my shield was tattered and of almost no defensive value anymore, that one arm was missing and another moved only fitfully. I knew that I should just retreat and seek what safety I could find, but my men and women were out there fighting still, many of them in as bad a shape as I was, and I knew I could not stop. So I went on killing.

When the light first cracked in through the hatch, I was disoriented. I couldn't actually recall how I'd gotten from the battle to the position I now found myself in, which seemed to be a reclining one of some sort. The bright light came from above me, which seemed to be to my left, so I turned my head to the right.

"Captain, you okay?" It sounded oddly like Fullerton. I thought I remembered him getting shot. "I don't see any blood, he looks okay to me. Give me a hand with him." I didn't think he was talking to me so I stayed silent.

It sounded as if at least one person climbed down in the cockpit with me. Someone must have because I felt my restraining straps being undone. My helmet had already come off somehow. Strong hands grasped my arms, pulling me upright. Then their grip shifted to my arm pits and it felt like I was handed off to another set of strong, waiting hands.

I tried to open my eyes, despite the brightness and the pain it induced. Everything was a bit blurry, but it looked like I was standing (well, being held) up on the side of my Man O'War. It looked a bit beat up, but then, I had been using it pretty hard. The area around us was a dry, cracked desert scape. Broken war machines littered the surroundings, and it looked like several rescue teams from both sides were sifting through the wreckage in search of survivors.

"You okay, Captain?" I peered in the direction of the voice, looking at the man who was helping me stay on me feet. It kind of looked like one of the infantry team squad leaders, Briton. I tried to nod but I'm not certain how effective I was. I wanted to be put down, to just go back to the bliss of unconsciousness. Something inside me said that I couldn't, that I was still alive and thus still had a duty to perform.

"I think so," I got out. "Let me down, would you?" Briton nodded and helped me find a stable perch to sit upon. Fullerton appeared next to me, having crawled clear of the cockpit.

I surveyed the strange scene before me. It looked like our infantry were working side by side with their Imperial counterparts to free those injured still trapped within their ruined tanks and Man O'Wars. There certainly was no shortage of those, burnt and blasted machines were as plentiful as sand on a beach.

"What's going on?" I asked, almost rhetorically.

Fullerton replied anyway. "After that Hughes plowed right through you, the Minuteman commander offered terms. He said we'd be allowed to get our fallen, treat the wounded and bury the dead if we stopped fighting. They still outnumbered us so badly they could have finished us off with ease, but instead their offer was that we could keep anything functioning if we agreed to the cease fire. Lieutenant Siddiqui accepted their terms."

I couldn't fault that decision. "How many did we lose this time?" I didn't want to know, but I had to ask. I already knew the answer was too many.

"I lost eight, Prav lost fifteen."

That hurt. So many lost on his first ever combat mission.

"How's he taking it?"

Fullerton shook his head. "I don't think he knows. The medics are keeping him pretty drugged up. He lost both legs."

Chills ran down my spine. Sub-lieutenant Prav was only twenty-one. He had a fiancée back on Terra Kai that couldn't wait to see how many medals he'd earned by the time he returned. His mother had cried when she'd pinned his rank on, and his father had cried when he'd been assigned to ship out to Madrigal. Somehow, war didn't seem so glorious anymore.

I swallowed hard. "How many warriors?"

"Lieutenant Siddiqui lost three from your old patrol. Lieutenant Russell's entire patrol is gone save for three badly wounded. Russell took a couple of nasty wounds, but he'll be okay if he doesn't lose his eye."

I swore, loudly and at some length

"This game isn't much fun anymore, is it, Captain?"

I had nothing to say to that. It was true.

Chapter Thirteen

Tango Niner Five Area of Operation: Roundel
Metropolitan Nanton, East Parsi
Madrigal
Unified Terran Republic

January 7, 2653

"What brings you down here at this time of night, Captain?" Short asked.

I turned to face him and smiled briefly. "You ever get insomnia, Short?"

"No, sir," he said, furrowing his brow. "Usually the problem I have is staying awake." I could tell by the look on his face that he was immediately having second thoughts about the wisdom of confessing such a shortcoming to his company commander while standing watch.

I smiled to try and reassure him that his confession wouldn't get him in any trouble. "That's because you're still nineteen. Give it a few years and a couple more stripes on your sleeve and it'll be different. Anyway, I just thought I'd take a walk. The bay seemed like a good place to stretch my legs."

"Yes, sir," he said. Obviously, to him I was talking nonsense and he was only trying to appear to be paying attention because of my rank. His discomfort amused me somewhat, because I could easily remember a time when I too was intimidated by captains. Those were good days, filled with camaraderie and adventure; days not long past, but gone forever all the same.

"Carry on," I told him.

With a brief acknowledgment and wishes for a good night, he turned on his heel and resumed his patrol. I watched him go, wishing I was able to sleep as easily as Short claimed he could. I also wished that I was as free of the burden of command as he was. After a moment I went back to my own patrol.

I hadn't actually lied to Short. I tried to avoid lying to my troops as much as possible, both for religious and personal leadership reasons. I really could not sleep, but that was because I hadn't yet worked up the courage to try.

It was only about a week after our retreat from Yang-tze that I was first visited by ghosts. Faces came drifting up to haunt me in my sleep, and sometimes I heard voices asking me why they'd died and why I'd killed them, why I'd killed their children. Sometimes the faces were ones I recognized. Good friends, valued comrades, loyal soldiers, and trusted advisors all came to haunt me. Some asked if I'd remember where they were buried, others wanted to know why I'd sent them back to Earth in a cold, black bag. Far too many just wanted to know why, and to that I didn't have an answer.

It wasn't long before I recognized several other symptoms of post-traumatic stress disorders beginning to appear in my behaviour. Ever since Huang-tsu I had this tendency to jump at loud noises, my hands sometimes shook without any apparent reason, and I would often wake up drenched in cold sweat. When I did sleep, which was often difficult even when no ghosts haunted me, I felt I was gripped tightly by some unnamed, unknown terror. Waking from this terror was like being brought in from the cold and wrapped in warm blankets. I thanked God every time he woke me, especially when it was from those awful nightmares. They were coming more frequently too, as if the ghosts were growing ever more insistent for answers. Answers that I didn't, couldn't, have.

Eventually, I grew to fear sleep itself. I was unable to slip into what was once a blessed release without curling into a fetal position and softly weeping. I knew I had to sleep, or I wouldn't be able to function as a leader, and that would just get more people killed. That didn't make it any easier.

I didn't dare tell anyone of my symptoms and problems. While they might not be severe enough in nature to have me sent home in shame, they were certainly enough to make my troops and my colleagues lose faith in my courage and resolve, or so I believed anyway.

Oscar Wilde's claim about truth never being simple aside, the simple truth is that many, many others were having the same reactions. Most of them were as scared as I to come forward and confess to the reality of psychological trauma. A few, perhaps braver, perhaps more scared, did seek treatment, but we all looked at them in disdain as if there was something unnatural in not being able to kill people day in and day out without having any problem. We acted as if we were above them because we did not admit that risking death on a daily basis for a world that hated us shook us to our cores and frightened us more than we'd ever thought possible. Perhaps we simply felt better belittling those that suffered, pretending that we did not see our own selves in their torments.

I walked slowly around the Man O'War bay. It was really just a recently renovated factory warehouse that had been commandeered for our use, along with most of the rest of this industrial park, but it served. I'd seen the other areas in the city that had been commandeered for troop housing, and it was all pretty much the same: large warehouses and factory complexes in industrial parks. It was a bit more spartan than the comparative comfort we'd enjoyed during our down time, but it was still better than what we'd had most of the time in Yang-tze.

Our company had been in transit across most of the length of Parsi, and therefore out of combat, for almost a week now. We'd taken wet-navy transport along the shore line, blissfully secure in our knowledge that at least the seas still remained under Republic control. That wasn't surprising, it's pretty rare that a nation will expend the huge amount of cost and effort involved in actually transporting a battleship from one planet's ocean to another's. Since we carpet bombed any shipyard in danger of being captured, we'd foiled our enemies' attempts to contest our domination of Madrigal's waters.

During that blissful week, it had seemed almost as if no war at all was being waged. I'd been able to sleep in a bed every night for a full eight hours, though the ghosts still came twice that week, and I ate real food cooked fresh from the ships galleys, three square a day. I could get used to that if allowed, but tomorrow we'd be once again going out on combat missions as we swept around the city to see just how far the Confederate forces had pulled back.

I never did fully understand the purpose of fighting in Roundel. Certainly, it was a major port city, but we'd already lost more than our fair share of those, one more seemed of little importance. In fact, it seemed to be of such little importance that even the Confederates had simply packed up and withdrawn well beyond the city limits when our first forces moved against the city a few weeks ago.

It seemed pointless, yet here we were, all set to lose more lives in the meat grinder of war. Maybe there was some important information that I wasn't privy to that rendered the city of greater value than I believed.

Even today, I very highly doubt that. It is the way of wars and militaries to fight and lose lives over things of relatively minor importance. It's a horrible way to treat life, especially that belonging to the grunts doing the fighting, losing, and dying.

When my impromptu tour of the Man O'War bay brought my to the foot of my Crossbow, I stopped and stood for a moment, just taking in the enormity of this miraculous technological construct that allowed me to deal death in ways barely dreamt of by my ancestors. For some indefinable reason I felt as though I were looking at it for the first time, the kind of feeling I should have had when I toured the bays in high school. A slight tingle ran along my spine as I admired the sleek, humanoid shape that allowed it to function so well in so many different terrains. I was pleased to see the fresh urban camouflage paint so pristine across its surface, interrupted only by the large number of barely visible kill marks trailing across the left breast. I thrilled at the power implied by the Bolt missiles mounted on shoulders, arms, and hips. I gazed in awe at the deadly beauty of the bullpup rifle that once again adorned the right arm, matched on the left by the shield that had proven so valuable in close quarters combat. I wondered at the effort and ingenuity, the planning and the extensive engineering that had gone in to building such a wonder.

I gave a slight chuckle. I wondered what the designers were thinking when they gave it such a stupid looking head. No doubt they were more concerned with function than form, but every now and then I looked at my Crossbow and wondered if the engineer who had designed the cockpit had spilled something on the designs, causing them to run and blur. Jonny used to joke that it reminded him of my toy Man O'Wars of old, the ones that I melted with lighters and magnifying glasses.

Concern over its somewhat peculiar visage apart, I took pride in the power of that machine. Sin it may be, yet pride is what I felt. I also felt very proud to know that my nation, the greatest nation in all the Charted Territories, entrusted me with this power. That was why I couldn't give in to the ghosts and their questions, because the living still counted on me to do my duty, to fight against the forces of aggression and injustice. They trusted me and I couldn't let them down for something as insignificant as my own sanity. My parents had taught me to do the right thing.

I let my gaze wander over to the Man O'War parked next to mine. Siddiqui had managed to get one of the brand new Tarantulas assigned to his lucky self. Now there was a Man O'War that was built as much for its looks as for its fighting ability. It had roughly the same silhouette as a linebacker in full gear. For armament it claimed not one but two forearm mounted HEPCs and an additional two racks of anti-armor rockets, externally mounted to preserve internal integrity in the event of a catastrophic failure, of course. Aside from the ball mount anti-infantry machine guns in front and rear torso, it had no internal weapons pods of any kind, proving that the brains in weaponry design had finally admitted that there were dangers inherent in internal weapons systems. Personally, I saw advantages and drawbacks to both systems. Given that both are widely used across the Charted Territories, I'm probably not the only one with that amazing insight.

I sighed, I don't know why. Perhaps I just realized the sad irony of taking so much pride, and seeing so much beauty, in these monstrous killers. So much effort is put into perfecting every inch of a gun barrel; I wonder if an equal amount of effort is put into the prevention of any need to use that gun.

It actually sounded like a fairly small firecracker went off, but the effects were anything but small. All the windows blew in, flinging glass and other debris throughout the bay. I raised my arms to protect my face from flying shards of glass and stumbled behind my Crossbow's leg. I cannot recall any other noise, but often that is the case with people hit by powerful concussion waves. The moment the glass stopped flying I was bounding up the ladder to the greater safety of my cockpit. I've never made the journey so quickly in my life. It was only a few heartbeats after that that my well practiced hands had all of my combat systems ready to go.

The channels were filled with voices, each trying to figure out what was happening, many asking for help. I already knew what had happened. The whole picture seemed so clear, as if the entire thing had crystallized in my mind the moment the proverbial shit hit the fan. I cursed myself for not having anticipated this.

Not all of Madrigal loved the Republic, less every day in truth, and no one had ever bothered to stop and ask the residents of Roundel if they welcomed our return to liberate them from their oppressive conquerors. It also should have occurred to us that when the Empire pulled outside the city limits, despite what the Taurus Conventions say about arming civilians, our Confederate friends just might have left a few toys behind for their partisan allies.

"...south perimeter..."

"Fires on Tac One and Tac Two!"

"...hit in three, maybe four..."

The dozens of jumbled messages coming through outlined a chaotic picture of multiple strikes against our base. I tapped my throttle up and moved for the door, wondering just what I could do. I wasn't equipped or trained to fight fires; neither was I the best choice for anti-infantry work. Still, I had to try.

"...pinned down, need support, over."

"Where is the air support..."

There wasn't time to go through the niceties of exiting the bay. I just burst right through the bay door, not even bothering to slow down when I encountered the corrugated metal. It screamed at me as I tore a hole in it, but I ignored it, distracted by far greater worries.

Fires were burning in every direction, factories and warehouses spewing flames into the night. It seemed like all around me had become one of Dante's circles, but for now I stood in perdition, neither heaven nor hell.

"Captain, what's the situation?" Fullerton asked. I glanced at my display and saw that he was in full armor and perched on the rooftop opposite me like a gargoyle watching over the sanctity of our temporary home. I wondered if he ever slept.

"Your guess is probably as good as mine, but I say that we've got some sympathetic partisan problems," I told him. "There's just no way Imps got this far back into the city without our knowing. How many of your troops are armored up?"

"Just over one platoon." The man was amazing. I reminded myself to have a talk with Mr. Fullerton about what exactly his duties were.

"Hold a defensive perimeter around our position. Tell Siddiqui to form up the patrols and send them to join me at the south gate. Once the patrols have deployed, take your platoons and join up with the 171st and lend them a hand in whatever they're doing."

"Affirmative, sir. Good hunting."

I acknowledged that, even though I was already a block away. Here, many vehicles had been tipped over and flattened by the first explosions, and I had to carefully step over and around them lest I be the cause of my own fall. Broken glass littered the ground everywhere around me. I saw at least two dead bodies lying in the street. Perhaps there were more but I did not want to look for them. Thankfully, this time at least, neither of the two I did see belonged to anyone I knew.

Another shockwave rocked the ground and a huge fireball blossomed to the south. I could hear the screams and shouts through my audio pickups, and I hurried even more. I stepped through a narrow alley between two structures to access the main road.

"How many out there..."

"...lost Alpha, lost Bravo..."

"...hold off much longer, they'll be all over us! Need some help here!"

I tried to isolate this last communication, pulling up the sub-frequency they were using. "Give me your coordinates and a sit-rep. Reinforcements are en route."

I could barely make out the response over the background sounds of combat. It sounded to be somewhere off to the southeast.

Another huge explosion almost knocked me off my feet. A moment later I was showered by debris falling from the sky. As soon as I regained my balance I slammed my throttle up to full and pounded down the street at top speed, heedless of the danger in my rush to get where I could do some good. I pounded around the last corner and caught sight of the remains of a small foot gate that I hadn't been shown in the quick tour of the base I'd received when we'd arrived.

The gate itself had disappeared, replace by a still smoking crater. The wall that had met atop and around the gate was missing enough so that I could easily have walked my company through it in ranks of three without crowding either the Man O'Wars or the remains of the walls. Through the gap I could see a small paved path that ran out to the steep edge of the river valley. Apparently a small pedestrian bridge used to span the valley's width, but now it was missing a large section near this side, and the rest of it was burning convincingly.

A small squad of infantry was spread out around the hole, firing into the dark. I was shocked to realize that several of them weren't even armored. At least a dozen bodies littered the ground in the area. Only two of those were armored either.

Yet again a huge fireball erupted to the east, in the direction of the main gate. The ad hoc base was coming to life quickly, lights were on everywhere now and aircraft of different types were starting to appear overhead. The infantry continued firing down into the valley.

It took me a moment to realize that what I was hearing bouncing off my Crossbow wasn't debris kicked up by the explosion, it was small arms fire. A quick scan showed fire vectors coming in from two and eleven o'clock. I chose two and pushed out through remains of the gate. The infantry gave me a ragged cheer as I went.

The river valley was dark and heavily wooded, and my opponents seemed to be equipped with enough gear to foil most of my scans because I wasn't finding anything. Thankfully, some of them continued firing on the infantry defending the gate, the stupider ones even kept firing their anti-personnel rifles at my Man O'War occasionally. Following their intermittent and mobile fire vectors was slow work, but after maybe five minutes of moving through the trees I tracked them down, a half dozen hicks with hunting rifles playing at soldier.

Apparently they weren't so stupid after all, playing on my own pride and sense of omnipotence. A heavy terrain truck came barreling through the trees on a collision course. I pivoted with a quick sidestep and fired a short burst from my anti-infantry turret into the truck's rear as it raced by me. The explosion knocked me back a half dozen steps. That truck had been loaded with some sort of "soft explosive," as they are euphemistically called. That's just a gentle way of saying non-military grade, which in turn is just a gentle way of saying it takes twice as much to do half the damage. A small truck load might not be enough to seriously harm a tank, but it would cripple a Man O'War with ease. Fortunately for me, the truck bed had been designed to shape and direct the lion's share of the blast forward into whatever target was struck. It confirmed in my mind what was causing all of those explosions around our compound.

Another significantly smaller explosion sprouted on my left kneecap as someone tossed a satchel charge at me. Then another one went off near my right ankle. More small arms fire was pinging off of my armor, all too often off of the cockpit window, and I could hear another vehicle approaching.

That was enough of that. I stood up and cut loose with my anti-infantry weapon, spinning around to send some rounds in every direction. I didn't stick around long enough to see if I'd had any sort of substantial effect, I just took off. At full speed I raced back up out of the river valley, cursing myself for a fool. I'd thought myself smarter than the enemy and I'd actually allowed myself to believe the propaganda that Man O'Wars are invincible. Nature has a unique reward for hubris: extinction, and I'd almost become a dinosaur.

It only took a couple of minutes to return to the foot gate and whatever dubious protection the remains of the wall could provide.

"Hey, Crossbow, on top of the building at eleven thirty!"

I looked up in the direction indicated and saw the slight silhouette of an armored infantry suit crouched behind a chimney.

"Thanks for buying us some more time to get into position, sir. My squad should be able to hold things here now, but they could probably use you over at the main gate."

I didn't even bother to acknowledge the comment beyond a quick grunt, I just turned and headed out. I wasn't hurrying, just keeping a good pace, having learned my lesson for the day about stumbling in to ambushes. My audio pickups were providing that distinct rumbling sound that means the same thing as the more common whistle: incoming artillery.

I flattened out completely, though it turned out to be unnecessary as the rounds impacted farther inside the compound. One of the office buildings that was being used to house non-combat personnel exploded. A few more fires started. I resumed my journey at a slightly faster rate. Another salvo air-burst above the compound, scattering anti-personnel shrapnel all over the place.

"Siddiqui," I tried broadcasting, "you get everyone up and running yet?"

"That's an affirmative, sir." The answer came through clearly. "Where you at, Captain?"

"I'm about a minute away from the south gate. I was lending a hand to some of the PBIs that got in trouble. You?"

"We're at the south gate, sir, or what's left of it, anyway. We've seen multiple vehicle bombs, a whole bunch of unarmored infantry, and now artillery fire. Command channels are out, they took out our communication network."

Anything else he was going to say was drowned out by the next explosion. "That's not coming from a homemade mortar," I said. "Someone's playing around with military grade hardware." I hesitated for only a brief moment. "Let's go get it."

Siddiqui was understandably perplexed by my decision to run full tilt *into* a hostile city armed with who knew what sorts of weapons. "Beggin' the Captain's pardon and all, sir, but why the hell would we want to do that when we could, conceivably, just hit it with an air strike?"

"Because we want proof that the Confeds are arming civilian populations and breaching the Taurus Conventions." That would give us some moral and political ammunition that the boys in power might be able to apply well.

"Oh." I assume he was thinking all of that through, but I didn't wait for him. I just marched right past him and out the front gate. My cocky self-confidence only lasted about three steps and then, as more explosions leveled another building in the compound, I decided I wanted to be a target no longer than necessary and ran like hell.

"Close it up!" I shouted. Another Molotov cocktail exploded, this time dousing my left arm in flame. So far, these homemade incendiaries weren't doing much damage beyond ruining paint and causing a little bit of extra heat buildup, but if one were to hit a damaged Man O'War and get inside its armor, that would be a whole different story.

"I got him," Johansson said, by now a veteran patrol leader and a good man under fire. A brief moment later his chain gun was blowing holes through the side of the building next to me. When his fire subsided, there was no further activity from the would-be Man O'War killer. Either he had gone down under Johansson's withering fire, or he'd fled the area. Regardless, we were pushing on.

A green flare went blazing up between the buildings, bathing the streets in a sickening hue that reminded me of hospital operating rooms. Like soldiers and lawyers, doctors also seek to hide the blood, and the preferred color is green. Lieutenant Fullerton was signaling that his special weapons squad had set up in their next support positions where they could once again provide infantry sniper fire or some Dragon support if it was called for. His other squads were scurrying around behind us somewhere, two platoons worth of the powered infantry that are so necessary in urban warfare. As much as I sometimes missed the firepower provided by traditional armor units, they would have been completely useless in these tight confines. Besides, since Prav's maiming I was unsure of my own abilities to safely deploy armor in combat, and the chorus of ghostly voices I carried with me agreed whole heartedly.

We continued our hunt through the streets and avenues of the concrete jungle of Roundel. Siddiqui had spoken accurately, someone had called in an air strike on the offensive artillery. I suppose they couldn't wait patiently, getting blown up one building at a time, while we stalked our adversaries. As luck would have it though, the aviators reported spotting one or two other deployments of military equipment, and I wanted to capture one of those before it was blown up or moved. As the other kind of luck would have it, plenty of Imperial fighters showed up to contest the sky above us, cutting us off from further air support or spotting.

"Mudslugger, six o'clock!" The warning was broadcast on all company channels. I confirmed the warning on my active scans, an Imperial attack plane was indeed bearing down on us, using the street to perfectly line up his strafing run.

"Cover!" I ordered unnecessarily. Everyone was already doing their best to find whatever cover they could. Some ducked down back alleys, some found side streets and a few were able to dive behind trees or fit partially into damaged buildings. All too many of us were still left in the open though, merely crouching down or flattening against building facades. There was no way for everyone to avoid all the fire that could be put out by such a missile and cannon laden plane.

A puff of smoke and fire announced the first launch from the plane. The deadly projectile sped away from its launch rack just before a missile traveling in the opposite direction slammed into the plane, disintegrating its tail section in a ball of fire. While the plane had been launching its first air-to-ground missile, Seanic's Crossbow had been launching a ground-to-air missile. I hadn't even known that he was carrying the fairly useless rounds instead of the standard issue Bolts, and I would have berated him heavily for doing so if I'd known five minutes ago. Now however, I was duly grateful. The aircraft, or what remained of the aircraft, suddenly veered left and out of our line of sight, plummeting like a meteorite, fiery tail and all.

I was certainly pleased to see Seanic's lifesaving kill, if I can use such an absurdly offensive oxymoron. I was even more pleased to find the Man O'War killing air-to-ground missile that had been launched had been successfully confused by our counter-measures. When I realized that the offending warhead had instead been delivered into the fifth floor offices of the Roundel chapter of the environmental activist/terrorist group GPI, I almost cheered over all channels.

Once again we had proof that God still watched over us and that he had a sense of humor. Still, we needed to be up and moving again.

"Johansson, move it out."

We stepped off again, working our way down Libre Avenue, heading for the Capitol Building. Supposedly it was there that we would find our proof that the Empire was breaking the Taurus Conventions. Unfortunately, the good Republican citizens of Roundel hadn't been too patriotic today, in fact the whole city seemed downright displeased with our presence. I wasn't certain whether I should empathize with them or condemn them. Either way, they were forcing us to kill an awful lot of them.

A flash and an explosion; one of my Roughnecks lost an arm. Someone spotted the culprit. "Dragon on the rooftop, three blocks at eight o'clock!"

My troops were good troops; disciplined, ordered, and smart. They were professional and decisive, but they were human, very young, many inexperienced, and prone to making mistakes. Understandably, given the circumstances of being in a hostile city, surrounded by friends-turned-enemies, and wandering around in the dark with no definite goal in mind, they were also very jumpy.

Much like a group of greenies just entering training, just like I'd done when I was green, the majority of my Man O'Wars turned into the direction of the attack and, when one pulled his trigger, quite possibly by accident in an excited state, they all opened fire. Their only target was the building itself, they weren't even trying to hit an individual. Worse, they were using anti-armor weaponry. Their armor piercing cannons, rockets, and lasers ate away huge amounts of the offending structure in an eye blink.

I had a sudden, awful flashback to the scene of destruction I'd witnessed as a child. Something small, young, and mostly innocent cried out in fear and horror at the history being repeated. For an instant, I wanted nothing more than to ensure that here, now, no five year old bore witness to a similar scene.

"Cease fire!" I yelled. "Cease fire!"

Abruptly they held up.

I stomped my Man O'War up and down our line, trying to convey menace and displeasure through its artificial visage. "That was the most disgraceful display of a lack of control I have seen in my career! This is friendly territory you are chewing up! You shit for brains had better smarten up, because I promise that the next one of you to fire an anti-armor weapon at anything other than an armor target will get out of his Man O'War, walk over to the impact site and retrieve the spent round! God help you if you use an energy weapon! Anti-infantry weapons only! Do I make myself clear?"

I shuddered as I realized that I sounded like Thayne. Maybe I should thank him for the lessons he taught me. Too late for that too, though.

"Pash, take your patrol north at the next intersection. Siddiqui, you go with him. Go three blocks then turn back east and parallel us. I'll stay with Johansson and sweep up and along Tranh Avenue here."

Their acknowledgments were quick and as soon as we reached the intersection of Tranh and Libre, they split off. I waited for a few minutes, covering their movements and allowing them to get into place. Then we moved out again, patrolling slowly despite our hurry, scanning every building, every vehicle, and every bit of landscape that could possibly conceal partisans, bombs, or military units. It was very slow going and my worries that we would arrive too late combined with my concerns over being a big target in a small bull's-eye to rub my nerves raw with anticipation.

It took a long time to approach the Capitol Building, a long time. The fact that we encountered no further resistance simply made me more jumpy. I almost did jump when my comm gear snapped on.

"Special Weapons squad reports confirmed contacts, sir," Fullerton relayed to me, loudly. "Armored infantry about ten blocks up. Possibly mechanized support. I've told the snipers to engage at will, but try to concentrate on anything that looks like it might be anti-armor capable."

"Thank you, Lieutenant," I said, forcing some calm into my voice. "Get the rest of your platoons ready. As much as possible, we'll try to limit collateral damage, but that means you'll have to actually go in and secure the people and the Capitol building itself. We'll cordon it off, you sweep it clean. Whatever goes down, we need prisoners and hard evidence. If things go sideways, you take that and get the hell out of Dodge, we'll be doing the same. You got all that?"

"Yes, sir. We're ready."

"Let's go then."

That plan lasted about as long as it took us to actually enter combat; not an altogether atypical result. I had just crossed the intersection running between the arboretums bordering the reflecting pool when a missile blew into our ranks. One of Johansson's Mercuries went down in two separate pieces. A second missile streaked into the downed form, removing the head and ensuring that the pilot was dead.

That tore it. "Weapons free! Siddiqui, hold position and hit whatever looks menacing! Fullerton, get in here now! Now!" With that I too plunged into the fray.

Call it bravery, call it foolhardiness, call it what you will, but I have never been capable of leading from the rear. Perhaps I'm a berserker deep down, but in every combat situation I always find myself in the lead, putting myself at the greatest risk. Other commanders do it differently, but even now I think my way was better.

It's not much, but I guess that is one positive thing. All told though, there's plenty more that outweighs that small thing.

I splashed my Crossbow right through the reflecting pool, shattering the tiles and retaining wall as I went. I was heading for the trenches and sandbagged positions at the main steps but I wasn't being very subtle about it. According to my training, I should have come through the trees, or at least circled back and around to the far side. My instincts, though, said screw that. I ran straight ahead, throttle wide open, shield up and rifle and machine guns all blazing.

The gun nest to the left of the stairs had a recoilless rifle. I noticed it about the same time they got a bead on me. I turned to the right as sharply as I could, letting loose a salvo of rockets. Their shot decapitated the exceptionally ugly statue of Ruth de Naudier, the founding mother of Roundel, that stood in the fountain and my shot decapitated all of them. It seemed fair.

At eighty kilometers an hour, it doesn't take too long to cross a courtyard, and I was almost on the steps now. The other nest had been hit by cannon fire from my Man O'War and at least two others. Only the small barricade at the top of the steps remained, and they seemed to be using only small arms.

Maybe I was tired of killing, maybe I just didn't want to fire on anymore hunters when no one was really at risk from their weapons, or maybe I just had another God sent instinct, but I slowed to a crawl when I reached the steps. I switched on my external speakers and blared out a demand for their immediate surrender.

I don't know if they wanted to accept my offer or not, because the whole building blew up, flames bursting forth from the windows moments before the very walls gave way like a dam burst. For the second time in one evening I was knocked on my backside, though this time was quite a bit harder. My teeth clacked together sharply and a small piece of my tongue got caught between my jaws and tore open.

My ears were ringing and my head was spinning, but I rose up once again, very cognizant of the fact that other buildings were exploding. Despite the incessant buzz in my head, I could still make out Siddiqui's words.

"Those are our own bombers, Captain! What the hell is going on here? Why are they attacking civilian targets?"

I shook my head to try and clear it a bit, and dabbed at my bleeding mouth with one hand. "Some idiot screwed up royally once again." There are those who believe that any job that calls for a bullet can be accomplished just as well with a bomb. "Have the company withdraw to the fall back point on Libre. We're heading back to base."

More lives lost for nothing. Five more minutes and the operation would have been a success.

"Fullerton, you copy that?" I asked. There was no response. "Fullerton?"

"Captain, this is Horenstein." The leader of the special weapons team. "The Eltee took half the platoon into the Council Chambers across the courtyard."

I looked to the building he was speaking of. It no longer stood, save for a portion of one wall with meager flames licking at its base.

"Sir, Alpha squad reports we have one captive. Also two crates loaded with assault rifles and one box of Dragons. They are withdrawing in good order." Under happier circumstances I could have kissed the man. Now wasn't the time for celebrations though, I'd gained another ghost.

Returning to our base was fairly simple: we ran like hell. No one wanted to come out and take a shot at us with the aviators all but carpet bombing the city. Perhaps there was some good in that after all. I just hoped the propaganda value of those weapons would be worth what we'd paid in human lives. I really hoped.

Chapter Fourteen

Tango Niner Five Area of Operation: Tabletop Mountains
Formosa, East Parsi
Madrigal
Unified Terran Republic

May 11, 2653

"Get on top of it!" I shouted. "Support, lift fire!"

The assault team hit their jump jets, riding plumes of smoke up the face of the cliff. The support teams walked their fire across the enemy position one last time, then stopped firing altogether, preparing for their own assault run should the primary one flounder. Fortunately, like the well trained unit they were, the assault team burst through the enemy armor and infantry like a hot knife passing through butter, quickly causing the enemy weapons to fall silent too.

"We're all done here, Captain," Saunders reported.

"Thank you, Lieutenant, and well done." I switched to the XO's channel. "Let's bring the company up on line."

Siddiqui rounded up the three patrols that had laid down cover fire, and we all trotted up the far side of the hill. He quickly set up a defensive perimeter, including attending to our losses and whatever information and prisoners we managed to get from the Imperials, while I took quick stock of our situation and prepared to report to command.

It always sounds so much simpler saying it than doing it. A few words about the amount of information required doesn't do justice to how much detail is actually put into each of those reports. Sometimes it seems so amazing that battlefield commanders can do it at all.

Putting everything together gave me a brief opportunity to survey our newly won position. This was a wonderful defensive location, easily accessible from the rear allowing for easy re-supply and retreat. The front was a sheer drop making it difficult to assault by almost any force. Too bad they'd been preparing for an armor assault. I guess sometimes our counter-intelligence kids actually do something right. Actually, our whole military had finally started to do some things right.

Roundel had provided some wonderful political propaganda against the Empire, bringing international pressures to bear on them as other nations began to distance themselves from the Taurus Accords breaker. It didn't seem like much to Joe Foot Soldier, but in reality it cost the Empire a lot of time, resources, supply chains, and political backing that they would rather have spent on Madrigal's field of battle

Even better, after the Rangers and the 33rd Light Foot began striking all across Sunni held worlds, razing large parts of their industrial base, that particular nation was forced to retreat to protect their other worlds, leaving only two players in this high stakes game. The war went much better for the Republic after that, at least on a strategic level. When all one considered were the numbers, the kill ratios, ground gained versus ground lost, percent of land surface and resource production under control, and other such measurements it did indeed appear that we were doing much better.

On a tactical and operational level, of course, the war continued to be hell. It is the demonic nature of this beast that someone has to actually go out and kill the enemy, all too often being killed in turn. Worse, someone has to give the orders and be fully responsible for the lives lost on both sides, and when those whose freedoms you are fighting and dying for seem to be singularly ungrateful, as the local population constantly demonstrated, the one sending good men and women out to die bears an impossibly high burden. At least the end was now in sight, and victory assured if we acted quickly enough.

"Tango Niner Five, this is Charlie Foxtrot One One, standby for sit-rep." I waited only a few seconds, then launched into my report, unwilling to stay here any longer than necessary. I was fully aware of how many big guns sat atop this mountain waiting to pour hard death onto us. "Have taken hill five three six. No losses. We have five, I say again, five papa oscar whiskeys tended and awaiting pickup. Combat effectiveness remains above niner zero. Over."

I was waiting for the acknowledgment and confirmation of some staff personnel, perhaps a relayed order to move on, but nothing beyond that. Instead, Colonel Schwartz's voice buzzed in my ear, the signal blasting through what little jamming was being attempted. "Aarons, that's a helluva job you're doing out there. Now get that last gun emplacement at the top of the mountain."

I nodded, even though he couldn't see me, flattered by the Colonel's praise and his confidence in me. "Yes, sir!" I flipped channels once again. "Siddiqui, have the patrol leaders bring it up in a wedge. We're going to the top."

"Incoming," someone warned. We flattened our Man O'Wars, availing ourselves of the dug in positions prepared by the prior occupants of this hill. Scores of rocket artillery exploded around us as the last surviving battery in the Tabletop Mountain range tried to blot us from their sight like the offensive stains they took us for. They hadn't wasted any time at all in their counter-strike, I'll give them that.

It was time to end this game. The people of the Republic had unified as never before in their support for our wars, and the fighting had ended on most other worlds. Now the focus was shifting to this battle, the one that had dragged on and on and somehow become symbolic of everything that we fought against. Our leaders, both military and political, were pumping more forces and logistical support into Madrigal than we'd ever had before. The final push was on to drive the last of the foreign invaders from our borders, to make the Republic whole and strong again.

To take leave of our ghosts and our memories, to go home, heal the wounded and bury our dead, forever listing the names of the fallen by embossing them in the walls of our hearts.

The instant the last explosion of the current salvo faded, Siddiqui bellowed out a truly barbaric sounding, "Follow me!" With that, he had the entire company up and moving out, each patrol spreading out to fan across the entire mountain slope. He went with Johansson and Hart on the left and left it to me to take Pash and Yamamoto on the right. We raced up the steep slopes, terrain too open for infantry and too rugged for tanks, like humanoid mountain goats, explosions blossoming around us. I felt so very alive, even faced with the prospect of being so very dead. God forgive me, but I loved every minute of it.

It was the perfect scene, like one taken straight out of a movie. The bad guys were dug in at the top of the mountain and fortified with artillery, armor, infantry, and a bit of augmented armor. The good guys (in theory, that was us) were racing up the mountain at nigh on a hundred kilometers per hour, deadly flowers of explosions sprouting all around them. I saw Man O'Wars fall, crippled or destroyed, but the bloodlust was in me and I didn't care. I felt the excitement that only the madness and dangers of combat can bring. It didn't matter that the Roughneck next to me disappeared in a ball of fire, or that something smashed into my left shoulder, almost knocking me over. I didn't care that one moment the terrain in front of me was an even slope and the next a large, smoking crater yawned open to swallow me. None of it mattered. I was a warrior at war, fulfilling the very purpose of my creation, and, for that moment, I was at peace with the myself and the universe, and all my ghosts fell silent.

Our first line hit the Imperial's outer perimeter like a tsunami going over a seawall. Siddiqui immediately engaged the defending units, then swept them to the left to open a path for the next wave. We passed through the opening Siddiqui had created and swept in on the artillery and air defense batteries. My targeting system was catching lock-ons faster than I could pull the trigger and for one brief instant I actually had all twelve Bolts in the air at the same time. They convincingly struck tanks and mobile cannons, triple A guns, missile launchers, and sentry towers, and my salvo was not the only one.

My missiles spent, I hunkered down behind the burning remains of a tank. When I saw another tank fire on one of my subordinate units, I sent a full burst from my rifle into it. The rounds mostly glanced off of the heavy front armor, though one or two may have penetrated. It wasn't enough. The turret swiveled in my direction and sent its own hundred and twenty millimeter round in my direction. The explosive shell burrowed deep into the dead tank that I was using as cover before it exploded. Pieces of armor went everywhere, including a few into my own now less-armored form.

Cover blown, quite literally, I did the last thing any tank commander would expect, I charged. Yes, I did that almost every time, but, as it turns out, sane people don't normally run screaming down the still hot barrel of a tank that outweighs them by a hundred tons or so, so it's not unsurprising that most tank jocks still don't expect it. That's why it works; that's why I did it.

The gunner had a tough time bringing his gun to bear as I ran straight into him, firing as best I could at the sensors and view ports. I admit, at the time I wasn't entirely crazy, I didn't run straight down the barrel, I did angle slightly off to the right making a lucky shot less likely.

Once I was far enough to the side to no longer be hitting the heavy front armor at its best angle of deflection, I emptied my rocket racks into the tank. Half of that number probably would have done the job, but that close, knowing that my armor had already been breached, I wasn't taking any chances. The whole turret blew straight into the air as the front half of the tank disintegrated.

This base was better defended than I had initially thought. Our charge, which should have pounded straight through the firebase, had stumbled, faltered, and ground to a halt. Most of the company was crouched behind cover trading fire with tanks that outweighed them three to one. We wouldn't last long in this stalemate. I stumbled my Crossbow into a shallow trench and laid low.

"Siddiqui, bring everyone into my position," I ordered. "I'm calling in fire."

He didn't waste either time or breath acknowledging my command. I knew he'd heard though, because everyone was picking up from their positions and beating feet to get somewhere close to me.

"Sierra Zulu, this is Charlie Foxtrot One, request smoke on Tango Romeo Papa three seven. Range shot. Out."

It only took a few seconds for that smoke round to reach the mountain top and it fell right smack dab in the middle of the Imperial controlled portion of the firebase. This artillery unit was good!

"Sierra Zulu, this is Charlie Foxtrot One, smoke is good. Request fire, heavy rain."

A few more seconds waiting and then the thunder came to life and marched all over that mountaintop. High explosive rounds combined with proximity detonated anti-infantry shrapnel rounds to quite literally shred the remaining opposition. Our artillery support personnel must have been using live feed satellite observation because they were incredibly accurate in delivering on target. I almost felt sorry for those tanker drivers, it's very hard to crawl one of those beasts into a foxhole and we'd already driven them out of their better prepared areas of retreat.

"Charlie Foxtrot One, this is Sierra Zulu," the message came. "Be advised, rain will stop in fifteen. Out."

I started my countdown. "Siddiqui, pass the word!" It was so nice having an XO to look after all of those messy little unimportant details that we call reality, it freed up my time for more important things like not getting killed. "We're over the top in twelve!"

Those seconds ticked away quickly. The time you want to drag rushes past, and the time you want to go quickly takes forever. Still, there's no denying the devil his due. It was only a few breaths later that the sky stopped falling.

"Over the top!" I broadcast on all bands and even cranked it out at full volume over my external loudspeaker. The remaining scenery was very different from what had been there a few moments before. Every building, entrenchment, tree, large rock, and fence post had been hit at least once by artillery, and our mountaintop looked more like a moonscape than anything of a more terrestrial nature. Even so, plenty of things still moved out there, many of which were still more than capable of shooting back at us. Our company formed one long, staggered line and advanced at moderate speed destroying what remained. For a moment it seemed that the entire mountain top was on fire as we leveled what remained of the entire camp, from bunkers to artillery pieces. Then, almost surprisingly, things were very quiet. We had no time to enjoy it, though.

"Hart, you and Pash set up on perimeter." My mind was already running at light speed and my mouth was trying to keep up with it. "Yamamoto, police up this area for POWs. Get a body count and see what we've captured for weaponry. Put someone on that big ass lobber over there and see if it's still functioning. Also check the triple-A guns, we might need them soon. Johansson, get out there and scout around, see if anything's moving our way. I don't like surprises and I doubt that the Confeds want us here for very long. Siddiqui, try and locate us some support drops or flybys or whatever you can find."

A series of acknowledgments played through the comm channels, but I was already switching mental gears, preparing to report to higher.

"Tango Niner Five, this is Charlie Foxtrot One One, objective achieved. Standby for sit-rep." Once again I scrolled through the information updates my patrol leaders were feeding me, even while they started on their various assigned tasks. It took considerably longer this time because we actually intended to stay for a while and I expected my patrol and team leaders to feed me some fairly detailed information. When all of that was compiled, I smiled. What I saw there on my display, and passed on in my report, was a welcome surprise. It was perhaps the only time when none of my people died.

"Tango Niner Five, this is Charlie Foxtrot One One. One eight Mike Oscar Whiskeys lost, seven warriors Whiskey India Alpha. Estimate combat effectiveness at eight five percent. Minimum three zero Papa Oscar Whiskeys, may find more. Will hold till further notice. Burst transmission to follow. Out." I uploaded all the detailed information about our exact situation, including food and water supplies, ammunition levels, armor damage to the various individual Man O'Wars, and everything else that could in some way possibly impact our performance. That was all sent out in a microsecond burst on a scrambled channel.

This time I received no immediate feedback, so I began the job of preparing our defenses. It seemed that, given the strategic importance of the Tabletop Mountains as defensive points, the Imperial forces opposing us were rather unlikely to just sit idly by and let us stay there. Company was coming, and probably sooner rather than later, to deny us too much time to dig in.

The previous occupants had obviously expected their perimeter defenses lower down the hills and mountains to hold off any real threat, at least to hold them off long enough for this fire base to rain some serious firepower down on them from above. The strongest defense looked to be series of underground, reinforced bunkers, the kind designed to withstand orbital bombardments. Apparently they'd originally intended to hole up and bring in outside support.

All of that meant that the trench work and fortified positions weren't very well developed and, lacking that orbital support capability, they'd relied instead on strength of arms and numbers to try and throw us back. Considering how much damage our assault had wreaked on those proto-defenses, we had a lot of work to do to give ourselves much of a chance against a dedicated assault.

Pash and Hart seemed to be well on their way to giving us a workable defense. They'd already reinforced the trench line and deepened it somewhat, and they were clearing fire lanes out from the encroaching vegetation line.

"Siddiqui, we got any support coming our way?" I asked.

"Some, sir," he said without much enthusiasm. "Support says they can drop us a bunch of expendables, including plenty of reloads for our Bolts. We can also expect a good load of mines and tank traps, Man O'War tangle-foot, and good old fashioned infantry concertina wire. Word is that we can have just about any physical munitions and equipment we ask for."

"Outstanding. What about personnel?"

There was an uncomfortable silence for a moment. Finally he confessed, "Nothing, sir. We aren't priority for personnel right now."

I'm certain my mouth dropped open. "That isn't right," I said. "Let me get on the horn."

Something had to be wrong, there was no way we were going to really hold this position without backup, especially infantry support. It's true that Man O'Wars and tanks are great for taking territory, but until the PBIs come in and hold the ground, the war isn't over. The aviators will tell you they do all the real work but those of us who live and die on the ground know that infantry are what make or break defensive battles.

"Schwartz, this is Aarons," I sent, ignoring all communication protocol. "Please respond, over."

I waited a moment listening to the faint hisses, buzzes, and pops that indicated that somewhere distant someone was jamming communications. It was far enough away that it didn't affect local transmissions, but it was definitely getting stronger on the more distant communications.

"Aarons, this is Schwartz. You're wondering where your support people are," he said.

"Affirmative, sir. It will be difficult indeed to defend against any sort of dedicated assault without infantry support. We need snipers and mortars, Dragons and anti-aircraft…"

He cut me off. "I'm not a stupid man, Captain, I understand your predicament. Now you need to understand that you don't know everything. There are attacks all up and down the line right now and there isn't anyone who can be spared. You're the only unit that is currently forward of the line, and you are in a position that we very dearly need to hold, but there's no one who can get to you yet. For now, you're cut off. You are going to have to do everything you can to keep that mountain under our control or there is going to be holy hell to pay all through this valley. So, Captain, you are going to dig in tight and keep the Confederates off of there, whatever the cost."

"Do we have anything at all?" I pleaded.

"Aarons, I'm giving you every piece of materiel that you could ask for. Auto mortars, sentry cannons, mines, AIL batteries, everything short of a nuke. If and when someone becomes available, you'll get reinforcements too. Until then, you have priority for tactical air strikes only, so don't count on more than one arc-light, which you'd better save. Probably no direct arty either, until things change down here. Now I've got other things to worry about than wasting breath yakking with you." He cut the link.

We got lucky. It was more the eight hours before we heard anything out of the Imperial forces opposing us. We weren't idle in that time. Colonel Schwartz had been true to his word. We didn't receive any personnel, but we got everything short of that. Even the helicopter that dusted off our POWs dropped off toys we put to good use. When the Confederates came calling, we had all sorts of nasty surprises ready.

For nearly three kilometers we'd leveled the forest down to the bedrock. Pash had expressed his worry over how much effort doing such a thing without engineers would involve, but I just called in a couple of air strikes with daisy-cutter bombs. That did the trick.

Once we'd cleared all the approach lanes we mined the area so heavily that at every step a Man O'War would set off at least five mines. We even threw tactical smart mines throughout our own position, trusting that their tiny little computer brains would recognize us for the good guys and not go off every time we turned around. I admit that I used my newfound procurement power without shame. I feel no remorse for that. Perhaps Schwartz hadn't envisioned that I would completely empty out his supply depots, but I was in no mood to take chances. I had this thing about dying.

Some things change.

Throughout the mine field we'd also planted a veritable wall of tank and Man O'War traps. They were basically just pointed metal stakes of different shapes and sizes that would force an onrushing enemy unit to slow down or get stuck. Either way, it made them better targets and forced them into our kill lanes, our concentrated fields of fire. Beyond that, there wasn't much more we could do outside our position. Inside, however, was another story.

Just as Colonel Schwartz had suggested, we had auto-mortars that our designated fire control officer could control from his Man O'War, and we had AIL batteries strung all around our mountaintop to pick off advancing foot soldiers. We had automated rocket launchers, guided missile racks, anti-artillery lasers, anti-aircraft cannon, and about anything else we could dream up.

It seemed like a lot, and it was, but in a battlefield where the dominant weapons are electronic in nature, it's hard to put all your confidence in remote or computer operated equipment. So we kept busy. We dug trenches and set up barricades, we sandbagged and we laid wire, we stockpiled reloads and we checked and rechecked and checked again every last piece of equipment we had. We ate, we slept, and we prayed.

I felt confident. I would have preferred to have reinforcements, like about two companies of infantry and one of armor, but this was better than I'd expected. Also, for whatever reason, the Empire had made a mistake in not counter-attacking immediately. An entire company can do a lot in eight hours, and we took full advantage of every minute. When night fell we settled in to rotating watches and just waited.

"Contact, Captain," Johansson said. It had to happen eventually.

"Where are you?"

"We're at the base of the draw on hill eight." That wasn't very far away.

"What do you have?"

"It's hard to tell, sir, we're getting a lot of localized jamming. Visual counts suggest one patrol and a platoon of PBIs. Probably scouts."

I thought that over. It was unlikely that they were coming all the way up here just to look at our defenses. They still had enough orbital positions to get a pretty good look at us from overhead. More likely, they were looking to see what approaches were least contested.

"Keep an eye on them, but let them pass."

He acknowledged.

"What's the status on reinforcements?" I asked my XO.

Siddiqui was on the front lines, checking the security posts. I could vaguely make out the shape of his Tarantula through the cockpit window. The enhanced view of my tactical overlay showed it quite clearly, though.

"Nothing, yet," he said. "I don't think the Imperials like us being here at all. They're throwing everything but the kitchen sink at our lines."

"Then why aren't they hitting us?" I asked for the fifty-eighth time. As he'd done every time after the third time, Siddiqui just ignored the question.

"I wonder..." I was cut off as the skyline lit up in front of me, silhouetting the Tarantula against an artificial display of lightning and fire. A second later the sound wave rumbled over us. It sounded for all the world like the noise made by the cement truck that ran over the dog Mom bought Jonny and me after Spice died. It was the sound of impending doom.

"Positions!" Siddiqui bellowed.

The anti-artillery lasers started going nuts, and dozens of explosions blossomed in the air above us, bouncing us around with their shockwaves. Not all of the shells were destroyed by our defenses though, there were far too many. Those that survived fell squarely on our position, shredding machines and lives together. I found a deep foxhole, well sandbagged, and crawled as far inside as I could.

"Johansson, what's going on?" Nothing but static greeted my comment. I switched back to my XO. "I can't reach Johansson. Get everyone ready for the worst as soon as the arty shifts!"

Those lasers saved our butts. The Confederates rained enough high explosive down on us to dig an impressively deep crater in our position. Lucky for us most of it was detonating high up in the air.

Then it was quiet. Siddiqui broke into that, loudly. "Ready for it!"

I crawled out of my foxhole and moved forward to the perimeter. My sensors were being dampened by that localized jamming Johansson had mentioned. Still, I could feel enemy movement in my bones. I knew they were close.

"Flares!" I ordered, acting on a hunch. Dozens of white hot phosphorous flares rocketed skyward, effectively turning night into day. There, fully exposed, were dozens of infantry sappers methodically moving through our kill lanes and removing our mines and traps. The jamming units they carried with them effectively nullified our auto-mortars and other automated defense systems as easily as they confused our scans and other detection sensors.

At least two dozen different Man O'Wars opened fire on them. Rockets and beam weapons, kinetic rounds and explosives all converged on the five or six different groups of sappers out there. They died quickly, and took their jamming with them.

With that, our mortars and AILs leapt to life, spewing death into the forest beyond our kill zones. Mortar rockets knocked over trees and started fires, and laser beams stabbed into the shadowy recesses aiming at unseen targets.

The imperial commander only had two options at that point: charge or retreat. He wasn't really in a position where he could afford to delay any longer, so of course he charged. I had expected a counter attack along the lines of a battalion, I was in for an unpleasant shock. My tactical board lit up like a Christmas tree, the kind of tree that you soak in gasoline and set afire, that kind of lit up. The enemy stretched for kilometers. My computer put the count at around a division's worth of armor, infantry, artillery, and augmented armored infantry.

"Oh shit," Siddiqui said on our private channel. I couldn't have said it more eloquently myself.

It was good that we'd prepared so well ahead of time, because there was no time to think. Several hundred targets varying from 200 kilogram infantry all the way up to 200 ton main battle tanks came pouring out of those woods. Scans showed another wave close behind them.

"Snipers and Bolts only! And energy weapons if you have 'em! Free fire with anything anti-infantry!" I ordered. As long as we still had lots of mines and traps and our automated defenses in place, I wouldn't waste ammo double tapping our enemy.

I locked on to a tank just peaking around the vegetation line and sent a Bolt hurtling into it. The fire that blossomed all across its front left corner spread to the tree it was sheltering behind, but the green wood really wouldn't burn well. I was almost disappointed by that, imagining what havoc a forest fire would have played on enemy morale and plans. Still, considering that the daisy-cutters hadn't started anything burning, I shouldn't have expected anything better.

Armored infantry were bounding across the slope to my left, using the remains of the forest as cover and concealment for most of their movements. I couldn't get a lock, but I fired several sustained bursts in their general direction and didn't see any more heads bobbing up and down. I don't know if they were killed, if they retreated, or if they merely moved more carefully. I didn't have the luxury of worrying about it.

Too many enemies were milling around back in that forest. We lacked the true heavy artillery needed to inflict real damage on them from here, and I was not about to leave our secured position to root them out. We'd be down to fighting them in the open soon enough without going looking for it. I just hoped enough of the mines and traps had survived the artillery bombardment to have the desired effect on the enemy when that time came.

I received my answer to that question quickly enough. The enemy charged en masse. The entire first rank of infantry and armor evaporated, showing that even ten percent of the mines we'd laid was sufficient for some effect.

I lifted my prohibition on general weapon use and let everyone go weapons free. We scythed through their front line, raking back and forth through their ranks. Like dominos, armor, augmented armor, and infantry all fell in turns. I put one full burst straight through a charging Pyro's chest, causing a spectacular fountain of flame to burst forth like a phoenix rising from its own ashes. The fuel for its flamethrowers was exhausted quickly enough, but embers and single tongues of flame continued to flicker inside that burned out shell for some time. Oddly, it never fell over, it just sank to its knees and sat there frozen, burning in its own funeral pyre.

Their numbers were overwhelming though, and they steadily ate up the ground between them and the top of our little hill. Infantry teams were bounding up the slopes, finding cover behind the larger traps and obstacles. As often as not they were decimated by mines and our directed fire, but those that fell were quickly replaced and the charge barely wavered.

Once a few tanks were ruined by our mine field they simply resorted to the rather artless expedient of lobbing high explosives ahead of their path to clear as many mines as they could. Enough of our mines survived to provide an impediment, but no real barrier to their advancement.

Our automated weapons systems were showing their limitations as enemy sappers successfully used directed jamming to eliminate them, or indirect fire was lobbed onto them, or they simply ran out of munitions. The ones that continued to be effective could only cover a small area of our perimeter, and Siddiqui was madly trying to shuffle enough of our reserves around to cover any blind spots that cropped up. It couldn't be enough.

Though it seems like a half hour in the retelling (it seemed far longer living through it) it really only took a handful of minutes for our position to be overwhelmed. We fired on them with great effect, they fired on us with limited effect, but their numbers were so much greater than ours that they would be upon us in only a few more minutes. I had Siddiqui hit the command detonated mines.

Close to a hundred tons of military grade high explosive went off in perfectly coordinated shape and angle, washing the slope with air and fire. The shockwave that rolled down the mountainside was like a miniature volcanic eruption. It leveled everything in its path. For a few moments nothing stood between us and the tree line, but I knew even that would not be enough. We needed something far more powerful.

"Siddiqui, call in the arc-light," I ordered. Then I paused for a moment before adding, "Bring it down on this position."

"Excuse me, sir?"

"Just do it!" I shouted. "We can't let them get through us!"

He didn't question me twice. Maybe he figured we were about to be overrun anyway, maybe he still believed in me and thought I had one more clever trick to pull from my sleeve, or maybe he was just too busy to question the wisdom of blowing ourselves up when many, many fine Imperial troops were willing to do that very thing for us. Whatever the case, he followed his orders and put in the call for fire to the distant circling planes.

"En route, Captain. ETA in six."

I nodded to myself. "In four, call everyone back off the line. We'll shove everyone into the bunkers and blast the embankment down on top of us."

Siddiqui sounded grudgingly appreciative of the plan. "So they'll rush straight into the arc-light trying to catch us unprepared while we're protected. It's probably the best we have. Thanks, Captain."

I hadn't quite thought it through to that extent, but I didn't tell him that. No need to undermine his confidence. Besides, maybe he was right.

That was all the time we'd bought, the Imperials were charging again and we were back to the grim business of removing limbs and heads.

I grow weary of describing every minute detail of the slaughter we engaged in on that world. Suffice it to say that for two minutes we killed and were killed in turn. I saw friends and enemies alike separated from this vale of tears in an eye blink. We pushed them back and were pushed back. We fired and we reloaded, we lived and we died, each in turn.

Two minutes before we were to fall back Johansson's voice broke through the background jamming. "We're coming up the back side, Captain, and we've got backup."

My heart skipped a beat in hope. "How many are with you?"

"We've got half of my patrol and one other, plus three platoons of infantry and two of armor. We're loaded for bear too." He sounded excited, he didn't know what we were really up against. I hated to crush him, but while the reinforcements would make things closer, much closer, they wouldn't, couldn't decisively tip the scales in our favor.

"It's not going to be enough, Johansson. We've got an arc-light coming in. You'd better get clear if you can."

"It's too late for that, sir, the infantry will never get clear. You've got to call it off, Captain. We're here now, we can hold!"

I swallowed. Hard. "I can't. There's just too many of them."

"You have to call it off, sir, we can't just let them die by our own guns!" Siddiqui broke in on our private channel.

"If we let them come, most of them will die defending this hill anyway," I told him. "This is too important to risk."

"We can be there in time, sir!" Johansson pleaded.

"Just do you're best to get out of here. Save who you can."

"You're killing us!"

"That was an order, Lieutenant!" I cut the channel. Visions of Captain Kay lecturing me about the effects of killing your own troops welled up out of my memory. The feeling I'd had when he'd told me how morally wrong the decision is, even when absolutely necessary, almost made me follow Johansson's advice. I pushed that feeling aside, it had no place here, and I had no other choice. The lives of a few who would have died anyway, sacrificed in order to achieve the mission, weighed poorly against the far greater number of lives that would be saved by our success. That was how it was, this was how it would have to be. It was time.

"Fall back!" Siddiqui called. Our retreat wasn't very organized, we just up and ran. Likely, that led the Confederate forces to pause, wondering if they were being led into a trap. It didn't matter. Soon enough they were picking their way through the firebase, wary of the mines and traps we'd laid, yet confident in their dominance. We sat hunkered down in our bunkers, the ones the Imperials had dug so deep and then not thought to put anyone in, waiting for the tremors to start.

My heart squeezed tight in anguish when I received that last call from Johansson at the same time as the roaring overhead started. "Captain, we're still not clear! Call it off, call it off!"

Then the lights started flickering and flashing and everything started spinning as we were tossed to and fro. The only sound I could hear was the rumbles and roar of a thousand explosions tearing open the face of the planet and laying waste to whatever was found beneath.

My Crossbow pitched forward, the stroboscopic effect of the flickering lights making it all appear to happen in slow motion. Something jarred me from the side, then another something from the back. I felt a tightness in my chest and everything went black.

Chapter Fifteen

Tango Niner Five Area of Operation: Tabletop Mountains
Formosa, East Parsi
Madrigal
Unified Terran Republic

May 12, 2653

Someone was whanging a hammer against my head. That sort of conduct pissed me right off, but I was too tired to really care. I let myself doze again, despite the hammer.

I was thirsty. I tried to find my water tube with just my tongue, but I didn't have much success. Some salty liquid trickled across my left cheek, but I wanted water, not blood. I groped around with one hand, I cannot remember which, until I found the tube hanging back near my ear. I popped it in my parched mouth and quaffed several large swallows.

I hadn't even realized I'd gone back to sleep until I awoke again. I lifted my head clear of its rest. Pain stabbed from my brain stem right through my eyes and I passed out.

This time I just slowly turned my head sideways. I couldn't see anything. I blinked several times to assure myself that my eyelids actually were open. I still couldn't see anything. Some small part of me started having a fit, trying to convince me to panic because I was blind, but the rest of me just said that panicking was too much work and it was time to go back to sleep. I tried heeding the latter exhortation but there was a voice buzzing in my ears.

"Captain? Lieutenant? Anyone?" Someone was lost and scared. *Why doesn't security just take that kid to the customer service desk and find his parents? Don't just let him make his own public announcement*, I thought.

"Anybody out there? Come on guys, I don't want to be down here all alone."

Me neither, but that's better than being down here with you annoying me.

I fumbled around without even trying to open my eyes until I hit or flipped something that made the voice stop. That was good, now I could relax again.

"I'm blind!"

That dream wasn't a good one, which might explain why I woke up screaming. Of course, waking up from a dream where you're blind to a reality where you're also blind is a pretty quick way to induce a heart attack. Apparently my body parts had had a good long debate while I'd been out of consciousness and come to some sort of consensus that it was now okay to panic. Lucky me.

I touched my eyeballs, confirming that my eyelids truly were open. That stung, but what mattered that if I was blind? Thoughts of Russell filled my head.

I tried to sit up again, slowly, but the pain was still severe. I shivered in fear, but that hurt too. I don't know how long I just laid there in a literally blind panic, but it certainly seemed like a very long time. Somewhere in the recesses of my swollen brain a little voice cried out that maybe there wasn't any light down here. That gave me a glimmer of hope and made me feel better.

Now I could see. I couldn't see any actually thing, but instead of everything being dark, now something very near to my face was very, very, bright. I opened my eyes but that made the light painfully bright, so I quickly closed them. I heard voices speaking, but I couldn't understand the words. Hands were moving around me and touching things in the cockpit. They touched something near my shoulder that made me arch my back in pain. That made them momentarily stop both the chatter and the touching.

The medics cut through my restraining straps and gently removed my helmet. It seemed strange at the time that they would be so soft and careful in getting me out when the journey that had brought me here hadn't been gentle at all. Perhaps I'd finally earned some kid gloves. They were even more careful as they examined my shoulder area.

This all seemed familiar somehow. I seem to recall something about once before having been awakened by rude people trying to pull me out of my comfy command chair whilst I wished for nothing more than to return to a painless sleep.

Even after the medics sprayed my ears I was incoherent for a time. I didn't really understand what was being done as they used a laser-cutter to free my shoulder from the metal shard that had skewered me. It was about a hand's span in width and they just cut it free without pulling it loose. In my disoriented state that made me mad; damn it, I didn't want that thing in me. I tried to yank it loose, but only succeeded in making myself scream in agony. The medics quickly controlled my hands, I think one of them gave me a shot of some sort, and guided me out of the shattered cockpit of my Man O'War.

They continued on, leading me up out of the hole in the ground where my Crossbow had somehow been buried. I couldn't focus, so I can't actually say what my reaction was to the devastation and destruction that surrounded me. The pit that had been dug to excavate our buried force was already huge and the engineers were busy enlarging it. A breastwork of ramps and scaffolds lined the hole. Some of the engineers' excavation equipment towered high above me and I remember leaning far back to look at it, almost overbalancing the poor medics trying to guide me to their field hospital.

When we reached the top of the dig site, it vaguely registered in me that this mountain was now very bare indeed. Its pockmarked face held nothing to suggest that a brief, yet pitched battle had taken place during the night. No bodies littered the land, no war machines lay broken and burning, no forest remnants poked through to show where enemy forces had gathered to contest our possession of the area. Nothing at all remained. The face of the planet had been scoured clean of the infection that our conflict represented.

"Where's Siddiqui?" I asked. For some unnamable reason that information seemed important.

The medic just pulled me along gently by the arm. "We'll find all of them, Captain. You're only the fifth one we've managed to get out so far. Just come along."

I followed, all bemused. Something about what he said wasn't quite right but I couldn't put my finger on it. Instead of worrying about it, I just allowed myself to be led across the way to a field hospital that had been parked nearby. The huge tracks were folded underneath and the walls had been expanded to allow for more working room. A triage center had been established in one of the pavilion tents nearby and that is where my guides led me. They sat me down in a chair, very careful to arrange some sort of support for the spike skewering my shoulder, and left.

I can't say for certain how long I sat there simply staring off into space. It must have been some fair amount of time, as my head injury was likely of low priority. I didn't even want to think about my shoulder. I still didn't want to look at it and everyone else also seemed to have some sort of hole in them, anyway. I remember noting how strange it seemed that there should be so very many people in this tent if I was only the fifth one saved. I don't recall how many were there, though.

I do recall that someone briefly shone a light in my eyes and asked some questions, but I can't remember what he or she said either. Slowly, very slowly, I became more aware of my surroundings, more cognizant of what was happening around me, more able to understand what was happening. I wasn't fully back together though, not even close; just better.

I realized I was very thirsty.

"Water?" I asked a passing orderly. She was a cute blond, and she smiled. Maybe that's why I can remember her better than most of the others. Whatever the reason, she brought me a canteen of water and advised that I drink slowly, then departed. I ignored her admonishment and drank the first half in two huge swallows. Then I sat there sipping on the rest of my water, trying to focus, but I felt so out of it, as if I was missing something very important but had long forgotten what that important thing was, left only with the certainty that the knowledge had once been there and was now missing.

Someone was shaking my good shoulder very gently. "Wake up there, sleepy."

I guess I'd dozed off. I forced my eyes to focus on the voice and saw a couple of doctors sporting the pips of majors looking at me. The man took his hand from my shoulder when he saw he had my attention, then he and the woman both moved to take seats, one on either side of me.

"Can you tell me your name and rank?" the woman asked.

I thought for a long moment. Was she really asking me that? What a stupid question. "Yes."

She just stared at me, then prompted further. "Well, will you share them with me?"

That took a moment. It was there, it just wasn't coming out right away. "Chase Aarons. Captain."

She smiled and nodded at that. "What unit are you with, Captain?"

Why all of these questions? I looked at her hard, trying to figure out why she was so curious about everything. "Eleventh augmented armor," I said. Something about that didn't seem right, though.

She looked at me puzzled. "The Eleventh was disbanded months ago, Captain."

Disbanded? Oh, yeah. "We transferred into the Eighty-Ninth. Those of us that were still alive."

"Everyone who was left from the entire division?" the man asked. He was waving something square, black and annoying over the back of my head. I began to dislike him, fluttering his hands around all over the place just centimeters from my scalp and now asking pointless questions. I partially turned to face him, but the supports around my skewered shoulder limited my movement more than I had expected.

"There weren't very many of us left. We were absorbed pretty easily."

The man gripped my hand and told me to squeeze hard. I tried to grind his knuckles together and crush his fingers but my grip felt pretty weak. He shone another light in my eyes, then clamped my knee with one of those tripod reflex devices that doctors always carry. Going off the frown on his face, the results didn't satisfy him. He pulled out what appeared to be an ice pick with a pizza cutter on the other end and jabbed my leg with the pointy part. Naturally I flinched which sent shards of agony radiating out from my shoulder.

I cried out at the pain. "That hurts you stupid prick!"

"You took a bit of a beating there, Captain," he said. Now the woman was touching the back of my head with something. I wasn't sure what it was but I wanted her to stop it. "What do you remember of it?"

I shuddered, the pain that movement caused bringing tears to my eyes. "Russell was blinded. Prav lost his legs. I killed so many I…" I trailed off. For a moment I said nothing, then, "I've never been shot out of my Man O'War before. Jonny's going to rub that in."

"That's all in his file; he's juxtaposing the two incidents." The woman was speaking over my head to the man. To me she said, "That was with the Eleventh, Chase. Tell us about last night with the Eighty-Ninth."

How did she know my name? What file? I was so confused I blurted out the first stray thought that went passing through the short-circuited synapses of my brain. "Johansson didn't get clear." I could hear his cry still echoing somewhere in my head. It was the most painful sound I'd ever heard. I can remember accepting in that deluded state what I would try to justify away for many years.

I don't think they understood what I was referring to, but they still seemed to greet this as a more positive sign.

"Anything else?" the man asked.

I didn't understand his question; I didn't want to. That single memory was so painful alone that I didn't dare risk anything that might hurt like that did. I just shook my head very slowly and carefully.

"Well," said the woman over my head again, "he shows mostly sub-cortex symptoms. There's some tertiary occipital hemorrhaging as well. We'd better get him in for a DGT before anything worse surfaces. I think we can probably do the shoulder once we take care of that, it's just a minor reconstruction."

The man nodded and they both just walked off without another word to me. A moment later the cute blond came back. She picked up the empty canteen that I didn't remember dropping and smiled gently as she wiped up the spilled water with a towel she carried. Then she carefully helped me rise, taking great care to stabilize my shoulder against unwanted movement before she led me off by the arm. We wandered through fabric hallways that I hadn't suspected could exist within these tents, seemingly turning at random as we threaded our way through the maze that medical types love to construct in order to disorient patients.

At some point we entered the hospital proper. It was a testament to my state that I never realized exactly when the walls became more substantial that cloth. We passed a window and for some reason I stopped to peer out. It had started raining lightly and I vaguely wondered what the engineers were going to do about all the mud. My blond gently guided me away from the view, but I could hear the downpour that started moments later. That pit was definitely going to flood; I wondered if anyone was still down there.

My cute blond took me to a small cubicle, gave me some vague instructions about not going anywhere, and then left again. That struck me as silly. Not only did I have no desire to go anywhere, but I wasn't sure how to get out of here either. I just rested my head to one side, careful not to jar or put pressure on my shoulder, and closed my eyes.

I fell asleep again. I dreamt of blonds gently massaging my scalp and shoulders. That was okay because they all looked like my orderly and they were all naked. Their fingers on my scalp felt like pure heaven as they worked the pain and stress of a hundred lifetimes out of my body. One of them caressed my arm slowly and gently with her long fingernails, lightly scraping the skin. For some unknown reason she suddenly jerked her hand back and stabbed her nail deep into my arm, forcing it down all the way until it scraped hard and long against bone.

"Ow!" I jerked upright and stared hard at the nurse as he finished pulling that huge needle from my biceps. "What the hell are you doing?" Then I didn't care. I felt really good. Mellow, relaxed, and carefree, that was me. The nurse's proffered apology was totally unnecessary. Nothing bothered me now. I tried to stand up and walk off, but the nurse pushed me back down.

A horrible, god awful pain shot through my shoulder, but even that didn't matter. This was a nice development.

"Someone will come for you in a minute. Just sit tight, Captain."

I actually shrugged, which also hurt like hell, but I didn't care because even harsh pain didn't matter. I didn't care about anything, and wanted nothing. Well, that's actually not quite true, there was one thing I wanted. Another one of those needles would have been very nice indeed.

Sooner or later, either one was good and it didn't matter which, the nurse returned and guided me into the DGT theater. I seemed to have lost all of my clothes at some point along the way, but that didn't matter either. Naked felt pretty good too; maybe better. I sat on the chair as they indicated, uncaring that it was cold enough to shrivel everything that contacted it. I positioned myself to their specifications, fitting my neck and torso into the supports and allowing the whole team to gather around for easy access to my head and shoulder. The apparatus moved, which was so cool at the time, turning me upside down and spinning me around at the doctors' will.

They removed the metal piece from my shoulder first, by way of the rather direct if indelicate solution of grabbing it with a pair of pliers and yanking really damn hard. I can see why they have to go through so many years of medical school to learn techniques like that. I knew that much about medicine when I was five, for crying out loud.

Even with the drugs, the pain made me almost faint, and when I returned to relatively full cognition they'd already finished fixing up whatever damage they'd found, or perhaps created. Either getting something that large shoved through your shoulder isn't as bad for your general state of well-being as it sounds or I was out of things for longer than it seemed.

I *do* remember the DGT, for which I am *not* grateful.

Anyone who's ever had a DGT can attest to the degree of discomfort and pain involved, both physical and psychic. It's a difficult thing to attempt to explain to anyone who has never experienced the process, and I was very glad to have received that shot first, even if it did sort of wear off toward the end of the procedure. There are a lot of centers in the brain ranging from pure pleasure to hellish nightmare, and stimulating those in varying combinations can result in some very disturbing patterns of sensation and memory indeed; sensations and memories that don't fade the way dreams do. Many of them linger to this day.

Even after the stabbing pain in my eyes stopped, and the deafening thudding in my ears subsided, I was not a happy camper. My shoulder hurt something fierce and I couldn't have moved my arm even if it wasn't taped to my body, I was still having vivid recollections of the DGT, and I was being led around the hospital vehicle and tent complex butt-naked and dressed only in one of those paper thin hospital gowns that leave a conveniently easy access for the enema nurse. I was, however, myself again.

The nurse took me to a place where I could claim new clothing, allowing me to change into an ill-fitting set of pants, shirt, and boots. Then he just left me there with no further instructions on what to do. I suppose he had other casualties to concern himself with, and I was no longer among the walking wounded.

I struggled to dress myself with only one good arm, fighting the fasteners and openings in the clothes that I'd never so much as noticed before. After covering my nakedness, minus any instructions to the contrary, I left. It wasn't that simple, because I had to work my way back through the labyrinth of halls and walls that was packed so tightly into this limited space. Even so, I did manage to make my way back to the triage center.

There were now several dozen injured strewn around the area in different states of repose. Some bled, many moaned, all looked like hell warmed over. They all appeared to be Republic soldiers, which made no sense because we'd been so far out ahead of everyone else, there should have been at least a few Imperial soldiers present. I continued to survey the room, wandering between the stretchers, stunned at how many soldiers were here, wondering why I could not find a familiar face, half afraid that I would among the seriously injured.

Indeed, it wasn't long before I did come upon a familiar form lying on one of the beds along the back wall. Johansson was propped up in a semi-seated position and his eyes were closed. A thin blanket covered him from the neck down. He didn't look too bad. Beyond being as white as the sheets beneath him he only sported a few scrapes and bruises, probably about what I looked like save for my shoulder injury. I was reassured to see him, that meant that he had made it to a place of at least comparative safety. If he'd made it, I had hope for the others that had been with him, especially the PBIs.

I approached him from his right, trying to be careful not to wake him if he was sleeping deeply. "Johansson," I whispered, "you all right?"

He didn't move, but his eyes snapped open, completely conscious and acutely aware. He stared at the roof above with eyes that bulged from his head as though they sought to escape the very confines of their sockets. Then his mouth contorted into an expression of pure anger and he turned his head toward me.

"You son of a bitch!" he shouted. The string of invectives and curses he hurled at me after that was both fluent and loud. By the time a pair of nurses had hurried over to try and calm him down, he was struggling to sit all the way upright and, having finished describing my genealogical heritage, he was down to calling me a murderer and traitor. "How many good men did you kill? Victims of our own guns! What of that vaunted honor and glory you always speak of, Captain? You should have died. Who'll trust you now?" He lobbed a gob of spit in my direction. I stepped back, quite puzzled, and it landed at my feet with a wet smack.

The nurses grabbed him to wrestle him back down to his stretcher. He put up a fairly impressive struggle, and his blanket fell loose, exposing the mechanical tourniquets that capped the stumps of both his arms, just above the elbows.

I wish I hadn't recoiled in horror, one more regret in an exceptionally long list of regrets, but I did. Johansson began laughing at my shocked reaction and continued to fight against the nurses holding his shoulders.

"Can't face your own handiwork? What, no more words for the unarmed man?" He continued describing my high crimes and misdemeanors at the top of his lungs, colorfully laced with every expletive I'd ever heard. Heads were turning our way, even amongst the injured, drawn by the spectacle of a patient railing on an officer.

One of the nurses instructed me, none too politely, to leave and let them handle the situation. I retreated to the sounds of Johansson's taunts and accusations. To this day I can still hear the echoes of his ranting.

Two steps backward, then I turned and, not quite running, quickly moved out into the setting sun. This was insane. I'd done what was necessary to accomplish the mission, to save lives. Captain Kay's voice reverberated up from my memory at that thought, warning me once again of the consequences of trading lives for expediency.

In my arrogance, I thought I understood Johansson's pain, and then I tried to minimize it and set it aside, despite his being a hero. He had tried, and done, everything he could to help me, his professed friend, even going far and away beyond the call of duty. It hadn't been enough and I'd been forced to use something more. He'd been severely injured in that action and felt both a failure and a cripple, so it was only natural that he'd lash out at me. Bearing that has always been part of the burden of command.

Having justified all of that in my thoughts, I was able to take a moment to catch my breath. It was cool now, and the rain still fell steadily. I stood just outside the entrance to the triage pavilion, sheltered somewhat from the breeze and drizzle by the bulk of the tent, watching the heavier drops stir ripples in the gathering puddles.

"Captain," a familiar voice called from my right. I turned to see a welcome, if serious, face.

"Siddiqui, you made it." It was a stupid thing to say, but it was the first thing that came to mind to say.

His only response was a nod and a cool stare. I lowered my eyebrows. "What's wrong?"

"You don't know?" His response was blunt.

Now my eyebrows raised at his insubordinate tone. "Are you referring to Johansson, Lieutenant?"

He flinched at my use of his rank, but didn't back down. "Yes, Captain, and many more like him; dead, dying, or crippled."

"It's not an easy thing, you know. We've both seen a lot of good lives ended or changed forever." I half shrugged with my good shoulder. "I'm tired of it too. I'm tired of watching my friends and subordinates get hurt or killed. I just pray for an end to all of this as quickly as possible so we can all go home."

"At what price?" His oddly insubordinate manner, so unlike him, and this line of questioning were making me extremely uneasy. "Not everyone gets to go home. Sir."

"I'm not certain I like your tone, Lieutenant."

"That's just too bad, isn't it, Captain?" He sneered at me. "Because I'm not certain I like you or what you've done. Maybe you should go spend some time in there with some of the people that used to be my friends." He tossed his head toward another tent, just across from our position. "Tell all of them about 'necessity' and 'expedience' and then we can talk again. Feel free to bring me up on charges of insubordination at that time." With that he stormed off.

I stood there dumbfounded. What world had I woken up to? Straight out of some science fiction novel, I felt like I'd been transported to an alternate universe populated with exact copies of all the people I knew, but the copies all acted completely differently.

With no orders, no Man O'War, and no unit, what else could I do? I walked the short distance through the mud to peer inside the tent my executive officer had indicated. I almost threw up. It was the morgue; the place they were storing the bodies until they were finished enough with the living to spare some time for the dead.

Confused over why Siddiqui should send me here, I slowly wandered around the tables. Apparently the medics had been too busy with those that could still be saved to take any pains at all with these poor souls. Their bodies were strewn none too neatly atop a series of cold, metal tables. It looked like someone had made an abbreviated attempt to match limbs and other parts with the proper head and torso, but without much success. Each body had been stripped of at least one boot and given a toe tag listing name and rank.

I have tried and tried again to convince myself that Siddiqui didn't know, couldn't have known, what I would find there. Yet every time I almost believe that, logic rears its ugly head to tell me he must have known. For that, I have never yet been able to forgive him. Maybe someday, God willing, but not yet.

I was in a great deal of shock, brought about from the combination of the trauma of my injuries and the disorienting behaviors of people I'd thought I had known so well. That's the only thing that could possibly account for why I would stay in that cold place and wander the ranks of the dead looking at toe tags, reading each one.

Hubert, Ronald; Staff Sergeant. Tran, Angela; Specialist. Godfrey, Ronald; Staff Sergeant. Harrison, Gosberg, Lee, Fran, Shelby, and Xiong. Privates all.

I stopped cold.

Aarons, Jonny; Lieutenant.

However poorly my brain had been functioning up to that point, it stopped working at all then. My body moved of its own accord to inspect the lifeless thing in front of me, so cruelly labeled with the same name as my brother's. My feet walked closer to the table, my eyes surveying the body from foot to crown.

One black leather boot, still tightly laced, covered its right foot. The left was stripped bare and sported the harsh white tag that obviously mislabeled the body. Its forest camouflage pants and tunic were rumpled and creased, spotted here and there with mud. Nothing you wouldn't expect for someone who had just been crammed into a power suit a few hours ago. Black gloves covered his hands, worn thin where they would have made contact with the power suit's receptors. The face was difficult to read, difficult to comprehend. It was much like looking in a fun house mirror in which you recognize yourself, but it's not really you at all.

I suppose it *could* have been Jonny, it looked somewhat like him. The body was about the right height and weight, and the facial features bore a superficial resemblance too, but Jonny was darker, never this pale. His face was fuller, stronger, it didn't hang sallow and wasted. Jonny always had a smile on his face, laugh lines already forming at the corners of his eyes. This man looked deeply saddened, the worries of a soldier marked in the crinkled brow, the eyes that showed a chronic lack of sleep. Most of all, Jonny was so very, very alive, and this man was quite convincingly dead.

No, this wasn't Jonny, just someone passing close in resemblance.

The body was intact and showed no visible cause of death.

It couldn't be Jonny.

I inspected the body more closely, looking all around for whatever trauma could have caused this death.

It was not Jonny.

No blood showing, no holes in the uniform, nothing to reveal the secret that brought this poor soul, whomever he had been, to this cold and unknown resting place.

Jonny?

I noted something odd about the way the body's patrol cap fit, then it dawned on me that this body actually wore a patrol cap when none other did.

No, it wasn't Jonny. No, just a fairly uncanny resemblance.

Infantry only wear patrol caps when they're unarmored, and all of these ones would have been suited up for combat, so someone must have put it on the body when it was brought here.

It was a very striking resemblance, though.

With one hand I gently pushed the cap back to reveal a gaping hole larger than my fist in the upper left side of his skull where hair the same color as mine should have lain thick and matted. Nothing but an empty space lay beneath.

"Jonny," I whispered, choking on the second syllable. I collapsed onto the table right there beside him. I hugged him close to me, needing my brother's touch, even this cold, hard, and unyielding embrace.

I had to know for certain. I grabbed his right hand and shucked off the glove that covered it. There was the scar that I gave him when we were eight, playing with the mower.

Dad had left it running in the backyard while he'd gone in for a drink of water one hot summer afternoon. Jonny had wanted to surprise him by helping out, and dragged me along. He had been clearing a big stick out of the way and I'd pushed a bit too fast, almost amputating his hand. He'd cried and cried and cried, even after the doctors had finished reconstructing everything, but he never once blamed me.

There also was his Harvard class ring, tarnished somewhat by the wear and tear of long, hard fieldwork. I remember well how he displayed it proudly at my commissioning banquet. He had explained to me and Rachel that it was a special design made available only to the top five percent of the graduating class.

I turned and rolled up the right trouser leg, exposing the pale scar that he'd earned at twelve. We'd found a bullet from a hunting rifle lying in the street and had tried to set it off by throwing it against the pavement. We succeeded and Eric, the neighbor kid, got shot in the arm. Jonny had fallen down at the shock and smashed his shin against the curb, scraping skin almost to the bone.

No, this wasn't Jonny, because Jonny was always, always so very alive.

I pulled the body's cap back on tight. I smoothed down the collar and lapels of his tunic, replaced the glove and pant leg I had disturbed, and even straightened his remaining dog tag. I leaned in to hug him one last time, not that that stiff, lifeless husk really counted as him. I kissed his cheek, brushed away the tears that had dampened his face, then walked slowly and deliberately outside.

The heavy rain of earlier had abated for the most part, but it had left plenty of mud behind. I sloshed through the thick stuff, struggling against the suction that threatened to pull my boots off with each step. The light drizzle cooled my face as much as the breeze did; it felt good, almost as if it were washing away a multitude of sins.

But it couldn't. I'd killed my brother.

I stumbled over a branch in the mud and splashed down on my one good hand and my knees. Vivid pictures of Johansson's gross injuries swam before my eyes. His accusing stare as he called me a murderer and a traitor to all those who trusted me floated before my eyes. I saw Jonny, lying there cold and alone, only one small injury separating him from the life he'd once had. I remembered Johansson's excitement at bringing infantry reinforcements. Had he known Jonny was coming? Putting himself at risk one last time for his brother's sake?

I vomited whatever contents my stomach had on the ground in front of me, the whitish chunks pooling along with the gastric juices in a small divot. Then I puked again. Johansson's last words before the strike, his pleading for me to save them all, echoed in my ears. My stomach heaved again. I told myself that it had been the only way, that those who died would have died anyway, and this had been the best way to assure some semblance of victory.

But I hadn't known Jonny would be amongst them, and suddenly that made all the difference in the world. I had killed my brother.

Now I was vomiting blood, but that didn't stop me from continuing. I grew dizzy, but I still couldn't stop. I huddled there trying to puke out my kidneys for a very long time indeed. I couldn't stop myself; in fact, I think I welcomed it as a penance, but nothing was undone because of it.

At some point I lost consciousness, perhaps I should be thankful for that, but it didn't last long. I was probably only out for a minute. I'd stopped puking but I almost started again at the smell of my previous work. I crawled to my feet and, uncaring of any danger, perhaps because of the danger, stumbled back to the crater the engineers were still enlarging in their rescue efforts.

Upon reaching the lip I could see that they'd uncovered the third bunker. I had no idea what I was doing. I just stumbled right over the ledge and splashed headlong through the mud, sliding as much as climbing down into the hole. It was just blind luck that I didn't break my fool neck. I didn't care if I did, maybe I was hoping I would.

Maybe it's too bad that I didn't.

By the time I reached the bottom of the pit I was covered from head to toe with a sticky black mud. I was cold and numb, body and soul, but I had nowhere else to go. I slogged through the knee-deep water to where the medical teams, warmly dressed against the elements, were pulling more lifeless bodies from the ruins, tagging and bagging. I saw men and women who I knew well, warriors that were very alive until I'd pulled the trigger on them.

I killed my brother!

I puked again, double handfuls of blood spraying forth onto the already saturated earth below. It was all too much. Too much gone wrong, too much guilt, too much anger, too much pain. I turned one last time and ran. I ran into the rain. I ran far across the blasted, muddy terrain. I ran until I entered the forest once again.

I didn't stop running, really, not until this very day. In fact, even being in here, I'm still just running away, I'm just not using my legs anymore.

Chapter Sixteen

Yellow Bird, Wilke
Hashama
New Paris Protectorate

February 11, 2654

When I ran into those woods on Madrigal, I'd taken no thought but to escape from the horror that I had unleashed upon my own world. Running seemed so easy and felt so right that I didn't stop. I excused myself from active duty (I went AWOL) and found a way to get on one of the few civilian transports headed off world.

The Empire was making a total withdrawal from the planet, and the Republic had decided not to contest their retreat. The confusion that created provided more than enough cover for my escape. I was far and away before enough dust had settled for anyone in a position to care was able to realize I had truly gone missing, much less do anything about it. It would have taken a long time for anyone to even suspect that I'd gone off planet of my own volition.

I couldn't stick around; I needed to run, and run, and run. It wasn't until many years later that I learned I was trying to run away from myself, which just doesn't seem to work, even though I've not yet managed to stop. At the time though, all I could think of doing was shipping myself farther from the worlds of the Republic, farther from any last tenuous connection with the event and place that had killed Jonny.

I was very successful in cutting off any and all ties that would have reminded me of anything from my former life. No country, no unit, no family, no duty. I left it all, abandoning what had previously given my life shape and form, hope and meaning. The only thing I couldn't get away from was Jonny's murderer, and my inability to achieve that one impossible goal was slowly driving me a little more insane every day.

And here I sit, so many years later and halfway back across the Charted

Territories, and I still can't get away from that man. I think, perhaps, that it is still driving me very much insane.

I'd saved up a significant amount of money, earning my regular salary and allowances (plus off world bonus plus combat pay plus isolation pay) for many long months. There had been no time to spend much of it on Madrigal, and really nothing to spend it on unless you were into prostitutes, which I hadn't been then. I'd occasionally put together a package for Liz, or spent a few days of leave carousing moderately with Rachel and Jonny, but that hadn't cost anything, really. The Guard had provided everything I really needed, and there had been no time for hobbies or luxuries.

Money can do a lot for a person seeking to run away, and I had plenty, so I ran far away indeed.

I left a brief note for Rachel, a pathetic scrap of paper to ease the pain of my abandoning her and everything else. It was mostly just a scribbled mess, soaked in tears and written in a horribly shaky hand, telling her that I loved her. I tossed it in the mail drop at the starport. There was nothing else that I could think of to write. I couldn't explain to myself what I felt, much less put it into words for someone else to understand. I certainly couldn't face her. She'd loved Jonny as a brother and I'd killed him for the sake of my own pride and bid for omniscience. I asked Rachel to tell Liz that I was sorry. Worse, far more cowardly I think, I asked her to tell Jonny's wife I was sorry, and to tell my niece that I had loved her father, to actually go back to Earth and hold them all while I just ran away.

I wonder if she ever did tell them. I wonder how, or if, she managed to explain to them that I'd killed Jonny and then ran away, playing fugitive to fate and fortune in an attempt to control the demons in my soul. I wonder so many things. I wonder why I never had the courage to find out the answers to my questions.

I promised Rachel, in that letter, that I'd find her again someday. I don't know why I said that. I guess I knew that I'd be gone far away for a very long time, though consciously I'd formed nothing resembling a plan, I was merely running on instinct. To find her again, in this great big galaxy, what a pipe dream that was. I guess I thought I owed her, at the least, that small tenuous hope that I could love her enough to come back for her someday. Maybe that just made things worse. Maybe she hoped for me and prolonged her own suffering. I don't know and never will.

In any case, I moved from world to world as fast as I could find transportation, desperate to avoid any brush with Republican authorities or contacts, burying myself in an alcoholic stupor whenever possible along the way. That didn't make the pain go away, but it did seem to dampen its sharpness, and it certainly made me care a whole lot less about my own misery. I tried to make sure that I always had at least one bottle close at hand, whatever the place or time of day. I ran all the way to Hashama, a provincial backwater Fringe world in the New Paris Protectorate.

The trip took me almost two months, but it seemed to be just one long blur of drunken self-loathing and guilt. I slept wherever I could find a horizontal surface, whether in starports or on transports, ate whatever was handy, and drank to ease the pain. At first I'd tried to talk to others, passersby, fellow travelers, social workers, anyone, but I didn't get much sympathy or help once they learned that I was a drunkard and a deserter. The listening ears always dried up rapidly, leaving me alone with my sorrows once again. It didn't matter, not in the slightest, because they couldn't give me the forgiveness I truly needed anyway.

Only I can provide that, I suppose, and yet I find that despite all the years that have intervened and all the other events I've been a part of, that particular commodity is still in very short supply.

Hashama has a reputation of being a good place for criminals and deserters to disappear, never again to be seen by those looking for them. It is, to be truthful, a wholly undeserved reputation, played up through the media and preyed upon by a certain amount of organized crime. Perhaps the Reavers actively sponsor the rumor in the hope that it will attract a greater pool for their recruiting efforts.

In truth, Hashama is a world like most other worlds, varied in climate, terrain, culture, languages, races, religions, and peoples. As everywhere else in the Charted Territories, it has an underworld element, but that is by no means the dominant face of Hashaman society.

None of that is to say that I was disappointed with what I *was* able to find there. I was easily able to come by everything sufficient to meet my needs: privacy, alcohol, and distance from the Republic. Hell, I was about as far away from Madrigal as I could get without finding my own private yacht with which to go off exploring the distant stars, an idea that was only rejected because of its prohibitive expense.

To my eternal regret, I found that location alone could neither salve my guilt nor mend my broken soul. No place or substance, no distant location or exquisite brew could give me what I truly needed most, because what I truly needed most was the close family support and love of Rachel and Liz.

No, that's not true. What I needed most was Jonny back. Lacking that what I needed was the family support and love of my parents, all of which had been taken from me.

What a joke I'd become, I was twenty-seven and wanted nothing more than to have my mother hold me close and rock me so I could cry myself to sleep every night. I needed my father to tell me that everything would be all right while my mother rubbed my back.

I certainly cannot deny that I needed Elizabeth to hug me tight and assure me they'd all be there for me, or for Rachel to kiss me softly and wipe away my tears as she heard my confession. I needed human contact with those that knew me the best, with those I could trust to forgive me and accept me no matter what sin I'd committed.

But Jonny was gone, as were my mother and father. Liz and Rachel remained, far away as they were, but, goddamn it, I couldn't look myself in the mirror without horror, how could I trust anyone else to forgive me? Instead of turning to the people who probably could have helped me, I ran far and hid deep. When that alone didn't work, I turned to experimenting with other forms of therapy.

I take no pride in relating what methods I used in my attempts to overcome my guilt and pain, my sorrow and self-loathing. I do not and cannot congratulate myself, nor do I not seek to brag about or justify the myriad sins I've committed. I simply confess to them, a long list that but heads up the introduction to my many weaknesses.

Drugs were my first attempt. When alcohol alone no longer comforted me, when being drunk was no longer enough, I ran the full gauntlet from hollows to stem-stims and hit everything in between. If it came in a pill, powder, crystal, cigarette, or needle and you could drink, smoke, eat, swallow, or inject it, I tried it. Several more months passed by in that manner, months I cannot recall in any manner of real detail. Not that I would try very hard to do so, even if I thought I could. I made a lot of new friends, though, friends that were always more than willing to help me trade some of my useless money for another packet that would make the pain go away, for a time at least. They called my the Republican and they never asked prying questions.

Perhaps they were the best friends I'd ever had.

I frequented prostitutes, usually trading some small part of my stash in exchange for a few moments of physical contact. It was the only thing I could find that even came close to the real, legitimate physical affection and acceptance of friends and family, the contact that I needed so desperately. I cannot say I was wholly unsuccessful. The carnal sensualities of the flesh would combine with my chemically altered mental state to push away the pain, if only for a few moments. But moments were more than I'd had before, and they were at least as addictive on their own as every other substance I was abusing added together.

Such is the nature of the human body that it quickly becomes inured, though, even to abuses as extreme as mine. In a matter of only months the peaks were disappearing, the highs were losing their potency. I could no longer achieve the perfect nirvana I'd once touched so briefly when I began my experiments. Still, I persisted, convinced that sooner or later I'd find the right combination or dose of drugs, at the right party, with the right group of girls, to suddenly feel at peace with myself.

It didn't work, of course, it never could have. My immoral practices and betrayal of Rachel brought with them still greater mental and emotional guilt and anguish, often accompanied by a fair amount of physical pain. The drug euphorias were no longer strong enough or long enough to count as true escape, and when I sought to make them greater, well, I was five times treated in hospitals for overdoses. I needed more, or I needed something else, something new and different.

Then, one night, I killed someone again.

He'd probably seen me paying off a dealer or a pimp and realized I had some money. I didn't know he'd followed me to my apartment until he stabbed me in the back as I fumbled my keys in the door. I think he used a screwdriver; not the wisest or most effective choice of weapons, but he'd probably had to improvise on the spur of the moment. The pain was excruciating whatever weapon he'd chosen, and my body reacted badly to being punctured between my shoulder blade and my spine. Despite what my brain may have offered as an opinion if consulted on the matter, my body still wanted to live and that made me move reflexively as best I could in order to promote that survival.

I flung the door open all the way and fell forward onto the floor, breaking my fall on my forearms. I crawled forward slightly then kicked back as hard as I possibly could, trying to kneecap my attacker. This wasn't an action movie, and I no hero; I missed completely and got a series of three hard-toed kicks to the thigh for my trouble.

Again I scrambled forward, trying to put my back to the floor and get my hands and feet to where they could ward off blows and defend me. I felt a strange sensation flowing through me, one I'd not felt in so long, one I realized, in the depths of my soul, that I'd missed. It was the feeling of combat, the rush of a blood and endorphin tsunami driven by whatever amount of adrenaline was able to work its way through the current chemical cocktail pumping through my veins.

As I tried to roll I was kicked hard in the side and I felt more than heard the ribs cracking. The momentum of the kicks helped to turn me though, which meant I was able to partially deflect my attacker's killing blow as it descended, propelled by the entire weight of his body. The screwdriver bit deep into my shoulder instead of my heart, the same shoulder that hadn't ever been quite right after Madrigal, scraping the collar bone and going right out through the back side of my trapezius muscle. When it thudded into the floor beneath me, my assailant lost his grip momentarily.

I cried out and arched my back at the pain. I kept on whimpering as I tried to focus on defending myself, especially as he reached to grab the screwdriver's handle again. I did manage to get a death grip on the wrist of that one hand, despite the agony and my moans. I had no intention of letting that hand loose.

That particular effort didn't do much good, however, as he simply got his knees under him and basically sat on my chest, from which position he just started punching me in the face with his free hand. That dazed me pretty quickly and I lost my grip on his other hand. He must have realized how effective this tactic was because he didn't even try to retrieve the screwdriver once he had both hands free, he simply started beating me with both fists. On one of those shots my head bounced off the floor and I lost consciousness when my ascending head met his descending elbow.

It might have been only a few minutes before I regained consciousness, or it may have been half an hour, I don't know, but he was still there ransacking the place when I came to. He'd already found one of my drug stashes and some money. Obviously, he was looking for more. I should have just stayed where I was, feigning unconsciousness or playing dead until he left. Instead, unable to think quite straight, I tried to quietly raise myself off the floor. I must have moaned or grunted because he turned to face me.

He smiled when he saw me, that rat bastard actually smiled at me. His head tilted to one side, studying me for a few short seconds, as though amused by the idea that I was even still alive. It was as if he was saying that my coming back to life for more punishment was a welcome event indeed, just the thing to completely make his evening a good one. He approached me almost lazily, crossing the distance with three measured steps.

There was nothing lazy about the boot he delivered to my face. The kick flung me backward and almost erect, leaning against the wall. This time he did retrieve his screwdriver with a lightning quick snatch. It was all I could do to hold myself semi-seated upright against the wall as I screamed at the top of my lungs. He didn't care about the noise. In this neighborhood no one was going to call the police or rush to my aid. He put the screwdriver right back in through the same hole it had come out of, then pushed it down to lever against the bone. I dropped all the way to the floor, my weight actually pulling him farther onto me, leaving him almost mounted on my chest again.

I flung a hand out reflexively, pushing the index finger of my right hand into his left eye. I didn't just jab or poke him, I actually pushed until his eyeball literally burst with a spurt of blood and some clear liquid. He shrieked in pain, jerking back spastically, his hands reflexively covering both eyes. I staggered upright, pushing against the wall with my good hand. I knew I had but a brief second while my opponent was writhing in agony, so I stumbled across to the kitchen hoping to find a knife or a pan that could be used as a decent club. I was far too slow.

His kick caught me directly in the small of my back, sending me flying into the kitchen's none-too-clean counter. My broken ribs ground together, but that was of secondary concern because I thought I'd been paralyzed from the waist down. My legs buckled when my body impacted with the counter and I dropped, once again, helpless to the ground. He was shrieking and sobbing hysterically at me, apparently upset about his ruined eye. I thought he would kill me now, yet it was all I could do to flop over onto my back again, my legs feeling useless at the other end of my body. I couldn't defend myself.

With only one arm working properly and no legs to move or kick with, I warded only a few of the repeated kicks he directed into my ribs and neck. He actually hauled me upright to lean against the kitchen counter so he could beat me with better form. It didn't work very well because he only managed to punch me a dozen times or so before I slumped to the ground again.

He grabbed me again and I thought he would repeat his previous attack but he surprised me instead by yanking the screwdriver free again. Thanks to this gift of deity which so many claim is my greatest blessing, I can recall quite clearly every single one of the twenty-two times he punched that dull tool into and out of my abdomen. I don't really think he was trying to kill me at this point, not unless he was truly intent on it taking a long time, because he didn't aim for anything truly vital. I think instead he merely wanted vengeance for the way I'd crippled him, he wanted to torture me and see me suffer. Then again, he may have just been lashing out insanely from the pain and panic, with no thought or direction at all to his relentless attack.

He finally tired of perforating my bowels, and left me dying on the kitchen floor, my body's fluids and innards leaking across the soiled tile. I could hear him in the bathroom, sobbing, and I saw that the light was on. Likely he was inspecting the damage done to his eye. I personally was far more concerned with the bluish loops I could see poking out of some of the larger holes he'd made in me. That and the blood. There was blood everywhere. So much of it, and all mine.

My assailant came out of the bathroom, delivered one final kick to the ruined mess he'd made of my gut, then left with the drugs and money he'd found. He simply ran out, leaving the door open behind him and a dead man on the floor.

No, I wasn't going to allow that to happen. I didn't want to die, and I certainly had no intention of going alone when I did.

I dragged myself over to the bed stand, the one that hadn't yet been looted when I interrupted my guest. I tipped it over so I could open the drawer and retrieve the gun I kept there. It was just a cheap slug thrower, something to protect my place with. Some good that had done. Still, I had it now and I told myself that I wasn't going to die with a full magazine.

I dragged myself, so slowly and so painfully, to where I could rest slightly against the wall below the window. With a heave and cry of pain I raised up high enough to rest on the sill. I teetered there and, for a moment, feared I'd plummet the four stories to the pavement, finishing in the street the dying that I had already started doing in here tonight.

The building's front door opened and a figure staggered out. My vision was a bit blurry and I wasn't completely certain if I had the right target or not, but I knew this was my only chance. I aimed, then squeezed the trigger as rapidly as I could. On the fifth shot the gun exploded, sending some small shrapnel pieces into my hand. Cheap Dominion export piece of crap.

I dropped the now useless weapon and peered down to the street. A form lay crumpled on the front stairs of my apartment building. At least one shot had done its job, now I had to get on with surviving my experience.

I crawled around painfully again until I found the phone. I reconnected it and called for an ambulance. It probably would have made more sense to call first, and then get the gun, but I was lucky to be able to do anything even vaguely rational, much less critique the finer points of my carefully crafted plan.

Having summoned aid, and unable to think of anything more productive, I went ever so slowly back to the bed stand and retrieved a hollow to chew on. It couldn't have been more than twenty minutes since I'd come home, but I felt so terribly tired. I thought about my gun. I chewed the hollow and tried to ignore the sight of my own intestines bulging out, and the smell that accompanied them. I thought about that damned screwdriver. I felt the hollow burning out the inside of my head and welcomed the escape from pain. Sirens approached from the distance, but I no longer felt anything at all inside save for the brief thought that I'd somehow enjoyed killing again.

"Aarons? Benoit Jordan, public defender."

I shook his hand slowly, both out of respect for my injuries and because I had a difficult time accepting that anyone would just come right out like that and admit to being a lawyer. He wore a pretty impressive suit though, I'll give him that. Apparently the Parisians were more generous to their public defenders than most other parts of the Charted Territories were.

"You are in some serious trouble, Chase," he stated abruptly.

Apparently that was true, since a public defender was showing up in my hospital room the same day I got there, although you'd think still being alive would count for something positive in my life. Maybe not, since that very survival carried all the baggage and burdens of my life along with it.

"Why should I care?"

He shrugged. "It's your funeral. Quite literally, actually. Though I can't honestly say I understand why you'd fight so hard against an intruder only to get executed by a judge and court for shooting a wino." He smirked at me. "Don't look so surprised. I did my research, I know everything about you."

That was a good question, though. I'd done a lot of thinking about that and several other questions. I hadn't intended to shoot the wino. In my pain and drug induced haze it had never occurred to me that crawling to the window had taken a very long time and that my attacker was long gone. Why I had shot the wino was not the real question, though.

Why had I fought so hard to live? I was pretty certain that I would warmly welcome death at this point, so why resist? I knew it was more than instinct, because instinct didn't make me find a gun before seeking help for myself. No, I really think I just enjoyed the killing.

"You have a better idea?"

"Only one. This isn't a criminally tolerant society like the Republic is, and if you go to trial the nature and seriousness of your crime will buy you a death sentence for sure. The only other choice you have is putting your talents to work. You could help the Protectorate and her citizens." He actually seemed sincere. Maybe he really believed that crap, maybe he'd simply polished his speech through long hours of practice.

I snorted as rudely as I could manage around the breathing tube shoved ignobly up my left nostril. "No thanks, I'm not interested in that 'service' crap."

He set his case down on the table next to him, flipped the latches and opened the lid. He actually pulled out a glossy brochure and shoved it in my face, almost vehemently. "I'm not talking about picking up garbage at some kiddy playground, you stupid man. I'm talking about cleaning yourself up, healing yourself up, and getting back in the cockpit of a Man O'War. I'm talking about turning your life around and getting out of the hell-hole you've dug for yourself. I'm talking about the challenge of combat, the thrill of the hunt, and the glory of defending innocents from the predators who would threaten them. I'm talking about not having to pay for hookers anymore and getting a rush that no chemical stimulus will ever be able to duplicate."

I pushed my head back into my pillow as far as I could, trying to focus my eyes on the brochure and whatever ludicrous promise of fulfillment it advertised. I laughed bitterly when I read the cover. "You think I want to get back into the military? I think I've caused enough harm there for one man in a single lifetime, so how's about you go shove your foreign legion or Reavers or whatever you call them, okay?"

He tossed the brochure on the table beside his case and looked around, likely checking for witnesses. Then, finding none, he put one finger on my philtrum and pushed. Hard. It hurt, and when I squirmed to get away it hurt even more. I found myself in the extremely humiliating situation of being held down quite painfully by a single digit.

"Listen, you stupid man," he said, leaning into his words, almost bringing his nose into contact with mine. "I make my living watching idiots like yourself hang for stupid crimes that didn't have to happen. Kids pulling convenience store robberies that go bad, drunks and druggies too incapacitated to understand what they're doing when they're trying to find their next hit, spouses who find their partner cheating on them and lose control. I'm not talking about a mob hit-man, but about everyday people who just made a stupid choice or found themselves in a bad situation and someone died. They all get a rope stretching just the same, but it doesn't sit well with me. I get tired of seeing it time after time because there is so much wasted potential in those lives.

"Now here you are, filled to the gills with knowledge and training ten times greater than most of those others will ever have in their entire lives, and you won't take the one option that will keep you from swinging from a tree branch. At least try to get yourself killed in combat, you fool."

I said, "Urgk."

He jammed down harder than before, forcing my head down at an angle that made it a challenge to breathe. "The statistics are there, Chase. Everyday two hundred people are killed by separatists who think they can win their cause by blowing up school children and pregnant women. Everyday Jarvyn sponsored raiders strike in the disputed zone or across the border and kill another five hundred citizens. Every *single* day, you stupid twit, at least one major factory in this country gets bombed by heaven only knows who with an average death toll of thirty-five. That means that each day that you are still alive to see the sun come up, as useless as you may think that particular blessing is, seven hundred and fifty Parisian civilians who would appreciate that chance don't get it because of terrorists and insurgents. Our main military forces are meant for major combat, they aren't designed for these kinds of operations and police operatives can't operate effectively on these terms. That's why we have the Reavers.

"So, here you sit, a warrior with the kind of training and abilities that only nations the size of the Republic can provide, but you're washed up, drugged up, and useless. In two weeks you will stand trial for murder because you shot a man for revenge, not even in self-defense, and you got the wrong man anyway. The case is open and shut. No matter what I try to say, you will hang one week after your trial, and then you will have achieved your self-destructive goals and have rendered yourself totally useless." He removed his finger from my upper lip area. "Unless you join the Reavers."

I glared at him and curled my lip back into its comfortable sneer. "Why would that make a difference? What kind of screwed up justice system do you subscribe to?"

"It makes a difference because the protectorate rewards those who serve.

Would you rather we tell the Republic's Home Guard that you're here? They'd ask for your extradition, of course, but it would be denied because you stand accused of a capital crime. But assume we did, what second chance could you get there? A dishonorable discharge at the very least, and a stain on your permanent record that would haunt you for the rest of your life. You'd find no job for any government agency or any government contractor, which most major corporations are. No, you'd likely spend the rest of your life bagging groceries." He lifted his head higher to look down his nose at me.

"But among the Reavers, no one will ever ask for your background check, criminal records, or anything else. In fact, once you join you will receive amnesty for everything you've done before joining. Any outstanding warrants will be dropped, charges will be quashed, and you'll receive the full protection of the Parisian government from any claim another nation might level against you. So, as long as you join between now and your execution, the government will extend clemency and you will be able to go free."

He kept up a good prattle. Every point he made was legitimate, I just didn't care about most of them. That didn't mean I was really, honestly ready to die. Somewhere deep inside I still wanted to live. Maybe something in me recognized that I was sick and needed to get better, and the only way to accomplish that was to go on living.

"And how long would I have to serve?" I asked, suspicious of anyone's good motives. "If I were to join up as you seem to expect."

He put his hands on his hips. "We're not seeking slaves. You will incur a three year obligation, after which you will be free to do as you wish. Perhaps you'll elect to stay on and help the way our most distinguished officers and training cadre have done. I'm certain they'd welcome your experience and expertise."

Yeah, that was likely. No one was ever going to welcome a deserter and a fratricide. "You'd not offer this to a man you believe a murderer if that was all there was to it. What's the casualty ratio for your precious Reavers?"

That made him pause for a moment. I'd touched on a tender spot so I pushed for the kill. "What's the ratio, Jordan? What are the odds that I'll die out there as surely as if I'd let them put a noose around my neck right here? What is so risky that you'd let a man as terrible as me go free for accepting the assignment?"

To his credit, he looked me straight in the eye and didn't hedge his answer. "On an annual basis the Reavers experience a thirty-three percent fatality rate."

I snorted. "So you figure if I manage to make it through three years I'll have dodged death enough to justify a release?"

He nodded. "That's it. I'm not here to lie to you, I'm here to give you a second chance at life. It's not the best chance, but then, you put yourself in this position, no one else did."

That was true enough. I'd killed Jonny on my own and come to Hashama on my own, now I would live or die on my own as well. "Are all the members of this suicide squad of yours marked for death?"

"Most of them," he nodded. "A few of them are military or law enforcement who wanted to be a part of it and volunteered. Most of those will have higher officer ranks or cadre positions. Generally, though, your comrades in the field will be murderers, rapists, child molesters and ilk of that sort." That was a pleasant thought. "But none of that will matter to you, or to them. All of you will put the past behind you, and serve justice and repay the Protectorate by fighting for the good of the society that you have wronged."

"What choice do I have?" I knew that answer already.

"None at all. That is why I give it to you. If you had other options, you wouldn't need me."

I sighed. "Leave your brochure, I'll look it over. But I'm not committing to anything yet."

A tight smile flashed briefly across his face as he retrieved the glossy and handed it back to me more gently than the first time. "You all say that exact same thing, even though you only have one real option."

I nodded my understanding. "A noose or a battlefield death. Tell me Jordan, do you get paid a commission for each recruit or does it just count as time off for your own dirty deeds?" It seemed such a ludicrous concept, one that I said half in jest, but I had a gut feeling.

"I get a commission, of course," he admitted frankly. "But that doesn't mean that everything else I said was just a sales pitch, or that we don't need people like you. People that have screwed up badly and want and need a chance to make a difference again, to atone for the wrongs they've done, are doing just that, and I'm proud to be a part of it."

I laughed at his assuredness. "You have no idea what you're talking about."

"You'd rather swing?" His eyebrows raised slightly.

"I don't care about that either. If I go, it'll only be because I'll get the chance to kill again."

I thought that would stop him, or wipe away some his confidence. It did neither. He merely shrugged. "You're not the first one to say that, either. Of course, most of those never quite manage to finish their full three years, so you might want to reconsider who you go around telling that."

He retrieved his case and made a casual salute as he exited my room.

Chapter Seventeen

New Paris Protectorate Legionnaires (Reavers) Basic Training Camp
Unknown Desert, Unknown System
New Paris Protectorate (Assumed)

March and April 2654

"You filthy maggots are only here because you can be of more use to the Protectorate dead on a battlefield than you can be dead swinging from a tree! If you think for a minute that that means I won't shoot you dead here anyway, then think again!"

Adjutant Chef Martel's face was as hard as a granite cliff, his complexion similar, his voice reminiscent thereof. He paced in front of our loose formation, slapping his thigh with a hard riding crop, almost a sjambok, to emphasize each word as he spoke.

"Let's get this straight from the very beginning so there will not be any misunderstandings later on. You have all pled guilty to crimes that carry mandatory death sentences. By entering that plea you have been allowed to escape that immediate punishment by serving your country one last time as a Reaver, where you will have the chance to die with an honor that you most assuredly do not deserve. However, if you screw up now, or just piss me off, then I will simply arrange for your death right now. Hundreds of Reaver recruits die in training accidents every month. I can't give you an exact number because no one cares enough about you scum to actually do an accurate count. What I can tell you is that you could easily be one of them. Do you understand me?" The last was shouted.

I knew what to expect here, of course, but, like the others, I made no response. The adjutant put his nose right in the face of a man to my left.

"I repeat, do you understand me?" he shouted.

"Yeah, man," the man said. Then he fell to the ground doubled over his groin from the hard knee Martel had delivered.

"Anyone who addresses me without using the honorific 'sir' will meet an even more severe punishment. Do you understand?"

"Yes, sir," the group said, almost as a whine.

"Gods above, you are a pathetic lot. Here you stand: rapists, drug peddlers, and murders, and not one of you has a spine strong enough to keep you vertical." He began whipping the fallen man with his crop, yelling right in his ear. "Get on your feet and back in formation! You gave up the right to lie down on the job when you raped your ex-wife, Tanner." As the man clawed his way upright again, Martel delivered another strike to the groin, this one with the riding crop, dropping Tanner again. Now Martel moved on.

He walked down our ragged line and began laying about with his crop whenever he saw something he disliked. "Stand up straight! Suck in that gut! Eyes forward!" Each command was punctuated with a smack of the crop and a wince or cry of pain from the recipient. One schmuck found himself on the receiving end of a whole list of critiques. "Shoulders back! Back, not up! Stomach in! Farther! Pretend you're not as fat as a whale!" Again each sentence came with a lash of the crop. Apparently this recipient didn't care for the brutal treatment. He rushed Martel, winding up flat on his back after a single palm heel strike to the chin laid him out.

"Anderson, you big ape, you are as stupid as you are ugly!" Martel yelled down at the man. "Get up and get back in formation!" A booted toe that probably cracked ribs emphasized the order. The kicks continued, only getting harder until Anderson rose to one knee.

With a cry that sounded like an enraged bull elephant charging a cameraman on a nature show, Anderson flung himself at Martel. His wild rush wasn't even slowed by the powerful punch Martel delivered to his midsection, and then he was literally lifting the adjutant up half a meter into the air by his own neck with one hand. Martel calmly gained a grip around the huge man's wrist and pulled his body up to twine his legs around the limb, preparatory to locking and breaking the elbow. Anderson cried again, this time more in pain, but still in anger. I guessed he was probably convicted of a murder or two, likely committed after flying into a rage.

Anderson flung Martel to the ground, then dropped onto him, wild punches flying left and right. A loud bang rang out. Anderson threw one more halfhearted punch, then slumped sideways, a neat little hole in the back of his head. Martel regained his feet, holstered his sidearm, then dusted his hands and straightened his uniform.

"There's always one," he murmured. Then he resumed shouting. "Start looking like the professional cannon fodder you are. If you pay attention to what we teach you here, you just might live long enough to earn your way out of your sentence. Though I seriously doubt that."

He paced all the way around our formation, occasionally lashing out at a recruit for no discernible reason. He continued speaking while he walked.

"But the real truth is that you fat pukes are all going to die! That is one fact I am quite confident stating. Nothing short of a God-given miracle is going to bring any single one of you back from even your first mission. I personally believe that's a good thing." He stopped, once more in front of the formation. "Do you see that building over there?"

We all looked into the distance where we could just make out a pillbox, looking to be as close to the horizon as possible without falling off the edge of the world. Martel was not happy with our response. He ran along the front rank of the formation and lashed everyone at least twice across the stomach or shoulders.

"I asked a question! Do you see that building over there?"

"Yes, sir." The group had learned to say the words, but not how to sound enthusiastic about it. That would come quickly enough. For now, as I'd fully expected, Martel was going to assign us the same task every military in the galaxy first assigns their new recruits.

"You will run there and back, right now," the adjutant chef ordered. "The last ten people back, I will shoot. Now go!"

As we ran past Anderson's still bleeding corpse I had no reason to doubt that he would indeed follow through on his threat.

"I said start with your right foot first!" Martel was right in my face, bits of spittle flicking out and hitting me in the forehead and temple. I just met his gaze with a loathing stare, the kind that let him understand that I had no reason to respond to his arbitrary accusation. Moreover, it let him know that I knew full well that it wouldn't matter what I said in answer to his denouncement, I'd just earn another lash from his ever present crop.

He seemed uncertain exactly how to handle the situation to his best advantage, he probably wasn't used to working with the most educated people. I wasn't giving him any overt justification, though I knew he'd come up with something eventually. I could almost hear the gears turning over in his head as he tried to figure out how to best humiliate and punish me, and the entire unit with me to turn us against each other—though the idea that he treated us as if we were some sort of supportive cohesive group was laughable.

"But you said left foot first, sir," someone half an IQ point under stupid said from somewhere ahead of me in the formation, rescuing me and Martel from our impasse while calling down wrath upon his own head. I rolled my eyes slightly and caught a ghost of a smile drift momentarily across Martel's face. Whether it was because of my expression or just his anticipation of another thrashing that caused the smile I didn't know. No, actually, that's not true. It had to have been from his own sadism, because he wouldn't have been amused by my look, he would have used it as an excuse to inflict more physical punishment. He lashed me a stinging blow across my left cheek anyway before he turned and stomped over to confront the moron.

"Are you calling me a liar, boy?" A lash across the chest before he'd even stopped in front of the man. "Are you questioning the words coming out of my mouth?" A lash across the outside of the thigh hard enough to cause one knee to buckle. "Don't you know your left from your right?" A lash to the shoulder, the left one. "Do you think I am as stupid as you obviously are?" Three lashes in quick succession over the top of the head, the final one opening a cut in the man's scalp that trickled blood slowly down his face to drip from his nose.

"Now, you will all repeat the exercises again!" Martel resumed pacing through the formation, contempt dripping form his every word. "You will not be excused for mess privileges until you have mastered at least these few basics of marching and turning as a formation! You have already been here an entire week, been introduced to proper military discipline, had the rules explained to you a thousand times over, and yet you still haven't managed to complete a full day without bringing needless punishments down upon yourselves!" He sneered back to where I still stood at attention. "I guess for today's difficulties you can all thank Messr. Aarons!"

I started up the log in turn, trying to stay somewhere toward the middle of the pack, the position least likely to stand out or in any other way draw attention. The woman in front of me slipped on the wet wood of the log, slick in this rain, and slammed face first into the log before bouncing to the side and slumping to the ground two meters below. I just ran right past her, barely even sparing her a glance as she lay there on the grass bleeding and crying. I was, however, careful to avoid the slippery spot which she had discovered and the fresh blood she'd left to mark it. The rain pouring down would clean that away soon enough, though. Too bad for those coming behind.

I vaulted from the end of the log, catching the rope hanging about a meter away, and began climbing. The rain-slicked rope was almost impossible to hold securely, and my death grip on it caused it to bite hard into my flesh, my calluses still redeveloping. As I got my feet under me, gripping the rope tightly between instep and sole, and slowly started to work my way up the rope, the entire thing suddenly started swinging back and forth. Martel stood at the bottom, a firm grip on the rope, trying everything he could to break it free of my grip. The tough material cut deeper into my skin, but I would not release it. The pain grew excruciating until finally the line simply ripped free, liberating a chunk of flesh off of each of my palms as it went.

I fell the two meters with my limbs flailing briefly and landed on my back in the thick mud, the impact knocking the wind out of me. Before I had a chance to recover even slightly, Martel was there, kicking me in the ribs repeatedly with his boots and lashing me across the shoulder with his crop.

"That was a teammate you left back there! She was only slightly injured, not dead, and your successful completion of the mission might depend on her being with you later on!" It was hard to listen and cover my vitals at the same time. I had no wish to go through training with a broken rib, or, far worse, lose an eye to Martel's crop as one trainee had done last week. I couldn't even form a word, the only sound escaping me was a groan as my lungs tried to convince my diaphragm to restart the air exchange process.

"Now get back there and help her up!" he shouted, finally leaving off the kicks, if not the lashes.

I struggled to rise, both against the mud and Martel's beating, only to see that the woman, whom moments before had only broken her nose and cut her forehead, now looked like her face had gone through a meat grinder. Her hair was missing at least one patch and her shirt had been torn completely open to the waste, leaving the fresh lash cuts on her back and breasts humiliatingly plain to see. Apparently the adjutant had gone to her before coming to me, and taken his fill there by beating her savagely. There was no way he'd even had enough time to explain to her why she was being beaten.

"Come on, Aarons, wake up, it's a blanket party for Taqa."

I struggled to open my eyes, pulling myself from dreamless sleep back to the bitter reality of the waking world. It was still very dark, though I could make out the shape of someone going from bed to bed shaking each person awake with the same announcement she'd given me. Apparently this news, despite causing a loss of already precious sleep, was being well received as most everyone else leapt to their feet to assemble some sort of makeshift blackjack out of bedding and toiletries or whatever other components came easily to hand.

I didn't care about what was happening. I wasn't even certain who Taqa was, having purposefully and successfully tried not to get even remotely attached to anyone here. It didn't matter to me how much of a screw up Taqa was, or what everyone else intended to do about it. Nothing mattered anymore. I only briefly looked around, fully intending to go back to sleep.

The only person in the platoon not awake now was the target, and she still lay sleeping blissfully, or at least unconsciously, unaware of the impending brutality. Something deep inside protested that this wasn't right, to gang attack someone in her sleep. I ignored the message.

Taqa's first notice came when four people grabbed the corners of her blanket and yanked them down tightly, pinning her to her bunk as she came wide awake, terrified if still ignorant of what was about to happen. A fifth character moved quickly to throw a make shift gag over her mouth, preventing any random screams from escaping and alerting the cadre. She found out then what she had in store as each person took a turn bludgeoning her with their blackjacks and other improvised blunt weapons. Again I felt almost a twinge of guilt for not intervening, but I smothered it next to the incomparably greater guilt I already felt for the events that had led me here.

But those bastards, they beat that poor girl black and blue from neck to toe for almost thirty minutes. Her crime? Simply that she was the one always screwing up the marching, always slipping off the logs, always getting the whole platoon punished for not being as coordinated as everyone else. Certainly everyone made mistakes but not on such a consistent basis, and Martel always made certain to punish the rest of us for her slipups.

Only one person there that night didn't take part in the beating, and I just turned my back to it, closed my eyes, and tried to go back to sleep, ignoring her stifled sobs and pleas for mercy and help. In truth, her choked cries bothered me little enough back then, and I quickly slid back into slumber.

We sat eating our mystery meat on a shingle, that tasteless grayish paste they troweled onto a piece of stale bread and said was healthy. I was about finished choking the foul concoction down when the dumbass across from me decided he needed some conversation with his dinner.

"So, Aarons," he said around a bigger mouthful than I'd ever been willing to risk taking of this sludge, "what are you here for?"

I was mildly surprised to realize that he knew my name, I hadn't bothered paying attention to anyone else's, and for some reason I guess I'd assumed everyone else would do the same unless there was a particular reason to, like there had been with Taqa. I chewed the rubbery substance in my mouth for a moment, mulling over what answer, if any, I should give. While giving an answer might encourage more questions, I decided that remaining silent would probably present an irresistible challenge to my bone headed dunce of a companion here.

"I killed a man," I said shortly, knowing full well that he'd ask at least one more annoying question.

"No shit," he said chewing loudly, masticated food quite visible through his wide open mouth. "We seem to have a lot of those compared to most other platoons." I was once again surprised by his knowledge. How he knew about other training platoons when we rarely saw them from closer than a hundred meters and never talked to them was a mystery to me. He indulged himself in some more open mouth chomping, combined with a lovely sounding snort to clear his nasal passages, before he continued. "Still, you don't look the type. What did this guy do to you that you had to kill him?"

I swallowed the last of my meal and stood up with my tray, readying to return it to the receptacle. "He asked me too many questions." I turned and walked away.

"What the hell is your problem, trainee?" a voice shouted at me. Thankfully, it was an officer and not Martel. That was how successful he was becoming. Despite what I told myself, what I wanted to believe, I was very much afraid of the man. This one though, the officer, I wasn't afraid of, though he seemed to have a problem of his own. He probably needed to impress himself or someone else around here. He walked over to stand just in front of me. "There is no talking during meal times!"

I made no reply, just narrowed my eyes and glared at him, willing the wordless communication of my pure hatred, letting him know that if I ever again needed to murder someone, his name was quickly moving to the top of my list of targets. Apparently he got the message, unscrambled and in the clear, for he broke eye contact with me and walked rapidly away.

"You will touch your weapon only upon my orders, and at no other time!" Martel's voice echoed clearly up and down the length of the range. We'd been in the simulators several times, but this was the first time we were to be entrusted with live ammunition.

I stood in my foxhole like everyone else, an unloaded assault rifle to one side of me, a grenade launcher on the other. "Place your right hand, and only your right hand, on the T-38 assault rifle. Pick it up. With your left hand, retrieve an ammunition clip from your LBE. Insert the clip into your T-38 and assume a firing stance aiming at the targets down range and directly in front of you! Then you stupid slugs will await my further instructions!"

I followed his directions precisely, doing no more and no less than told. When my hand closed around the familiar feel of the assault rifle's hand grip, I briefly considered how easy it would be to simply pivot and put a magazine's worth of bullets into our friend Martel. I want to believe that I discarded that option as unlikely to produce the results I desired without the unwanted side effect of dying in turn, but I think I was simply too scared. I wanted to, but his towering presence, far bigger in my mind's eye than in my physical one, cowed me into spineless obedience.

I believe everyone must have had that thought, it would only be natural, but I'm not certain how many others were honest with themselves about the matter. I wasn't, it's only in retrospect that I can see the truth.

Someone else, though, either wasn't as thoughtful on the matter or wasn't as scared I was; maybe she just had other, bigger fears. I had a fairly clear view of Taqa in the foxhole next to mine, and when Martel began lashing her once again, she stood oblivious to that pain. In fact, she quite calmly, and for once with great coordination, put a magazine in her rifle, chambered a round, then spun and put a burst of full auto right through Martel's forehead. Her victory was short lived, literally, as the range snipers removed large portions of her own skull.

The range officer's voice echoed out from the range PA system. "All of you, stand where you are! Remove all ammunition from your rifle and person and stay facing down range or you will be shot! Be sure to empty the chamber and your LBE carefully and slowly! Now place the rifle on the ground to the right side of your foxhole, then climb in front of it and kneel down. Remain motionless with your hands behind your head. Range officers will police this range."

I did what I was told as the instructions were repeated again. I always did what I was told lately. It was odd to realize that I wasn't even glad that Martel was dead. In some ways, I was actually upset because it just meant more inconvenience for me. I was confident they'd find another adjutant at least as sadistic as Martel to take over the duties of what he had referred to as discipline.

There was one lighter moment in those dark days.

"You used a machine gun patch to clean a rifle barrel?" The shocked exclamation echoed all around us.

Adjutant Chef Aster wasn't quite as bad as Martel had been, he was only mean, not sadistic. He didn't carry a crop, though he was blinding fast with his hands and feet when he wanted to be. He'd told us that his background had been in special operations with Diane, that his job was to make us effective soldiers for hunting down other scum (emphasis on other), and that he would kill all the rest of us if that's what it took to train just one person properly. Somehow, that didn't sound reassuring, though it didn't frighten me either. He couldn't frighten me, not really, he wasn't Martel.

He was however, successfully frightening one poor kid, the one with his cleaning rod jammed halfway down the barrel of his T-38. Aster loomed over the kid who visibly shook so hard I expected him to fall over in a dead faint at any moment.

"Yes, sir. I thought it was the same as the rifle patches, sir."

"You moron! It's four times the size! How could you possibly think they were the same?" Aster snatched the jammed rifle barrel away from the recruit. "Go sit over there and finish cleaning the rest of your rifle."

The kid swallowed and returned to the group where he retrieved the other pieces of his disassembled rifle and tried to clean them. The indoor range was far more comfortable than the hot sun we'd have been expected to work under if Martel had still been here.

Aster took the rifle over to his own work station, where he had a few specialty tools for fixing problem weapons. He looked over his choices before setting the barrel in a vice and picking up a small sledge hammer. When he started bashing the cleaning rod, trying to knock it loose, all conversation on the range stopped, every head turning to watch this bizarre dance. The kid whose rifle it was shrank in on himself, knowing that his stupidity would be rewarded harshly.

Every time we took a weapon into our hands we were drilled on the need to treat it with care. It was not a tool to be used for prying or hammering, it was not a crutch for support when hurt, and it was not something you ever, ever dropped. So when Aster growled in frustration, snatched the barrel up by the jammed cleaning rod, pulled it free of the vice and began slamming it repeatedly against his table, the wall, and then the floor, we just stared in amazement. Several people looked over at the poor kid, expecting him to end the day with a new hole between his eyes. Those sitting next to him moved away cautiously, trying to remove themselves from the zone of the impending blast.

With a snarl from Aster and a final superlative blow, the barrel came free from the rod and flew across the range to clatter to the floor and roll to a stop quite some distance away. Aster, breathing heavily from his exertion and anger, walked over to retrieve it. He briefly examined it before stomping back to the soon-to-be-dead trainee. The kid stood up, trying to take what was coming like a man, though he still cringed when Aster thrust the barrel at him.

"That," Aster growled, still panting, "is the cleanest barrel I have ever seen. Carry on."

Then he turned and walked off as almost everyone except me broke into spontaneous applause at the performance.

It was just another day, one in a long list of them, spent out on the dusty, hard packed dirt of the parade ground, trying yet again to force a group of mostly uneducated, violent criminals to march in good order. I wondered what the point was since every year a third of us would be gone and we'd never be asked to march. I supposed it was meant to drill in obedience and swift response to orders.

Of all the miracles, Aster had granted us a break, unheard of under Martel's rule. A chance to sit in whatever shade we could find and just rest while he went off on some errand or another was just about as good as any drug high I'd ever had. I shook my head, that way was still too tempting, too addicting, and I wasn't yet certain if I should stay away or go back to it.

"Aarons!" Aster yelled at me from where he approached across the field. "Get over here!"

I got up, brushed off some of the dust that clung to my fatigues, and trotted across the field on the double to see what he wanted me for. "Sir," was all I said as I stopped at attention in front of him.

"Your file says that you were a warrior before. Is that true?"

So, apparently Jordan hadn't just stuffed me into the ranks of the PBIs to die ignobly on some dinky foreign and lifeless rock. That meant that it had been Martel who had suppressed the information. I tried again to be glad he was dead, again it just didn't matter to me.

I like to pretend that Martel had no effect on me, that he never broke me, but that's just a lie I tell myself. While he hadn't broken me down completely, he'd certainly taught me not to open my mouth with the same method most people use to teach their dog not to whiz on the carpet: pain. As a result I had no wish to say anything to Aster. So I didn't.

I still had a large stubborn and rebellious streak in me, one that resented what had been done to me. That part just stared Aster straight in the eye, letting him know that I didn't fear him, telling him that he should fear me. Another mistake. This man had been successfully dealing with rebellious criminals for a long, long time. He dropped me to the ground, doubled over by a lightning fast kick that was too swift to see. It hit me in the pit of my stomach like a sledge hammer.

"Don't be giving me that attitude, boy!" he yelled while I blew chunks all over the ground at his feet. "When you stop puking your liver up, get your rotted carcass over to augmented armor, they'll take care of you from now on. You can go be their problem."

Devine looked across his desk at me as a man might look at something odd his dog has just dragged in off the street. He probably wondered how he would work me into a training rotation that had already been in swing for over five weeks. He probably wondered if he wanted a former officer in his group.

"You don't need basic augmented armor training, so your technical and tactical skills are probably fine, but how well are you going to work with the team?" I assumed he was merely thinking out loud, not actually asking me a question. It wouldn't have mattered if he was asking anyway, I wasn't going to jump up like a well trained animal and tell him how well I could perform tricks just for his satisfaction. "Oh, well, I guess we'll find out."

Now he rose from his seat, pacing a quarter turn around his desk to shuffle some more papers. "Don't expect the perks you were used to before as a warrior, Aarons. You couldn't even amongst regular forces, this isn't the Republic. Maybe they think their warriors are so elite they should all be officers, but here you'll be lucky if you live long enough to make warrant officer." He just stated this as a fact, not as an accusation, condemnation, or anything else. "You'll stay a private, and don't expect anyone to go easy on you because of your past rank."

I didn't say anything because I didn't care about that part. I hadn't expected anything more than this, or if I had, it hadn't meant much to me. I was, I'll admit, excited to be out of the PBI ranks and back into the augmented armor, the one thing I knew I was good at, but any desire for perks or creature comforts had been burned out of me by torment and torture. I'd also given up any claim to such things the day I walked away from my duty and the responsibility for my own actions.

"Nguyen," Devine said, motioning to an aide to come in from outside the open door, "take Aarons and get him set up in a bunk with the other warrior trainees. Make sure he knows when and where he's supposed to be for duty each day, and get him squared away on everything else he needs."

To me he said, "Get settled in quickly. You've got plenty of catching up to do."

A low whistle echoed around the water and throughout the open area of the showers. I wasn't certain from whom the sound originated, though it was obviously going to be yet another someone who didn't know how to mind his or her own business by keeping a closed mouth.

"Damn, Aarons," a larger man said from down the row of nozzles, "where did you get all those scars? You fall gut first on a rack of knives as a kid or something?"

Once again I weighed the benefits of silence versus answering; once again I felt that saying something was better than saying nothing. I was probably wrong, but that was what I felt at the time.

I shrugged. "I met a man a while back who figured he needed my money more than I need my intestines. We argued about if for a while, he won."

The big man nodded and turned his back on me, gesturing in my direction with a thumb and stage whispering to those around him, "What a pussy."

I then understood why the Reavers needed strong authority figures like Aster, even if they occasionally were psychopaths like Martel. Without that actual fear restraining them, some criminals—like me—with all of their anger and problems were just too difficult to control. Martel was gone, Aster wasn't around, and Devine wasn't intimidating in the least.

I grabbed the big man by the back of his hair before either one of us really knew what I was doing. I smashed his face straight into the bare shower pipe, dropping him to the ground. When he rose up on a hand and a knee to spit out a couple of teeth I kicked him square in the jaw with the ball of my foot, feeling his mandible break satisfactorily. That was the closest I came to winning the fight, the closest I think I've ever come to winning a hand-to-hand fight since E and P camp.

As the big man was sinking back from my kick he caught a hold of my withdrawing ankle and pulled hard. My other foot, lacking any real traction on the wet tiles, slipped out from under me and I landed hard on my back, smashing the back of my head against the floor. For a moment I couldn't see, and that was long enough.

What I could see, when my vision cleared, was the big man carrying a small wooden bench over from where it had rested against the wall. I scrambled up to a crouch before he struck me with it. I took the impact on my arms, which hurt, but a lot less than taking the blow in the head would have, even if it did drive me back to my knees. A couple of people started shouting at him, trying to stop him before he killed me. Two women even went so far as to grab his arms trying to restrain him, but he literally brushed them off.

The next blow came in sideways, catching me in the kidney area and dropping me to the tiles completely. I felt paralyzed, scrambling to get my legs to obey my will and get back under me, not in fear of the fatal blow being raised above my head, but still in a wordless anger that demanded I complete thrashing my enemy.

I was unsuccessful, and still lay on the floor as the big man raised the bench high over his head to strike down into my own skull. Apparently another man felt things had progressed far enough, and he ended the fight by the simple expedient of kicking the larger man hard in his bared genitals.

No one ever asked after my cuts and bruises. No one ever mentioned the incident again.

Whatever anyone may have thought was wrong with my head, there was nothing wrong with my hearing. The officers continued speaking, oblivious to my existence even as I approached them. I held my gloves in one hand and used the other to wipe the beaded sweat from my brow and fling it from me. Those simulator pods get hot sometimes.

"...expected to be good coming out of the Republic, but this! Wow."

"...hope there's no trouble, I've seen what happens when cadre lose to trainees before."

"At least we know he's got what it takes!"

"Then I just hope he lives long enough to come back and teach himself someday..."

That comment almost made me smile. Living long and coming back to this place; two things that weren't really high up on my list of priorities.

"Quiet, here he comes."

They turned to face me, three field grade officers with the pips of the regular army. I nodded toward them, briefly wondering if they realized that I wouldn't have saluted them even if we had been outdoors where it was mandatory.

"Congratulations, private," one said to me, "that was a fine performance in there. You're exactly the kind of warrior the Protectorate needs to defend her citizens."

I snorted as rudely as I could as I continued to stomp past them, giving far less than two whits about either the Protectorate or her citizens. They were all part of the reason I was here, after all. Of course they resumed speaking to one another, even before I was out of earshot.

"That kind of attitude..."

"...confident that Devine will reign him in..."

"If he doesn't, he can always get killed in the field quickly enough."

I laughed out loud at that last comment. In fact, I was so amused by it that I actually turned back to the officers, witnessing the somewhat startled looks on their faces. I barked out another guffaw.

"That, sir," I said to whomever had spoken last, "would suit me just fine. Just don't get in my way or I may take you with me. Sir." I laughed again then turned and proceeded on my way.

Chapter Eighteen

Slave Lake, Rudyard
Yardsmith
New Paris/Jarvyn Disputed Zone

June 24, 2654

This is not the first time someone has tried to treat me, it is merely the most recent. With varying levels of success, there have been quite a few others. Most successful, in the long run at least, was Father Patrick, chaplain to the Reavers' 1st Mechanized Battalion.

Among the Reavers we were officially encouraged (which is simply a polite, social euphemism for saying required) to attend confession before every mission. I guess since they expected at least a third of the unit to die each year, they wanted all of them to be as ready to meet God as they could be, especially considering the state of most of our souls.

So, without the Father's signature testifying that a particular individual had indeed been through confession, no one could go out on a mission, which didn't sound so bad in and of itself. Of course, to counter that disincentive, if you did fail to get his sign off before a mission you were supposed to be on, you could be summarily discharged, which would mean having any previous charges or warrants reinstated against you.

Somehow, they forgot to mention that part of the program in the recruiting materials that I had been shown.

I sat in that office, a bit too warm and much too tightly confined. The bench I sat upon was comfortably padded, but poorly shaped for extended periods of sitting. Patrick's chair looked much more comfortable, one of those insanely expensive ones designed to be comfortable to sit in for twenty-four hours straight. Between the two of us, a modestly sized, hardwood desk sat cleared of all books and papers. How he had ever managed to convince the bean counters in requisitioning and the tight wads in allocation to allow a simple chaplain to have a desk of that size and weight, in an office this size, on a military transport, I'll never know. Maybe he was more than a simple chaplain, maybe he'd just heard too many confessions and knew too much. He certainly knew a lot about every one of us.

Patrick leaned against the desk, resting on his forearms. "What is it that you honestly want out of all of this, Chase?"

I leaned away from him, resting against the wall behind me. "Death."

A simple answer to a simple question. It gave him pause, though. He looked down at his clasped hands before he asked, "Whose death? Yours?"

"That one would do."

"Truly? Despite God's condemnation of suicide?" He raised an eyebrow questioningly.

I sneered at him. "What God? The same one that you say loves us all? The one that you preach has a purpose and a plan for all of us? Is that by any chance the same one that brought me here by virtue of setting me up to murder my own brother?"

He shook his head sadly. "None of us can presume to understand the mind of God. I can tell you, though, that He does not look upon your brother's death the way you do. He knew what He was doing, and He welcomed Jonny to Him. He also has sent you here for a reason."

Now it was my turn to shake my head. "No, I'm here of my own choice, a consequence of my own actions. I'll not believe in any such God as you preach. Why should He get to claim some unseen benevolent plan for His misdeeds when I must suffer and be judged for mine?"

He sighed. "You look on things with mortal eyes, through a temporal point of view. His eyes are immortal, and His point of view eternal."

"You delude yourself," I shot back. Then I shook my head some more. "Trust me, I've gone where you have not, done what you would not. Believe me, there is no more God, and I've abandoned all faith in Him. You would do well to follow my example."

"Then what end dying? To simply cease? What of all the pleasures and experiences that life yet has to offer? What of the good you do here?"

I barked a laugh at him, loud enough to make him sit back, slightly startled. "I'm here because I have nowhere else to go, because I was pressured into being here, because I get to kill people on a regular basis, and because sooner or later some other idiot will get in a lucky shot and end it all for me." I choked out another bitter laugh. "Remind me to put something in my will to thank whomever does me that favor."

That wasn't an entirely honest answer, though I didn't realize it at the time. Truthfully, I still wanted to serve, to do good in the universe. Jordan hadn't been all that far off in his sales pitch, I did want to make things better somehow. At least, I'd like to believe that I did.

"If you believe in neither God nor the good of a life, yours or anyone else's, then what stays your hand from ending it all yourself? Why not simply step in front of a transport or do a swan dive off your Man O'War?"

I ground my teeth in frustration, angrily clenching my hands into fists where they rested against my thighs. I didn't know how to answer that question because I didn't realize then that I didn't truly want to die. I just thought I did.

"Maybe it's because I'm chicken shit!" I exploded. I could feel the intense heat in my face, it must have been virtually glowing a throbbing red. "Is that what you wanted to hear? Does that make you happy? Maybe it's because no matter how much I hate what I see in the mirror I can't just stick a barrel in my mouth and pull the goddamn trigger! Maybe it's because I've got plenty of hell right here in this life without going to the one in the next just yet!"

He wasn't phased at all by my shouting. Father Patrick had balls of solid steel. He just leaned forward again and gently said, "Then your faith is not as dead as you believe." He paused, but I made no rejoinder, witty or otherwise. Now he leaned all the way back in his chair, crossed one leg over the other, and rested his elbows on his knees. He tented his fingers in front of him in that mannerism many people use to try and look like they're thinking something profound.

"But something is not quite right with your protestations, Chase. I mean, you could have stood trial for murder and been done with life that way. A quick six foot drop, a quick snap of your neck in a noose and life is ended. Or it would be simple enough to allow yourself to be killed in combat, would it not? Just stand around and try to get hit by whatever is out there. We've had Reavers that actually did want to kill themselves, and they always put forth a lot more effort and showed much more creativity than you have in achieving that goal." He raised his hands to tap them against his mouth. "Now you, you continue to take steps to ensure that you go on living. Why all that if you do not truly wish to live?"

I had no answer, and that pissed me off even more. I stood up to storm out. "We're done here. I've got people to kill."

"Perhaps you do," he threw at my retreating back, "but in doing so remember that you also have people to save. So do I. You do your part to save lives and I will do my part to save souls, and mark my words, your soul is very high indeed on my list of targets."

I just stalked off, ignoring, at least by all appearances, everything he said. I didn't even bother to close the door behind me. I was the last on the list to see Patrick, and that meant I had to hurry to get strapped in and ready for our drop.

Our initial entry into the camp on the outskirts of Slave Lake was mostly uncontested. That fact alone seemed so strange, given what we knew about the fanaticism of our opponents. Two months ago, the New Popular Jarvyn Front had lost a cell on Whitaker to the 3rd Mechanized Battalion, and all thirty of them had committed suicide rather than be captured. Last month, we'd accidentally found a shop during a sweep on Caen and they'd thrown everything but the kitchen sink at us before it was all over. That fight had been so brutal I'd been the only survivor of my team, of my whole squad for that matter.

With that kind of response history, it made little sense now that a group as territorial as the NPJF would just let a Parisian task force walk all over one of their main camps with nothing more serious than a few sniping shots at our troops, snipers that were quickly neutralized by our own infantry.

I think it was my surging popularity (I jest, of course) that had won me the honor of being on point. Everyone else was probably hoping that would get me killed off, but it suited me just fine as it gave me the best chance of getting the most kills. Also of getting killed as they hoped, but that was of no consequence. Our infantry had already secured the perimeter, so I led the augmented armor platoon in, three squads strong, my Will O'Wisp bobbing ever so slightly as I moved it forward in a random zigzag pattern. We broke up immediately, first by squad, then by team, to cover the entire area.

Something tickled the back of my neck as I approached the intersection created by a quad group of hangars. It was nothing that I could place my finger on exactly, but something wasn't right. I paused ever so slightly to better examine my overlays. Oh, that's what it was. These hangars to the right were bouncing off too much of my scans to be just the sheet metal they appeared to be. I could still get proper readings from the inside, but something outside of them was putting out a low level of jamming. It was just enough resistance to disguise unarmored infantry on the far side, nothing bigger. It was subtly done, and would have gone unnoticed if I hadn't double checked my hunch.

I slammed my throttle to full, bringing my Will O'Wisp to a headlong sprint, then, with a deft touch, spun it sideways allowing my feet to pull out from under me, laying me down. I slid forward on one side, cannon and rocket launchers ready. The waiting ambushers hadn't anticipated such an insane and unusual maneuver, and their first shots, about a baker's dozen direct fire rockets, flew through the space my torso and head should have occupied. They landed somewhere in the distance with a fairly impressive series of explosions.

I didn't bother to track their flight, I had more pressing matters to attend to. I squeezed my own triggers, unleashing a laser and machine gun salvo sufficient to kill the five of them two or three times over. I'd have launched a rocket burst as well if the stockpile of rockets they had brought along as reloads hadn't gone up so nicely, caving in the sides of the hangars with the force of the blast.

The charred remains of the bodies jutted up from the ground at weird angles, completely unidentifiable as human. The rocket system they'd been armed with was demolished, as were the five rapid personal transports that had been parked behind them. The walls of the hangars had been bashed in, about two meters deep at the center of each crease, and flames licked at the corners of the blackened paint.

Then the talk started. It was all the same words, once again reconstructing familiar phrases.

"Did you see him duck that? No one reacts that fast."

"I know! I saw him just turn and…"

"…cut the chatter, boys and girls. But damn…"

I pulled my Will O'Wisp back to its feet, briefly surveying the damage around me while I only listened to the talk with one ear. On Madrigal I'd long since grown used to new units having this reaction after seeing how I fought for the first time. My berserk style awed them for some reason, when it should have convinced them I was completely stir crazy and to be neither trusted nor admired. Such a reckless disregard for one's own safety and well-being should not be a laudable characteristic under any circumstances, and yet those kids from the Republic almost worshiped it.

Perhaps in the end, it is the world that is crazy, and only those of us that are in here who are truly sane.

At least I can say that the Reavers most certainly didn't worship me. Most of them were convinced I'd put a bullet through the head of anyone who annoyed me too much. Some days I was tempted to do just that. I certainly did do my best to encourage that fearful belief in everyone around me as it had the most desirable effect of making all of them keep their distance and ensured that any annoying questions they might have about my personal history were directed to someone else for answering.

The smoke rising off the burns on the caved in sides of the hangar drifted almost gently across the azure sky. I hated it, it looked too poetic and perfect for the death and destruction that we brought here. I needed to kill something more, these five had not been enough. I flirted momentarily with the idea of trying to shoot one of the birds circling lazily on the warm updrafts, but they were too small to target effectively. Besides, small, inhuman targets do so little to satiate a bloodlust.

"Let's have a look at this hangar complex, Aarons," Prathouvang said, indicating which one with a gesture from his rifle. "It looks to be the biggest, and this is where they set up their ambush, after all."

Neither one of those reasons made any logical sense, but I let it go. I wasn't going to debate our leader on his hunches, maybe they were as accurate as mine. Instead of saying anything, I stomped my Will O'Wisp right through the corrugated metal doors on the hangar to the left, ignoring the awful sound that made, looking for enemy targets. I got lucky right away. A trio dressed in fatigues was squatting around a quad TOW launcher, struggling, it appeared, to attach the optical guidance unit.

I fired a burst of machine gun fire into them, decapitating one rebel and removing large chunks of the second's torso and inner organs. It also had the bonus effect of shattering the launcher in a rather impressive way. The third rebel opened her eyes wide in shock, then threw her hands high in the air, dropping the rifle she'd had slung over her shoulder.

"I surrender!" she called out clearly, the terror in her voice most evident.

I looked at her and studied her for a moment, giving the rest of my team a chance to fall in around me. She probably wasn't more than seventeen, more likely only fifteen or sixteen. Her ivory-skinned face and pale blond hair were in dire need of a good washing, but she was certainly pretty in a perky sort of way. She was obviously young enough and idealistic enough to get involved with a group she likely shouldn't have, but possibly she was reformable. Given time in the right education and treatment facilities, she could probably become an upstanding, productive member of Parisian society.

As I studied her, for a passing moment I had a flashback to my first year in COTC. I remembered holding a gun on a helpless Cadet Marsh as he wondered what had happened to his unit. I'd shot Marsh to cruelly humiliate him, to cause him a kind of pain that he didn't deserve, to boost my ego and salve my own wounded pride. This poor girl was no different, standing helplessly before me. Marsh had deserved better than what I'd given him. This girl deserved a far better chance than the one I gave her.

I fired a quick, two round burst. The first shot amputated her left arm just below the shoulder. The second shot smashed through the corner of her jaw and converted the lower half of her pretty face into a pulpy mist.

"Mon Dieu, why did he do that?"

"How can anyone be so inhumane?"

"Inhuman, more like it..."

It didn't matter. They should be thankful I was here to pick up on ambushes and remove resistance like this with quick, decisive action. That meant they could all wake up for at least one more day and that would bring them another day closer to getting out of the Reavers and maybe making a normal life for themselves.

I smiled grimly, finding a sort of ironic humor in the thought that these questions, while broadcast on team frequencies, were not actually asked of me directly. Apparently I was being quite successful in warding off question of any sort.

"Shut up, both of you," Prathouvang said. "She would have done the same for any of us, given half a chance." He was grasping at straws, but trying to fit his image of how a leader should behave anyway. I could have laughed; I could have wept.

"But we could have interrogated her and..."

"That's enough. Keep us moving, Aarons."

Prathouvang was wrong, that wasn't enough. I needed more targets, bigger kills. That couldn't be all of them. I accelerated just as we'd practiced so many times before, heedless of the confined spaces, and rushed through the rest of the building's offices and attached parts, unsuccessfully seeking any sort of movement or life. We swept into the main hangar bay, the ceiling soaring high even over our Man O'Wars. I immediately stepped right and crouched, sweeping the area for targets. As each team member behind entered, they too took their appointed positions. We must have looked much like some large scale SWAT team as we knelt and turned every which way looking for threats.

Nothing surfaced immediately, but there was so much clutter it was hard to be certain. Heavy equipment was strewn across the entire area. I could see what appeared to be hard cutting tools, lighting equipment, and several dozen generators. Parts of various weapons systems were readily visible, including armor and augmented armor weapons, and, tellingly, several empty munitions racks. In the far corners stood gantries and scaffolding, the ones on the left draped heavily in hoses and wires.

Collem let out a low whistle. "Looks like someone got a fresh support payment from the Jarvies, and they were putting it to work too."

"Split left, Aarons. Take Berring with you. Check those rigs in the corner especially closely."

I clicked a wordless transmission to signal my understanding, then moved off, Berring following some distance behind. His Roadhouse with its heavy multiple launch rocket system and HEPC cannon would be almost useless in this confined environment, not that Berring was anything much above the level of completely useless as a pilot anyway. He was a chatterbox too, when he got nervous it seemed he couldn't shut up for a second.

"What's the plan, Aarons?" he asked inanely.

Naturally, I didn't bother to respond. We'd gone through enough training and standardized exercises to know our positions and responsibilities by heart. Well, most of us had, Berring was probably still clueless.

"So, um, did you know what it was that got everyone here? I mean what they did to get stuck in the Reavers?"

This time I did answer, albeit tersely. "No, I don't. And frankly, I don't give a double damn on a rolling donut. So shut up and pay attention."

He was persistent, though, I'll give him that. Even my bite-your-head-off reputation didn't dissuade him from his need to talk. "Well, Prath was a drug lord, I heard, the biggest on all of Genevieve. Maybe that's why he's such a natural leader, huh?"

I just shook my head in pity, really, as I tried not to get distracted from the task at hand. The man was going to get himself killed for more reasons than just his piss poor piloting abilities. We had to move slowly and carefully, checking every little niche and cranny, so as not to blunder into a quickly fatal ambush or step on a life altering mine. Even a Man O'War can take a long time to cover a single kilometer under those constraints, and the slightest misstep or loss of concentration can have permanent consequences.

Berring continued his annoying if informative lecture. "Collem, no one talks about it too much, but they said he had this thing for little kids. Pretty sick, huh? But I guess he's no worse than the rest of us now, and he's a brother Reaver besides."

Now I was being distracted. I'd known all along that my comrades in arms would be felons of various sorts and forms, but I now understood how one or two ill-made choices could bring one to walk down that path. I'd discovered a tolerance for the mistakes of others I'd never suspected I would have. This thing with children, though, that was something else. I shook my head again, more sharply this time, trying to refocus on the task at hand.

"Me, I was just a commuter pilot until I got a bit too drunk one night after work and ran a family of six off the road and into a tree." He gave a short, nervous little laugh. "I guess that makes me just like you."

That was too much. I spun in place and leveled my main laser cannon straight at the Roadhouse's cockpit window. The end of the cannon actually butted up against the shell and that hundred millimeter barrel must have look very large indeed from where Berring was sitting.

"Get this straight you baboon: you are nothing like me. You are an idiot who took the lives of innocents because of your own stupidity and because you believed you were infallible. You are nothing like me...at all."

I dropped the weapon back to its guard position, then turned to continue on, but that didn't mean I could get those phrases to stop echoing in my head. Berring had struck a raw nerve with an accuracy uncanny for one so incompetent, and I'd provide the wording for my own condemnation. *Because you believed you were infallible.*

Berring changed his topic, but still couldn't halt his chatter, even though he must have been worried that I might kill him. Maybe it was that very fear that made him keep talking.

"Would you look at all this stuff? It's worth a small fortune. If they left all this behind, imagine the value of what they took with them!"

He had another point there. Something very, very important must have taken priority in the evacuation if they left things like this behind.

Eventually we worked our way through all the various pieces of debris without incident, finally getting close enough to the gantry to see what they'd been working on so hard in here. It wasn't pretty.

"Prath," I sent out, "we're done over here. Call in EOD and Hazmat, they've got some bad things to take care of here."

"Copy that, Aarons," he returned. "We've got something here too. Probably the actual payload, if you're looking at the delivery system."

I clicked a wordless acknowledgment again and very carefully began moving back the way we'd come.

"What is it, Aarons?" Berring asked.

In my surprise and preoccupation I forgot that I was supposed to be an intimidating jerk, evidence that perhaps it was more an affectation than my natural state. "It's a bio weapon delivery system. I saw a few types demonstrated in a Guard briefing before we went to Madrigal."

"You fought on Madrigal?" His tone of voice made it clear that he found this even more interesting and surprising than the germ weapon. I cursed my loose tongue and wished to haul every syllable back. "Cool, wait till I tell the others."

I guess he had a very short memory for some things. He needed a gentle reminder of the importance of my privacy and the shallowness of my temper and tolerance for others' stupidity. Again I stopped, and again he stared down the barrel of my laser cannon.

"You'll not tell anyone about that. Ever," I instructed him. "That is my business, and mine alone, and it will stay that way."

I actually heard him swallow. "S-s-sure, Aarons. Whatever you say, no problem. Your past's safe with me."

I didn't believe that for an instant. At the first opportunity for gossip, Berring would make certain that everyone in the unit knew I'd fought on Madrigal. That would be followed by wild rumors and rampant speculation. So be it, it was too late now. The cat was out of the bag and it was my own fault. I turned and led the way back to regroup with the others outside.

"Back to extraction," Prathouvang told us. "All the sweeps are finished and the whole camp is being quarantined for the lab boys. We're the lucky ones who will be taking a suborbital hop over to Camp Pike to see if we can't find something more substantial there."

I snorted. That seemed unlikely, but was typical military intelligence. It would take us a full eight hours to get to Pike, and the NPJF would definitely know we were on the way by now. If they stuck around, it would be with plenty of advance notice and lots of preparation time to make those nasty little surprises. Still, someone had to go check it out for further clues to their operations and other bases, and I guess we, of the teams sent to Slave Lake, had drawn the short straw to go to Pike.

It was early spring in this part of the world. The air was crisp and clear, and patches of brilliantly white snow were still visible in the deepest shade, even in the failing light. Game trails were abundant, as were other signs of animal life. We made too much noise for them to remain visible, but they were all around us.

Pike was a gorgeous little camp, literally built in the forest. The trees were a distinctly blue form of a coniferous type and grew thickly in between buildings, or more accurately, only enough trees had been cleared to construct each of the buildings. Intelligence said it was originally built as a retreat for political leaders and think tank members, but evidently had fallen into disuse until the NPJF had bought it up with one of their front companies.

None of the buildings were big enough to house armor or augmented armor, and that meant we were relegated to providing security for the infantry as they went door to door in their own searches. That explained why only one augmented armor team had come along. I hated it. I would have preferred combat to just crouching behind a tree for a half hour, then getting up and moving two hundred meters only to repeat the same boring process behind a yet another tree. Nevertheless, that's how it went for three tedious hours.

"Aarons, Collem," Prathouvang called out. "The EOD team is breaking up to cover more ground. You two move up to the far side of camp and secure it. Move back this way as they clear the buildings and we'll meet in the middle. Be careful, we've already found more than one mine around here."

It sounded like a stupid plan to me, dividing our already small force, but we were out in the middle of nowhere and unlikely to actually be attacked, so I didn't protest. I just clicked a confirmation. Across the camp, barely visible, I could just make out Collem's Mirage mirroring my own movements as I rose from my crouch and slowly worked my way through the trees. The infantry and EOD units we were to escort were already bounding ahead of us, but we kept the pace slow anyway.

"So," Collem said on a private, scrambled frequency as we reached our first security point, "it's just the two of us working together."

Unlike Berring, Collem had never before evidenced any great need to talk simply for the sake of talking. There must have been a reason for him to start the conversation or he'd not have done so. As was my usual wont, I said nothing, I merely concentrated on moving slowly and carefully through the trees, looking for a good place to hunker down. I stepped gingerly, alert for any suspicious signs of an attack, ambush, or booby-trap that I wouldn't easily see now that night was falling.

"Berring says you fought on Madrigal."

So that's what this was about. Again I didn't reply, I had nothing to add. I was confident he'd continue.

"So do you think that makes you special, Reppie boy? Think that makes you tough? Berring, he told me you were a coward who ran away ‘cause you couldn’t take it anymore.”

I smiled. If only that had been true. I almost laughed aloud at the thought. If only, Jonny, if only.

“He told me you think you’re tough, too, threatening to kill him twice back there.”

This had taken a nasty turn. I’ve noted before the nature of some humans to push everything to the limit. In my polite moments I call them stupid. When I’m not feeling so civil, I have other terms involving a lot more expletives. So be it, if he wanted to play pecking order we could do that.

“Interesting,” I said without expression. “He told me that you enjoyed little boys and girls.”

He laughed softly through his nose. “I still do, Aarons. Remember our little excursion on Io? It’s not like they don’t want it though, and I never killed any of them.” He clicked his tongue. “Does that bother you, Reppie? Still think you’re better than me? What if I tell you I’ll go right back to it once I’m out of the Reavers, out from under their thumbs? Are you going to threaten me the same way you threatened Berring? Are you, tough guy?”

A glance through my displays confirmed my hunch that he had most of his weaponry focused directly at me if not yet locked on, even though he was still walking forward and ostensibly searching for a secure spot. I smirked and casually put a nice thick tree between us. Then I pivoted in place and doubled back on my tracks, activating my electronic counter measures as I went.

Collem realized what was going on when he lost all contact with me. “Aarons? What the hell are you doing?” I imagined I could hear him quickly hitting switches and making control adjustments as he realized that he couldn’t see me through my camouflage and electronic screens in the low light.

I smiled even more tightly as I paced my Will O’Wisp carefully through the forest, hunting after Collem’s Mirage.

“Aarons?” Some tightness was starting to bleed through in his voice. Apparently he was remembering all those rumors about me and how little respect I had for human life. Maybe he was remembering how callously I’d executed that girl back at Slave Lake. Whatever, I was better than him and he knew it. “Knock it off, man, I was just trying to make a point.”

“So am I,” I told him. The fool only now engaged his own ECM package. The Mirage’s ECM suite was actually superior to the Will O’Wisp’s, but you wouldn’t notice the difference unless you were in something like an airborne detection unit. To everything less, they were equally invisible. In any event, it was too late for that, I already had a direct, if rough, visually enhanced fix on his position.

He started moving off, slowly, as if uncertain of what to expect from me. "Aarons, this isn't freaking funny!" Good, he was panicking just as I'd hoped. Now to push him over the edge.

"Do you know where I am, pedophile?"

The response was slow but honest. "N-no," he stammered out. "Hey, you've made your point. You're the big man, I'll knock it off. Let's just stop all this and get back to work."

"This is my work." I said it as low and threateningly as I could, forcing my voice to personify brutality. Like Oppenheimer so very long ago I softly, quoted from the Bhagavad-Gita, "I am become death." I fired a carefully aimed shot from my laser. The invisible beam sliced off a heavy tree branch which bounced off the Mirage's shoulder before crashing to earth. "The destroyer of worlds."

Collem turn ninety degrees and ran. "You're crazy, man!" he shouted as he darted his Mirage deeper into the woods.

That wasn't what I'd intended, I had thought he'd run back to the others. He was supposed to be scared, to get the point and learn a valuable lesson about messing with me and talking about kids. He wasn't supposed to step on a mine.

The explosion was very impressive, as would be required to kill a Man O'War, lighting up the twilit sky with a riot of colors. I cut my ECMs and carefully picked my way along the path that Collem had followed through the forest. The Mirage was lying in a heap, burning quite heavily, shattered almost completely by the force of the explosion. I carefully picked my way around the fallen giant, careful to watch for any secondary explosives that hadn't gone off already.

"You bastard," Collem choked and coughed at me. His broadcast signal was weak and I had no doubt that, even if were he to try, he couldn't call out to the others. No doubt he was injured in some way by that blast, he probably wasn't going to be able to save himself. I tried to think about how to best get him out of the wreck. I decided I'd have to actually go down and use the emergency manual access hatch.

I was halfway out of my harness when he spoke again. "You son of a bitch, I just wish one of those kids had been yours, or your little brother or sister."

I paused. "You what?"

A fit of coughing, likely from the smoke. "Yeah, just me and your brother. That would have been fun, eh Aarons?"

I held myself there in mid-motion, but I didn't say anything.

"Yeah, maybe when I've done my time I'll go visit your family. You'd like that, wouldn't you?" I could hear metal scraping on metal. He was probably trying to pry open the escape hatch from the inside.

I sat back down in my couch and put my harness back on. The Mirage was almost completely consumed by the flames now. Soon, enough of the cockpit would be enveloped. I added the team frequency to our communications, keeping our local one open so Collem could hear.

"Prath, this is Aarons."

"Aarons," Prathouvang said immediately. "What's the sit-rep?"

I looked down at the shattered Man O'War and the evil man inside, weighing my options. "Collem stepped on a mine, a big one. His Mirage is totaled."

"What about Collem, did he eject? Can you get him out?"

I carefully lined myself up with the cockpit window. "No, he didn't make it."

The scraping from Collem stopped. "Aarons? What are you doing?"

"Saving my soul."

I kicked the cockpit full on. Three more times I reared back my Will O'Wisp's gigantic foot and crashed it down into the Mirage's cockpit assembly. I stopped and examined the burning wreck, confirming that, if the pilot was still alive, he had no hope of escaping the all consuming flames.

I turned and walked back, alone in the night.

Collem stayed and burned, alone in the night.

Chapter Nineteen

Reaver Carrier *Justice*
Jump Point Zulu Three: Inbound To Komodo
Morganin Chain
Jarvyn

April 3, 2656

"No more innocents will die." Marcy thumped the pulpit for emphasis. "No more citizens killed in their homes, no more children slain in school, no more elderly burned in their beds."

There are no innocents, I immediately thought, *not anymore. They don't exist and even if they did they've no right to, not while the rest of us struggle so hard and still suffer.*

The minister surveyed the room. "Today we will crush the heart and head of the BLA with one decisive blow. We will show them the fate of terrorists and send a warning to all others of their ilk. We will hunt them out from amongst their rocks and we will end this here and now, on our terms and by the grace of God, but on their soil!"

Applause and cheers echoed around the room. For some reason the entire assembled might of the Reavers greeted this call to battle as some sort of righteous cause blessed of God. I harbored no such delusions. I didn't really believe in any God, but if one were to exist, I doubted He would countenance the murders we were plotting. It didn't matter to me. One more murder on my soul would be like dropping another handful of salt in an ocean, but neither was I going to lie to myself about the true nature of the deed.

My sneer and snort were not terribly subtle and I'm sure Marshal Davis would have appreciated it if I had been more tactful. That was just too bad, though, since he wanted my experience and training in a leadership role, he would have to put up with me as myself. If he'd wanted tact he should have promoted someone else. Also, he should have known better than to put me in the front row of the auditorium.

I guess the Marshal had his reasons, though. He hadn't even known me from Adam until I'd been commended for heroism above and beyond after that debacle on Summersand. It must have been some ingrained instinct that had made me take over command when the shit hit the fan. Still, I couldn't understand why that would prompt the man in charge of the Protectorate's entire special operations command to take a personal hand in guiding my career. Maybe he too saw a destiny I'd once believed in.

Everyone rose when Marcy stepped away from the head table, and several of his retinue of ass-kissers glanced my way repeatedly. Two of them spoke to one another in those subtle whisper-behind-a-hand moves that only serve to advertise to the whole world that you're talking about someone.

The room broke into a hundred separate conversations as the assembled officers began discussing what we'd just been told by the Minister. I resumed my seat and waited as the pair that had been exchanging whispers finally talked themselves into coming down off the podium and approaching me.

"You don't seem to agree with the Minister, Capitaine," the bald one said. His name plate read du Smith and his rank and uniform branded him a colonel in the regular forces. He wore the insignia of augmented armor, but that didn't mean much, most Protectorate field grade officers do, regardless of whether or not they have ever actually served in that role.

His companion wore only civilian clothes and a bland expression, so I had no idea of his exact position. Obviously, though, his comparative rank must be close to du Smith's else they wouldn't be together thus. Likely he was some fairly powerful government attaché, an undersecretary or some such.

As was usually the case, I was in the perfect mood to pick a fight. I blatantly refused to rise to my feet again, even going so far as to lean back in my chair as though I were the one dressing them down. This had every hallmark of being a good conversation, just the type I enjoyed with so-called superiors.

I raised my eyebrows at the two men. "I can't comment on the man's ability as minister of foreign affairs, though he certainly talks a good line to stir up the troops, I'll give you that. He certainly made everyone want to go down there and kick some butt. Unless you've spent your whole life listening to Parisian propaganda like you local boys, however, you'll know he's full of shit."

"Excuse me?" The colonel's eyes bulged out a bit at my vulgarity. I almost smiled, but that would have ruined the effect.

"New Paris has stomped on the BLA every single time they've so much as organized a political party. You've left them no way to be heard, no opportunity to air their grievances, and then you act all surprised and wronged when they have to blow up government buildings and school buses to get attention. Maybe you should have just listened to them. Oh, but then someone else might hear what they have to say and think they were right, and you couldn't have that."

"That's a pretty serious accusation, Capitaine," the civilian said softly.

"It's not an accusation, just a recounting of the truth," I shrugged. "Until five years ago the BLA had never harmed a fly, and then they suddenly began to bomb schools and office towers for what you called 'no apparent reason.' The general population is ignorant and bought your official story about 'madmen' and 'evil incarnate' and such, but you and I know better, and so would anyone who took the time to do their research." I started ticking points off on my fingers. "Three times the BLA has tried to organize a national political party, three times they've been dismantled by force and barred from public office. A total of eighty-four different high level sympathizers have been 'disappeared' in the last two decades when they tried to run on other parties' tickets. Ten local elections have been overturned, and the head of the BLA has been in jail for twenty-five years now, yet no one has ever filed charges against him."

"That's a very impressive bit of research," the colonel's companion said, his cool expression not changing save for a slight raising of the eyebrows.

"I like to know who I'm killing, it helps avoid unpleasant surprises like getting killed. Just who the hell are you, anyway?" I blurted, pointing a finger directly at him.

He smiled as though sharing an impressive secret. "I'm the Minister's intelligence analyst. Colonel du Smith and I collaborate on much of our work."

"You're a spook," I accused him. He continued smiling, yet nodded a confident little acknowledgment.

"Too bad your theory's all crap, Capitaine," du Smith put extra emphasis on my rank to drive home his own superior one. "These are murdering scum who chose their own path to walk down. You've seen the footage from Rein, how can you not think they are evil? How can you not think they deserve the justice we are about to bring them?"

"Colonel," I said with a shake of my head, "I cannot deny that the people we are about to go down and kill are murderers who have slain, as you term them, 'innocent' men, women, and children indiscriminately. They have made attacks without warning and without taking responsibility for them afterwards. They now seek nothing less than the total overthrow of the Protectorate's established government. But whatever they may be now, you must accept the fact that you are the ones who made them what they are, you are the ones who are responsible for each and every single one of those deaths. Now you are going to go down there and kill the monster you created, and you label that justice. A bold faced lie, I call it."

Du Smith flared angrily. "How dare you?"

Now I rose, coming to stand face to face with the colonel. I curled my lip and tilted my head slightly to one side. "I dare because it's me that's going down there to do the killing and the dying, Colonel, and not you. Now, I'd bet that you probably wouldn't understand what that's like, since you regulars decide whom to promote beyond field grade command on the basis of some outmoded notion of nepotism. Maybe to you being related to a career politician is an important qualification for leading men into battle, but for those of us who have actually been there in the crucible, that means nothing. We think you're a joke, a very bad one."

That had the desired effect of tightening his collar. "Boy, I have attended the finest warfare colleges and institutions in this galaxy and learned everything there is to know about modern warfare. By damn, I'll wager that I've forgotten more about organizing and fighting a war than you'll ever know."

I snorted. "I've killed more men in a single morning than you've done for in your entire career. Go away, Colonel, you're bothering me."

I don't know which entertained me more, the fact that he was so flustered at my insubordination that he couldn't reply, or the fact that he actually *did* go away. One could get used to that sort of thing.

"That was ill done, Capitaine," the spook said. "The colonel has proven himself in combat on at least two occasions now. Not a lot by your standards, I know, but more than you give him credit for. By all accounts he is a fair warrior, good enough to have survived some very tight situations. Besides, he and his brigade will be dropping down with you, so doesn't that say something?"

That surprised me. "Why in heaven's name would he do that?"

He shrugged. "I guess maybe you don't know everything that you think you do, Capitaine." Then he walked away.

"Whatever you say," I called to his retreating back, though I didn't pitch my voice loud enough so that he could hear me, "just don't expect me to bail him out of whatever trouble he finds down there."

"All troops prepare for drop! All troops prepare for drop!"

The announcement blared over the ship's intercom a bit sooner than I'd expected. It didn't matter, I was just sitting with my platoon leaders in our briefing room doing nothing but make-work. Ostensibly I was getting a brief back from them, but the discussion had pretty much degenerated into a debate over whether I was right or wrong to be riding down in Thomlin's boat since it would land first, God willing. The point was moot, I wasn't about to go to all the trouble of moving my Man O'War from where it was already parked in the boat. I let the argument go anyway because I understood that they just needed something to defuse their nerves and keep them from thinking about the risks of the coming drop.

"All right kids," I said at the alarm, "go get your little ones and tuck them in tight. Let's see if we can't bring everyone back together one more time, non?" They all wished me luck as they left, Gurgi waving her hands over my head and invoking some sort of blessing on me as she went. Even after they'd all left, I lingered behind, mulling over my own thoughts about the mission.

That poor bastard Berring, eighteen months dead now, God have mercy on his soul, had been right. These people were my brothers and sisters now, all of them. Thomlin was a former freedom fighter/terrorist himself, Gurgi a major crime lord's head of prostitution. In fact, as Jordan had said so long ago my entire company was filled with murderers, dope peddlers, rapists, and terrorists, but every single one of them had changed. All of them were trying to make things work out better this time around, trying to make their lives mean something. I knew that for a fact because I'd built this unit up from the refuse pile it had been a little over a year ago. After a few more Collem-type incidents, we'd sorted the chafe from the wheat. Together, as a unit closer and stronger than any I'd ever seen, even in the Guard, we'd come through more missions with less losses than command believed possible.

This was my family now, and that bothered me.

I pounded the table with a fist and swore loudly. This was most definitely not the time to be getting all maudlin about how much I'd come to care for these misfits of mine. We weren't going off on another lighting strike or raid against a cell, we were off to a real war this time, with a real enemy awaiting us planet side. Sentiment could come later, round about the same time as we buried our dead.

I stood, tugged my uniform straight, slapped on my cockiest smirk and followed Thomlin to the launch bays.

I caught up with him just as he was counting the last of his warriors through the dropship's upper drop bay hatch. "Good to go, Greg?"

"Yes, sir. Everyone is ready and we are set."

I clapped him on the shoulder. "Let's do this."

He started to smile, then focused on something over my shoulder. "What's all this, sir?" He pointed with his chin.

I turned to follow his gaze. He was looking at the situation board where it displayed live feed reports on fleet position, air cap cover and the like. The board, normally green and friendly, had gone livid with angry reds and yellows, spewing out a list far too long to be accounted for by what resistance we had expected.

"I have no idea," I frowned. "That's an awfully large number of orbital defenses. Something's not right."

The picture feed showed a group of fighters streak by, strafing one of the other carriers, eating up plenty of turret fire in return. Something really bothered me about that, but I couldn't place my finger square on it. Thomlin figured it out though.

"Where did all of this stuff come from? Sir, combat fighter craft are a hobby of mine, and those are Krupp Pfeils, I'd swear to it! And that platform is a Mark XII, straight out of Gottenheim!"

"This isn't what we planned for," I admitted. "Look, we've already lost a tenth of our orbital fighters." That was scary too, because these were Protectorate regulars, the Reavers had no aviators. "This, as the ancient proverb warns, just got interesting."

"What of the mission, sir?" Thomlin asked. "Is this changing our plans?"

I turned back to him. "Why would it? Command is sitting in their war rooms right now with a much better idea of what's going on. When they decide to change our orders, they'll let us know. Unless we hear differently, we're still on because some very smart people still think we can accomplish our objective down there." I sure hoped that was true. I was just afraid that too many people making decisions were as petty and shallow, not to mention just plain stupid, as Colonel du Smith appeared to be. "Besides, since when did we worry about a few extra fliers buzzing around in the sky?"

He nodded, but opened his mouth to say something anyway. Whatever it was, he didn't get the chance, because the com system blared loudly once again. "Five minutes to drop! Five minutes to drop!"

We both dove down the hatch, one right behind the other, literally sliding down the ladder. We split apart the moment we hit the drop bay floor, racing to our assigned machines. I cursed myself for finding a spot so far from the hatch, but I'd wanted to be right in front of the landing ramp so I could be out quickly. Now I wondered if I'd make it to my seat in time to avoid being splashed into multiple pieces when the boat started its decent and requisite high G maneuvers.

I almost ran right by my Man O'War, I was in such a hurry. I skidded to a halt and dragged myself up the ladder. Halfway up the rungs the next announcement came.

"Two minutes to drop!"

I hauled myself into the waiting open cockpit and quickly strapped myself in. Even before I did a final systems and safety check, I was calling all my platoon leaders for status checks. They probably wondered why I was breathing so hard, no doubt sounding like an emphysemic humpback whale with a bagpipe stuck in its throat, but they didn't mention it. Everyone reported in fine; Man O'Wars and warriors alike ready for the trial ahead.

"Drop in thirty seconds!"

We were all locked in tight, crammed as firmly in our dropships as sardines in their cans. I now made absolutely certain that every one of the seven clamps that held my Will O'Wisp was fastened properly, I wasn't any more intent on getting smashed into pieces inside my cockpit than I'd been outside it. These Flurry class dropships, big and bulky as they were, were also fast and maneuverable, and they proved it all the time with various jinks and jukes. Even with the partial acceleration shields and velocity shunts a vessel that big carries, it was hardly the most comfortable way to get to a planet's surface. The Flurry's various high-speed maneuvers avoided all kinds of nastiness coming the other way, though, and that meant it got you there quick and usually in one more-or-less contiguous piece. That was pretty important to me and all the folks with me.

That was probably the first moment when I consciously realized that I did not want to die anymore. What's more, it dawned on me that I never really had wanted to. It was not the most opportune or welcome time for such an epiphany, just before I was probably about to die anyway, but that was when the realization came nevertheless.

I felt the rough shudder as our boat released from the carrier's belly, then a fairly noticeable shove forced me up against my restraints as we accelerated rapidly away from the gigantic ship. I hurriedly patched myself in to the boat's tactical feeds. Some pilots have no problem relaxing on a combat drop, blissfully and thankfully unaware of what is happening on the other side of the boat's walls. They play music or games, some even read books. I was definitely not one of those people, I had to see for myself what was going on.

It wasn't a pretty sight. Actually, from an aesthetic point of view, it was very pretty if you discounted all the dying and such. Brightly colored columns of plasma rose everywhere, causing the most amazing colors shifts in everything close enough to reflect the light. Beautiful fireballs blossomed around us, sometimes very close to us. Anti-aircraft fire from the orbital platforms, and even a fair amount from the surface, was filling local space with missiles and cannon fire that streaked through the starry heavens, often reflecting brilliant flashes of light as they went.

I'd programmed my displays to back trace the different weapons, and color them in different hues according to type. Everywhere around us the invisible streaks of energy pulses put on a show that most performers could only dream of. It was terribly beautiful, and, frighteningly, terribly deadly as well.

Our aviator banked us hard, just avoiding a plasma stream and the satellite that emitted it. The boat behind us was not so lucky, exploding instantly in a superheated ball of flame. An entire company of infantry had been on that boat. So many dead, so quickly.

A cannon shell the size of my Man O'War rushed up from the surface at incredible velocity. It tore past us and smashed into the side of the *Justice*. The explosion was amazing as a corner of the ship tore loose, it's venting atmosphere burning up in the blast. The comm channels went haywire with calls for rescue coming in from fighters, escape pods, wounded dropships, and even individuals ejected from their craft yet still alive in their environmental suits.

I admit it readily, I was scared. I'd never felt so helpless in combat before. Always it had been me in the pilot's seat, me making the decisions, all me. It didn't help that this was my first truly contested combat drop, either. It was nerve wracking, and I knew we'd chosen to land in an area fairly close to their base in order to minimize their reaction time. If resistance here was so heavy, what would it be like at our drop zone?

We swooped down through the raging orbital battle, our gunners taking opportunity shots at whatever they thought they could hit. At least one of them tagged an orbital fighter that was chasing one of our own dropfighters. It took only a moment for us to pass through that level of combat, then we hit the atmosphere.

The jolt of impact smashed me hard to the side of my cockpit, only my helmet tether preventing my head from bouncing off the wall. I guess that's one of the reasons why we wear the things. The tactical feeds showed heavy energy weapon fire inundating the sky around us. Our jamming and interference were successful enough to make it inaccurate, but it only took one or two lucky shots to end one of these trips unpleasantly, and there were a lot of shots out there.

As if the thought alone had summoned it, we were hit by something. I can't say whether it was an energy weapon or not, but it blasted into the drop bay on the other side of the boat, shaking the whole dropship violently. We didn't lose any vital systems, but our hull integrity had been severely compromised, and three Man O'Wars were torn free of their harnesses and sucked out to plummet to the planet below. If that shot had hit the cockpit or the engines, we all would have been like those warriors and had a few minutes to enjoy free fall before we buried ourselves several meters in the ground.

Almost as soon as we were low enough for them to be effective, two atmospheric fighters were vectoring in on us. One of the other boats' gunners capped the first one with a missile, the other cut off after an aborted strafing run, chasing one of the dropfighters that had made atmospheric entry with us. Likely, that would be an easy kill, no dropfighter could compete one on one with a dedicated atmospheric.

That observation made me think of Rachel, something I'd tried very hard not to do for a very long time. Tears leapt unbidden to my eyes and I wanted to weep, but my body was already gripped tight in the throws of panic, it had no energy to spare for sorrow and regret. The blast shields of my heart descended again as I took hold and forced myself to concentrate on the present.

We were within range of the flak cannons and other projectile weaponry now, and we were feeling it. The explosions hadn't hit us yet, though several other boats that I could see were not so lucky, but we were being buffeted hard by the shockwaves. Occasionally I even heard a piece of shrapnel clanging off of the hull.

I watched as a small flight of our bombers was able to make a quick pass over the drop zone, a trail of flashes and fire igniting behind them. One of them appeared to just snap in half when it got hit by triple A fire. The rest of the flight just sped onward. Quickly behind them, a fur ball of fighters from both sides tangled over the fate of the bombers. Then we were through them, too.

The ground rushed up so fast I thought we were going to be drilling a deep crater on impact, and then a huge weight shoved me to the very bottom of my chair as the pilot decelerated at maximum power. I almost lost consciousness as all the blood in my body rushed to my feet, my larger physical stature and height proving one of the reasons why women are better aviators. I did a few funky chickens but managed to recover as we touched down.

That term is not really an accurate description, of course. We actually slammed into the ground like an elephant trying to chase eagles over a cliff. We hit the surface hard enough that one of the Man O'Wars in the rank behind mine broke free of its harness, all of the clamps simply ripping free. The machine, completely loose, bounced several times and slammed to the floor hard before rolling to a stop leaning against the legs of another pair of Thomlin's soldiers.

I'm not certain how well the landing struts absorbed such abuse, but my spine complained noticeably. Even so, the very second we made contact, even while still bouncing around, I powered up all my systems. As soon as the boat stabilized I disconnected my umbilical (which provided my feeds; local communication; even power and air so that I didn't deplete my own supplies) and released the clamps gluing me in place. The ramps were already dropping to let in the darkened sky.

Despite my rank, I was once again the first out the door. I'd always done it that way, and nothing was going to change that. Besides, I was getting positively claustrophobic sitting in there waiting for something to shoot us.

The infantry were already on the ground, the DZ secured. Flares were scattered through the air, sailing gently across the sky, lighting an atmosphere darkened by night and the cloudy haze from the contrails of missile and shell fire. The Flurry tossed another half dozen flares into the air just as I stepped out onto the planet's surface, followed by several bursts from its large cannon. A salvo of rocket artillery came next, targeted to hit somewhere in the unseeable distance.

Smoke rolled over us almost immediately; some was created by both sides' attempts to screen the other, some a byproduct of all the shooting and burning going on around us. The terrain was lightly wooded and very hilly. Infantry scampered across the landing zone in numbers greater than I'd ever seen in combat before as the Protectorate marines and regular army troops joined with their Reaver counterparts.

I accelerated away from the boat, Thomlin's platoon right behind me. Maybe a heartbeat later the next boat over from ours took a direct hit from an artillery round. Shrapnel spattered against my armor as the shockwave bounced me forward, but, since it didn't kill me, there was no time to worry about it.

"Thomlin, can you see if the other boats are down yet?" I called out.

"Yes, sir," he replied promptly. "Marshall and Vinde are..."

Those were very nearly his last words as a kinetic round tore the head off his Man O'War and smashed it into a very small package. I didn't see how he could possibly survive, but a brief instant later his ejection seat successfully rocketed away from the ruins of this cockpit.

I dashed my own Man O'War right up the side of the hill ahead of me and laid it down on the slope just short of the crest. Infantry and augmented armor from a dozen different units joined me there, somewhat sheltered from an overpowering hail of fire that decimated those left more exposed.

"That's a lot of armor and augmented stuff out there," said one of the infantrymen nearby. He spoke to no one in particular. "What the hell is going on?"

As more fire whipped past us and rained down from above, I figured we had two choices, either go win this battle or get back in the boats and hightail it out of here. Two more boats went up in impressive fireballs, and several more took off for safer locales, effectively removing one of those choices.

"Follow me!" I shouted out the ancient infantry phrase across every channel and at maximum amplification on my external speakers. I hoped it would motivate all of those around me, because we were going to do the single most difficult thing anyone can ever do in war: we were going over the top. The response was overwhelming. At least a hundred voices responded to my own shout with various wordless battle cries of their own and, as a single mass, we stepped over the top.

Kinetic weapons sliced through the infantry ranks, knocking them down like dominos. Energy weapons and bigger kinetic weapons did the same to our augmented armor. Explosions from artillery, rockets, missiles, and cannons decimated our ranks. None of that mattered. We surged forward, as relentless and unstoppable as the waves of the sea.

An endless wall of opponents greeted us, or so it seemed. Armor, infantry, and a few scattered augmented armor units hunkered down in their prepared positions and fired away at us. Their defenses were not truly hardened, just some holes and trenches with earthwork thrown up in front, exactly what you would expect from someone with foreknowledge of an invasion but little time to prepare for it.

It had been a long time since I'd fought on the line like this, and never in such numbers. It brought its own rush with it, unique amongst all of human activity. It's the rush of being a part of something so scary, so dynamic, so hugely important, so much bigger than your small and insignificant self, and so everlastingly alive in the face of so much death. Anyone who has ever been in the midst of a hometown crowd when their team wins the final game of the championship playoff has felt a similar sensation. This phenomenon is about a billion times more powerful, though. It's a heady drug that makes cowards into warriors, boys into men, and men into heroes.

It also makes warriors and heroes into corpses.

A series of explosions bloomed between me and Thomlin's platoon. I wove away from them, separating myself from my Man O'Wars. It didn't matter. There were plenty of infantry bouncing along beside me. I fired off all of my rockets, taking no time to aim them, confident that there were sufficient targets to guarantee that something would be hit. My laser cannon throbbed and grew hotter with the sustained fire. I ran, I jumped, I dropped, I rolled, and I got up to keep on running.

It was as if my berserk fighting madness became horrifically contagious and took hold of every man and woman there. Together we surged forward, heedless of our innumerable losses, until we dropped into the enemy's very trenches, foxholes, and sandbagged positions.

Farther up the hill a mortar platoon began lobbing rounds down on us, unconcerned about their own troops being exposed to the blasts. Anyone left in the open quickly took shelter in the trenches. Those that were too slow flattened out and took their chances in the open with the heavy mortar barrage.

I rolled my Will O'Wisp into one end of an armor trench, burning a hole through the first tank's weak rear armor as I fell. The explosive pressure and heat created as the laser passed through the internal compartment, superheating everything it even grazed, killed the crew. Then I pulled up close beside it so the armor could protect me somewhat. There I crouched while the mortar platoon showered us with every bit of ammunition they had.

Our initial mad charge had worked far better than it should have, another indication of our opponents' lack of preparation, but now we risked being stopped cold. If something didn't change we would sit here until we were eventually pounded into the ground.

I moved cautiously from around my precious tank, literally crawling through the trench on hands and knees. When I reached the first bend I peered cautiously around, wary of meeting a large bore gun coming the other way looking for me. Luck was definitely with me, this portion of the trench at least was occupied by our infantry, and what sure looked like Gurgi.

"Susan," I called to her as I trotted forward. "Where's the rest of the platoon? Where's the company?"

"I've only got two squads here, this one and one up clearing the trench. The other two are over with Greg. Last I saw he was diving into the next trench over."

"We've got to get closer so we can rush those mortars." Another long series of explosions underscored my comment. One round landed close to the lip of the trench, partially collapsing one wall and spraying all of us with dirt. "Come on."

More troops, mostly infantry, were managing to find the relative safety of the trench, and it was becoming crowded. The last thing we needed was to be bunching up, but we couldn't very well stay out in the open right now.

Gurgi and I worked our way far enough forward to catch up with her advanced squad. They'd killed a half dozen tanks and two score infantry and moved us far enough up the hill that we were no longer directly targeted by the heavy bombardment.

"Let's go," I told them all. We stepped over the threshold just in time to see three attack fighters swoop down on the hilltop, releasing several bombs. They pulled up sharply, racing off into the wild blue yonder while the hill sprung a new fountain of flame.

A cheer rang up from all of us, infantry and augment armor alike, and we resumed our mad rush up the slopes. We crested the hill at flank speed, and there we stopped. In the far distance of the valley, maybe ten or twenty kilometers away, we could see what appeared to be thousands of units positioning themselves. Giant Titan-class dropships, originally designed for transporting ore to orbital manufacturing facilities, stood in the distance disgorging troops. The arms of Krupp stood out boldly on their sides.

Their air cap swarmed thickly through the skies.

"Tabernacle," Gurgi swore. "How could we not know of all this? How could they hide it all?"

"What do we do now?" someone else asked. Her answer came quickly enough.

"Fall back to the boats! Reavers first, Regulars will cover!" That voice sounded familiar. Was it really du Smith? I searched my boards and located the speaker in a Lance not too far over.

"Fall back!" This cry was taken up even more readily than the attack had been, and instantly every Reaver was bouncing and running back for the boats. The Regulars spread out their line, slowly moving backward even as we could see aircraft and ground units vectoring our way.

I trotted toward the Colonel's Man O'War. "Colonel, you can't hold this. Bring your troops back with us, we can cover each other."

"Aarons," I could easily hear the disdain he put into my name. "I am not a coward and I am not going to run. We will cover your withdrawal. Now get moving!"

I cursed his folly, even as I activated my ECM suite preparatory to being attacked. The stupidity of his willingness to sacrifice so many soldiers (for there was no way they could successfully retreat if they stayed put long enough to actually engage the Krupps) merely to prove that his courage was up to the challenge angered me. I wished someone would put a bullet through him right then and there.

Then the Krupp aircraft were strafing us, and someone did just that. The colonel's Lance folded in on itself, the torso missing between the chest and hips. My computer grabbed a quick lock and I put a laser beam through the engine of one of the attack craft. It spun lazily to earth, heavily spewing smoke. The aviator ejected safely, something du Smith had yet to do.

Then our own aircraft were there, God bless their courageous souls. Without their insane dive into the Krupps' superior numbers, we would have been blasted flat by repeated air strikes.

I can't tell you why I stood over du Smith's wrecked Lance then. I hated the man; I thought he very much deserved to die and that it would be good for all of humanity if he did so with haste. By protecting his fallen Man O'War I was making myself the most conspicuous target on the battlefield, yet I did it anyway.

After the aircraft had passed we received the first wave of augmented armor. The infantry met them on the horns of Dragons, and I put one down with my cannon, but the infantry kept working their slow way back to the boats. Only one small team with red crosses painted conspicuously on their unarmed armor broke away to approach us.

The next wave of augmented armor to break over the crest was likewise received in the Dragons' maw, but nine or ten remained even after the infantry expended their armor killing weaponry. Now useless in the face of so much heavy equipment, the infantry lit off in rout as much as retreat. Only a half dozen Man O'Wars remained to back me up, and they were far behind me.

In true Krupp fashion our opponents accelerated into us, firing everything they had. I'd like to say that I accounted for most of the enemy, but that wouldn't have been true. What I did manage to do was mess them up sufficiently to allow my allies to eliminate them.

It must have been so frustrating for them, rushing down that hill straight at me and wondering why they couldn't get their targeting systems to lock on. That gave me enough time to successfully drop to one knee and skewer one of them, taking its leg off at the hip. I rolled sideways as they opted just to shoot in my general direction with cannons and rockets. Earth and rock kicked up all around me, a few shots even tore into the left side of my armor, but I was still functional.

The warriors behind me were not inactive, and their missiles and energy weapons removed half of the remaining Krupps from action. Gravity and momentum brought the enemy hurtling passed me, unable to stop in time, and I quickly shot two in the back. It doesn't seem terribly honorable but it got the job done. The rest were accounted for by the others.

A simple look told me that the medics had successfully retrieved the colonel from his fallen Lance. Only my lunatic stand had kept the enemy away long enough for the PBIs to pull the colonel out. I wondered if he realized who had provided the cover for his rescue, and if he knew why, because I surely didn't. I wondered if I would regret what I'd done, then shrugged. One more regret to me was as inevitable and immaterial as living one more day seemed to be.

Chapter Twenty

Point Machia, Namur
Glory
Mauren States

November 19, 2656

"It's been a long haul. I don't know that I can do this anymore, Father."

It was the only time that I recall attending confession on a planetary surface. I think Father Patrick understood the kinds of vices most soldiers, especially Reavers, will freely engage in whenever they are on a non-hostile planetary surface. Also, he likely wanted to make certain that he heard confession as soon before anyone died as he could make it. That usually meant in orbit or transit, given the short, brutal nature of our missions. It was unusual in the extreme that he'd come to visit us at any sort of camp, but then, this was an oddly unusual mission.

We were officially on down time, training with our counterparts in Mauren while command decided where to send us next, but that was just a cover. We'd really been sent in to provide heavy augmentation to the strength of the Maurenine Takers as they hunted an elusive cell of NPJF, one that had an annoying habit of crossing the border to strike, then crossing back to hide. Intelligence anticipated a strike on another planet within two weeks and arranged for us to try and intervene. We'd been here for ten days already, so either they were wrong or we were getting very close to whatever was to happen.

We talked under a tree of all places, on a grassy little hill, warm in the spring sunshine that filtered down through the budding leaves. I sat with my arms folded around me knees, my back resting against the rough bark on the trunk of the tree while Patrick stood on a lower part of the hill looking slightly down at me. He wore his cross and collar underneath his camouflage fatigues, but from a distance he just looked like any other Protectorate regular commandant.

"What is it that you cannot do?" he asked softly.

I raised my hands in an expression of dismay and confusion. "I can't kill anymore. I don't want to, at least not for something that so often seems so trivial. I have enough ghosts haunting me for one lifetime. Maybe more." An understatement and a half. If only I'd been wise enough to quit collecting them when I could.

"You think this is trivial?"

I shook my head violently. "Not this, no. These people need protection, and we're giving them that. We've seen first hand just what kinds of pain the NPJF is willing to dish out on a population base whose only crime is failing to overthrow their own government." I paused. "But lately, it seems we're so...I don't know, political. We're not fighting terrorists half the time, not the real ones who put bombs on trucks and drive them into playgrounds, anyway. This last six months how many times have we dropped on actual armed opponents? Two? Maybe three?"

He rocked his head from side to side, then nodded. "Probably about that, yes."

"So three times against training camps or staging sites and, what, three, four dozen drops on factories and small resource communities that we're 'suspected' of collaborating with the enemy?" I tried to keep the bitterness from my voice. "We've killed security guards and destroyed peoples livelihoods all on a suspicion. How many times were we wrong?" I scratched an itch behind my left ear.

"And it's not just that. It's like we're purposefully being kept away from any real conflict. Thomlin says it's as if Komodo scared the high ups away from making any more decisions that might get people killed; as if they can't stomach the thought that we might possibly lose that badly again. Gurgi just thinks someone at the highest level has been bought off, that Krupp won in more ways than one. Either way, I don't think it's in me to kill someone just because he's supporting, in a non-violent manner, the independence of a group of worlds he believes shouldn't be subject to the current government. Should they die or have their lives ruined simply because said government is unhappy with that attitude?" I shook my head again and plucked up a blade of grass to roll between my fingers. "I've no wish to play God anymore. I've tried it before and didn't much care for the feel of it. It's not like I was any good at it anyway." I threw the blade of grass away bitterly.

Father Patrick dropped to one knee next to me. He didn't say anything until I raised my head and made eye contact. For the first time since Madrigal I was able to look up at someone and hold that eye contact longer than a few moments, not shifting my gaze back to where my hands lay cradled in my lap until he began speaking again.

"You've changed much since I first met you, Chase." Well, no shit. There was a helpful comment if ever I've heard one. When we first met I was a drug addicted whoremonger, who, to plagiarize Keats, was half in love with the idea of his own easeful death. Would that I could undo much of that, but I cannot.

Would that I could undo so much of my life, but I cannot. Can life itself be undone?

"You know that Lucifer was cast down because he thought he should be God," he continued.

I snorted. "I've heard the Sunday school stories, Father. I never gave them much credit, especially these last few years. Maybe I should start listening to them again now that I've lived through most of them as a principle. I almost feel sympathy for the devil."

"You should," he said. "The fall of the Son of the Morning was tragic. It's not something to revel in or rejoice over, it's something to feel pity and sorrow for. It's nothing less than the greatest tragedy in all of history."

I looked up at him again, more than slightly puzzled. "Just where are you going with all of this?"

He shrugged and gave me a sardonic half smile. "I have no idea whatsoever." We both laughed. "But, really, I'm doing what priests do best: quoting obscure, general passages of scripture to make it appear as if I have all the answers, right? Wouldn't want to spoil my reputation for omniscience." I shook my head and smiled even more widely.

He extended his hand to me as he rose to his feet. "Come on. I'm afraid there's little enough more I can tell you, and we've still got God's work to do you and I. There will be time to speak further at another time."

I muttered a rather noncommittal syllable as I gripped his hand firmly and he hauled me upright. We walked in step back toward my office.

"I've always wanted to ask you something," he said. "Why didn't you take your discharge?"

Now it was my turn to smile and cock my head. "You always wanted to ask me, meaning you never have? Since when did you back down from asking anything?"

He laughed clearly and I joined in when he said, "Frankly, if I can borrow one of your more eloquent lines, you scared the piss out of me every time I had to sit alone with you in that office."

That made me grin again. "Good, I'd hate to think all of that effort was wasted."

"Don't dodge the question, now that I've finally asked it. Why didn't you go? You could have done so many different things in these past months."

"That's true," I agreed, then shrugged. "I guess I wasn't ready to go back then. Some of these guys grew on me, kind of fungal like, and I had nowhere else to go, nothing else to be. Besides, I hardly thought saving du Smith was worth any kind of reward."

He smiled at that. "Was it because you were wrong about the BLA, maybe? Because they weren't the misunderstood political group you thought them to be?"

I shrugged. "Maybe, or maybe they were just unfortunate pawns being used in a bigger game played by larger nations. It's so hard to tell the good guys from the bad guys anymore, and that's another part of the problem with the Reavers, we're all former bad guys.

"I've seen the dark side of humanity, I've walked there and called it my home. But I wasn't evil, at least not in the ultimate sense of the word. I no longer think anyone really is. Some make poor choices, others have rough circumstances, mostly we just have different points of view. When those choices aren't overtly violent, like funding subversive political groups, is that worth killing each other over?"

"Is that why you referred to being unready to leave in the past tense?" He was a perceptive bugger. That's probably what brought him so close to saving my soul.

I could only nod. "Yeah, I've made my decision. Davis wants to promote me again and send me over to the Diane Group. He wants me to help them integrate better augmented armor tactics into their supported rapid deployment units. I've decided to accept that offer. I'll be discharged from the Reavers as soon as we get back."

Patrick clapped me on the back heartily and grinned broadly. "Good for you, son. I'm glad to see you doing something to make a difference, though we'll miss you here."

"Miss me?" I blinked. "I thought you'd be glad to see that you actually did manage to carry out your threat to save my soul."

He laughed again. "Your soul was saved thousands of years ago at a place called Golgotha. I just helped you remember that." He stopped to study me.

"I'm proud of you, Chase, most people that live long enough to get out of the Reavers still don't have the level of faith you do."

I didn't let him stay there staring at me, I continued walking. "That was my parents' doing, you just reminded me of a few things I'd forgotten."

"Have you forgiven Jonny's killer?" he called after me.

That sudden change of tactics hurt. I didn't stop walking but I muttered under my breath, "You bastard."

He understood anyway. "Someday you'll have to. Jonny would want you to."

I said nothing because it was true. I could feel his gaze burning into the back of my neck even as I continued walking. He was obviously awaiting a response of some sort. Conveniently, my buzzer went off. I didn't even wait to excuse myself, I just started running for my Man O'War.

We'd gotten lucky in our search for the NPJF. One of the remote drones the Maurenines are so fond of using to scout large areas of land had been shot down up in the mountains of Namur, not too far from the city of Turmai. Naturally that doesn't sound particularly lucky, no one was rejoicing that one of our drones got shot down, but the bloody thing had crashed right through a rather elaborate physical and electronic camouflage screen to land smack in the middle of a camp that obviously didn't belong there. My Maurenine counterpart, one Captain Escobar, had his units, and two of my own platoons, on maneuvers a great deal closer to the area, but since our transports were right here in camp ready to go, and they didn't have to come find us, a sub-orbital hop and drop would probably put us at the sight while the Maurenines were still in transit.

Escobar told me in no uncertain terms that I should engage any enemy present as soon as possible, he would catch up. Three times I made him repeat those orders, until he likely thought me deaf or mentally deficient (which is okay, because I had similar suspicions about him on a daily basis). His instructions were making me very nervous. The idea of carrying out an act of war on foreign soil without direct supervision from that nation's command staff made my palms sweat. The opportunity for disaster tripled.

On the face of it, this seemed so routine for the Reavers. Another mission, another terrorist training camp, but we hadn't actually gone into a live camp in months, certainly not one with active resistance, and I worried that our reflexes had grown dull, that we wouldn't be on our toes the way we used to be. I briefed both platoon leaders in detail while we were in flight, and I know they grilled each squad leader, each passing it on in turn until the lowest individual in the company sent it back up the chain. When my platoon leaders recited everything back to me to my satisfaction I started to relax. Then I would look at my map, or my altimeter, or something else that would remind me we were going into an actual hot zone for the first time in almost a year, and I would panic and start the whole process over again. Everyone else in the company must have been nervous too, because no one told me to knock it off.

We dropped uncontested high up the mountain, between Turmai and our target. If anyone was going to be shooting, we wanted them to have to come shooting through us before they could reach the city. In most cases we had standing orders to be between the enemy and the civilians, but I'd learned long ago on Madrigal not to trust that the civilians will still be on your side when you actually get there to fight for them, so it always made me uncomfortable to have possible partisans at my back.

The camp we worked our way up to and through was strictly mobile, all tents and trucks. Plenty of camouflaging nets and electronics were there, as well as a good deal of personal effects, not to mention the wreckage of the crashed drone sitting squarely atop a now-squashed truck, but no sign of any actual people or the weapons that made them dangerous. Fresh, deep treads left the camp going deeper into the interior of the mountain range, but they ended within a kilometer when we tried to follow them.

Once we'd completed an initial sweep, I sent Thomlin out on a spiral patrol. Gurgi set up a secure perimeter and I dismounted, taking two or three of our more analytical and technically minded warriors with me and we went through a few of the tents. We started with the biggest. It had detailed maps inside; maps of every starport on Glory, and lists of the security procedures at each, including the military ones.

"Looks like someone wants to nick themselves a dropship," McCree said.

"What for?" I asked. "They've already got them."

McCree shrugged. "Maybe there's something special on this one."

I wondered how we would ever be able to figure out every little ploy or plot being hatched, or find all of the people behind them. I wondered if there was really a point to it, I wondered if the governments and nations involved hadn't brought this all on themselves. We all knew what was going on, but for the most part we usually chose not to speak of it. Other countries had been nervous about the Protectorate since the failed attack on Thule sixty years ago. That single, poorly planned act of aggression, carried out before my parents were born and motivated over a rather simple and minor border incursion, meant that the Parisians would find few allies within the Charted Territories, and many enemies both open and hidden.

Those nations that knew the truth, that the Parisians had actually deployed nuclear weapons to be used aggressively in that conflict, saw the Protectorate as an unstable, lethally dangerous nation, despite the fact that national leadership had changed hands at least a dozen times since then. It probably seemed only logical to them that they sponsor as many internal factions as they could in order to destabilize the government, that way the Parisians would be more worried about problems at home than abroad, and less likely to repeat the mistakes of the previous generations. I remembered a quote I'd read somewhere about the punishments for the sins of the fathers being passed down to their children and grandchildren. It was certainly true here.

I sighed. This NPJF group obviously wasn't operating on a shoestring budget, which confirmed they had outside sponsorship, just another pawn being used to punish a lapse in judgment made so long ago. I wondered why it was so hard for others to forgive the mistakes that had been made in the past. Immediately I heard Father Patrick's voice echoing in my mind telling me to first ask myself that question.

The equipment we found in that camp was sophisticated and expensive. Going through the other tents and vehicles we found communications and anti-surveillance equipment that was years more advanced than anything I'd ever seen before. This was the stuff they were willing to leave behind too, so there was no telling what they'd taken with them. The job of the Reavers was just going to get harder and harder. I almost felt bad for getting out, but there would be enough violence to go around, no matter where I went.

I rolled up the design prints that I'd been flipping through, plans for another aerosol missile delivery system that had been found lying open on a table in the last tent we searched. They had been left open so blatantly it was as if we were being challenged to try and stop them. In a pique of anger I crumpled them up and threw them to the ground behind me as I turned. Enough of this, let some local Taker team come collect the evidence, it was time to go kill someone.

I felt no sympathy for the plight of this particular group of bastards, they had chosen to fight for their cause by killing civilians and attacking non-governmental targets, and they were researching weapons of mass destruction. No one respected that, the callous disregard for the sanctity of human life, and it just wasn't right. That was the norm for these groups though, and I'd been dealing with that for a couple of years now. What really made me mad was seeing how willing they were to prostitute their cause to foreign national interests. I remembered a blonde teenager, dirt smudged face and worn uniform, who had been far too young and naive to have known about all the political maneuvering being carried on behind the scenes. She'd died, not for her beliefs, but because someone in another country, someone who didn't care one whit about her, her ideals, or the victims of the attacks, was using her as a simple tool. It's the civilians and other innocents that suffer for the decisions of governments, both foreign and domestic.

It always is.

I was just exiting the tent when Shelley, one of Gurgi's squad leaders, came pounding up to me, her Stalwart screeching to a halt just in time to keep from squishing me. I felt vaguely insignificant as I stood there looking way up past the huge shield and oversized cannon to where Shelley sat.

"You've got to come quickly, sir," she blared down at me. "Lieutenant Thomlin says he's made contact with a group of them, and he says they've got hostages."

"Capitaine, slow down," Gurgi said from behind me. "Don't startle them or anything."

That seemed like a reasonably good suggestion. I slowed to a more normal walking pace about two hundred meters from the cleared area. I chose to stay on the road so that the hostage-takers would see us coming and not panic like they might if we just suddenly appeared out of the forest.

"He demanded to talk to you, sir," I heard Thomlin tell me. I couldn't see him, but the computer had him located about ninety degrees around the glade, on the front side of the temple. "I told him I could talk but he just shot out one window on the top floor there and threatened to start pushing hostages out if I didn't get you out here. I didn't have any better ideas."

"It's okay, Greg," I reassured him, "you did right." If I had no idea what to do in this situation why should I expect my subordinates to know any better? This wasn't what we were trained for, we were supposed to just shoot everything in sight. I eased slowly up the road to where I could see the entire temple.

The first thing I noticed was the child. She was about eight and stood at the lip of the window, her bottom lip quivering as she bravely fought back the tears threatening to fall. An angry red welt on her forehead and some bruising around her left eye were clearly visible upon magnification, and testified that she had already been maltreated by her captors. A pale white face poked around the corner just long enough for me to make out a tall nose and blonde hair, then it disappeared back inside again.

The temple itself was a beautiful construction, a work of art. Its graceful spires soared heavenward, its stained-glass windows each an explosion of beautiful colors arranged in a magnificent display of different religious themes. I didn't know what denomination, sect, or cult had built this structure, but it was inspiring.

The window at which the child stood depicted the Crucifixion, but the bottom half had been broken open, shot out Thomlin had said. I doubted the symbolism of that choice was mere coincidence.

A voice blared outward, amplified many times more than was necessary for me to hear. "No farther! You stop there! I'll kill them all if you come any closer!"

I quickly brought the teams to a halt. Thomlin continued to spread the rest of the company out around the perimeter of the building, cutting off any escape routes. I cursed our lack of infantry support, but Escobar was bringing plenty of them with him, ones experienced and trained in this sort of action. They were supposed to be here very soon.

"I have over a hundred hostages in here! Do as I say or they will die!"

I moved slightly, as warriors are always apt to do when concentrating on other things, unconsciously turning to speak to Gurgi.

"Quit moving! I'll kill them, I will! Watch the girl and see!"

I immediately froze, waiting long seconds for something to happen. Nothing did.

"Wait," I said slowly and calmly over my external loudspeakers. "We can talk this out. You're in charge here, no one has to die." I didn't know what to say, I wasn't a trained negotiator. The only choices I knew how to provide were surrender and death. Somehow, I didn't think my friend over there would find either of those rather limited options appealing, so I was trying to think of something else. I eased backward a step, trying to appear unthreatening.

A loud shot rang out and a small body toppled slowly out the window and to the ground. The sights and sounds of that cold blooded execution have never left me. I can still see the small spurt of blood made as the bullet exited from the left side of the child's skull. I can hear the report and echo of the gunshot, fading like the light from the girl's eyes. I can still watch, with agonizing slowness, the body slump forward, bereft of the life it so dearly deserved, and plummet the five stories to the waiting earth below. I can even hear the sound it makes when the body impacts, much like a sack of flour heaved off the back of a supply truck and onto the waiting cement of a storage barn.

"You son of a bitch!" I screamed, horrified beyond what I'd thought possible. "I said we could talk!"

"Shut up," he told me, "or another will be following right now! You were told not to move!" I closed my mouth and bit my tongue.

Sure enough, another young girl, this one maybe five and weeping openly, was shoved forward to stand at the window's ledge. She tried to shy back, to pull away from the height, and a hand holding a pistol lashed out to strike her in the head. She stumbled back, falling against the window sill, almost dropping over the precipice. She shrieked, and kept on crying.

"We have children and old people in here, and they will all die if you do not do as I say! Now, move all of your men back, deeper behind the tree line. Now!"

We complied, what else could we do? I didn't break the perimeter that Thomlin had established, but I did push it back through the tree line as ordered. I had Gurgi take her team back and see if there was any way she could work in closer or set up a better shooting site.

"Capitaine," Thomlin said, "there are only maybe twenty five armed people in there." I'd also counted that up, our thermal imaging, resonance burners, and other scans more than capable of penetrating the temple's walls. "Where are all the others?"

I sighed. "I don't know. They obviously beat feet when that spotter crashed on them. You should have seen how much stuff they left behind, some really advanced ECM stuff especially."

"So they arranged this little stunt as a distraction to keep us off of the important ones' tails. But are we seeing what's really going on in there, or just what they want us to see? You said they had some pretty advanced stuff."

Thomlin raised some good points. Those questions and many more needed to be answered and I didn't know how to do that. I needed more information, and the only people with that commodity were the ones holding children as hostages.

"This is Capitaine Chase Aarons of the New Paris Protectorate Legionnaires," I shouted out, giving our official title. "Let the hostages go, surrender yourselves, and we'll let you live." It was true that I really only knew how to provide two choices, and I blurted them out like an idiot as soon as the pressure was on.

"Capitaine," came the response. This was a new voice, not the one that had been shouting out orders and, presumably, shooting children. "My name is Olav Haakon, head of this alting. You must know by now that we have forty-five hostages under the age of ten alone in here, and that should remind you of who is making the demands here. You know that we cannot do as you say. You may let us live, but those in power will execute us anyway. That is why you must provide us with sub-orbital capable air transport within the hour. Otherwise we will kill these people."

He had a legitimate point about the executions, no one in power was going to let these bastards live. They had a simple choice: fight and die here or surrender and die in a public execution. All of us in the Reavers were familiar with that choice, that's how most of us had gotten here. At least I had a name now. Dredging up my education in neuro-linguistics I tried again.

"Mr. Haakon. Olav. Even if what you said was true, and it isn't necessarily, that would only apply to your leadership. Would you really sacrifice the lives of everyone, from the children to your own men, just to protect your leaders?"

For a time, nothing happened. I wondered what was going on inside. Likely they were discussing what I'd said, perhaps weighing their options. I was starting to think I just might be able to handle this. I wiped some of the sweat from my palms, hoping they'd answer soon. They did.

Another shot echoed through the glade, shattering the stillness of the forest. Another tiny, lifeless body plummeted five stories to smash on the ground below.

"Stand fast!" My platoon, squad, and team leaders repeated the order up and down the line, reminding each of my soldiers that they had to restrain their impulses to start firing or things would just get worse. I swallowed hard. So many hostages, so many hair triggers on both sides just waiting to send everyone to an early grave, and all of us, especially me, at a loss as to what to do next.

"There, you see, Capitaine?" Olav said. "My people are willing to do all sorts of things for me, and for the freedoms that we fight for."

"Is that what you call them, you bastard?" I shouted. I was regretting every word I'd ever spoken in defense of any separatist. "The freedom to kill innocents? To kill our young and defenseless children? You're nothing but filthy baby killers!"

Another form was thrust quickly to the window. This time, it was a poor little boy who'd obviously lost control of his bladder who stood shaking and crying on the ledge. I could see myself in that boy, so many years ago.

"Be careful what you say, Capitaine. I lead my people, I do not control them, and some of them have taken offense to what you say. You do not understand us. Now, arrange our transport for us. You have ten minutes to respond favorably."

Okay, this was somewhat better, at least he was giving us some time with no one firing. I bit my tongue and pulled my hands away from my firing controls, just to be safe. Then I sat there chewing my nails because I hadn't the slightest idea of what to do next.

"Capitaine," Thomlin said, "I'd like permission to go down there on foot. I think I might be able to at least stall for some more time."

"Why would I let you get killed like that?" I asked him, truly puzzled.

"I used to be like these people, sir." The regret in his voice was audible, but so was his self-confidence. "I was sixteen when I got recruited, and I thought I was doing the right thing. It's been a long, hard struggle to atone for those mistakes. I wasn't part of the NPJF, but I still think they might listen to one of their own kind. They said that you don't understand them, sir, but I do."

Briefly, I wondered if Thomlin looked to join them in their struggle. I immediately banished that thought as terribly unworthy. That man had saved so many lives during his service (ten long years he'd been sentenced to) and never wavered even in the face of the most difficult of assignments. Besides, he was at least smart enough to know not to go over to the other side when surrounded by half a company of Reaver Man O'Wars.

I nodded to myself and said, "Okay, but be damned careful out there. These people aren't trustworthy. Make sure you take a set with you too, I want to be able to talk to you down there."

He clicked back an affirmative. Dimly, through the trees, I could make out his dismount and descent. He slowly walked about halfway to the temple with his hands held out to his sides. Dust puffed up at his feet and he stopped suddenly, another report echoing out to us.

"Don't do anything," Thomlin told us all. "They're just testing my resolve. If we break, they'll shoot me down."

I held my breath as he resumed walking ever so slowly forward. Another shot, according to my displays, whisked past his head. The trajectory calculation said it passed mere centimeters from his gray matter. I magnified in on Thomlin and saw that he wasn't even breaking a sweat.

"It's okay," he reassured us again, his voice rock steady. "Now they'll listen to me."

I don't know how he knew that, I want to say that he shouldn't have, but he was right. After that second shot they allowed him to walk right up to within two meters of the door, which they opened slightly. There they made him halt and remove his set, which he threw a few paces behind him. I swore. I wanted to hear what was going on, I needed to know what was happening down there.

"Capitaine," Gurgi said, "FO says the Maurenines are here, and they brought our boys with them."

That relieved me somewhat, at least I wouldn't have to shoulder the full responsibility anymore. Soon Thomlin's security line had four times as many people on it, half of them infantry. Gurgi joined me as I fully briefed Escobar on what was happening, the two of us towering our Man O'Wars over his tiny armored form.

"Dogs," Escobar called them in that thick accent of his, the one that always made me think he was stupid. "How good is this Thomlin of yours?"

"I honestly have no idea, we've never been negotiators. Maybe we should call in the professionals," I suggested.

"We are the professionals, Capitaine, and we don't negotiate either." He sounded like a kid attempting to sound tough in front of his friends. "Our snipers can hit every one of them before they have the chance to react." He started giving orders to his infantry to set up for that very task while I bit my tongue. I don't think it was just his accent that made me think he was stupid, but I didn't want to step on his toes in his own backyard.

At the temple, Thomlin was continuing to talk to someone inside. The door had opened all the way now, giving us a better view of a pale figure holding a machine pistol. That gun didn't waver a millimeter from its deadly focus on Thomlin's heart.

"What about Thomlin?"

"That is your call, Capitaine. If you wish, my snipers will take them all down and he can make a run for it. Otherwise, you can wait until he fails and gets shot before we take them out." The fool's confidence in my lieutenant was underwhelming.

"They made him take off his set." I'd already told him once, but figured I'd better repeat it for him, just so it would have twice the chance to sink in. "I can't tell him to make a run for it."

"We are here, Capitaine," Escobar said, "and he knows that. If everyone drops dead, I am certain he'll figure things out quickly enough. In the meantime, we can let him proceed while we get our firing patterns perfected. Who knows? Maybe he'll even get lucky, though I doubt that."

The man at the temple door motioned Thomlin to raise his hands higher. Thomlin complied slowly. The man stepped fully out of the door, crossed to stand directly in front of Thomlin, and placed the barrel of his gun directly against the Lieutenant's forehead. I held my breath again.

Another single shot rang out and I shuddered, but it was Thomlin's tormentor who fell back dead. One of Escobar's snipers had decided he wasn't going to watch Thomlin be executed. A big mistake.

Thomlin turned to me, lowering his hands as he did so, and looked straight at my Will O'Wisp. His look was plaintive and his lips moved. I couldn't make out the words for certain, but I think he was asking me why I'd killed him. He was cut down from behind by a hail of bullets from within the temple.

"Fire!" Escobar commanded his snipers, half a second too late. They did so in almost perfect unison. Thirty shots rang out and all of the twenty-some-odd figures holding weapons inside the temple fell. It seemed so easy. Then someone inside shot the little boy.

"No," I said, shaking my head in denial.

A small explosion popped one of the spires off, tipping it to crash through the temple's roof.

"No," I said, louder and more forcefully.

Another, larger explosion went off in one of the larger rooms inside, where many of the hostages had been held, and three more sent the rest of the spires smashing through the roof.

"No!" I shouted, long and loud. The explosions kept going, one after the other. Inside, school children, young mothers, elderly grandparents; societies weakest members and they all disappeared right alongside their captors, burning in a roaring hell created by a madman and sparked by an idiot.

Three days later, I was delivering Thomlin's eulogy as Patrick presided over the funeral. I added Greg's name to the number of ghosts I carried around with me. His question echoed in my ears every night, even after I accepted my promotion and transfer.

That same day, right on the schedule intelligence had established, the NPJF successfully stowed away on board a dropship bound for a Protectorate medical supply transport. The transport was hijacked and jumped away from Glory. The target was not chosen randomly, nor for its humanitarian abilities.

The components being transported back to New Paris were to be used to treat HWS, but could easily be used instead to manufacture weapons grade quantities of the disease.

Thomlin and all the others had died for nothing.

Chapter Twenty-One

Juruko, Ibaraki
Iwo Jima
Iwaki Confines

June 23, 2657

Most people know what happened next, everyone watched the reports live on the news networks. The Hegemony invaded Iwaki in December with the sort of speed that we'd always thought impossible, overwhelming and occupying Kobe and Kira almost simultaneously. The two planets had already fallen by the end of January.

I'd thought I'd seen all the evils that the life of a soldier has to offer on Madrigal, but I was wrong then. After my years in the Reavers I'd thought no enemy cruelty could shock me, but I was wrong once more. Humanity's capacity for brutality surprised my yet again, and the invasion of Iwaki was an entirely new lesson in the depths of our race's depravity. If there is anything that can be worse, I do not wish to ever find out.

I was on Liberty with Diane when the news came. Diane had long used the outpost as a staging area, and we'd gone there to ascertain the viability of using hired guns to supplement certain covert ops. After only a few days my soul was aching from spending too much time in the presence of these soldiers of fortune, for the most part men and women of weak morals living the kind of life I'd sworn to never again experience. That cold, lifeless moon was home to all the habits I'd once embraced, legalized and marketed as a place where mercenaries could gather to remind themselves that they were alive before taking another assignment. Then we heard about Iwaki.

I couldn't sleep for two days after watching those first images, smuggled out by two reporters with more guts than most special operatives I've ever met. The pictures of Yonago, on Kira, burning brightly against the darkened sky sent shivers up and down my spine. The number of casualties there was horrific as the Hegemony used orbital bombardment on the city, making it an extremely brutal example to others. Apparently the lesson was not learned well, or the experience was addictive for the Krupp forces, because five more cities were leveled in similar manner before the slaughter slowed.

The suffering did not end there though. Maybe worse than the pictures of Yonago were the images of all the women in Mira between the ages of ten and forty being rounded up and forced into mass prostitution camps, camps where they reportedly were systematically raped by the Krupp soldiers, male and female alike. Those same pictures showed the other concentration camps, the ones where the males and other females, those too old or too young, were kept; gigantic enclosed areas, segregated into smaller pens for easier control, where hundreds of thousands were forced to live like caged animals in a zoo, with nothing to eat but their own dead.

Naturally, the Confines appealed to the Republic for help in defending against this incursion, citing the mutual defense treaty they'd signed along with so many other nations after the armistice had ended the Unification War. My motherland, however, was still hurting from the memory of the that great war. So much effort and so many lives had been thrown into that conflict, most especially the battle defending Madrigal where fully a third of the war's casualties occurred, that the Republic had lost its heart for more warfare. After Madrigal successfully seceded in January, taking advantage of the obvious anti-war feelings rampant throughout the Republic, many of us half expected the nation to break in two again immediately. In the end it broke up a lot farther than that, but that didn't happen until later. At the time, the Republic simply abrogated the treaty, telling their former allies to stand fast on their own.

Iwaki turned to the general international community to plead for help, only to receive similar responses from the other superpowers. Humanity in general was still hurting from the memories of the Unification War, and no one wanted to see superpowers clash again, at least not so soon. Every nation was afraid to send its sons and daughters off to die again. It was easier to ignore the threats and pretend they only affected Iwaki than to accept the possibility that the only way to preserve the future was to see the entire Chartered Territories plunged into war again.

It was the smaller nations that acted, the dozen states that bordered on either Iwaki or the Hegemony. It was they who realized the true danger in the Hegemony's unrestrained aggression, and they who banded together as had never happened before. They each brought with them other small nations, ones that shared their borders or were mutually dependant upon international trade, and together we sent an impressively large task force to reinforce Iwo

Jima when it came under attack. The brutally aggressive Krupp advance, we swore, would be stopped there.

When our orders came down exactly as expected, confirming that my Diane group would be going to Iwo Jima, I was more than a little wary. Though extremely thankful to be leaving Liberty, I wasn't certain how well I would be able to work alongside some of our fellow task force members. After all, I had witnessed the Jarvyn sponsored depravities within our borders too many times to feel comfortable around them, and after Glory I didn't trust the Maurenines to know their heads from a hole in the ground. Besides all of that I still blamed the Sunni for Jonny's death. Granted, it's not like I held them solely responsible, I also managed to blame myself and the Empire for their respective parts. There was plenty of blame to go around. If the Sunni hadn't decided to get greedy and butt into a war that wasn't theirs to start with, however, Jonny might still be alive and back on Earth hugging his daughter and wife.

Still, I gritted my teeth and tried to bear up under the burden. I knew we needed allies as never before if we were to have even a chance of victory, and we couldn't exactly get choosey about whom we'd allow to proffer their help. Marshal Davis and General-major Evans circulated an essay written by Colonel Rutger two hundred years ago on Aubaine which talked of the healing that can be done when two enemies are given a common task, and I read that essay a dozen times over. I tried to imagine Father Patrick telling me about how I would know I'd made progress in my own spiritual growth because I'd be able to forgive everyone I blamed for my own problems. I guess I wasn't making as much progress as we'd hoped for in that department, but at least I'd returned to regular prayer and scripture study, so there was still hope for me; or so I believed.

It was, admittedly, amazing to see so many nations, many of them traditional enemies, join together to face down such a great threat to international stability. It sent a powerful message to the superpowers, the great bears of nations. It was a sharp reminder that too many wolves can take down even the biggest Kodiak. Maybe that's why they all resisted so hard; maybe that's why they turned so terribly destructive.

All of that would come in time, but for now we were off to Iwo Jima.

The thrice damned Roughneck bucked under me in its horribly annoying gate as it lumbered along. Again I wondered idly just how difficult it would be to control in combat if it was this hard to simply walk it down a game path. I cursed it and wished fervently for the return of my Will O'Wisp, or even something like my old Lodestone of so long ago. Sure, I welcomed the extra armor, heavier than anything I'd ever had before, but the much rougher ride was very difficult to get used to and, despite my often reckless style of fighting, I was unnerved by the Roughneck's design for close quarters battle. I missed, in an extreme way, the unique abilities of everything else I'd piloted since graduating from OBT. The Lodestone's jumping abilities and multi-directional firepower, the Crossbow's ability to reach out and kill an enemy at extremely long ranges before they even knew I was there, and my Will O'Wisp's knack for disappearing from enemy sensors; these were all things I'd gotten very used to, each in turn, and I missed them very much.

The rest of my Diane team worked their way slowly through the night darkened foliage all around me. Intelligence suggested that somewhere out here was a Krupp field grade officer, likely an Obertsleutnant, with his own special operations unit, probably working to counter the previous Diane incursions made in the area of Juruko. Normally I wouldn't trust military intelligence to tell me if it was raining outside, but Diane intelligence, a refreshing change from other organizations I'd fought in, was smooth.

The bloody Roughneck, now that was something else. Originally designed and built by the Terran Dominion to be an economical and effective mainstay augmented armor design, which it certainly was, it was nothing more than a mud slogger. To be fair, it is surprisingly capable of being combat effective even after taking twice as much damage as would put most other Man O'Wars out of action permanently. The huge auto-cannon it was designed around is highly dependable (as in you can roll it through the mud and still fire it without any consequence more serious than a rude, gastrointestinal distress sound), equally effective against armor or augmented armor, and lethal with only a short burst (which further conserves the already cheap ammo). None of that meant that it was in any way graceful, comfortable, or subtle.

"Commandant, Delta group reports contact at one tree seven seven. Suggest it may be a trap. They would like to spring it with our help. Request we provide security coverage."

I clicked back an affirmative understanding and followed slowly and carefully as our point turned us in the appropriate direction. That took me off of the easy going of the game trail and back into the dense undergrowth where I had to be careful with every step lest I find some hidden log that rolled under me and put me on my back, possibly damaging my Roughneck and jeopardizing the mission. Everyone else was being similarly careful, which slowed our progress to a crawl. That was good for the infantry, it let them keep up with us easily enough without distracting them from their other tasks.

I must admit I'd always taken the Roughneck warriors for granted, assuming they were just bitching and complaining about minor details when they talked of the difficulties they faced. Now I had a new admiration for all of those warriors I used to command and how well they really had handled their machines in battle.

My real mistake had been in allowing anyone I didn't know personally to touch my ride. That and trusting a superior officer to be able to take care of the small details of anything. Marshal Davis had assured me personally that it was more important that I stay with him to aid in drawing up the Diane deployment plans than anything else. He told me not to worry about moving my own machine around, he said his people would take care of everything from outfitting and calibrating my weapons systems to loading my Man O'War onto our dropship. Not only had they somehow forgotten to load my precious Will O'Wisp into the same dropship as I was on (so that it could be deployed at the same time I was, that small, unimportant detail), but they'd forgotten to load it onto *any* dropship in the whole Protectorate expeditionary force whatsoever. Communication with Liberty base confirmed that, indeed, my machine still sat in the 4th Diane Mechanized support bays, sporting a pristine new night camouflage paint job and standing very alone in an otherwise empty hangar.

It wasn't long before we crested another slight rise and were able to see what Delta group had spotted. On magnification and on every other scan it looked like an infantry camp comfortably set up for the night, probably about a company's worth spread out over about a kilometer. It wasn't anything obvious that made it feel like a trap (like a campfire or some of the other stupid things I've seen in movies), but it just seemed to be too perfect of a find knowing, as we did, that somewhere in this area a high level Spezialkraefte team was working against us. They, however, didn't know that we had four whole Diane groups out here hunting them: us, Delta, and Gamma and Epsilon off to the east a ways. At least, I fervently prayed that they didn't know that.

I was so unpleasantly surprised to find myself suddenly busted back to the ranks of the PBIs without even having the protection of an armored suit that I was ready to bite someone's head clean off. It was the one and only time in my strange career that I got to rant and rave, literally yell and swear, at a general officer without fear of being reprimanded. That didn't magically teleport my Will O'Wisp all the way to Iwo Jima, but it did motivate someone to find me something with long legs, some armor, and a big gun. Of course it just happened to be a Roughneck.

On the slightly more positive side, this Roughneck had been modified a wee bit from the original design. For one thing, it had a ghost suit grafted onto it. While not as effective as the specialized stock packages of the Will O'Wisp or the Mirage, the prohibitively expensive ghost add on went a very long way to rendering me less visible to active scans, and almost invisible to passive ones. At least my own team wouldn't vote to leave me behind out of fear that I'd give them away every time I powered up. Whomever had modified the Roughneck had also ditched the auto-cannon in favor of an almost as lethal, and much quieter, even if shorter ranged, HEPC.

A dozen tents could be made out at the camp, with the likelihood of more back in the trees somewhere. My tacticals quickly spotted at least a half dozen guards on watch, all armored. None evidenced any heavy anti-armor weaponry, but that wasn't a guarantee that such weapons were absent.

We rolled around to the north of the camp, allowing ourselves a direct line of superb visibility from which we could attack or cover a retreat if necessary. Delta sat tight in their assault positions, more than ready to take out their target. They could have done it by themselves easily enough, but we saw no reason to let overwhelming numerical superiority go to waste.

"Bandsaw," I called back to my communications support. Nicknames are very important in Diane, but all the good ones I could think of were taken before I got there, so for the time being they just called me by rank. Once everyone was arrayed to our satisfaction, it was time for action. "Have Delta start this game."

He relayed my message and they sprang into action with a swift and silent deadliness that amazed the eye with its near invisibility. About half of the sentries fell in a silent and invisible volley of laser and silenced slug fire. Then infantry and augmented armor rushed forward together, quickly and quietly neutralizing the remaining enemy sentries. As rapidly as that, they set up their own security and searched the camp, ready to move out at a word.

Equally silent and efficient, I moved my units around to provide a better augmentation to Delta's perimeter. We watched the shadows around us, wary of the attack that had to be coming. Yet nothing came, even when we waited some more.

"Delta reports the tents are all empty, sir, no sign of having ever had anything in them, either." Just as we'd suspected, but then where was the trap?

"Any prisoners?" I asked.

"Affirmative, they've got one only slightly wounded. He's not very cooperative so they're just going to have him pulled out."

I agreed with that plan, let the analysts interrogate him and we'd get back to doing our job. "Then tell them we'll shadow them to their extraction point, and tell them to get going, I don't like staying here any longer than we have to."

He clicked his acceptance.

"Atlas," I called one of my infantry leaders. "Break it north and parallel Delta. Falcon, you're with Atlas. The rest of us will lag back one klick."

Delta group wasted no time leaving their destruction behind them. They bundled their prisoner up and were off so smoothly and quickly that I almost didn't see them go, and I knew what to be looking for. Atlas and Falcon took their respective infantry and augmented armor teams north, and I just sat there for a couple of long, long minutes waiting for Delta to get a kilometer ahead of us. They were moving fast though, and soon enough we were on the move as well.

"Commandant," Whisper, my other infantry leader, said, "we just had a flash of active scan sweep over us. Only a burst, then it was gone, but it was definitely pointed our way."

"What's the likelihood they came up positive?"

"Computer says only twelve percent, but they didn't scan anywhere but here, so I'd say higher."

We cut south eighteen degrees, just to help throw off anyone looking for us, and sent Tchaikovsky to pull Falcon and Atlas a bit back to help cover us as well. We moved swiftly and silently through the overgrown terrain, pausing rarely. A half hour later, our friend with the sensor array was back.

"Directed active scan, Commandant," Vigil said. She was on point in her Mirage. Everyone froze where they were. The scan played around the lead edge of our formation for about ten seconds before it disappeared.

"Positive?"

"Not on a Mirage, sir." She spoke with a confidence I couldn't quite bring myself to share.

"Good. Whisper, you get a triangulation on them?"

"No, sir. Some pretty high local interference in that thirty seconds."

I expected his answer, as I'd already gotten the same results from my own efforts at triangulation. Someone was definitely out there, packing at least as much ECM equipment as we had, and their scanning abilities seemed to surpass our own. They obviously had a pretty good idea of where we were, if no other solid information about us as of yet. We'd now officially become the hunted.

"Tchai, move up and find out if Delta has been getting pegged as well, then sweep out and ask Vulcan about it too." He affirmed then sped off to make secure contact. No point in blurting out our position just yet with any kind of broadcast that ran even the remotest risk of possibly being detected.

"Where are you, Obertsleutnant?" I asked the ether quietly. "You know someone is out here, and you know we have your bait, when will you strike?"

Tchaikovsky returned promptly, reporting that neither one of the other groups had experienced any kind of directed scan, so they remained invisible. I certainly hoped so as we meandered across the mountainside for the next two hours. Twice more we caught flashes of directed scans, none of which actually tagged us, or so we believed. We were almost rid of our burden, and then we could go hunting ourselves.

We made it all the way to the extraction point, high atop the mountainside. It turned out to be a breathtakingly gorgeous site from which you could see the beautiful twinkling lights of Juruko. We had no time to admire the view before we got hit.

Delta's infantry were busy stringing their prisoner up for high-speed plane extraction (basically they tied the poor sod into a straight jacket and threw a balloon up in the air with a line for the plane to catch as it went whipping by) when one of them fell over. Even knowing how these ops are done, it still took me a moment to realize he'd been shot, especially since the offending shot didn't register on my overlays. Fortunately, those PBIs are experts at saving their own skin, and they'd all disappeared.

Now the game was truly on as two Diane groups hunted through the dark for their Spezialkraefte nemeses. The one thing I can say is that I am truly glad I wasn't that Krupp soldier laying helpless on the ground, looking up at the sky waiting for a plane to pluck me up like so much fuzz picked off of a sweater, and listening to powered infantry and augmented armor stomping all around me with the occasional exchange of gunfire.

As it was, it was the most surreal experience of my life; the most surreal that didn't involve some sort of illicit substance, anyway. Every one of us on both sides of this little exchange had state-of-the-art stealth technology in the forms of passive and active ECM suites and camouflage materials, was operating on years of hard training and battle hardened experience, and none of us were stupid enough to just start running around flailing our arms in the air to make ourselves obvious visual targets. The very real concern over hitting a friendly unit became a frightening reality if anything blocked the secure IFF transmissions.

We had drilled exercises similar to this a number of times, and we all went into action without any need of instruction or debate. I lumbered my Roughneck over a slight ridge, then immediately dropped prone as I entered a slight divot. The rest of my group quickly joined me in going gopher while Delta worked an intricate search pattern. A flash of superheated metal and one of Delta's Man O'Wars fell.

I couldn't make out what had fired the shot or where it had been fired from. My computers were being blocked from even getting a decent fix on the ballistics of the weapon used, and it all happened so silently.

Another two flashes of light, given as Delta infantry exploded, confirmed that we needed to do something fast or the odds would soon be more even than we cared for. Delta was moving around in the woods and getting picked off, yet we sat with nothing more to do than wipe our sweaty palms and keep hoping someone would slip up and let us see them. We sat there for many more long minutes as a half dozen Man O'Wars and four more power suits were destroyed or severely damaged.

"I got it," Vigil said finally. I said a quick prayer of thanks as she lashed out with her laser and blew a hole through an enemy Ausdehnung. The light from the burn showed another Man O'War not far behind. I quickly sent an HEPC burst through its cockpit. That machine's containment coils burst with a stunning display of pyrotechnics. That brilliant flash of light blinded us all and outlined most of Delta in the open. The Obertsleutnant didn't hesitate once his cover was blown, he took immediate advantage of that distraction and the trees erupted as we were assaulted full scale.

He could not have accounted for all of our numbers, else he'd never have attacked in such an all out manner, yet it seemed as if his units showed no surprise at all when we rose from our hiding places to double the numbers they faced. Perhaps their confidence and resolve were greater than ours, perhaps they simply didn't realize the truth until the trap was sprung, but the final fight was quickly over.

I rose from my prone position and vaporized two infantry suits with a single blast as I dashed straight into the teeth of the Krupp charge. A laser removed the left arm of my Roughneck above the shoulder, but that piece of junk just kept on going, only shifting slightly to compensate for the changed balance. It was slightly awkward trying to carry and target my weapon with only one hand, but again my Roughneck was up to the task.

I was able to snap off two more quick shots, one into another group of infantry and a final one into the side of a Man O'War before we were in close combat range. I triggered my anti-infantry cannons repeatedly without really targeting them, just to make the PBIs keep their heads down, and lashed out at a Versteckt with a kick that caused its knee joint to buckle backwards. The Man O'War fell forward but began to roll to its back. I stopped that maneuver by virtue of shooting it in the back of the head. The warrior inside was likely shredded by the particle burst, and the Versteckt stopped moving.

None of the Man O'Wars were using kinetic or explosive weapons because of the noise those weapons produce (they cannot be easily silenced like their infantry counterparts) and the ease with which they may be backtracked. That leant a silence to our battle that I'd never experienced before. Man O'Wars fizzled and died, infantry burst open with puffs of red vapor, and men and machines crippled and killed one another with little more than the occasional whiz or whine of superheated gases escaping.

One of Whisper's infantry squads was duking it out with a Krupp group to my left. I sprinted right over top of the Spezialkraefte position, sending powered suits scattering for cover and allowing the Diane team to swarm over them and quickly finish them off. The PBIs immediately returned my favor by firing their lasers into the view ports and sensor equipment of the Ausdehnung that was trying to skewer me with a focused beam. The infantry fire did a perfect job of dazzling the warrior and blinding the Man O'War, giving me sufficient time to put a double blast of high energy particles through its chest and into its engine.

All around me Diane members were double and triple teaming their opponents, finishing the battle quickly and decisively. There wasn't anything else left for me to shoot at.

"All right, teams," I called, panting slightly from the exhilaration of the fight, "bring it back in. Give me a sit-rep ASAP. Whisper, Atlas, let Delta police up the bodies and check for survivors, I want you out there looking for anything we may have missed. Vigil, you and Falcon are on heavy security, one klick radius. Tchai, Bandsaw, stick close with me."

I took a moment to admire the lights of Juruko while I gathered my thoughts. I know that sounds like an insane thing to do in the middle of combat, but it was just a moment, a few seconds maybe. Then I was striding across the battlefield, looking for my Delta counterpart who was not answering her com; her and the Obertsleutnant. I spent some time searching for both of them, with no luck. Dawn was starting to lighten the sky, it was time for us to be moving on.

"Commandant," Bandsaw relayed to me, "Delta has gone over everything. This wasn't a Spezialkraefte team, just a Ranger unit. Looks like intelligence missed the boat on this one."

My knee jerk reaction was to conclude that my earlier assumptions of the abilities of Diane intelligence were premature. That thought was unfair though, no one can be completely accurate all of the time, they just did the best they could which was usually the best anyone could hope for. That, and I had a hunch about something else that didn't seem quite right.

"Bandsaw, who has the scanning and ECM that we witnessed earlier?"

"Apparently they all had some pretty extensive stealth tech, let me check on the scans, sir." A few seconds passed while I awaited the answer. I took the time to move out to the perimeter and begin gathering my units back into a traveling formation. "None of them, sir. No explanations are available. Scans came from another unit."

"Understood." I hated mysteries, they usually led to surprises; unpleasant ones. Our opponent was good. "Let intel worry about it. Call in a boat for extraction, let's be gone from this place."

"Affirmative, sir. Delta is doing the same."

An impossibly bright flash from behind me reversed the night, painting everything an unbelievably harsh white. It disappeared almost instantly but left me half blinded. That would be a good description of my Roughneck as well, as its EMP shielding partially failed and a good number of its circuits and processors reversed polarity and shorted out. I crashed to one knee, fighting the controls for all I was worth. My HEPC rifle fell from my weakened hand, cartwheeling down the hill a couple of turns. All of the Man O'Wars I could see simply dropped as though they were mere puppets and their strings suddenly snipped. Instinctively I tried to keep upright. I shouldn't have bothered wasting the effort.

A sound I imagine is somewhat akin to standing on the launch pad underneath a Riese class dropship as its gigantic engines slowly push it away from gravity's dominion thundered all around me, vibrating every organ in my body from my lungs to my kidneys. A flash of panic and butt-puckering fear rushed through my body, standing every hair on end and giving goose bumps to my goose bumps as my sphincter took a solid grip on the cushion beneath me. My whole Man O'War was thrown forward like a rag doll discarded by an angry child in the midst of a tantrum. The Roughneck sailed forward in an amazingly flat arc. I watched as the ground flew by below me at high-speed, then rose up just as quickly to smash into me. The planet rejected my rough treatment of its surface, possibly offended by my previous rejection of its safe, gravity bound confines. I was once again tossed into the air that rushed by, perhaps to show me how an airborne Man O'War is truly a fish out of water. Again I flew, this time tumbling so that I could see the earth and the sky, each in turn, cartwheeling past my view ports in rapid succession. Of all the miracles you would not expect, I landed on my feet. Much good that did, though, as both legs crumpled and sheared off from the incredible force directed against them.

The torso of the Roughneck tore free and continued its descent into the ground, straightening its course upon impact and sliding along at an impressive speed. I held onto my restraining straps with a death grip, certain that I'd cheated death for the last time and expecting to see a bright light calling me home at any moment. I hit a rock and began tumbling again, flipping over and over time after time, bouncing into the air for brief moments only to be returned to earth with a vengeance. Finally I slowed, tumbling to an almost gentle halt.

I had just enough time to take a few deep breaths before the air that had so quickly rushed away from me came hurtling back at high speed.

This time wasn't as bad, though that's like saying a kick in the head isn't as bad as a kick in the groin: they're both bad, it's merely the degree and type of pain that differs. I tumbled back the direction I'd come, meaning I was now going downhill, slamming into the ground more often than before as I caught less air and more rock this time. I was jounced and jingled, scared that my restraints would break away as they'd done on Madrigal and leave me to the mercy of fate and God, both of whom had never before seen any grand need to spare me either pain or suffering.

Eventually the amusement ride ended with me face down on the hard ground, my weight resting on my chest. My communications equipment was broken and fried along with everything else in the cockpit. I seemed to be the only thing left functioning, which did elicit a most heartfelt prayer of gratitude.

I tried to open the hatch, but none of my systems were responding and that included the hatch. I swore and tugged at my restraints, which also would not come undone no matter how hard I slapped the release. With a grunt I disconnected my head-tether, then pulled off my helmet and allowed it to drop free. A bit of contortionist stretching allowed me to get my hand and ankle close enough together that I could then draw my boot knife. I used its serrated back edge to saw through my straps with difficultly. The knife would catch in the fibers of the strap regularly, annoying and distracting me so much that I almost forgot to catch myself when the last fibers tore through and I actually dropped forward.

A quick manual inspection confirmed that the hatch had completely deformed during my little joyride and would be impossible to open even with my emergency escape tool, a fancifully hopeful name given to the crowbar installed in every cockpit. Standard protocols suggest that the view port is the best way out of an inactive Man O'War, but my current alignment precluded that possibility unless I was ready to start tunneling my way to freedom. I retrieved my helmet and did what I have always done in dire circumstances: something stupid.

I placed my helmet firmly on my head and fastened the straps tightly. With my face shield secured and every part of my flame retardant suit double checked for security (I didn't want any bare skin exposed for this) I reached across and activated the eject mechanism before I could think through the wisdom of my actions. Explosive bolts strategically located within the cockpit seams removed the major portion of the cockpit walls, or tried to anyway. At least one failed, leaving the armor totally compromised but still loosely attached. Then the rockets under the command couch ignited, bathing me in an intense blast of heat as it smashed my seat into the ceiling of the cockpit hard enough to dislodge the hanging scrap and render the chair a piece of designer modern art. I would have been more pleased with the fact that I hadn't been on the chair if there had been any air left to breathe in that confined space and I hadn't just given myself a second degree burn on a good forty percent of my body.

I stumbled out of the shattered remains of my Roughneck's skull, gasping for breath and peeling my very hot uniform from the blistered skin beneath. The blasted terrain made it difficult to orient myself immediately. At first all I saw was a lot of ground stripped of topsoil and vegetation, and dotted with a few broken pieces of augmented armor and infantry power suits. I suppose I knew what must have happened, but I didn't really accept that until I managed to get my bearings by locating Juruko, or what now marked its place.

The mushroom cloud billowed high into the air, marking the final resting place of over a million civilians. That confirmed everything I had subconsciously expected, and I again pulled my helmet from my head to gaze unimpeded and in wonder at the spectacle. Then I turned from that marker of infinite destruction and looked in amazement at the battered remains of my Man O'War's head and torso.

God works in mysterious ways, and apparently He'd blessed me more than I'd realized when He'd left my Will O'Wisp behind. Of all the Man O'Wars I'd ever piloted, only a Roughneck could have taken the abuse dished out by my being this close to a nuclear explosion of that magnitude and still allowed me to walk away. My much more delicate Will O'Wisp, with all its specialized electronics and spanking new paint job probably would have shattered into a million pieces, and me along with it. I finally appreciated the hunk of junk I'd been given.

I watched for a few moments before realizing that others were still alive, also clawing their way free of the various augmented armor and even a few power suits still present on the battlefield. All looked more than a little dazed, shell-shocked by the enormity of what had happened. The looks on their faces when they saw that huge cloud extending kilometers up into the atmosphere spoke volumes.

That drove home the full impact of what I was seeing. For the first time in over three centuries, nuclear weapons had once again been used in warfare, and against a civilian target. Chills raced up and down my spine and I knew Iwo Jima marked but the beginning of this new war, not the end.

Chapter Twenty-Two

Camp Penticton, Building 83 (HQ)
Jin, Ibaraki
Iwo Jima
Iwaki Confines

October 30, 2657

Not even the destruction of Juruko was enough to convince the superpowers to get involved, despite the fact that it completely discarded the Taurus Accords and any semblance of civility those documents lent to this most uncivilized practice of warfare. The big nations justified their stance by saying there was little difference between orbital bombardments of civilians and nuclear bombardment of civilians. They were right, of course, there was little difference, which is why they should have become involved at the outset. Yet still they clung to their naive hope that this was a limited conflict, one that would resolve itself quickly and return the balance of power to its former equilibrium.

We knew better. We'd hurt the Hegemony on Iwo Jima, even forced them to withdraw despite their parting gifts, but the war wasn't over. Intelligence suggested that the Krupp forces were redirecting their assaults, choosing new targets and new tactics, not abandoning their quest for dominance.

We knew we had to hurt the Hegemony quickly or they would merely gain more momentum and wash over many more worlds with their brutal lightning war. Too many others would die, and the Hegemony would merely move to once again threaten those of us that remained. It was time to take the war to them.

Even the Hegemony couldn't be a completely unified whole, there had to be political factions of some type interfering with the Chancellor's rule, otherwise we probably would have seen more than one nuke on Iwo Jima. We needed to take advantage of that confusion, and to do that we hatched an audacious plan. We were going to capture and hold, at least temporarily, the Krupp Hegemony capitol world of Gottenheim.

I sprang to my feet the moment he walked into the room. He wore no rank insignia, as was his usual wont, but that was just another sign that this was indeed who I thought it was. I'd studied his picture and history in detail over the last two weeks, ever since Marshal Davis suggested I take the attached position he'd negotiated, and I knew almost everything that was publicly available about this most remarkable leader of men. He did wear the snarling dog's head insignia of the Dogs of War, though I wouldn't have needed even that to identify him. The fact that I was waiting for him in a small conference room just down the hall from his office also helped.

"Marshal Matheson, an honor," I said, extending my hand.

"You seem to actually mean that, Commandant," he said, shaking my hand firmly. It wasn't exactly a question, though it did sound as though he were genuinely surprised by my presumptuousness, but an answer seemed to be required nevertheless.

"Yes, sir. Your reputation precedes you." Nothing too original, but not too kiss-ass, either. I could live with that. "I've been finding quite a lot to read about you and your organization these last few days. Most of it has been quite positive."

Matheson smiled. "I should hope so, seeing how much we pay our public relations officers."

I just blinked. I didn't know the Dogs of War actually employed public relations personnel. I suppose it made sense, every military and para-military organization in the Charted Territories does the same, but somehow that didn't sit with the image I'd built in my head of the Dogs being purely on the up and up.

Matheson bade me be seated again. He also took a seat, across the table from me, relaxing in a manner that still implied instant readiness for any required action. Everything about him, from his posture to his expression broadcast supreme confidence and moral assurance. Here sat a man who had found his destiny, accepted it, and made a difference in the lives of so very many. I wanted that.

His first words surprised me. "Commandant, what do you know of the Dogs of War?"

I hadn't expected to be tested quite like this. I frowned slightly and narrowed my brows as I tried to recall all I'd read in the last several days.

"I know you are the martial arm of the Uryist Enclave, a political, almost quasi-religious sect with affiliates on almost every inhabited world, with, if you'll pardon the clichéd expression, a 'home world' established on Ury itself in the Yreka province of Ioannina. You select your members from across the Charted Territories, regardless of national origin, focusing instead on ideals and beliefs. Still, you reportedly have some of the toughest selection criterion of any military organization in existence, most certainly the strictest outside of a national military. Your combat record indicates a superbly organized, trained, and led outfit almost the same size as the entire Iwaki Defense Force, a fact that has not always pleased some of the larger nations in the Charted Territories."

He simply brushed that all away with a wave of his hand. "That's merely details, Commandant, trivia. Please, tell me who the Dogs really are."

I squirmed slightly and tried again, attempting to take a more philosophical tack.

"The Dogs see themselves as the moral descendants of Mo Tzu. You even base your organizational designs and philosophies around that of the ancient Chinese philosopher. When aggressions break out between unevenly matched nations, or within nations when directed at under-defended groups, you offer to mediate an end to hostilities. If denied, you usually join your forces to those of the weaker side and fight the war to a standstill, whereupon you again insist upon mediating a settlement to the conflict. As often as not that offer is accepted."

"Good," Matheson nodded. "You have been doing your reading. Now, you've been to a couple of combat academies, give me a SWOT analysis of the Dogs of War. Just a short one, so give me the high level brief and be candid."

I swallowed. It's a good idea to never get comfortable when a superior asks for either honesty or candor, especially when asked about themselves.

"The Dogs have an incredible strength in their organizational structures, both military and political, as well as a legacy of being the good guys. That organizational structure ensures rapid decision making at all levels, despite allowing an extreme amount of organic communication given your nature as a military group. The great opportunity here is to lead an effective and decisive strike of the League of Nations against an aggressive superpower, thrusting the Uryists to the forefront in terms of political prestige and general leadership."

"And our weaknesses and threats?"

This was the part that made me nervous, most people in positions of power got there with the help of a sense of self-confidence bordering on hubris and simple do not take criticism well. "The greatest weakness with the Dogs is that they are so idealistic that they sometimes forget the realities of politics and the evils of warfare. Within the last eight years you have three times been betrayed by allies in the field, and twice been allied to groups that committed more crimes against humanity than you can shake a stick at. Some of which apparently were committed with the help, or at least complacency, of your own people, which did little to bolster your international reputation.

"Moreover, while you've had a great deal of success in forcing people to the negotiating table, you've also had numerous failures. Some of those have been quite high-profile, and several ended with the Dogs having to either withdraw from the conflict or become bogged down in serious peacekeeping operations which waste both time and precious resources and, in the end, generally fail anyway.

"The threat of any one of those outcomes will be disastrous on Gottenheim. We haven't got the manpower or the resources to fight a protracted conflict against the Hegemony, we have to force peace talks immediately. Protectorate projections suggest that if we haven't fully secured our objectives by July, with a settlement no more than a year after that, we'll be forced to retreat from the system. If that happens, we'll have lost our gamble, coming up short on the balance sheet, and everyone will blame you."

I stopped and waited for the denials and accusations.

"That was blunt," he said blinking. Then he grinned and slapped his hand on the table. "That kind of commitment to the truth is exactly what we want in the Dogs." He rested his elbows on the table and leaned his weight onto them. "There is much conflict in this galaxy of ours, as you may have noticed in your career. Too often the parties have no wish to understand or communicate with the other side or sides involved, they simply want to be right. When one of those parties has a significant strength or power advantage over the other, war becomes almost inevitable. It is simply too easy to destroy a smaller, weaker group that you disagree with than to try and find ways to coexist, but in the end that simply breeds more hate and bitterness, leading to more conflict."

I nodded my agreement, thinking of some of the groups we'd fought against in the Reavers, and their sponsors too.

"You're right," he continued, "too often the Dogs of War have been less than one hundred percent successful, but at least we're trying. We can't stop all of the wars, we can't win every battle, and we certainly haven't had much success in limiting the depravities and crimes against humanity that so often accompany these violent outbreaks, but no one else in this corner of the galaxy is doing even half as much to make a difference." He stopped in mid-thought. "Well now, I asked for your candor and when you give it to me I surprise you with a long tirade trying to justify our short-comings by lecturing you like a new recruit. Sorry about that. Commandant."

Actually, he'd not surprised me at all by trying to defend his ego, such an action is a mainstay of people in power, but his apology was setting off more alarms in my head. A powerful figure willing to apologize to an inferior rank is a potentially dangerous novelty.

"Let me ask you something more personal, Commandant. Chase, if you don't mind." Even if I did mind, would I tell that to a field marshal? "Why do you want to take this attached position?"

This one I could answer. "Because I believe that Marshal Davis has the right of it when he says that the Dogs of War are closer to the ideal military organization than anyone else currently active in the Charted Territories right now. While others have comparable records of accomplishments, the Dogs do it with an idealism and civility, not to mention underlying morality and end goal, that all others should aim to accomplish. The Marshal would like to learn and adopt many of the methods and philosophies you utilize." I smiled. "Besides, I'm intrigued, and that hasn't happened for some time."

"Good. We can always use a good man when we're riding to the rescue. There are a lot of damsels in distress out there that need a hero."

I raised an eyebrow. "Are we white knights then?" Notice how I'd already assumed that I'd be made one of their own? I was presumptuous, but I did not think my confidence unfounded.

"Knights? Hardly. History shows us quite convincingly that those particular individuals were more often rogues, rakes, and scoundrels than heroes to the masses. We would definitely be more."

Now his face grew quite serious. "Here comes the hard part. We don't have purely ceremonial advisors or attachés in our organization, we never have and we never will. That means that if you decide to come with us, and, a bigger if, if we decide to accept you, you'll be given a command under my direct staff. You'll be dubbed a full major in the Dogs of War, you'll be put into the leadership of a line unit once again, and you will be asked and expected to face combat. I know your immediate history these last few years has been with different special operations units, but I'm certain that you could make the switch back comfortably. I'm also certain that you realize that the knowledge you have gained in those areas would be of invaluable aid to the soldiers under you."

He leaned in toward me. "But are you willing to accept those terms? Will you slug it out on the front line again?"

Back to the line? The closest I'd come to that since fleeing Madrigal had been those brief hours on Komodo almost two years ago, and I'd still been leading a much smaller Reaver unit then. Was I ready to lead a large unit again? Was I ready to once again face a life where every single day I woke up knowing that people under me were going to die? Did I have any other choice?

"I'd be doing us both a disservice if I answered you right away, sir."

"That's also the kind of honesty I want to see in my Dogs," he said with a gruff nod of understanding. "However, I need to see some decisiveness as well, and you don't have the luxury of spending a long time thinking this over."

"Agreed." I made my decision, trusting my gut. I looked him square in the eye and said, "I want the position, Field Marshal. I know we can both benefit from my presence among the Dogs of War. I can help you on Gottenheim, and you can help me find the better way that this galaxy so desperately needs."

He clapped his hands together once. "I expected no less. I've worked with Marshal Davis many, many times over the years and trust his people judgment. However, since you will be given a combat unit, you'll need to gain the acceptance of the officers you'll be working closest with. Meet me back here in four hours and we'll see how everyone else takes to you."

I stood and saluted. He dismissed me.

I did a lot of thinking and soul searching during that walk back to Marshal Davis's temporary office. I know it didn't make a lot of sense to want to be going back to a line unit, but it felt right. I believed I could make a difference in all of this, perhaps touch some small part of that destiny that had motivated me so strongly before. God knew how much we needed to find a better way than war, and how badly we needed to end this conflict.

Other smaller, balkanized nations throughout the Charted Territories had taken heart from our united defeat of the Hegemony forces on Iwo Jima and started redressing their own lengthy list of perceived wrongs. The Confederate Empire found itself the target of at least thirty different planetary assaults or revolutions sparked or backed by smaller foreign powers. Thirty. An impossibly high number, yet there it was. I lost no sleep over the difficulties facing the Empire, but I also wondered what that boded for the future. It seemed to me to be just the beginning, that we were only starting to get a feel for what results when various peoples are willing to fight for the ideal laid out so very long ago by Abraham Lincoln when he said, "No man is good enough to govern another man without that other's consent."

These days, it seemed no one was granting that consent anymore.

Even the Republic was feeling some small effects of this uprising of smaller, autonomous groups. Several worlds had experienced some form of rebellion, nothing as major as Madrigal's secession, but violent uprisings nonetheless. A few border incursions and subsequent skirmishes by the Sons of Terra had also shaken up a few Republican citizens.

In fact, of all the major nations, only the Al 'Ayn Emirate had escaped attack so far. I wondered if that would last, or if it would only be a matter of time before war swept across the entirety of human civilization and exploration. While the Unification War had affected most every nation, it had only involved a very small percentage of settled worlds. This new form of war, instability across every part of every nation, threatened everyone, everywhere.

There had to be a better way, and maybe joining the Dogs would give me a greater insight into finding that way.

Davis's door was already open, and I could see him hunched over his desk, furiously scribbling something on the paper in front of him. He looked up quickly when I knocked on the door, almost as though he were afraid I'd caught him doing something wrong. For a brief moment, I saw a face wracked by the stresses of long years of killing and more killing. The weight of the life and death decisions he made daily was evident in every line of his face and, oddly, a strange amount of fear and even guilt seemed to be hiding just behind his eyes. That kind of face was one I was familiar with, it was the one I went to bed with every night and woke up wearing every morning. Then he smiled and beckoned me to enter, his entire expression and demeanor changing, and that all seemed to fade away like a dream upon waking. I only hoped I could hide my own baggage half so well.

He motioned me toward the other well padded chair beside his desk, which I sank into gratefully. When I started to speak he silently held up a single finger for a moment while he finished jotting something down, then shuffled his papers around sufficiently to preclude any attempt I might make to read whatever he'd been writing. After that he sat up straight in his chair, folded his hands together and rested them on the desk while he looked at me.

"So, what are your thoughts?"

I had no hesitation. “I want to go, sir, if they’ll take me.”

He raised an eyebrow. “No concerns?”

“None, sir,” I said with a shake of my head. “I’ve done my research, and Marshal Matheson seems to bear out my own conclusions that you were right, we do need to learn their methods.”

“What of taking a line command?” He hadn’t told me he’d known of that ahead of time, he could have had me think it over before going in blind. I supposed he had a good reason for not telling me, hopefully something less petty than simply another test, and I didn’t really want to pursue that line of thinking.

“I can do it, sir.” I took a deep breath, then decided to change the subject before he could press me on it. “The Dogs are an amazing organization, and I’d like to learn more of what they have to offer. It could make a huge difference to the Protectorate and her citizens.”

He accepted my maneuvering with grace. “That it could, which is why I wanted to arrange this position, and why you, with your varied background, are still the best one for the job.”

I changed the subject again to avoid any more embarrassing comments. “I’m supposed to go back this evening and speak with some of their officers, to see if they’ll accept me.”

“Yes, I was told that would be their methodology. I’ll go with you when you’re ready.”

I glanced at the time. “It takes a little while to walk over there, sir. Shall I meet you back here in two and a half?”

The interview was not going well. Actually, the two generals and one of the colonels I would be working with as part of Field Marshal Matheson’s command each in turn seemed to think I was a great candidate, and even said they looked forward to working with me. This last colonel though was a bird of a different feather.

“I’ve faced tactical nuclear weapons on the battlefields of Vai-xing,” Colonel Jamieson said, looking down his long, pointed nose at me. “What have you done that compares to that?”

“I was in Juruko, sir, my Man O’War and a good portion of my unit were destroyed by the blast. I have some appreciation for the concept of nuclear warfare.”

“Other than that,” he said.

“Excluding what we’ve just experienced here, sir, I’ve done nothing that compares to nuclear warfare," I tried not to let my annoyance show, though I was growing very annoyed, very quickly. "But with all due respect, Colonel, nukes were never used on Vai-xing." I hoped he truly realized just how little respect I felt he was due.

"But they were there," he snapped quickly, thrusting a finger in my face, "and we could have been hit with them at any time."

"Oh," I said, trying to control the anger building inside me, "well if that's the case, then I faced biological weapons on Yardsmith, Komodo, Summersand, and Glory, sir. And I'll say this again, unlike your unit, sir, mine was actually in Juruko."

He ground his teeth together audibly, tensing his fists on the tabletop. I didn't understand, what was his problem, why this hatred of me? Even if I'd offended him somehow in some previous life, did we really need this pissing contest?

"I've been credited with over three score Man O'War kills, and I've fought in conflicts as bloody as Akjoujt." He said it like a challenge, one I did not want to accept.

"I'm not criticizing your abilities as a warrior, sir," I said placatingly, trying to sidestep the confrontation he was dead set on provoking. "Your accomplishments are significant. All I want is a chance to join with the Dogs in this conflict and learn how to use what you have to help the Protectorate better position herself in trying to help find some lasting peace in this galaxy."

He sneered at me, literally pulled up one corner of his mouth and sneered at me. "I said, I've been credited with over three score Man O'War kills, and I've fought in conflicts as bloody as Akjoujt. How do you think you compare to that?"

I shrugged. "I killed more than sixty Man O'Wars before I even became a captain, sir, and I fought in a line unit on Madrigal, the biggest, bloodiest conflict this galaxy has seen in three hundred years."

He slapped his hands down on the table and leaned forward. He pitched his voice low so I could hear the disdain flowing freely. "I know you for what you truly are. You are a deserter, a turncoat, a murderer, and a fratricide!"

I would have jumped over the table and beaten the holy shit out of him right then and there if Davis hadn't placed a hand on my shoulder. Every muscle in my body strained against whatever discipline I had, begging to be unleashed and deliver the kind of ass-kicking Jamieson so richly deserved for his comments and attitude.

"Colonel," Davis said to Jamieson, "in the Protectorate, a man who has successfully served in the Reavers is absolved of all former crimes and misdeeds. We do not mention them again."

"That may be interesting to a Parisian, but I fail to see how that..." This time it was Matheson who cut him off.

"The Marshal said we do not mention them again, Colonel. Do not make him repeat himself."

Jamieson fumed. Turning to Matheson he said, "I've no further questions, sir. Let's shove him in a simulation and see if his skills are up to par for a Dog of War."

"If you will, Commandant?" Matheson asked.

"Gladly."

I ran my hand over the smooth top of the simulator pod, smiling as I remembered my first encounter with these machines. I idly wondered if one day it would be me hunting brand new warriors through simulated forests and congratulating one out of thirty of them for actually managing to damage my paint job. The thought wasn't without its appeal. Perhaps when this was all over. For now, there were other things to do.

"We're ready for you now, sir," the tech said from the control station. I gave her a nod then pulled open the pod hatch. This time I didn't bang my head against the panel as I entered, I had learned a little bit here and there in the years I'd been practicing in these things.

"Okay, sir?" the tech checked on me. "If you'll begin the startup sequence, you're in a Crossbow II. As per Colonel Jamieson's request, you'll be in the Tabletop Mountains on Madrigal."

That son of a bitch. I appreciated the tech letting me know whose idea that had been. I wondered if she knew as much about my history with that world as Jamieson did, of if she was just being courteous; maybe she liked me. I shrugged, I wasn't going to let Jamieson get to me. I carried the ghosts of Madrigal with me every minute of every day, being in a simulation wouldn't make them any worse. It would certainly pale next to the nightmares I suffered from regularly.

I pulled my helmet in place and ran through an abbreviated startup. After all, it was just a simulator, nothing should be wrong with it. Everything seemed to be fine, and I signaled the tech that I was ready.

Madrigal's Tabletop Mountains, one the shortest ranges on that world, materialized around me in all of their former glory. This program apparently hadn't been updated to account for the few landscaping changes we'd made to the area back during the Unification War, which was just as well. It would have been a different hunt if there hadn't been any trees.

I started jogging my Crossbow through the trees comfortably, I'd survived much worse combat than this in this very area, this would be a cake walk.

"You have three opponents, Commandant," the tech's voice told me. "A Sniper, a Thug, and a Mirage. They're off somewhere to the northwest of your current position. Good luck, sir." I imagined I could hear the smile in her voice. No, I wasn't ready for any romance yet, and I was probably just projecting onto her anyway.

"I don't mean to make your job difficult," I said, "but do you suppose you could tell me how a three on one Man O'War duel resembles true combat in any way, shape, or form? I mean, this is movie material, something straight out of a poorly written book, not real life combat."

She laughed, almost giggling, which I found cute, but any attraction I felt bounced off of my thick emotional scarring. "I had similar thoughts, sir, but the Colonel seems to believe this is the best test of your skills. He's a strong believer in the dominance of augmented armor versus anything else on the battlefield."

"Well," I told her, "isn't that special. Do you know how many I have to kill to pass this farce of a test?"

"I have no idea, sir, they don't let me in on things like that."

"I didn't think they would, but I had to ask. Thanks."

I turned almost due north and sprinted through the trees, running up the mountain side looking for the high ground. As my altimeter rose and the slope grew steeper my spirits soared right along with them. I felt good, really good. At the risk of sounding ghoulish, I found myself actually welcoming this virtual return to Madrigal. I'm sure Jamieson picked the venue in an attempt to disconcert me, but it backfired. Instead of being haunted by ghosts, I was remembering what it felt like to be young and alive, living the greatest adventure imaginable. I couldn't lose, especially not in this simulated mockery of combat that Jamieson believed was real. I started questioning his claim to sixty combat kills; maybe he was referring to warriors he'd *gotten* killed.

I veered west at the tree line, staying back where I had some cover and concealment. Apparently the Sniper pilot had different ideas because there he sat, as obvious as the nose on my face, astride the rocky ridge looking for all the world like he'd just come out of a recruitment poster. It was the stupidest thing I'd seen.

I had a brief flashback to my time as a Two in COTC. I had been looking at a series of promotional posters on the classroom wall. One depicted an infantry officer standing up in plain view and shouting inspirationally while all around him enlisted soldiers took cover; the caption read "Infantry: learn to lead." Captain Kay had drawn a bull's-eye around the man's head and written "Sniper: learn to shoot."

I took that advice to heart, drawing a big bull's-eye around the Sniper with my targeting systems, and launched a Bolt. The Sniper had just enough time to react to the incoming fire by turning toward the missile's smoking contrail before the warhead removed all of his limbs and large portions of his torso.

"Nice shot, sir," the tech complimented me. I think that definitely qualified as flirting, personally, but I was kind of busy looking for two more Man O'Wars, though I regarded them as significantly less dangerous than the Sniper. Despite the Mirage's near invisibility, it didn't have a big punch, and was rather a delicate machine. The Thug was just a Sunni version of a Roughneck; plenty of staying power and it packed a wallop, but lacked anything much resembling finesse.

That cockiness almost got me killed as I was working my way down a steep rock slide that had cut a big swath through the forest, trying to close the distance to the intermittent blip I was picking up on my scans. The Thug came charging right across the fallen rock field, almost literally bouncing and skipping across the boulders and gravel, practically dancing. That's the rough equivalent of doing a waltz on a floor covered three centimeters deep in marbles. The shots he was firing were too far out of range to be effective, and the footing made accuracy a chore, but they were definitely worrying me as I stood there. I fired a brace of Bolts, but the Thug did its little waltz right between the two of them, successfully dodging at the last minute and shaking the locks.

A good lesson there. Finesse is in the pilot, not the machine.

Still, I had my own tricks. To start with, I stepped on a loose rock and slid halfway down the slope rolling ass over elbows. That slip saved me from being skewered by a half dozen shots that would have done nasty things to my hide. Lying on my left side I fired both wrist cannons, scoring direct hits on the Thug's massive, curved chest. The shots literally bounced off. I was slightly concerned at that point.

The Thug fired at me at the same time as I hit my jump jets. The sudden thrust rocketed me across the ground like a drag racer, heading straight for the Thug's legs. The rocky surface scraped off several unimportant things like my communications array and one of my anti-personnel guns, but the sudden, unorthodox move caught my opponent off guard. He hit his own jump jets and rocketed up to get away from my flying tackle.

Similar to the maneuver I witnessed as a child, I rolled fully to my back and launched a rack of rockets into the Thug's pelvic structure. The explosion tore off a leg and warped the Thug's spine, sending it flipping through the air, at least one jump jet still burning. The crash the Thug made when it hit the ground made me wince in sympathy.

"That was amazing, sir." Did that really sound like she was clapping?

"Thanks," I said again as I dragged myself to my feet. Something was partially jamming my left knee joint, probably a rock had lodged itself there, and the potential loss of maneuverability concerned me. "I was lucky. Who was that?"

"That was Captain Lapenda, sir. She's something of a living legend in the Dogs augmented armor ranks."

"She was amazing moving like that," I agreed, "almost floating right across the most treacherous of footings. I've never seen anything like it."

"But you were better, sir."

"I got lucky," I told her once again. I didn't add the old saying that it's usually better to be lucky than good. Since the simulation didn't end, I had to keep going. Now came the truly hard part, hunting a Mirage that didn't want to be found before it found me.

After a good half hour of wandering about aimlessly, which did manage to dislodge the rock in my knee, I realized just how stupid I was being. No way was I ever going to find a Mirage running its Shift ECM suite and running around a fair sized mountain range all on my own. I needed to let him come to me. I went back to the rock slide and climbed back up to the top, an area with very limited approach vectors. Then I cranked up every active scan I had to full for ten seconds, then turned them all off, basically sending up a flare and a spotlight pinpointing my location to anyone out there. I wandered around the outskirts of the area repeating this performance every two minutes for ten minutes straight, chancing that the Mirage wasn't already right next to me. Then I would wait for a few minutes just watching, and then begin again.

There was really no reason for my opponent to come out and fight me, we could have both stayed in hiding forever, but I was announcing my presence and I was counting on Jamieson to be pressuring his warrior into taking an aggressive stance. Even if he didn't, I was confident I'd passed his little test to the satisfaction of any unbiased observers.

Sure enough, two or three minutes after I stopped my second series of scans, I had one of those feelings you get when you know someone is out there. I cranked up my audio and visual feeds, desperately searching for any sign of the Mirage. I heard the slight sound of gravel crunching and dove forward, the Mirage was right behind me. His first shot missed me completely but his second rendered my right arm useless even as I rolled for cover behind a boulder. I hit my jump jets as soon as I got my feet under me and rode a hot jet stream back a good hundred meters.

There was no sign of the Mirage, either visually or on any scan. That wasn't possible, it couldn't turn invisible. It must have hidden behind the boulders up there. A neat little bit of trigonometry on the computer's part and I was launching a spread of rockets in a high arc that had them landing just behind the string of boulders large enough to hide a Man O'War. Sure enough, the Mirage spooked at my shot and came charging out, eating two of the four Bolts I fired, losing the entire center portion of its torso in the explosion.

Davis and Jamieson were butting heads before I even returned to the room. I could hear them quite clearly from the hallway, and of course I stopped to eavesdrop.

"In case you weren't paying attention, or maybe you just didn't notice, he soundly beat three of your handpicked men, Colonel. Single handedly, I might add."

"Simulations aren't the same as the real thing!"

"And just whose fault is that? You're the one that decide on this stupid test, including the stupidest Sniper pilot I have ever seen. Don't complain when it's too easy for someone who, unlike you, has actually spent his entire adult life not just walking around in a Man O'War, but fighting to the death in one!"

"Just what do you think he will do when the heat is really on and he's staring death in the face?"

"If I were forced to make a guess, I'd say he'll probably do the exact same things he's been doing for the past five years. He'll make decisions, good ones, ones that will bring his people back alive. He'll fight hard with a skill you've never witnessed or imagined, and rack up more kills than you've dreamt possible. He'll make mistakes that cost and he'll get lucky breaks that level the scale; he'll win and he'll lose. In short, he'll lead." Davis paused. "He'll lead, and men and women will follow him."

"He will get them killed, like he's always done!"

I could hear Matheson's voice at that point, but the voice was pitched too low to make out the words. Quietly, I worked my way back down the hall and began my approach to the room again, trying to make it look more natural. As I almost reached the door, it opened and Jamieson came storming out, almost bowling me over.

"You better not screw up out there, Aarons," he threw at me, "not with my people's lives at stake."

I bit my tongue hard, with no effect.

"Go to hell, Colonel," I said. My tolerance for stupidity, never all that strong, finally exhausted, and my frustration boiled out. "How many combat missions have you actually run? How many times have you faced death on the battlefield? How many times have you actually been there? Triple that number and you might start to reach my scratch mark. Until then, maybe you're the one we should be worried about screwing up."

"Insubordinate!"

"Damned straight, Colonel. I've no use for any officer who cannot see reality through his own prejudice. Have people died under my command? You betcha, but are you telling me you've never lost a soldier? The only way that's possible is if you've never seen combat on the front lines. Judging from that ludicrous game you tried to pass off as a test, I'm starting to think that's a very real possibility. Sir."

"Aarons, if you ever speak to me that way again while attached to the Dogs of War, I'll see you behind bars." Then he stormed away.

"It's good to see you living up to the conflict resolution ideals of the Dogs, sir," I called to his back.

I tugged my uniform back straight and turned to enter the room where Marshals Davis and Matheson still sat conversing. They both looked toward me as I entered and rose from their seats. Matheson extended a hand.

"Congratulations," he said shaking my hand. "You've been officially accepted into the Dogs of War. Welcome aboard, Major."

Chapter Twenty-Three

Dogs of War Battlecarrier *Prometheus*
Jump Point Gamma Whiskey Three Six
Star System Alpha One X-ray Zulu Niner (Unnamed)
Terran Dominion

January 9, 2658

I once read a naval account that stated something to the effect that naval conflicts are determined by the combination of ninety percent positioning and ten percent weapons maintenance. You really don't appreciate the import of that statement until you experience your first broadside and see first hand the difference made by good positioning combined with a properly firing gun.

The same account also stated that non-orbital interstellar combat consisted of long days of bored waiting punctuated by an hour of pure terror. The statement comes close to, but ultimately misses, really capturing the true lack of romance inherent in interstellar conflicts.

"Helm, down six seven," Captain Halloway ordered, down being some arbitrary spacer point of reference that I didn't understand. Truthfully, Halloway was a commodore, but, by some odd naval tradition, because he actively commanded the *Prometheus* and not just the battle group, he was dubbed captain. No, it didn't make any sense to me either, but that's swabbies for you.

Lieutenant Commander Feye relayed his orders. "Steerage, down six seven."

A moment, then confirmation was passed in the opposite direction. "Aye, down six seven, Commander."

"Down six seven, Captain."

Do you understand how boring that is? Also confusing since I have no idea what any of that means. Now imagine that the bridge crew had been replaying this same sequence every fifteen minutes or so for the last two or three hours.

For two months we'd been doing our best to gather the coalition strike force together without alerting Hegemony intelligence of our imminent attack. The force that had been sufficient for Iwo Jima would not be enough for a full assault on Gottenheim. Even with a large portion of the Krupp forces pulled out of position attacking targets in Iwaki, the Dominion, and Lublin, we expected some heavy resistance when we tried to occupy their capitol world.

"This waiting is killing me," said the major to my right. "It's like having fingernails scratching down a chalk board over and over again." A glance at his branch insignia told me he was from the quartermaster corps, not a group generally accustomed to waiting in worry while an attack was imminent.

"You get used to it," I lied. I needed to try and do my part to maintain the mystique surrounding Man O'War pilots. It just wouldn't do if everyone knew that warriors get as scared as everyone else waiting for the shooting to start. After the shooting starts there usually isn't enough time to be scared. "Just take deep breaths and relax your shoulders."

We had jumped back and forth across a half dozen national borders, seeking allies, rendezvousing with reinforcements, and pretending we were being sneaky. Realistically, any half-assed intelligence service should have known something was afoot. We just hoped that they wouldn't be able to figure out what the real target was.

Still, this cat and mouse game of hiding in unnamed star systems, jamming mines and sensors buoys, sending out false trails only to double back or split up and join up again later, it all got very frustrating to a career ground pounder. While I could appreciate the strategy as similar to what we used, the distances and time involved were very foreign.

"What's going to happen?" the Major asked me. Great, another talker. I tried to bite my tongue and be patient, this was surely his first naval engagement as well, and different people have different needs. I still couldn't help myself.

"I'm going to guess that likely we'll zip in there and blow up all of their ships. They'll probably blow up a couple of ours." I was nervous too, and I guess that manifested itself in a sort of morbid cruelty. "If they follow the same strategies as us ground pounders, they'll take out the biggest ship first."

"That's us," he said, realization dawning. He swallowed hard and licked his lips. "You're kidding me, right?"

I shook my head, then shrugged. "Hey, I'm no expert, so maybe I'm wrong." That answer obviously didn't help him. He looked around nervously, then unbuckled his restraints, stood up, and left.

We'd jumped into this system three days ago and been startled by the rude (and loud) announcement that we were not alone. A small group (I don't know if fleet is the accurate term, I'm not a sailor) of Krupp vessels was also on station in the system, if a very, very long way away. It seemed prudent to me, and all I talked to, that we simply leave each other alone, but that has never been the Krupp way. The Hegemony force beamed off a message, likely a detailed one about the size and composition of our strike force, then, insanely, moved ever so slowly to engage us.

We weren't worried about the report they fired off, they couldn't have known who we were. The most likely explanation would have been that we were a Dominion task force moving to reinforce against the border incursions. If that was what they reported, it certainly wouldn't compromise the secrecy of our mission, the Hegemony had to expect the Dominion would not remain docile forever. In fact, we were due to link up with a real Dominion addition to our task force on our next jump, the last addition to our numbers before we struck out for Gottenheim.

I almost felt bad for what I'd done to the poor major. He'd annoyed me though, and at a time when I had no patience for being annoyed. It wasn't like I'd lied to him either, that very real concern was bothering me a lot. If we came out of this whole, I'd have to make an effort to hunt the man down and buy him a drink by way of apology.

It had taken the Krupp invasion of Thendas to make the Republic realize that they couldn't avoid the war, and how had they responded? By breaking apart. Five of the provinces from the original Free Terran Republic simply broke away, claiming they would no longer send their children to die for Dominion soil as they'd done during the Unification War.

They paid a price for that, but in the end, who can blame them for their feelings?

After the Krupp forces raced across Cancro, unchecked by the Republic's weakened Home Guard, the newly reborn Free Terran Republic had realized the depth of its mistakes, but by then it was too late, the ball had begun rolling and it was nothing but fighting from then on. Now they had the luxury of sending their sons and daughters to die for Republic soil, often in their own backyards.

As with so many other nations throughout history, the balkanization of the Unified Terran Republic, once started, was impossible to stop. Two more provinces went the way of Madrigal, even negotiating a non-aggression treaty with the Hegemony. As if anyone expected that to last.

I toyed idly with my pen, slapping it roughly against the scratchpad's hard plastic surface. The pad bleeped at this unusual treatment so I turned it off. I hadn't expected to actually get any work done anyway, it was just for show. Everyone else seated around the room also had various forms of camouflage from books to paperwork, one infantry captain (on ship we had to call him major, thanks to the weird customs of the swabbies) was even cleaning a rifle, but no one was actually getting anything done.

After arriving, the fleet had needed a few days in system before we'd be ready and in position to make another jump. That left us with no other choice but to detach a small number of combat ships and get rid of our opposition before they could threaten any of our relatively lightly armed and thinly armored transport ships. Besides, a real Dominion fleet wouldn't have run from the Krupp forces, not in their own backyard, and we kind of needed to play out that charade. All that was left was to win decisively and make certain they didn't find out who we really were.

At first I'd been extremely anxious, wondering how one goes about facing combat in space. My previous experiences with non-planetary combat had all been in boat drops that had only lasted a few seconds before entering the atmosphere, and I'd never been comfortable during those as I was just a spectator and someone else had control over my life and death. This promised to be even worse because at no time would I get to do anything that would make a difference, the whole battle, from start to finish, would be decided by others. I was just an observer, one who might die if things didn't go well.

After a full day of nervously waiting to close the distance to engage the enemy, I started to calm down a bit, realizing that it was going to be quite some time before there was any real danger. The next day went pretty smoothly, actually, save for the arrival of the news that Aurora had fallen to the Sons of Terra. Emboldened by the disorganization of the Dominion as it simultaneously fought on all sides in both a civil war and an international war, they had made the move they'd always dreamt of, the first step toward the reoccupation of Earth.

A mere three hours later we found out that Earth had also fallen, had hardly resisted in fact. I worried about Liz, and about Rachel, but things inside still hurt too bad for me to be able to dwell on the subject long, and I found myself easily distracted from those concerns. I didn't want to ask questions I couldn't answer there.

For certain, we now knew that the Dominion group we were going to meet in a few days would be much smaller than we'd initially hoped. Chaos gripped the Charted Territories, and it was so very hard to tell whether the good guys were winning.

This morning the combat alarm had blared and all of us ground pounders had rushed around trying to convince ourselves we were doing something of use, when we were mostly just getting in the swabbies' way. Finally I just said forget it. I quit tinkering endlessly with my TO&E, and bullied my way past a couple of marines into one of the combat control rooms just off the bridge. From there, those of us present (mostly army officers) would be able to witness the unpleasant drama unfold, and at least have a chance of staring death in the face before he took us all. Apparently I'd arrived much too early, for combat was, then, still hours away.

"Helm, come about to port one five. Roll thirty." Again the orders were passed along in that confusing manner and returned by the same route. These endless adjustments and tricks were tedious and mind numbingly dull. I was frustrated with it all and longed for the simplicity of actual combat, but approach calculations indicated that was still half an hour away.

Despite my first blush impression that this all seemed to be combat in slow motion, I wasn't completely correct. Million ton vessels trying to adjust vectors and attitudes just so in the hopes that they may precisely position themselves where they have all the advantage do not do so quickly, it's true. Lacking the velocity shunts and acceleration shields that make fighters so maneuverable those big behemoths seem truly sluggish, especially when they have to make course corrections of only a few degrees many minutes in advance if they are to successfully outwit and out position their foes.

While that all does seem rather slow on the surface of it, the proper term would be lengthy. When you add in the idea that the two groups to be involved were still accelerating towards one another, and had been accelerating in that manner for many hours, and you realized that they would be zipping past one another at extremely high speeds, something like three or four score kilometers per second or more, you understand that *slow* is not the word for it. The one who gets his positioning just right can fire for a longer period of time from a more protected angle at the weaker spots of his opponent. The one who gets it wrong usually ends up drifting through the endless expanses of space very cold, and very dead.

The bridge crew kept busy. Halloway presided over the oddly oval shaped area, packed tightly with consoles, crew stations, and displays. His chair sat toward the back of the bridge and up a bit, giving him the best position to hear and be heard. His own station was as complicated as anyone else's, probably giving him feeds from all the major positions.

Those other positions also had stations around the bridge, stations from which they coordinated the activities of their crews throughout the ship. Yeomen and other enlisted personnel did the real work, while the officers provided guidance and took the credit, just like other military branches.

Eventually the time did pass.

"Fire control, status?" Halloway asked.

The ensign did a quick double check. "Three minutes to energies. Torpedoes in ten and fighters away in fifteen. Guns in twenty and two."

"Estimate of conflict window?" The what? Now he was speaking that odd navy language that I didn't understand.

"Fifteen minutes plus or minus five from fighters." Good thing the ensign was there to clear up all my confusion with that response. I tried asking around the room just what they were talking about, but no one else had any idea what was going on either. They all just waved me down, trying to shush me up.

The only thing I did understand was that energy weapons in space have a very long effective range indeed. It's not quite line of sight, as a fraction of a degree off can account for a very large miss after a thousand kilometers, and there is a loss of beam cohesion over distance, but the range is still really far. Similar advantages and problems exist with projectile fire except that the slower movement means greater possibility of a miss or a successful intercept.

"Combat stations report fixed firing solutions ready for energies, Captain," the ensign at fire control said.

"Thank you, Mr. Hall. Weapons free at range, standard disbursement." Ensign Hall relayed those orders to the firing crews throughout the ship.

I watched the countdown on the board go down to two minutes.

"Mr. Hram," Halloway called communications, "reconfirm all ships that *Prometheus* group has the battleship and escorts. *Atlas* and *Hercules* have the cruisers at Foxtrot Six and Four, *Icarus* flight specially tasked on the boomer."

"Aye, Captain." He spoke into his set briefly, examining his displays as well. "Confirmed."

"Then we wait," I heard Halloway mutter under his breath. Apparently officers in the navy are as uncomfortable with the long minutes of waiting as army officers are. I guess we're all in a hurry to see just exactly how quickly the enemy can blow away the plans we worked on so hard.

The countdown ever so steadily clicked down toward zero. At the one minute mark I realized my mouth was so dry I could no longer swallow easily. That and my palms had grown weak and sweaty. This was an entirely new experience. Frankly, I missed the frustration and boredom of earlier as my body pumped adrenaline through my system.

"Thirty seconds to energies," Hall announced, oblivious to the fact that everyone else was also staring at the countdown.

"Helm free. Active counter measures, decoys away," Halloway ordered.

"Aye, Captain," Feye acknowledged, "Helm free. Roll fifteen on my mark, alternate combat procedure delta."

"Counter measures running," someone I couldn't see reported excitedly.

"Decoys away!" I couldn't identify the source of that voice either, it was a rather large and cluttered bridge after all.

"Four, three, two," Hall counted down for those amongst us who were blind or just ignorant. Maybe he felt the need to do something, however pointless, as strongly as I did. "Contact!"

Hall's last word was underscored by a brilliant light display traced across every screen and board on the bridge, likely throughout the whole ship. The computer traced each beam that lanced out from our ships to theirs and the ones they returned. An intricate web of invisible energy played across the vast expanses of space between all the ships trying to deliver death to the enemy's doorstep.

The initial volley quickly tapered off to a more steady thrum of intermittent blasts as those huge naval guns took time to recharge. Power levels throughout the ship dropped as weapons systems took priority from the generators. The lights dimmed significantly, almost to twilight levels, and the room grew perceptibly hotter as power was pulled from environmental control.

"Damage, Mr. Hram," the Captain called.

"The *Prometheus* has not been hit. Opposition appears to be targeting the escorts first. *Atlas* reports significant armor loss on all escorts. *Icarus'* group has lost the *Agamemnon,* which is venting, and the *Odysseus* has already turned to drop out of the attack vector."

"Bastards." That comment I understood. It made sense for the Hegemony forces to strike the smaller ships, the ones they could probably kill with one pass. This wasn't an orbital conflict with its lengthy stationary slugging matches where the giant ships would circle one another, it was an interstellar jousting match where the behemoths would rush past each other at incredible speeds, and the Krupps would want to kill something on this pass. Damaged ships could, conceivably, be repaired before the next battle, ruined ones much less likely. So the next time this group of ours faced off, it would do so with less combat vessels. That the tactic made sense didn't mean it seemed fair in any sense of the word.

The light displays on the combat boards continued, side displays showing various ship status reports changing colors as ships were hit. I saw clearly as the small frigate *Odysseus* faltered in its turn, holed through in a dozen spots. Fires flared across her decks and some blossomed into space. Another score or three of heavy naval batteries of varying size struck home, tearing her heart out and venting it to space. Chunks of her hull tore free and drifted away from the ship, I tried not to imagine how many people were also torn to chunks and left to drift in space.

"*Odysseus* is down," Hram said. "*Salvation* is en route for recovery, ETA is fifteen minutes. Preliminaries indicate half casualties."

Already we'd lost one, but quickly enough we evened out the score a little bit as one of the Hegemony vessels, a much bigger one than the *Odysseus,* faltered in its acceleration. I wasn't the only one to notice it. Shouts were exchanged across the bridge, and even a few in our war room, as different suggestions were voiced on how best to take advantage of the situation.

"Status on the heavy," Feye called out.

"Losing power," Hall confirmed. "Venting on three decks. She's turning about, breaking vector."

"Discontinue fire on the cruiser, discontinue fire on all escorts," Halloway instructed. He wanted to remove some of that firepower. "Focus on the battleship, let's take it down."

"Torpedo solutions ready!" Hall shouted.

"Fire at range."

A few more tense moments of crisscrossing energy fire, then, "Torpedoes away!"

I swear I felt the whole ship shudder as those huge Beluga torpedoes, armored and packed with their own stealth and ECM packages, tore away from the ship with a powerful acceleration. The entire battle group vomited out well over a hundred of the Belugas, and many other smaller torpedoes and missiles as well, holding back nothing more than was required by our weaponry's limitations. Our opponents did the exact same thing, though with a significantly lower number of projectiles.

"Twenty seconds to impact." Was that our impact or their impact?

"Anti-torpedo measures?" Halloway asked.

"Activated…locks slipping, we can't hold them," Hall responded. Those Krupp electronics were good, quality stuff, making it difficult to detect and defeat their torpedoes. "Manual targeting in five. The battleship has slipped its acceleration curve! Reading fires in forward gunnery stations!"

Every eye on the bridge focused on the screen that showed a blown up display of the battleship we were charging. While their fire was trying to eliminate our smaller escorts, our entire group's concentrated fire had actually done some damage, slipping in through the thick front armor of the Krupp ship. The behemoth was hurt and visibly shuddering, likely racked by explosions as its forward ammunition magazines cooked off.

With armor or augmented armor such an injury would be very fatal, with the big ships, thickly armored and segmented into isolated sections with blast doors and armored bulkheads, it was an inconvenience. It was an inconvenience at the wrong time however, as those shudders threw off the anti-torpedo batteries, allowing a greater portion than normal to do the job they were designed to do.

"Impact!" Hall shouted.

This time the whole ship really did shudder as three or four torpedoes tore across the upper decks of the *Prometheus*. I lurched against my chair's restraints, admiring the way the bridge crew didn't even flinch from their duties despite the ship bouncing all around them.

On the screen, the Krupp battleship fared far worse. Its broadside partially exposed by the abrupt turn the explosions had caused, it sat helpless as a full dozen warheads slammed into it all along its length, cutting deep inside. Secondary explosions wracked throughout and slowly, ever so slowly, the battleship broke cleanly in half.

A cheer went up across the bridge, and I was vaguely surprised to discover myself clapping and shouting right along with everyone else. I guess the swabbies had some impressive and worthy abilities of their own. The cheers didn't last long as more shudders ran through the ship and several displays changed violently.

"Roll forty-five," Feye instructed, rotating the ship on its long axis to keep our damage farther from the enemy's fire.

"Concentrate fire on that last cruiser," Halloway called. "Damage report!"

"Thirty percent armor loss on section forward three," Hram reported. "Minor breach in port scanning section, already sealed. *Minotaur* and *Cyclops* are dropping out. *Hercules* reports the *Echo* won't last much longer. Wait!" He held his hand to his ear, and focused on whatever he heard there. Then his hands flew across his panel and quickly changed one display to show our biggest battleship. "The *Atlas* is in trouble!"

Apparently the Krupps had decided our tactic was better, they began focusing their fire more toward the capitol ships. Even worse, with their superior targeting systems, they'd been able to better maneuver their torpedoes into the *Atlas*'s weaker points.

As we watched the display, energy weapons continued to play over the ship, destroying armor and weaponry. For some reason her captain wouldn't, probably couldn't, roll the ship around, and it was taking a horrendous pounding. Another half dozen torpedoes raced toward her, only four of which were successfully intercepted by counter-fire. The other two opened awful wounds all along her front quarter.

"Somer it, Ned," Halloway muttered forcefully under his breath, trying by force of will alone to make the great ship flip end for end to rapidly decelerate. "Drop out!"

It was too late for that though. The entire length of the *Atlas* cracked wide and fountained out air and flame, for one brief second burning as brightly as this system's star far above us. The reactor overload vent caused the massive warship to lurch sideways, slamming fully into the *Hades*. The two ships bounced apart like balls on a pool table, their lost acceleration rapidly dropping them behind the formation.

"Planes away," a new voice reported from the wing commander's station. Commander Boroma directed our attention toward the fighters and attack craft blasting away from the carriers in our group. Our counterparts had no carriers with them, giving us at least that much advantage.

One display showed a view of the flight deck. Dozens of fighters leapt from their bays, pilots giving each other the thumbs up as they bolted into the great beyond. Ground crew, dressed in their environmental suits, ran all around the bay in a chaotic pattern far too complex for me to follow, readying the next launch group with final preparations. A few seemed to be already preparing the capture mechanisms for the planes' return, others prepared crash equipment, rescue tools, and reloads for returning space craft.

Seeing all the activity, I felt vaguely guilty about just sitting around and doing nothing. That, however, is what officers are best at, or so I was once told by a fellow enlisted Reaver. It seemed so long ago.

The fighters raced bravely into the fray, heedless of the danger presented by the torpedoes that were still flying back and forth regularly and the veritable web of energy beams engulfing the dwindling space between the two groups. Their superior performance profiles had them racing in and about the enemy ships in only a few minutes, firing energy weapons and launching missiles from close range into the weakest armor.

Such daring was not without its own price to pay. More than one fighter disappeared from our active displays every minute, falling victim to the Krupp counter-fire. Once again I was fervently wishing for us to be miraculously returned to the time when I was bored and frustrated.

The display continued its inexorable countdown to heavy gun range. Once we got there, each ship would have about five minutes to blast away with their heavy plasma cannons, unleashing horrific destruction upon one another. Then we'd see how effective Halloway's endless adjustments had been, but with one cruiser crippled and their battleship gone, the Krupps could only hope to inflict a bit more damage, take a few more lives.

"*Echo* is dead in space," Hram said. "Life boats away. *Salvation* has the *Odysseus,* proceeding on the *Agamemnon*."

"The cruiser is coming about two one point two," Feye said.

"Attack planes have crippled frigates three and five." Boroma smiled.

"Guns!" Hall snapped.

Space turned that eerily beautiful bluish white color as artificial, miniature sun flares blasted out between the battle groups. It was strange watching the plumes move out so slowly after having relied on energy weapons and high acceleration torpedoes.

"Impact in five," Hall said.

"Planes clear," Boroma said.

"Two, one..."

This time we shook like we'd been hit by a fair sized earthquake. A couple of lighting systems and at least one display shorted out in a fountain of sparks. Little lightning bolts played across one corner of the bridge, burning one crew-member quite severely.

"Look, the *Icarus* is on the boomer," someone said beside me.

Boomers, as the navy calls them, more commonly called planet busters by us simpler folk, are stuffed to the gills with orbit-to-ground weaponry. They provide both local and general support, being able to strike targets as small as an armor company or, like we'd seen on Kira and Kobe, as large as a city. They weren't particularly dangerous in interstellar conflicts (we'd left our own boomers back with the main fleet), but after Iwo Jima the fear was that they now carried nuclear weapons.

On the display we could see that the *Icarus,* our largest close assault destroyer, had slipped out from behind our wake. It went flashing past the Krupp boomer at extremely close range like a bat out of hell. Normally, close range in space mean a few kilometers, the *Icarus* must have been within two hundred meters, almost touching the enemy vessel.

Guns all along the length of the *Icarus* belched out their deadly fire. The boomer was struck by at least two dozen plasma bursts at point-blank range. They boiled through the boomer's armor and into its delicate interior almost instantly. Deck plating, superstructure, and crew members flashed from existence along with any suspicious cargo that may have been on board. The boomer cracked open like an egg before being completely torn apart in the firestorm of released energies.

Us ground pounders whooped it up a bit at the kill, glad to see one or our main sources of fear torn to shreds before our very eyes. The navy boys and girls weren't so impressed with the easy kill, they had more pressing concerns. The ship bucked hard once again, actually catapulting one crew member, chair and all, into the ceiling. One of the officers near me bounced his head off the table. Then we were out of it.

"We missed the worst of it," Hram said without being asked. "Fleet has sustained twenty-five percent loss in combat power. Enemy retains only fifteen percent. *Prometheus* has lost thirty percent armor, fifteen percent firepower. Casualty reports still coming in from throughout the ship, estimate two hundred."

"Cruiser coming about to seven five," Feye said with a slight shout, "she's on collision course with the *Hercules*!" A shiver ran down my spine. At these speeds, even a glancing collision would be fatal for both ships.

Hall and Boroma spoke at the same time, even before Halloway could give any orders.

"All fire on the cruiser."

"Planes concentrating runs on the cruiser."

I think we all knew it we were just too close to make a difference, that nothing we did would work, but we had to try. I gripped the arms of my chair tightly.

The display showing the heavy cruiser painted a picture straight out of Dante's inferno. Our gunners had done their jobs well. Fountains of escaping flame and energy dotted her entire length, cracks and gaps showing everywhere in her armor, often all the way into her superstructure. Save for a few weak triple A guns still blasting away at our aviators, the cruiser's weaponry had fallen silent, likely destroyed entirely. Our fighters and attack craft raced along her length firing missiles and energy blasts into her interior, naval cannons of all kinds blasted huge chunks off of her, and the occasional torpedo still blew holes all the way through the ship. It wasn't going to be enough. Even if we disintegrated the ship completely, the pieces, all the mass of the ship itself, would still be on a collision course. We didn't even achieve that much.

I'll give all the props in the galaxy to the *Hercules* captain and crew. Despite the cruiser bearing down on them, they never flinched, the never turned away. It wouldn't have helped, but it would have been natural. They did manage to get a few life boats away first.

At thousands of kilometers per hour, the cruiser and the *Hercules* met almost head on. The collision literally disintegrated both ships, a huge explosion of released energy and gases blasted forth scattering the two hulls in millions of pieces, none much bigger than my Man O'War.

That was all I saw of the actual impact between the two ships, because the deck bucked violently under me again as we were swept heavily from stem to stern with plasma fire. For that brief moment we stood broadside to a half dozen destroyers, and they pummeled us with all they had.

Halloway and Feye were experts at their jobs, though, and when the Krupp ships were able to fire on us to their greatest advantage, they had our smallest profile to them. Our return fire was far more effective, timed properly and positioned right to grind the smaller vessels like garlic in a press. The broadside pass lasted only a heartbeat, but three destroyers winked off the boards.

When we broke through, more or less intact, the only thing of the *Hercules* left in one piece was a portion of the lower (relatively speaking) hull, about a third of the length of the ship. It floated dark and motionless, almost without movement, falling far behind us as we raced away from it.

"Guns beyond range," Hull said.

"Coming about on eight in four," Feye added.

No one else really had anything else to add. We were all a little shocked at what we'd just witnessed. For a tactic that had started with attempting to wipe out all of our escorts, the Krupp force had succeeded rather remarkably in destroying two of our battleships, trading two heavy cruisers and a battleship of their own for it. When we added up how many of their smaller ships we'd destroyed, it was obvious that the battle tilted in our favor. When we realized that we'd need every capitol ship we could get our hands on when we got to Gottenheim, it was obvious that the war was tilting in their favor.

"How many can we finish off before we lose them?" Halloway asked.

"Air-cap estimates forty percent of remaining," Boroma answered.

"And gunnery another forty," Hull said.

Halloway closed his eyes momentarily. "So at least five ships will escape." His eyes opened. "So be it. Concentrate fire on the larger ships, let's cripple them as much as we can."

"Aye, Captain," echoed across the bridge.

"Status on the first cruiser."

"Limping," Hram said. "Limited power. Intercept possible in ten."

"Launch boarding parties."

Marine boats, specially designed lithe, little craft capable of forcing an entry into almost any access hatch, zipped away from the ship, headed for the crippled heavy cruiser. On board were some very brave soldiers, those willing to actually board a dying enemy vessel filled with plenty of people that wanted to see them dead. Without thinking I saluted them as they sped off and was joined in that gesture of respect by everyone else in the room. We may trade jokes back and forth about the leather necked jar heads, but that doesn't mean we don't admire some of the things they do. Besides, these were *our* leather necked jar heads.

We continued to fire on the rapidly retreating enemy vessels as before, but now the return fire was thankfully light. Several more of the Hegemony ships disappeared from our displays as the gunners and aviators did their jobs.

"Reading energy spikes across the cruiser," Hram said. "Self destruct!"

Apparently the marines had noticed the same thing as their boats suddenly took extreme evasive maneuvers, likely flattening the marines inside as they overloaded their velocity shunts. The marine craft spread out in all directions, trying to get as far away from the overloading cruiser as they could before it released its full fury upon them.

The cruiser exploded in a dozen places, a victim of her own crew's refusal to be captured. It sent shards flinging out in all directions, propelled to extreme speeds by the strength of the blast. Several of the small pieces tore holes in a couple of boats, though they appeared to be still functional. One boat wasn't so lucky, a larger piece about the size of a two-story house crushed it entirely.

Licking their wounds and totally unsuccessful, though through no fault of their own, the marines turned to come back home. The fanaticism, the disrespect for your own people's lives, for your own life, it left a bad taste in my mouth. It left a bad taste in everyone's mouth.

"Air-cap breaking off," Boroma said. "Losses at thirty percent."

"Captain," Hram said, "*Salvation* reports that at least two of the *Agamemnon*'s life boats, confirmed ejected and functioning by witness accounts, cannot be recovered. Their tracking beacons were removed and left adrift in space. Suspect recovery by Krupp ships."

There was a silence across the bridge and throughout the adjoining observation rooms. All of us were mulling over not only the fate of our captured comrades, but also the impact this development would have on our mission.

"Bastards," Halloway said again.

Not only had the Hegemony successfully destroyed two of our most powerful warships, but now they likely knew we were coming straight for their capitol. I expected that our welcome to Gottenheim would not be a warm one.

Chapter Twenty-Four

Dogs of War Assault Carrier *Epimetheus*
Geosynchronous Orbit Over Drop Zone Alpha One Niner
Dogs of War Area of Operation: Grundorf
Vollstandigkeit Senke, Dammerung
Gottenheim
Krupp Hegemony

April 11, 2658

No one in the entire Coalition force was ever foolish enough to believe that taking the Krupp capitol would be easy. From the commanding generals down to the most junior private, each and every one of us knew this operation would be the test of our lives. The entire structure of the Hegemony practically guaranteed it.

With interstellar transportation being so expensive, most nations only ship luxuries and those essentials that are unavailable locally between worlds. The minerals and chemicals needed for such products as weapons and armor are plentiful on virtually every world mankind inhabits, so those things are almost always manufactured locally, then transported off world only in response to dire need.

The big exception to that rule is the Krupp Hegemony.

In the view of their current regime, absolute control of the nation's weapons production equals absolute control of the nation's populace and enemies, and everyone not of Krupp is against Krupp. More than half of the nation's entire munitions and military arms factories were located within the Gottenheim system. That's what made it the perfect target; that's what made it the perfect deathtrap.

The Hegemony also trains a great portion of its soldiers right there in the system. In fact, every resident is required to spend at least two years in the military just to qualify for citizenship, more if they ever want to be in government or positions of prestige and power, and all citizens are part of the reserves until the age of fifty-five.

The net result of all of this was that, to take and hold one solar system, we would have to defeat an estimated one eighth of the entire Hegemony military in their own backyard. That number would have been considerably higher if our allies hadn't been doing such an incredible job of convincing the Krupps that we were going to be attacking all along their border. That drew them out of position and left them chasing skirmishing units from a dozen different nations as they harassed the Krupp flanks.

We still had a huge number of defenders to face, and, after our interstellar engagement in the Dominion, they'd had three months to prepare for our arrival.

A surface-to-orbit gun battery is all but impossible to take out by direct ground assault. They're simply too massive and well-defended. The fact that they are usually built almost entirely underground ensures that even a nuclear strike, much less a simple air strike, generally can't take them out beyond repair. The only quick way to neutralize them is to blind them, and that would be our job.

This would be our baptism of fire, so to speak. My unit was a good one, drawn from the best the Dogs could offer, but none of them had fought under me before. Simulations could only do so much, and I wondered how well we'd work together when we finally hit the real thing. No matter, our task was to remove the central tracking stations that allowed the SOG batteries to be so dangerous. We would be plowing the road for the rest of the invasion.

While the aviators on both sides fought it out in the most massive furball ever imagined, every soldier in the Third Mechanized strapped in and readied his or her self for the impending drop. While the fleet moved in to engage the planetary defenses, we huddled in our ablative stealth shells and waited for the *Epimetheus* to get close enough to the planet to send us on our way. While that incredible battle was engaged and raged all about us, we sat helpless, merely waiting to be launched into the fray.

We stayed there for several hours, wishing for that moment to come, fearing that it would. I ran through every checklist at least a dozen times there in the dark. When that exhausted its possibilities for distraction, I patched myself into the tactical feeds to get a feel for how the battle progressed. My first sight was that of a crippled Krupp fighter deliberately ramming into an ambulance shuttle. Despite years of seeing killings on and off the battlefield, I still recoiled in horror.

It didn't stop there. My feelings of horror and disbelief just built over the hours as I witnessed barbarity heaped upon inhumanity. These outrages shredded every last rule of warfare. I watched an orbital gunship, engines leaking, use its damaged pylon to tear open the side of a thinly skinned, heavy infantry transport, spilling hundreds of bodies into the vacuum. I viewed with shock the brutal attack made against one of our unarmed and clearly marked hospital ships. Those bastards destroyed its engines and launch facilities, then left it to burn up as its orbit failed and it plummeted toward the planet below.

This wasn't warfare, this was cold blooded murder. In the name of defending their oppressive and aggressive regime, the Krupps were stopping at nothing. The difficulty in fighting an enemy like this would be in maintaining the moral high ground, restraining our own troops so that we did not fall to the level of the enemy. That would be an arduous task; we had known the Krupp soldiers would be dedicated, very capable, and equipped with arguably the best electronics and engineering in the charted territories.

We hadn't expected them to be so fanatical in defending the Chancellor.

I flipped from one camera feed to another, shaking my head almost in a state of sorrow. I was concentrating on the battle raging around us, not on the progress of the *Epimetheus,* so when the drop tone came it caught me by surprise. The assault carrier and its sister ship, the *Alpha Male*, had won through to the launch point. A second later I was slammed back by inertia's rude force as my pod was launched toward Gottenheim.

Suddenly I had other things to occupy my attention. A quick check of the status display showed we were all clear and away from the ship, heading fast for the surface. "Hounds, this is Pack Lead," I sent out. "Report by company." Our pods hurtled past dueling fighters, burning platforms, and the scattered debris left behind as vessels of all shapes and sizes came apart.

"Pack Lead, this is Alpha, all units report green."

"Lead, Bravo. We lost one pod on launch. All others good to go. We are ready."

"Charlie. Lost three to a couple of fighters. Everyone else is good." We weren't even on the ground and already we'd lost a squad of infantry and three Man O'Wars.

"Lead, this is Delta. We...hold on! No! Wait!" A loud pop from the communication equipment accompanied the destruction of Delta Leader, and a good portion of her armor company.

Less than two hundred kilometers to ground now. "All units, this is Pack Lead. Ionization blackout in thirty. Re-establish com as soon as you're out of it. Good luck, God bless, and give 'em hell." The replies were weak, masked by the static that was already starting to block communications and sensors.

The next minutes passed with agonizing slowness. I couldn't see or hear anything beyond the altitude and hull reports the pod was feeding to me. That has to be one of the worst feelings there is, not being able to do anything at all, not even watch, while those depending on you meet their fates.

The thickening atmosphere outside had begun to have a noticeable effect on my drop pod. I could hear the shriek of air rushing past, and I watched the external temperature reading climb from winter in the Arctic to midsummer in Hell in a matter of seconds. The outer ablative layers of the drop pod absorbed the intense heat, then burned clean away as the atmospheric drag slowed me somewhat.

At only a few dozen kilometers altitude, my computer decided it was time to discard the pod. Explosive bolts fired and the shell flew away along with enough decoys, chaff, flares, and jamming nodules to, theoretically, throw off the aim of any gunners with the skill to hit a falling rock. My first parachute also deployed, jamming me hard into my seat.

"Hounds, this is Pack Leader. Report." Nothing but static. I tried again. "All Hounds, Lead. Call in." It sounded like we were being jammed pretty heavily, as we'd expected, but still someone should have been close enough to overcome it at this altitude. "Hounds, report status." A few weak signals sounded faintly in my ears.

"Copy lead, Delta Three. Can't see…"

"…Bravo in jet stream, Alpha even farther off…"

Of Charlie I heard nothing. Shit. With intermittent contact with Delta Three and Bravo Lead, my computer pieced together the location of most of the battalion, and they were scattered all over the place. It didn't look like any two of us were going to come down within a klick of one another, much less land as an effective fighting group.

Since a Man O'War drifting gently to earth beneath a parachute makes a wonderful, helpless target, my computer cut me free. It had already done its job of stabilizing my descent and allowing me to re-establish contact with my unit, so it was time to free fall again. Once again I was riding an out of control lift bound straight for hell.

At ten kilometers up my second chute popped open with a tremendous jolt, again compressing the disks of my spine. My rate of descent slowed almost instantly from bat-out-of-hell to merely cat-with-tail-on-fire-going-over-a-cliff. The computer assured me that I was right on target, though alone, then made some minor adjustments to my position and attitude before cutting this chute free as well. At two klicks my final chute opened, signaling that it was time to put the heart back in my tin man and bring it to life.

Standard procedure for a drop is to activate just the major systems as the more delicate minor systems are more prone to damage from a rough landing. I didn't want to land unaware of what was going on around me, though, so I brought everything online immediately. I preferred the risk of losing a directional signal on landing to the risk of landing in a formation of enemy tanks without any sort of foreknowledge.

With about a kilometer left to fall I toggled my systems over to their rarely used look down/shoot down mode, hoping to find a safe, soft landing spot. I was fortunate in that there didn't appear to be any Hegemony units nearby, but the terrain itself was horrid—all razor-sharp ridges of bedrock spearing up from within the planet to heights of hundreds of meters with deep, narrow little valleys in between. Perfect Man O'War territory.

It would take a lot of canopy to bring a Man O'War to a soft landing using a parachute, and history taught that that would simply present too easy a target. That's why I cut away the third and final chute and activated the landing rockets attached to my legs and back. For the last few hundred meters I perched atop a pillar of fire, slowing to a halt just above the ground before the rockets burnt out.

I fell about half a meter, landing relatively gently in a valley barely wider than my Man O'War. I fired the explosive bolts that discarded the landing rockets, then set about my two most important tasks: securing the LZ and gathering in my troops. The first was easy enough, I hadn't actually gotten a fix on any hostiles during my entire descent. The second, now that was a problem.

More than four hundred of the soldiers in my battalion had made the drop, and not a single one of them was here on target with me. Armor, infantry, mobile artillery, augmented armor, everything; it was all missing.

I switched on my command frequency. "Eyeball One, this is Hound Pack Leader, requesting sit-rep. Over." My display began blinking a message that said "transmission error" in little red letters. The stresses of my rapid deceleration and landing had apparently done something unpleasant to some of my communication gear.

Now I was truly alone. For all anyone in orbit knew, I had been destroyed long before touching down, or I'd come down half a continent from where I was supposed to be like the rest of the Third. Part of a Diane motto popped into my head.

I will continue with the mission…

Destroying the multiple tracking stations that supported Battery Theta would be impossible for a single Man O'War. The Hounds had drawn that duty because Matheson felt our fully integrated combined arms gave us the widest range of possibilities, and the best potential for success. All alone, armed with nothing but my Will O'Wisp, it seemed unlikely that I would even live long enough to get within scanning range.

…though I alone remain…

With my orbital communications non-functional, I couldn't report to or coordinate with higher, and an evacuation was out of the question. Also out were the ideas of staying put and/or surrendering. I already knew more than I ever wanted to know about how Krupp treats prisoners of war, I had no need of experiencing it first hand. Staying put was as likely to result in my capture as surrendering was, so that really only left me with the option of continuing on to the target, hoping that others would also rally toward it, or that some other opportunity would present itself along the way.

I was not at all happy with the situation, but happiness is not required of a soldier. I set off in the general direction of Battery Theta, with only a vague plan and a heartfelt prayer in mind. My navigation systems showed it to be about fifty kilometers away, only a few hours march, even going slow over this terrain.

I'd only covered about a kilometer when the valley took a rather sudden turn leftward. Eyes glued to my passive sensors and guns at the ready, I snapped around the corner looking to surprise anyone who may have been on the other side, only to come to a very abrupt halt, a heavy metallic clang reverberating up from the lower torso of my Will O'Wisp

I pulled my triggers blindly and, images of limpet mines flooding my mind, had my hand half way to the ejection switch before I realized I had literally run right into the working end of a Paladin mobile heavy artillery piece. My computer belatedly gave off a tone, indicating that it too had recognized the machine, picked up an acceptable IFF signal, and overridden my command to fire. Since I was still more than a lingering red mist and a memory, the Paladin driver either had better control than I did, or had a computer working at least as well as mine.

"This is Major Aarons, Third Mechanized, Second Dogs," I said. "Identify yourself." Only after the words had already left my mouth did it occur to me that if this was a recently captured machine I'd just begged to be shot once the IFF override was enabled.

"An officer. Thank God! I haven't seen another friendly for hours. Half of my unit got wasted on the way down, then I landed who the hell knows where, and there wasn't another friendly in sight, and higher just said stick tight, but then all the heavy jamming started up and I lost all contact so I figured screw that, I was moving out because..."

The babbling voice sounded as though it belonged to a very young male who was currently scared out of his wits. I needed to get him under control before he lost what little self-possession he still had.

"Soldier! Attention!" I'd never really been one to lead through intimidation, even among the Reavers, though it obviously has its time and place. This was one of those times. "Name, rank, and unit! And get your weapon pointed someplace I'm not! Right now while I'm still young!" Though I'd never been a drill instructor, I'd had many up close and extremely personal opportunities to watch them at work. It was pretty easy to simply play the role as I imagine Thayne would have done. Hopefully this kid's parade ground reflexes would kick in and not his firing range ones.

The Paladin quickly swung its main cannon around to point away from me. "Sir! PFC John Watkins, sir! Fortieth Arty, Two Eighty Eighth Assault, Eighth ASDF Strike Arm."

I was slightly surprised at just how much tension drained out of me then. Not only was this kid a friendly, but he also came from a long-term ally of the Unified Terran Republic and the Terran Dominion before that. Even though I hadn't been a Terran soldier for many years, I still felt more confident with an Associated Stars soldier at my back than I would have with, say, a Sunni or a Jarvyn soldier.

Watkins and his Paladin, with its exponentially greater firepower, gave me great hope. He was a smart kid too, well aware of the problems we faced, and our lack of choices, which was why he was so glad to have an officer on whom to foist the burden of decision making. He wasn't terribly pleased when I told him my decision was to continue on to the objective, but he recognized it as making the best out of an impossible situations.

"How are we going to do that, sir?"

I pulled up my maps, though they were of limited use since the heavy jamming that Watkins had alluded to was even interfering with both my inertial tracking systems and my GPS systems. Oddly, the GPS wasn't complaining of any communication error in trying to establish satellite contact, so maybe the problem was just in the computer system itself.

"I'm trying to figure out just that. We still have to clear out those tracking stations."

Watkins said nothing for a moment, but my computer reported that it had made a firm connection with its counterpart onboard the Paladin. He was obviously looking at the maps.

"Might I make a suggestion, sir?" he asked.

I smiled, trying to be magnanimous. After all, the kids suggestion couldn't hurt. "Certainly."

"What about this dam here?" A circle appeared on my map around the particular terrain feature. "Does that give you any ideas, sir?"

I shook my head to myself. "That was discussed and discarded in the planning sessions. We originally wanted to just destroy it and let the flood wipe out most of the stations and their supporting infrastructure, but it wasn't feasible. The dam has some pretty heavy defenses of its own, and the valley is so narrow that we couldn't attack it directly without taking horrendous casualties. Besides, the engineers said it was just too strong to be taken out quickly without orbital bombardment, which, as you may have noticed on your way down here, we're not ready to be doing just yet. I don't think even your Paladin could scratch it. Nice try, though. Any other suggestions?"

He was quiet for only a moment. "If I understand it, sir, we don't need to destroy the dam, we just need to get the water out from behind it."

"Aren't those two alternatives essentially the same?"

"Not necessarily, sir. Have you ever dropped an ice cube in a full glass of water?"

I thought about that. "And just where are we going to find an ice cube that big? I could dig for a year with my I-tool and not have enough dirt to raise that lake more than a centimeter."

"Sir, don't just look at the topography as ups and downs. Look at the climate and what's up at the top of some of those mountains."

I was starting to catch on. "You're saying we should knock an avalanche down into the lake."

"Not one, sir, maybe a dozen. We can do *that* with my Paladin." His confidence was contagious, and I couldn't come up with anything better.

"That's a plan, I'll let you know if I come up with anything better."

It took us hours to cover the distance between us and the base of the mountains, circling wide of the SOG battery itself. I could have made it much quicker over this terrain, but there was no way I was going to abandon Watkins or his Paladin. With him, we had enough firepower and range to implement our crazy plan, without him, it would be nigh on impossible. Besides, I didn't want to leave anyone behind if it was at all avoidable.

The Hounds had dropped early in the local day, planning to complete our mission before the next morning. It was coming up on mid-afternoon when Watkins and I first caught sight of our goal, those heavily laden peaks, stabbing up into the sky above the lake. Naturally, there was a guard encampment right at the base of the valley we needed to go through. I told Watkins to hang tight while I took a closer look.

I activated my ECM suite and crept through the light woods, careful to use the land to my advantage. With much patience and effort (it isn't easy but you *can* low crawl in a Man O'War if you're willing to sacrifice a little paint) I crept to within a kilometer of the camp's outer boundary without detection. I checked every passive scan I had, even snuck in a few low power active ones. Of all the miracles it seemed my luck was good for a change. There was no sign of any armor or augmented armor. That made sense for the small perimeter camp this was, but it was good to confirm it. Of course, there were still several guard towers with moderately heavy weapons on them, and it looked like about a platoon worth of armored infantry.

I offered up a prayer of thanksgiving while I slowly slithered back to where I'd left Watkins. I thanked God that we weren't facing impossible odds, and asked Him to protect me and my young subordinate in the coming fight, even going so far as to pray that He have mercy on souls of our enemies. For some reason I felt all right after that, a rush of confidence, like nothing could go wrong, even if we failed. It was an odd feeling, and one I would most certainly welcome having again.

I could use some form of reassurance now, a sign from deity that everything will be all right, no matter what.

I explained the layout and situation to Watkins, and outlined our battle plan. He suggested three or four changes to my plan, all of them good ones. I wasn't stupid, I followed those suggestions closely in mapping out how we would attack the base. Then I turned and led my soldiers (every one of them) into the fray.

A mobile artillery piece like the Paladin isn't meant for direct conflict. It's a wonderful machine, with the ability to level huge areas of ground all by itself in an extremely short period of time, but it simply can't maneuver or reorient its weapons fast enough to take out a moving target. So our plan basically boiled down to Watkins bombarding the communications grid, the guard towers, and anything else that he decided needed to be blown up, while I worked my way around the perimeter jamming communications as best I could and taking out the infantry. We'd have to be quick, though, I couldn't jam them for long. It was a simple plan not that much different than many I'd practiced and run in the Reavers and Diane, save that the numbers on our side were considerably lower.

Positioning Watkins was easy enough, he simply drove to a point just behind the crest of a hill, out of direct line-of-sight from the target, and relied on my sensor and visual feeds to target the camp. I returned once again to the spot from where I had earlier observed the camp.

With my Will O'Wisp in position, kneeling behind a rocky outcrop, I took a few deep breaths to steady my nerves. Unsurprisingly, that didn't work. I wasn't afraid, but I was keyed up. I signaled Watkins to announce our presence in the time-honored artilleryman fashion: with a bang.

It's tricky even for the most advanced artillery piece to hit more than one target at the same time, but by varying arcs and propellant it is possible. Watkins was simply the best I'd ever seen. The four guard towers closest to my position and the communication array all went up in perfect unison.

Using that as my starter's gun I sprinted from my hiding place and down one side of the camp's perimeter while Watkins changed his position. My first target was a team of some four armored infantry, none of whom had any heavy, anti-armor weapons; too bad that didn't make them easy prey.

Professionals all, the moment they saw me they lit off on their jump jets and fanned out in an arc, preparing to surround and swarm me, firing their weapons almost continuously. They knew that the safest place for them would be as close to me as they could get.

I slammed to a halt where I was, brought my wrist cannons and anti-infantry guns up and to bear on the two outermost soldiers, and fired armor-piercing rounds through their bodies at short range. Even as their remains were still bouncing along the ground, I kicked myself back into motion.

The other two dodged around a lot as I closed in on them, their small lasers and cannons spattering against my armor. Their fire and movement spoiled my aim, though I must have clipped at least one of them with a shot or two. As they split to go around me, one to either side, I grabbed one in my left hand and squeezed him till he popped. I missed my shot at the one on my right, and he managed to get a grip on the back of my right forearm. I backhanded him against the trunk of a thick tree, shivering leaves and branches down onto the ground below. He lost his grip and fell, twitching slightly when he hit the ground. I didn't allow him any time to try and get up, I simply stepped on him.

I spun back to face the compound as Watkins sent up four more towers and what looked like two barracks buildings. I ran into the opening he created, confident now that he was good enough not to hit me, looking for more targets.

A Schwer tank turned the corner of the building ahead of me. It must have been hidden in a shielded shed. That was the only thought I had time for before Watkins had destroyed it too, pieces of the exploded turret pinging off my own armor.

The second infantry team to confront me was far better than the first. While Watkins and I were leveling the camp, they had ripped up a live power line; a risky proposition, even in a power suit. While the others distracted me, trading fire throughout a series of sheds that Watkins hadn't yet blown up, the one with the cable actually managed to climb on my back. He was trying to lever open an access panel when I followed the old fire drill we learned in elementary school: I stopped, dropped, and rolled.

I got up, he did not. The others, showing uncanny reaction times, were already trying to swarm me. I shot one at point blank range with my wrist cannons, splitting him from crown to crotch, then raked the others with fire from my heavy caliber anti-infantry guns.

"Major! I need some help over here!"

Presumably someone had tracked the trajectories of the incoming shots and realized that they weren't coming from very far away. The remaining infantry, at least two teams worth of them, were swarming away from the compound and headed for Watkins.

I fired one last burst into the armored forms near me, then took off in pursuit. I couldn't get a firm lock on any of them, though, they were too good for that, bouncing and juking as they ran. I raked the area with cannon fire, clipping a couple, and Watkins managed to blow up one squad with saturation fire. With no time to conserve ammunition, I launched a full flight of rockets into the nearest three.

The first one caught at least two of the heavy, unguided rockets square in the back and disintegrated. It was over so fast that he probably never even knew he'd been hit. The second must have picked up the explosions on his audio sensors, or had some other warning that trouble was coming up from behind. He bounced up and flipped in the air, turning to put his weapons at the ready, and catching one from my second salvo of rockets full in the chest. The rest of the salvo exploded all around, and the concussion and shrapnel ripped both legs off the third man. His screams, loud enough to be heard through his armor, were cut off by the left foot of my Man O'War.

I have spent many hours since that day wondering if I was right to kill a dying man who no longer represented a threat. My head tells me I spared him suffering, my heart says I was in the fury of combat. My soul says I murdered yet again.

One day God will let me know.

Watkins finished off the last two with his own anti-infantry weaponry, before he returned to systematically leveling the compound. I inspected my status reports, chagrined to see just how much damage those infantry had done. I had full breaches in my armor on every limb and three or four places on my torso, front and back, accounting for a total reduction of armor of more than fifty percent. My left arm and leg had suffered a twenty percent loss in motion and didn't feel as responsive as normal. One of my machine guns had been split in half lengthwise, another was outright AWOL. I'd expended all of my rockets and a third of my cannon ammunition. If we met up with anything heavier or more numerous than just another squad of infantry, my Will O'Wisp would be history.

When Watkins finally reported that he was done, I took one last sweep through the smoldering ruin of the camp to confirm that we hadn't left anyone behind to tell that we'd been here. I stood there in the center of the compound and surveyed the results of our actions. The place was a mess. Except for the power plant, the whole base was a smoking, burning ruin. The troops guarding it were either dead or had successfully retreated beyond scanning range. I hoped for the former rather than the latter, but, either way, the hard part was over.

"Sir, I'm getting intermittent connections with orbital communications. The jamming isn't as strong here." Probably because we'd just taken out a relay station along with the communication grid. I tried connecting with the Dogs' orbital command, but I was still getting a transmission error. I had Watkins route my signal through his comm gear instead.

"Eyeball One, this is Hound Pack Lead. Over." I waited listening to the various hisses and pops, then repeated myself.

"Hound...ball One. Status?" The message coming back was choppy and unclear, but at least it was something.

I relayed a brief summary of what had happened from drop till now and uploaded a full report from my logs. They acknowledged my report and promised to route all stragglers this way as reconnaissance showed it to be as safe as anywhere else down here.

I told Watkins the good news. "We'll have my whole battalion and maybe some of yours coming to back us up ASAP. Let's go finish this thing."

"We might not have to, sir," he said. "Look at the dam." Of course I couldn't see it from where I was, so I crested a low rise just opposite the one Watkins was currently parked on.

"What are you…" then I saw what he was looking at. Four Devil's Cross attack planes raced down the canyon, outside wingtips all but scraping the rock walls. The Dominion planes spewed white smoke as they launched full flights of AGMs toward the dam's base.

Counter-fire from the dam's defenses downed two of the planes and most of the missiles. The remaining two planes rose up out of the canyon and peeled away in different directions, then they were gone. The dam didn't even shudder under the impact of the half dozen missiles that struck it.

"That's why we didn't want to assault the dam in the first place," I said, almost smugly. "It's too strong."

We spent another half hour following the draw up to a suitable position, the terrain allowing Watkins to move at a much more acceptable speed. What we saw at the top was literally breathtaking in its spectacular beauty.

The entire valley opened up beneath us, a brilliant display of bluish mountains leading down to a lush, green vegetation line. The lake sparkled an amazing aquamarine back up at us, reflecting the white snow-capped peaks looming higher above us still. At the narrow end of the lake sat the dam, barely visible from this angle, the lake water lapping up against its upper lip. Beyond it the deep sand-colored scar of the canyon stretched away from us, curving to the north. I fought back a wistful sigh.

"All right, Watkins, we've played the odds long enough. Let's do this and get some reinforcements down here. You go get yourself set up out there. I'll cover you in case they manage to send any flybys our way."

I gestured with my left arm to an open area just in front of the steep drop to the valley below. It would provide an ideal position for hitting our selected targets, but it would be horribly exposed if any planes did come by. That's why I didn't bother to tell him that, even though I still had a full load, all of my missiles were anti-armor. I could only shoot down a plane or helicopter if it had the courtesy to crash nearby first. Though he'd done well, he was still green, and I wasn't about to give him anything more to worry over when we were only a few meters from our goal.

"Yes, sir," he said.

I watched him closely as he moved into position, his anti-infantry weapons moving enough to betray that he was still worried about anyone we'd missed. I smiled to myself. Smart kid, learned fast; maybe he'd make it through this war. I hoped so, he'd proven himself to be courageous, capable, and intelligent. I'd take him in my unit any day.

The Paladin came to a halt and its turret began pivoting. It stopped momentarily, definitely pointing the wrong way. Then, in a flurry, it spun around rapidly, the barrel raising and lowering as it moved, firing off a half dozen shots in as many seconds.

The rounds arced high above each heavily laden peak, detonating almost simultaneously. The entire valley rang and reverberated with the detonations, the unstable snow shaking loose easily. The avalanches built up speed quickly as they fell down those steep slopes, gravity accelerating their considerable mass toward the lake below. The noise was deafening, the vibrations impressive to say the least.

Watkins had been right. When all that snow and ice (not to mention the rocks and trees pulled along with it) hit the near end of the lake, the water leaped forward like a contained tsunami of muddy water and ice. It smashed into the dam at incredible speed, with a mass far greater than I'd really expected. Whether it was weakened by the previous attack or not I cannot say, but when that wall of water and mud hit it, the entire top third of the structure broke off, allowing even more water to rush down the canyon.

We watched the water pour over the now shortened dam at an incredible rate, a horrifying sight to behold. I shuddered at the thought of being in the path of that destructive force, and felt some sympathy for the Krupp forces and civilians that would likely find themselves in its path.

We retreated farther up the mountains, just in case someone decided to pay us a visit, but in the end it was unnecessary. It was only about a half hour more before we started seeing task force dropships landing in the distance. Apparently our gambit had worked well enough. We were going to be okay for at least one more day.

Chapter Twenty-Five

Dogs of War Area of Operation: Lienz
Ostlichbereich, Dammerung
Gottenheim
Krupp Hegemony

August 30, 2658

"By the numbers," I said. "Transports by columns in four, Man O'Wars in standard outrider escort formation. Move out."

The cockpit of my Will O'Wisp still had that brand new smell to it. It had finally been fully refurbished during our reassignment, and it looked and felt brand new. For some reason that just made me feel better, a whole lot better; refreshed and renewed to fight this war—and I needed it.

It had been a long and brutal five months. The battles we won were won only by the skin of our teeth, the ones we lost were catastrophic. We were steadily taking control of the planet, but not at the rate we needed to, and at a cost I wasn't certain we could bear. Similar stories were coming in from all across the Hegemony theater of operations.

Valiant offensive and defensive efforts on the parts of many had kept the main Krupp forces from turning to reinforce Gottenheim, but the cost was high. Throughout this part of the Charted Territories, Krupp forces were either winning stunningly, or only barely losing.

We set off across the plains of Ostlichbereich en masse, bound for the staging areas around the port city of Heid. The tall grass land made easy going for our transports, and gave us nice long, clear fields of fire, but that didn't make me comfortable with them. All my life I'd been taught that augmented armor has no place in the open; that's for armor and planes. I'd always worked in confined areas like mountains, canyons, and forests. Here I was feeling positively agoraphobic.

During May and June the Third Mechanized had been inexorably chewed to pieces in numerous battles across the entire continent. By the end of June, Dogs command had declared the unit hors de combat, and split up the survivors to fill gaps in other units. I found myself with a field promotion to Lieutenant Colonel and serving as XO to Colonel Jamieson in the Dogs' Second Division.

We both protested the assignment, but our pleas fell on deaf ears. The slot needed to be filled, and I was the one that the powers-that-be wanted filling it. I consoled myself with the thought that no one trusted Jamieson, and that's why they needed me here—to keep him from getting everyone killed. He likely deluded himself with some similar line of reasoning about me. I can't say which of us was right.

I pushed my throttle forward another couple of notches and moved up to take my place near the front of the column. Jamieson and I still did not get along, and the less contact we had the better we worked together. I clicked over to the general division channel. "All units, report in by battalion and company. Set all triple A and link fire to ID confirmation. Ground scan units, check for any indications of minefields or any other surprises. I feel like too good a target out here in the open, and I for one have had enough of that."

A chorus of affirmative responses came back. Everyone was doing the job they were supposed to, they didn't need me breathing down their necks or micro-managing their leadership. I was just uncomfortable with both my new position and the knowledge that our armor and infantry were elsewhere while we crossed the biggest, flattest, most open piece of land on this half of the continent. It was perfect terrain for an armor duel, but Man O'Wars just make nice big targets, and here we were, guarding a supply convoy all alone.

I had vehemently protested the situation to Colonel Jamieson as soon as I learned of it, and that was just another factor in our mutual loathing. Not only did he hate subordinates who talked back, he really did have some weird sort of heroic or romantic notion that Man O' Wars are invincible. He honestly had it in his head that they have no tactical weaknesses, and can overcome any opposition without the aid of armor or infantry, no matter what I'd been told in OBT. To this day, a part of me feels that he probably didn't believe in maintenance or air support, either.

By evening we were about halfway across the plains. We were making good time, but we still had to go slower than I wanted to so we didn't miss any signs of possible enemy activity. Not that those two hundred ton transports could have gone much faster anyway.

"X-ray Oscar this is Hotel Alpha One. Over."

I thumbed my mike switch. "X-ray Oscar here. Go ahead, One." This could only be bad news. That was one of my heavy recon teams about eight or ten kays out on our left flank, and there was only one reason a recon unit would call me directly.

"Oscar, Alpha One reports signs of recent armor presence niner klicks north of column's present position. No estimate on strength, Angriff class or heavier though. Infantry support probable as well. That's at nine klicks, nine o'clock relative. Signs appear to be at least one day old. Orders?"

"Thanks, One. Conduct spiral search from present location. Coordinate with Five on your left flank."

Another voice cut in on the band—one I was coming to hate more every day. "Jamieson here." The egotistical bastard felt that what was required of everyone else was optional for him. Things like comm protocols, chains of command, and respect for subordinate positional authority apparently meant nothing to him. "That's a negative, Alpha One. Resume outrider status and maintain position relative to column. Out."

My blood pressure soared and I actually had to fight the urge to keep myself from taking a potshot at Jamieson. That was probably why he was so fond of leading from the rear, it put him behind me and seemed to make him feel safer, somehow. I clicked over to the Colonel's direct channel. "Sir, with all due respect, just what the hell do you think you're doing? If there are tanks out there, maybe infantry too, they could cause us some serious trouble, even in small numbers. For our own safety, not to mention the security of the convoy, you have to..."

Over the open line I heard the distinctive beeps of a fire-control system IFF override. I felt a stab of shock. The son of a bitch was actually locking his weapons on me.

"Aarons, I am only going to tell you this once more. Then, if it comes up again, I'll charge you with insubordination and mutiny in a combat situation and shoot you myself. In my outfit we do things my way. And if I say that there's nothing out there that can hurt us, assuming for a moment that they are out there, you will act accordingly. Do you understand me, Mister?" The click of his weapons' safety releasing was plain over the open link. There was really only one thing I could say.

"Yes, sir, Colonel. I read you five-by-five. It's your way all the way." I clicked off my mike. *But if you really think I'm going to let you get me and this entire division scragged just to help you maintain your delusional self-image, you're wrong*, I thought.

There is a very ancient military tradition often employed in these situations. It's first recorded use was among the Norse raiders of ancient Earth, but it has been utilized, in one form or another, by just about every military in every conflict since then. Colloquially, it's called fragging. It usually involves some sort of horrible weapons malfunction and a dead superior officer. That's generally preferred to having a dead everyone.

I mulled the thought over and over in my mind. I'd killed many, many times to prevent harm coming to my soldiers. I wondered if it would make a difference if I killed one of my own to accomplish the same result; I wondered if God would see a difference.

As the day wore on, our scouts reported more signs of a recent presence—tracks left by armor to our right, recently spilled liquid artillery fuel to our left, and the footprints of evil little power armored trolls everywhere. Yet the signs all seemed to be at least twenty-four hours old, almost as if they'd been staging here the day before, then left just before we showed up.

Jamieson, of course, wasn't the least bit bothered by all of this. No immediate, obvious threat equaled no threat at all in his mind. I, on the other hand, was getting jumpier by the hour. I've never tried to hide the fact that I've always been an accomplished warrior. One of the things that had taken me through so many difficult situations was the fact that I was always willing to listen to that little voice in the back of my mind when it screamed of impending doom. Right now it was screeching like a wet cat and Jamieson wouldn't let me do anything about it.

It was about the supper hour when the heavy end of the hammer dropped on us. The sun was still hours away from setting, it stayed up late at this time of year at this latitude. We had ceased our forward advance for the day, and were just starting to circle the wagons for the night. Most of our warriors had finally decided that nothing was going to happen that day, and were thinking of nothing more than a hot meal and a bed under the stars when they came out.

Initially I wanted to push on, move all night and be in Heid by morning, but Jamieson was insistent. I admit I relented, I had begun to consider us past the danger zone. The Krupp forces had obviously moved on, and ambushes are best done in the early morning hours, when the body is naturally at its most sluggish.

I had just sent Jamieson the night watch rotation I finished drawing up. He turned his Titan and started to approach me. I expected he would take me to task for making the watches too strong. Wanting to limit the number of witnesses to our coming confrontation, I switched to our private channel.

"Colonel," I began. That was as far as I got. The Titan vanished in a dazzling explosion, leaving only two smoking feet.

I'm not sure whether or not the Krupp commander planned to throw us into chaos by taking out our CO first, or whether some gunner just got lucky. Under most other circumstances such a tactic may have worked very well indeed. For us, it may have been the only thing that saved us. It certainly saved us from Jamieson.

I dropped flat and, even as that first barrage of artillery rounds pounded down on our location, I was shouting out orders to a command that was suddenly entirely mine. I had a million and one things to do, and they all had to be done right now. "All Dogs, this is the X-ray Oscar. Charlie Oscar is down. I say again, the Colonel is dead. All units spread out and get down." Even as the words left my mouth, I was getting a fix on where the fire was coming from. "Activate all echo charlie mikes. Commence active scans, they already know we're here, don't by shy. Leads, keep everyone's head down, don't give them any better target locks than they already have. Ready for direct assault when the barrage lifts. Expect armor and infantry, possibly augmented armor. Keep an eye out for tac air. Transports, pull back. Avoidance patterns, but try to stay close. We can't protect you if you wander too far. Patch all sit-reps up the tac net to me as they come in. X-ray Oscar out."

Any replies were drowned out by the freight train thunder of more incoming rounds.

Most normal people have never been caught in an artillery barrage; no sane person would want to be. It's an extremely scary experience, almost like a DGT come to life. Lights flash everywhere while thunder roars all around. The earth quakes and tosses, heaving as though trying to throw you off in the hope that that will stop the torment being inflicted on it. Concussions slam into you from every side, tossing you helplessly about even inside a hundred ton Man O' War. Then, when all else fails, the churned and torn earth can sometimes actually try to swallow you, to cover up and forever bury the nasty man-things that have inflicted such pain and indignity on her.

I switched channels. "Eyeball Three, this is Delta Hound Two. We are under attack. Over." If we didn't get at least some help, our chances of surviving were in the slim to none range. The artillery would pin us down and work us over, then the ground units would come in and finish off whatever was left at their leisure.

"Two, this is Eyeball Three, we have you. Sit-rep, over."

"Eyeball, we are under heavy artillery barrage, twenty-five kilometers east of Tango Romeo Papa Bravo Six. Request immediate support, any flavor."

"Two, we have arty. *Golem* is moving to commence counter-battery fire. Be advised, tactical ground shows locals in your vicinity, orbital cannot get sufficient angle at this time. Expect engagement when rain lets up. Estimate numbers at one division, mixed armor and infantry. Also be advised, you are first priority for reinforcement as available. Will continue to monitor. Eyeball out."

One division. She almost made it sound like an even fight. Unfortunately, we were normally a combined arms unit, and Jamieson had allowed our armor and infantry to be co-opted into use elsewhere, leaving only about a brigade and a half worth of Man O'Wars at our side. All the enemy would be small, fast-moving armored infantry and heavily armored tanks. The actual odds seemed much, much slimmer.

While I was still digesting the grim news from combat control, the *Golem*'s counter-battery fire arrived and took care of our artillery problem. Somewhere up in orbit, the boomer received some fairly precise coordinates and vectored itself to the proper angle. Then it's big orbit-to-surface plasma and rail cannons opened fire. We were much too far from the artillery to see the results of the bombardment, but we did see the impressive, angry, red scar that ripped open the sky. We heard the rumble made on the way down, as well, and then, mercifully, the artillery simply stopped.

I'd never witnessed a demonstration of orbital bombardment from the ground before. I was stunned at the magnitude and abruptness of the artillery's demise. If the Hegemony troops were affected by the sudden disappearance of their fire support, they didn't show it.

"This is Tango Bravo Niner. Report contact. Infantry on the left flank! I say again, infantry and some armor at eight, nine, and ten o'clock relative. Coming fast."

"Roger that, Niner," replied her company CO. "Tango Company, stand by. Fire at will!"

"Contact, contact! Enemy aircraft on heading two eight one true. Multiple bogies, coming in fast and low."

"Gamma One to Gamma Company. Enemy aircraft acquired. Weapons locked. Missiles away! Point defense lasers firing on auto. All Dog units, watch for slip-through." My anti-aircraft units were already on the job.

"X-ray Oscar, this is Delta Prime. Enemy armor and Papa Bravo India at two and four relative, range two point eight klicks and closing fast."

"Roger that, Delta. All Dogs, this is X-ray Oscar. Weapons free, aimed fire only. Make them all count, people. It may be a while before the cavalry gets here." I didn't tell them that I wasn't even sure help was coming.

It seems odd that, despite my memory, I cannot refer to any of my people in the entire Second Division by name. It's not because I was trying to dehumanize them in any way, or even distance myself from them. It's just that I didn't know their names. I'd only been transferred in a few short days before, and I'd been so busy that I hadn't yet learned the names to go with the call signs and TO&E slots.

"Here they come," I heard Alpha Lead saying over the comm, "Pick your targets...fire!" Over a hundred Thumper heavy anti-armor missiles lanced out and away from our column with a great whoosh of dragon's breath. From where I stood, it looked as though the first wave of oncoming tanks simply self-destructed. Treads disintegrated, turrets shot off like holiday fireworks, ammunition stores exploded, all at once or shell by shell like the Devil's own popcorn.

It was pure slaughter.

The tanks' cannons had an effective range far less than that of our missiles, but as they closed the gap they began firing back, with almost as much destructive power and a lot more ammunition. At first the fire was almost random, with little chance of hitting anything in particular save by luck alone, but once they reached the outer ranges of their targeting systems my people began to die.

I had the entire Command Company acting as combat controllers while they waited in reserve, coordinating the entire division's actions and praying that things would not get so bad that we would be required to fulfill our secondary role and actually fight. That gave us the best seats in the house from which to watch the demise of the Second Division.

The Twenty-Fourth Battalion was the first to go. Composed mainly of fast, relatively light Man O'Wars, currently without the two companies of light armor that normally aided them in their reconnaissance role, they survived the first wave of Hegemony Stuka attack fighters fairly well by spreading out and staying mobile. They even managed to damage a couple of the retreating planes while taking only light damage themselves. In their efforts to avoid the Stukas, however, they ended up too far away from the heavy anti-armor units of the flanking First Brigade. In avoiding the fighters, they'd been unable to properly engage the tanks.

The tanks were more than able to properly engage them.

I don't know if I was the only one screaming over the comm net for them to disperse and fall back into position, but even as the words came out my displays showed those massive tanks barreling into what was left of the formation. The dying could be seen on the screens and heard over all channels.

I ordered the supply convoy to fall back along our line of travel, knowing that they could never get clear and that there was no safe place for them to hide even if they did. Then I moved up the Command Company to fill the growing gap that was forming where the Twenty-Fourth was being torn apart. I knew we were too late to stop the slaughter, they were all dying.

There was nothing heroic about it. They died on those plains for no noble cause, and for no good reason. Just a little bad luck, and a couple of poor decisions. On any other day, they may have lived, but dead they were, and dead they are, and while it may not have been my fault, it was and is my responsibility.

As we in turn moved forward into the meat grinder, I knew that we were going to lose most of our ability to control and coordinate the various units, but we didn't have much choice—our eighty plus Man O'Wars were desperately needed. I linked into the general command channel.

"All Leads, this is X-ray Oscar. Command is moving up to engage with the Twenty-Fourth. Leads to take over all control for individual units. Watch your backs, and your neighbors' too. Take it to them. Out."

I switched back to the local command channel to speak with my platoon leaders. "Move it up, wedge formation. We'll cut through them here, no stopping. If at least some of us can get behind them, we'll take the pressure off. Just keep everyone moving, no matter who falls."

I slammed my throttle wide open and headed out in the direction of our original line of travel. I'd picked a slight gap between the Krupps' armor and infantry in that area. If enough of us could get outside their lines, get far enough behind them, they would be the ones in trouble. They'd be faced with the choice of ignoring us and getting shot in the back or they could turn and face us, ruining their partial encirclement. The surrounded Dogs would have a new chance to tear into the Hegemony lines, causing chaos. That, I was hoping, would allow us to hold out long enough for some form of help to arrive.

As we drove our wedge for the gap between the tanks and infantry, I aimed my left wrist cannon in the general direction of an infantry squad loaded down with anti-armor rockets and cut loose. The white-hot depleted uranium penetration rounds tore them into bloody scraps. At the same time I fired off a salvo of rockets, taking off the turret of a tank to my right, and shot my main laser cannon at what looked like a mobile jamming unit.

We were badly outnumbered, out gunned, out armored, and up against an enemy force ideally suited to the terrain. We still had a chance, though, in that we were more maneuverable and a bit more agile in our killing abilities because a Man O'War can target multiple targets simultaneously.

Even as we ran, I watched the Catastrophe next to me take out one tank with a heavy missile, another with its main HEPC, an aerial spotter drone with a cannon burst, and two infantry with a machine gun burst. I reflected that it's an aptly named machine, even as I fired another rocket burst and my laser into the treads of still another tank.

"...help me! They're all over me. Get them off!"

"One Niner, you have suits on your back. Hold still while I burn 'em off." One Niner stopped to allow a Vulcan to wash him down with flamethrowers, then split in two when a cannon round took him full on. The Vulcan exploded only a second later.

"One One to all units, armor has flanked our lines! "

Not the news I wanted to hear. The edge of our flank was starting to crumble under the armor onslaught. Without waiting for a positive lock, I snapped off another laser shot at a tank that was lining up for a shot at me. I thought I'd missed, but then the top hatch opened and the gunner jumped out, trailing fire. He ran right in front of another oncoming tank, his limbs torn away from his torso as he was ground under the treads.

"All Leads, this is X-ray Oscar. Stay close. Watch that flank, and expect infantry trouble." I paused just long enough to launch a flight of rockets at an enemy squad as they bounded through my sights. Right about then, someone hit me in the back of the head with a dropship.

My Will O'Wisp tumbled forward, slamming head first into the ground. I was thrown hard against my restraints, and a shower of sparks fell all around me. One corner of my cockpit arced purple lightning bolts all across the console, the smell of smoke and ozone filling my nostrils. I continued to tumble fully over, first slamming onto my back, which knocked the wind from me, and then finally tipping once more to come to a rest face down, much like on Iwo Jima.

I struggled to suck in air, fighting the panic that accompanies that inability to breathe. It didn't help that the half of my displays that still worked had all turned an angry red. I closed my eyes and just tried to breathe. I could still hear my communications, though.

"X-ray Oscar is down!"

"Leads, this is Alpha Lead, I have command." That was good, at least she would be able to hold them together.

I willed my eyes open. My damage indicators suggested that most of my Man O'War from the hip area down was missing, as were the left arm and shoulder. I coughed twice from the acrid smoke.

"Leads, this is X-ray Oscar," I said. I got no response. I tried again with a similar result. I was still able to run a diagnostic, and I found the problem to be nothing more serious than a burned out board. I couldn't replace it, but I could route around it easily enough. It only took a minute, but already I could see on my displays that the Command Company was moving far away as they continued their drive. My sensors were out, but my data links were still operational, allowing me to see what the rest of the division could see.

"Leads, this is X-ray Oscar, I am resuming tactical control. Sit-rep." This time I got through.

"Oscar, this is Bravo Lead. We're holding our own, but just barely."

"Command Three, sir." That was the captain who was now leading the command company. "We made it out, and are moving to attack from the south. We thought we lost you, sir."

"Almost did, but I'm still here. I will be combat control." I toggled channels again. "Delta, what's your situation?"

"This is Delta Lead, sir. We're holding for now. We'll send a team over to your position."

"Negative, Lead. This position holds no value, use your troops where they are. Alpha?"

"We're fine, sir, but not forever."

The situation was grim, we were pinned down and taking steady losses, but it was about to improve. With the Command Company's heavy assault units ready to rip open the Krupps from the rear, and with everyone else maintaining good order despite our heavy losses, we could, just maybe, pull through to a better position.

"Three, this is Oscar. Sound off when ready. All Leads, standby for assault. I want you putting your units inside the Krupp formations as they start to turn their flank. Break them up and keep them from concentrating their firepower. We're going to force them back, make them withdraw and hopefully buy us enough time to regroup. Maybe even get some reinforcements."

That was something I desperately needed to know about. "Eyeball, this is Delta Hound Two. Request info update, over."

There was a brief pause and I wondered what would happen if everyone else was too busy to provide us with any help. "Two, this is Eyeball. What's your situation? Over."

"Eyeball, without reinforcements soon, *we* may be over. I have one shot at an attempt to break out of this encirclement. If it fails, we'll be sitting ducks. ETA on the cavalry?"

"Two, the Fifteenth Armored is en route to your position via suborbital hop. Will paradrop and LAPES. ETA is twenty minutes. Can you hold?"

"Unsure, Eyeball. Wish us luck."

A new voice broke in on the channel. "Delta Hound Two, this is Delta Hound Prime. Hang in there, we're coming. Good luck, God speed. Matheson out."

It seemed the Marshal himself was riding to our rescue. All we had to do was survive long enough to *be* rescued.

"Oscar, this is Three. We're in position, starting our rush now."

I wished them luck. "Don't hold back. We need this."

"Yes, sir!" he acknowledged. I patched into the company feeds so I could better follow their progress. "Rip into them! Company, stick with your partner, watch each other's backs! Fire at will!" A brief pause. "Yes, good shot, Thomson! Move in, move in!"

I watched the counterattack unfold on my tactical monitor. The Command Company teams tore into the rear of the Krupp tank formations with terrible ferocity. Heavy missiles launched by the dozen and Angriff tanks exploded. High-velocity cannons belched forth hundreds of rounds and armor splashed from mortally wounded land leviathans. Lasers burned, particle beams discharged, flamethrowers ignited, and all across the rear flank of the Hegemony formation, men and machines died by the score.

"Command One Tree," I directed, "you have Dragon infantry coming around to your left, attempting to flank. Turn to seven one and burn them when they crest the hill." I was the only one who had the luxury to sit back and watch the entire goings-on of the battle. I was also about the busiest man on the field. "Gamma Lead, looks like fighters inbound again. Discourage them."

"Oscar, Lead here. Roger that." Seeker class SAMs launched and Gatling guns belched out an incredible number of anti-aircraft munitions, all seeking their elusive, flying prey.

"Command Three, this is Oscar. Watch your left flank, it's starting to get out ahead. Bring it back on line. Are the Krupps turning to engage yet?"

"Negative, Oscar. Only in small numbers..."

"Oscar, this is Bravo Lead! Their flank is crumbling! They're turning away from us!"

This was what I'd been waiting and hoping for. "All Dogs, this is X-ray Oscar. Clear the field! Disengage and move on Bravo! Bravo, take lead and reform Hounds on your position." I felt the rush of adrenaline as surely as if I were taking part in the actual combat.

We charged right down their throats, not intent on destroying them, but on confusing their formations long enough for us to break free and reform. The Krupps had turned a significant portion of their line away from our column to deal with the counterstrike, and now it cost them.

On my screen the Man O'Wars of the Second Division surged and broke over the Hegemony lines like a cresting surf. Red and green symbols mixed, mingled, and winked out by the score.

"Able Four Five, three in the gully trying to get inside your squad. Stomp them..."

"...Baker teams, increase interval spacing. Don't let them force you back into a pocket..."

"Belay that, Delta Lead," I interrupted. "Send Baker all the way through."

"Affirmative, sir. But we are fully away from your position. Show Krupp units en route, your four o'clock. I'll send a team to get you out."

I swallowed hard at that. The Krupps would love to get their hands on a senior officer. Even though there was nothing I could tell them, they'd still put me through narc-interrogation, neural pattern extraction, and as many other painful and degrading procedures as I could survive. Then they would execute me. I briefly thought of calling for help, accepting Delta Lead's offer, but if I did so I'd most likely just end up getting more of my own troops killed. My first duty was to my people.

"All Hounds, this is X-ray Oscar." My screens showed nothing. As my units moved further away from my position they couldn't send feeds of my area, but my imagination had no problem pinpointing just how close the Krupp units were. "Fall back in good order." I could feel the vibrations caused by multiple heavy tank treads now. "It's too late for me." I heard infantry armor clanging against my Will O'Wisp as they sought the best way to rip me out of it. "Primary mission is protection of the supply convoy. Alpha Lead, you have command. X-ray Oscar out."

I slapped the release for my restraint harness and caught myself as I fell forward. I ripped my helmet off and scrambled underneath my command couch for the machine pistol stored there. My hands were shaking and I almost fumbled the magazine when I pushed it into its slot. I took a very shaky deep breath and pulled the charging handle, slamming the first round into the chamber. I recalled something Tchai had once said about facing capture when we'd first gone up against the Hegemony on Iwo Jima.

Save one last round for yourself...

The hatch suddenly blew off the back of the cockpit. An armored head with the Krupp arms emblazoned on the forehead appeared in the opening. All of my fine motor skills fled, and my training on precision aiming and controlled bursts went with them. I merely jammed the machine pistol into the soldier's face plate and fired off the whole magazine.

The armor suit fell away, the head of both occupant and armor smashed beyond recognition. I knew the next thing coming through the hatch would probably be a grenade of some sort, which meant that I didn't have the luxury of staying put. As soon as I'd clapped another magazine home, I grabbed the rim of the hatch and boosted my legs up on the back of the couch.

Explosions from outside rocked me around, causing me to fall back as I lost my grip on the edge. More explosions followed and I heard cannon fire being exchanged. I felt somewhat ashamed at the amount of relief I felt knowing that someone had come back for me, but that paled next to the anger that surged forth, knowing that my orders had been disobeyed and more valuable lives had been risked for no good reason. Whether I survived or not, I didn't need any more deaths on my conscience, especially not anymore faceless, nameless deaths; especially not for my sake alone.

I regained my grip on the hatch and raised myself back up to that level. Another armored faceplate loomed up in front of me. Too close to aim effectively, I batted it as hard as I could with the pistol. I doubt I had any damaging effect on the soldier himself, but I did make him slide back away from the opening.

I jumped up through the hatch, half sliding down the outside of the cockpit before I got my feet under me. The infantry soldier rose up again just off to my left and I almost fired off another magazine before he raised his hands and shouted my name. Only then did my brain register just what I was looking at.

His entire left breast was decorated with a subdued version of the same snarling mastiff head *supra* broken sword that decorated my own left shoulder patch. I lowered my gun and looked around. A handful of shattered Krupp tanks and a dozen broken power suits littered the area around my Man O'War.

Two hulking Goliaths strode patrol patterns not too far away. Again, the sigil of the Dogs of War subdued on their left chest. Behind them I could see Monolith heavy tanks, a whole bunch of them spreading out as they surged forward. Occasionally, several of them would fire into the distance.

I turned back to the soldier I'd almost shot. He had his faceplate open and he smiled. "I thought you were actually going to shoot me, Colonel."

"I almost did, Marshal. Thanks for coming."

He slapped me lightly on the shoulder, almost bowling me over with his augmented strength. "In the Dogs, we take care of our own."

Chapter Twenty-Six

Dogs of War Area of Operations: Heid
Heid Provinz, Dammerung
Gottenheim
Krupp Hegemony

January 17, 2659

I eased my rifle around the corner, then gradually followed it with the rest of my Cutthroat. Crouching against the wall to present as small a target as possible, I scanned the area with my passive sensors.

"Looks clear," I whispered into my mike. "Foxtrot Lead, you are okay to move west into one five six seven. Have infantry search each and every building for booby-traps, this area already scans hot." I waved my own company forward, and they fanned out to secure our area of responsibility.

As he passed, I snagged the arm of my First Sergeant's Man O'War. Switching over to as tight and secure a link as I could squeeze out of my comm unit, I whispered, "Top, get our demo teams into these buildings and check for mines ASAP. This area's too dense, we can't operate in all this clutter without clear communications, and I'm sick of having buildings falling down on us every time someone calls for help or switches on their active sensors." I took another look around our position, noting in passing that the clear sky would be perfect for an air assault drop. "The Krupps could drop another heavy regimental assault team, and we'd never know it until they opened up on us. This is taking way too much time. Circle the wagons and call Jason in for a powwow."

"I hear you, Colonel," Harris replied. He waved his Man O'War's arms to the infantry huddled not too far away, and they passed the signal on to their commander. Major Abate got the message, slowly. Without open communications, which were triggering booby traps, we were limited to these primitive hand signals and voice communication. Even directed line of sight like I'd used with Harris was being picked up if used over any sort of realistic distance. Abate activated his jump jets and bounded his armored suit over to where my sergeant and I hugged the wall.

"What's the word, sir?" Abate asked softly, opting for vocal broadcast. If he didn't want to chance directed links, even at this close range, then he likely had a very good reason for it. Harris and I immediately followed his example.

"These thrice damned, bloody booby traps are killing us. At the rate it's taking us to check these buildings one by one we are never going get out of here. The Krupps will be at the extraction point before we are, which isn't exactly the way I was looking forward to ending my day." There was no need for me to explain what would happen then, we all knew how preferable fighting to the end would be compared to the options the Hegemony gave to those who surrendered. Abate nodded his understanding. He was about the toughest, smartest tactician I'd ever worked with, and he knew a deathtrap when he was about to be stuck in one.

Abate was silent, and I knew he was examining the problem from every possible angle. He had a certain genius for coming up with outrageously successful solutions to impossible problems, which was why I had asked him to be my infantry commander in the first place. That, and he was a lousy poker player who couldn't walk away from a game. I didn't play often, but it was hard to just leave a game when Abate was losing so much.

"As I see it," Abate said, "we only have three real options, sir. First, we can continue to try finding and disarming all the traps in our path. But as you said, we don't really have that kind of time, not any more. Second, we can try sneaking through this sector to our extraction point without setting off any more traps. Only, they can also be remotely command-detonated, and we haven't the time or manpower to check every place someone could be hiding with a pair of binoculars and a transmitter. And third, we could pull back to an already secure area, and try to set off all the signal-trigger traps in a sector at once before we move in to it. That, of course, is going to make a huge mess that we may not be able to slog through, and might even do all sorts of things we don't want to have happen. That and it might not even work, depending on how advanced their equipment is." He shrugged his armored shoulders. "Personally, I'm not really fond of any of our choices, and I'm glad that you're the one being paid the big bucks to make this call, sir."

I wiped a hand across my face, momentarily closing my eyes as I made my decision. "Then here's how I think I should earn my money; if either of you see any holes in my logic, speak up now or forever hold the pieces you end up in." I licked my lips as I tried to rapidly, yet thoroughly think my way through our predicament. "We are out of time. Our rendezvous for extraction is in less than an hour. Disarming a sector one building at a time before moving into it is out. We don't have the time and it's still not all that close to being guaranteed safe. For all the effort, we need a bit more assurance. No, that's out.

"Trying to sneak a couple of thousand infantry and Man O'Wars through fifteen kilometers of city without being spotted is just plain ludicrous. We know that we're being watched, probably even right now. They might even be listening in on us because our ECM strengths may not be as good as their counter-ECM. They may even hear our plans as we make them.

"As insane as it may sound, I'm going with option number three. We need to come up with a way to deliberately set off all the booby-traps between here and the LZ. *And*, just to make things interesting, we also have to keep that battalion or so of Man O'Wars that's somewhere behind us off of our backs while we're blasting a nice swath through urban Heid on our way to the boats. Comments?"

Harris looked around a bit, probably half-heartedly checking windows for spies and snipers, then agreed with my assessment. "We're gonna have to move in a massive bounding over-watch then, sir. We'll have the over-watching half of the unit stay well back and running maximized emcon. They'll also have to try and hold off the Krupps if they get too close. The other half will have to spread out a bit and push their transmitters to emergency power and try to trigger all the booby-traps in the next sector before we enter it." He clicked his tongue a couple of times. "We could lose power packs doing that."

"The game has risks," I said, "but I think it's the best shot we have, anyway. Jason?"

I saw Abate nod through his visor. "The only questions are can we do it fast enough to get to the LZ in time, and can we keep far enough ahead of the Krupps while we're at it?"

"Those are the questions, but we don't have much choice. That's it then, we do it. Set it up, Mr. Harris. Make sure to divide the heavy assault Man O'Wars, the anti-armor infantry and, if we still have some, anyone with advanced electronic warfare packages more or less evenly between the two groups. And make it fast."

The battle for Heid was supposed to have been a cakewalk; it had even started out that way.

After staging on the plains west of the city back in September, we put the city under siege for three months. In December we had broken through their defensive lines, and had quickly smashed what little organized opposition had been left within the city proper. Heid fell within a week. It was one of the quickest battles the coalition encountered, and it was our swiftest gain of territory.

The units defending Heid had consisted mainly of tanks and other armor, and in the tight confines of an urban environment their limitations had done as much to kill them as had our missiles and lasers. No Krupp officer, a product of a dozen generations of the finest military minds in the Charted Territories, would have tried to defend a city with armor alone. It just didn't make sense.

The Coalition had struggled long and hard in deciding what to do once a city or town had been pacified. In the end the decision had been made that we were to set to work on obliterating the culture of martial conquest which had ruled the Hegemony for the last two and a half centuries. This meant destroying monuments, libraries, cultural centers, and government buildings and civic facilities. The idea was to raze the Krupp's aggressive culture totally, as they had done to so many others, and then hope that, if we left them alive, they would learn the proper lessons from all of that.

I didn't care for the idea of smashing a culture and then just leaving the citizens to pick up the pieces on their own. I felt, at the very least, that the Coalition nations should take enough responsibility for their actions to guide the Hegemony populace back onto a civilized track. It seemed to me that our current strategy would only invoke hatred, creating a new breeding ground for another aggressive nation bent solely on revenge. I thought it was stupid, but no one in task force command or the Coalition's group of policy makers was overly interested in the socio-political views of a lowly attached colonel from the Protectorate. In the end I simply followed the ancient maxim: shut up and soldier, soldier.

After finally accepting our role, the rebuilt and reinforced remains of the Dogs' Second Division, with me promoted again and now officially in command, had gone from being my vision of professional soldiers to some shilk junkie's nightmare of high-tech vandals. We had rounded up large groups of civilians, usually at gunpoint, marched them to whatever targets topped our list that day, and, like good despotic dictators everywhere, made speeches about how their own failure to stop the evils of their government had forced us to take these actions. Then, before their sullen gaze and angry sneers, we had, as our written orders put it so eloquently, "blotted out yet another monument to the evils of aggression, imperialistic conquest, and fascism."

Our plan of public demonstrations and focused terrorism appeared to be going fine, then one day there hadn't been any citizenry to round up. Over the course of a week or so, Heid had become a ghost town. We'd watched them leave, at first singly, then later in droves, but we were so spread out there wasn't much we could do about it but let them go. Besides, I for one was not about to start shooting civilians, and we lacked the prison facilities to simply arrest them all. Intelligence was divided on the issue. Some said they were simply trying to abandon our zones of control; others insisted that the entire reserve was being mobilized, but they had nothing concrete to back up that theory.

I immediately pulled the whole division back to our hold in Heid's northern industrial section. We sat there on a defense one alert status; everyone within a fortified perimeter, armed at all times, ready to move out in three minutes or less. Once I had all my chicks gathered into the roost, and felt secure enough to take the time to do so, I bypassed the chain of command and called Marshal Matheson directly.

What Matheson had told me made the hair stand up on the back of my neck. All across the planet, wherever there were major concentrations of Coalition troops, the same story played out over and over again: large numbers of the local population had simply up and disappeared. Ground forces command was operating in near chaos; some commanders sure that we were all now sitting with our pants down, while others saw no reason for any alarm at all, interpreting the migrations as a sign that our present rule was uncontested. As so often tends to happens in coalition situations, egos and tempers flared, and decisions were made according to expediency rather than competency. Matheson had his hands full fighting that battle.

As if large population migrations weren't nerve-wracking enough, to make the situation even murkier, fleet started encountering heavy, system wide communication and sensor jamming from locations throughout the solar system. Then the mines started going off. Sometime during the chaos of the assault on Gottenheim's orbital defenses, the Krupps had laid down a field of very sophisticated, inactive, and stealthy mines.

They were nasty little things, all but invisible to any of our sensors, and most contained enough explosive to punch at least a small a hole in the outer armor of even a heavy cruiser. While they only killed a couple of ships, they severely damaged quite a few, and they killed a lot of personnel. That tied up the lion's share of the entire fleet's resources and severely demoralized much of the navy. That's when the Krupp began their counterattack.

A message from Chancellor Krupp himself was broadcast across the entire world. In it he warned the Coalition to abandon Gottenheim or be destroyed utterly, assuring us that he was returning in force to reclaim for Krupp what was Krupp's. He promised vengeance upon the nations that had attacked the Hegemony, and called upon every citizen and resident to stand up and defend the Fatherland. He incited the entire populace to punish us with a violence unheard of in human history. All hell broke loose.

Across Gottenheim, wave after wave of armed Krupp citizens poured forth from hiding. Millions of them. They were armed with everything they could find, from reserve Man O'Wars and fighter planes to clubs and knives. Tanks, artillery, powered infantry; they all swept forth in a flood and pushed back the Coalition forces in almost every sector, inflicting incredibly heavy losses before most units could even try to scramble and throw them back.

The Dogs of War got lucky, if that's the term for it, for a couple of reasons. First, capitol units from the various coalition nations had usurped what they referred to as the prestige targets. The taking of the planetary capitol, the regional capitols, and the largest cities hadn't been of great strategic value, but they made for high-power propaganda bites when played for the folks back home. Not formally being from any nation, the Dogs weren't much concerned with that sort of thing, so our area of operations wasn't as important for the Krupps to recapture. That didn't stop them from trying.

The second reason we were lucky was that most of our unit leaders had, like me, made the wise decision to fort up as soon as we found our occupation zones active in a most unusual way. When the first attacks did come on our position, at about noon of that first day, we were at least nominally prepared. Unarmored infantry, many lacking even rudimentary firearms, began probing our defenses, locating our strongest fields of fire and mine emplacements.

It came as a shock to realize these soldiers were all old or crippled, but my intelligence analyst assured us that in the Krupp's manufactured society such people are only a drain on valuable resources. They would willingly throw themselves onto a grenade or attack a tank with rocks just to be of some seeming use one last time; they were just bodies to be used and discarded. I can't exactly say that we threw them back because they wouldn't retreat, but we did keep them from getting inside our perimeter.

The next attack, about mid-afternoon, was much more serious. The old and crippled came in waves, and they all had guns. They were accompanied by several armored assault vehicles carrying medium laser cannons and small HEPCs, and they managed to get right up to our perimeter lines in several places before we killed them all. Even with their weapons it still wasn't a true fight, just a slaughter. It was their numbers and armor that delayed us, that and our revulsion at the butchery and absolute waste of human life.

The third attack was the worst. Only a few hours before sunset, our observation posts and sentries reported children, literally hundreds of them, streaming toward our position, hands waving in the air and smiles on their faces as though happy to see us. I recalled something that General Gough had said so very long ago, and passed the order that no child was to be allowed within one hundred meters of our outer lines.

Despite all that we had already seen in that day, in that war, the entire division almost mutinied at that point. Even after months of fighting all across Gottenheim, and the reports that had come in from other worlds fighting the Hegemony, my soldiers simply could not believe that even the monsters who were Krupp would use children as human weapons. Many of my people kept clinging to that belief, initially refusing my orders to fire, right up until the first few children reached the forward observer and detonated their satchel charges.

The massacre was awful, something that tears at my heart whenever I think on it. The horror that comes when I dream of it is indescribable. I have never been willing to orders other to do that which I will not. I too stood on the line and pulled a trigger. The scars created by being a part of such a mass slaying of children, leading it in fact, run deep, and I doubt any amount of therapy can erase them.

The majority of my people started firing, but many of my soldiers, despite what they'd witnessed, still could not bring themselves to kill children. Many cherubic little four and five year olds ran or toddled right up to my infantry without ever being fired upon—then died anyway when the explosives they were carrying tore them and their perceived enemies to shreds. I remember most clearly watching and feeling completely helpless as one of my regular infantrymen, the tears pouring down his face easily visible through his raised visor, his whole body wracked with sobs, swept his rifle back and forth across the oncoming youngsters, killing at least a dozen. Finally he could bear no more; he simply turned his rifle around and shot himself between the eyes.

I do not think I can find any single experience in my life so positive that it outweighs that memory. It haunts me often enough, I'll not dwell on the details any longer. It won't bring back any of those soldiers, or the innocent children whose own parents used them as living weapons, and it won't make me less responsible.

We took heavy losses from the *kindergarten kommandos*, even once we started taking them down. Many of my infantry were killed and much of our perimeter was ripped apart. I ordered everyone to armor up, to cram into any armored vehicle they could find or even squeeze into the tiny space behind a Man O'War's pilot seat if necessary, in preparation for bugging out.

The *kindergarten* assault had told me enough about what kind of fanatical enemy we were facing, and what depths they would delve to in their fight against us. We were far from our own lines without orbital support or retrieval even possible in our current position. I was determined that that would be the last assault we experienced before we moved out.

At the crack of dawn we marched out, our Man O'Wars spreading out in the best formation I could come up with, a kind of massive version of a squad column with a succession of arrow shaped wedges alternately biased to the left and right. I ordered flanking and scouting parties out to our sides and front, each consisting of at least a platoon of armored infantry reinforced with a heavy weapons team or a Man O' War specially configured for urban combat. The more vulnerable armored vehicles, less adept at this sort of close quarters combat and jam packed with noncombatants and wounded, were in the middle of the column, well protected on all sides. Bringing up the rear were more than three companies' worth of heavy and assault Man O'Wars loaded for bear. I was damned if I was going to spend even one more hour as a sitting target for whatever else our implacable foe would decide to throw at us.

I didn't even call for a dust off until we were well on our way to the most likely extraction point, something big enough to allow us to evacuate a division worth of troops and equipment. Fleet granted me my request, but that came as no surprise, I wasn't giving them a choice.

"Here it is, sir." Harris sent me over a copy of the new distribution table he'd worked up for us. It had only taken him about half an hour. I'd spent the time shuffling patrols around, talking to the troops, and basically distracting myself with make-work. "Looks like we have about a reinforced battalion worth of infantry and two companies of Man O'Wars in each watch," he paused, took a deep breath, and continued, "but only one advanced EW suite left. Mine."

"Damn it. I want you in a better position to help keep the Krupps off of us. I don't need you wasting your time and effort on blowing up buildings." Then, from far behind us, I heard the echoed sounds of distant rocket and missile fire, seemingly growing steadily closer. We were out of time. "Harris, get up there and start blowing up buildings!"

"I'm gone, sir." And he was.

The sounds of weapons fire grew louder. Since I was already in a fairly good position, I stayed right where I was to coordinate between the two segments of my command.

An infantry suit bounced past me. "Sir, the local buildings are now cleared of traps, so you are safe to use general comms." Before I could register his name off the communications display to thank him for the news, he bounced away from me and toward the approaching thunder.

I switched my communications over from their tight, local settings. "Alpha Lead, this is Prime. Give me a sit-rep."

"Prime, this is Alpha," came Abate's voice. "We are taking indirect probing fire from roughly three klicks to our rear. No direct contact yet on passive sensors. Shall we go active?"

"Negative on that, Alpha, stay passive. We don't want to make their job any easier just yet. Keep quiet and let them think you're all up ahead with Bravo group." I tried to smile into my pickups and force confidence into my voice. "Maybe they'll even walk right out in front of you, and you can put some form of hurt on them. How are you fixed for heavy weapons?"

"Good but not great. I've got fifty-three heavy or greater Man O'Wars, each with at least three anti-armor missiles left. Also, some of my infantry companies are still packing a few Dragons around, but once those are gone, we're down to cannons and heavy lasers. All the HEPCs are up with Bravo."

I swore. That meant that all the heavy weapons with an endless supply of ammunition were with the current demolition section—where they would be of no use at all. It was too late to redistribute my augmented armor now. Over my tactical repeaters, I could see the first Krupp units now moving between buildings and closing on Alpha's position.

"All right, Alpha, tell everyone to conserve ammo, aimed fire only."

"Anything else I already knew that you'd like to tell me, sir?" I'd heard that turn of phrase before. It helped confirm my theory that good infantry commanders are cookie cutter stamped out of the same blob of dough.

"Good luck, Major, I'll cite you for your insubordination later."

"And good luck to you, too, sir. Alpha out."

I switched over to another channel. "Bravo Lead, what's your status?"

"We're almost in position and ready to broadcast, sir," Captain Stan Rock's gravelly voice replied. "Give us five and we'll be all set."

"Make it two, Captain," I fired back. "Alpha is going to have a lot of company in four minutes, and I want you ready to pass his people through your positions by the time they engage."

"Understood, sir. We'll be ready."

I checked on Alpha again. "Jason, keep talking to me, I don't like surprises."

"We've got visuals on Man O'Wars, sir. Looks like mostly mediums to a few heavies, but something's not quite right here. They're starting to just walk out into the open and stand there. They aren't searching or scanning or anything, they just stand there with their weapons down. After a minute they walk back to cover and another couple come out."

I felt some very big butterflies come to life in the pit of my stomach. "Go to active scans and watch for units trying to get around your flanks, especially infantry sneaking around your pickets by moving through the actual buildings. Start pulling back slowly so they don't get behind you, and keep me informed. I don't want to have to call you again."

"Roger that, boss. Alpha out."

I didn't have much left to do there, and we were going to be moving up soon, so I just moved my Cutthroat forward, up toward Bravo's location. I throttled up and called Rock up again.

"What's your timetable looking like, Stan? Alpha is on the move and running out of time quickly. The Krupps are up to something and Jason's going to need some maneuvering room soon."

"Sir!" The response was almost frantic, as if worried about what I was doing. "Get down!"

My Man O'War was slammed backwards by an invisible, silent fist moving at supersonic speed. My feet actually left the ground, and, airborne for a moment, I folded over forward. I quickly reencountered the ground and skidded down the street, quite literally ass first.

Even as I was bouncing ass over elbows along the pavement, the sonic boom caught up with the initial shockwave and washed over me, blowing out the external mikes. My computer silently informed me that my audio pickups were now useless, though I could compensate with vibrational sensors and internal pickups.

As I scraped to a halt, balanced on the backs of my shoulders with my feet folded back and hanging down in front of my face, I could see a kilometer wide column of dust rising in the middle distance. I shuddered even as I extricated myself from the rather undignified position. Either the sector Bravo had just detonated was laced with an awful lot more bombs than we'd found in previous areas, or we'd been extremely lucky to make it this far.

I rolled my Cutthroat over and levered myself back onto my feet. "Bravo Lead, just what the hell was that?"

Rock's voice was almost as shaky as my knees. "I've got a team checking, Colonel. Stand by." He waited for a minute, and I assumed he was receiving a report. I took the opportunity to do a thorough systems check on my Man O'War. Nothing seemed to be permanently damaged. "Damn it, sir, on replay analysis it looks like every floor on a lot of those buildings had built-in demolition charges. When we set off all those booby-traps at once, it set off the demo charges as well. I'm estimating that we just brought down about a hundred buildings." I heard him swallow. "Sir, they were willing to knock down a good chunk of their own city just to cap a few of us. How crazy are these people?"

That was the same question that had been occupying my mind since the first wave of their attack, and I still had no satisfactory answer for either one of us. I shook my head and forced myself to focus back on the here and now. We were still in the middle of a battle zone, and that is generally not a good place to stargaze and woolgather.

"Prime, this is Alpha Lead."

"Go ahead, Alpha," I said. "You're right on time."

"Colonel, we're withdrawing in good order back toward your position. The Krupps are taking their own sweet time about moving up to engage us. Looks like they don't quite understand what that big bang a minute ago was all about." Not that Abate could have had a clue either, but he trusted that someone would have told him if it was anything important.

It suddenly occurred to me that something else might be going on. I wasn't about to bet all our lives on it quite yet, but after all they'd thrown at us the last two days just maybe the Krupps didn't have any more firepower left than we did. The more I thought about it, the more sense it made. If they'd had such overwhelming firepower in the first place, they would never have sought to whittle us down with cripples and children.

I clicked my communication channels to allow for what I was going to ask. “Alpha, give me a visual feed from anyone and everyone who has a clear view of a Krupp Man O’War. Specifically, I want to check out their missile racks and ammo storage bins. Something is fishy about this whole thing, and I want to find out what it is before it gets us all killed.”

He clicked his mike in reply, and I started checking through visual and thermal pictures of the force pursuing us. The view the repeaters provided showed that my guess hadn’t been entirely accurate. From the lackadaisical manner in which the Krupps had been pursuing us I’d really begun to wonder if they still had a strong enough force to actually hurt us. What I found was not what I was expecting.

Once you rip off all the different electronics, weapons, and armor configurations, there are relatively few basic Man O’ War designs, and those are all based on the human form because of its versatility in almost any terrain. A good model design will spread from world to world, nation to nation, copied and modified by each organization that it passes through, but in the end it’s still basically the same machine.

Many of the Krupp Man O’Wars behind us were something else entirely.

While most of them were of the standard humanoid configuration, a significant minority of their number were not. Instead, I was confronted with a fantastic array of bizarre configurations, strange designs, and worst of all, unfamiliar weaponry. Augmented armor with reverse articulated legs that looked like giant ostriches sporting huge MLRS pods, low slung ones with four or more legs that skittered along exposing only the smallest of profiles, even squat wide ones that looked like nothing more than legs with weapons on them; all were standing in plain sight next to their more mundane humanoid counterparts.

I switched over to address both of my leads at the same time. “Alpha, Bravo, this is Prime. Bravo, get your people under some cover and ready to pass Alpha through your lines. Alpha, go to active scan on those Krupp units and fall back as fast as you can in good order. We need some information on those new machines behind us. Be ready to cut your scans and comms once you pass Bravo’s line. Uplink everything you get on those Man O’Wars to me. Do it now, people. Time’s out.”

I pushed my Cutthroat to a jogging pace and passed Bravo’s lines myself. I didn’t bother to stop, as I could see from both my visual scans and my tactical repeaters that Rock had the situation well in hand. I did make sure to give a thumbs up to the man in the Leviathan I passed closest to. I’ve always tried to remember those little things that I've always found help to keep morale up in even the worst situations imaginable.

Passing one friendly unit through the lines of another while under fire is about the trickiest combat maneuver there is. Under the influence of heavy electronic warfare and under fire, those holding the line often cannot readily tell friend from foe, and they tend to fire upon anything that moves or shoots. The moving unit, on the other hand, is often firing at a pursuing enemy force, and has little time for niceties like passwords and checks. It's textbook dogma to charge when you catch the enemy doing this, and I was expecting the worst.

"Be ready," I warned Rock.

"Dogs of War commander," a voice popped in my ear. It sounded male, harshly accented, and supremely confident to my ears. "I am Obertsleutnant Henning Keitel, commander here."

What was this? Since when did the Krupp leadership allow their field officers to send messages to the enemy?

"Colonel Chase Aarons, attached, Dogs of War Second Division. What can I do for you, Obertsleutnant?"

A chuckle. "You cannot *do* anything for me, Colonel. But there are those in the Hegemony that do not always approve of the way the Krupp family utilizes their power."

Surprised, I blinked a few times while I tried to figure out what to say, I certainly didn't want to overplay this if it was what it appeared to be. "I imagine there would almost have to be. What about them?"

"Look around you, Colonel, and you will see some of the finest warriors and soldiers the Hegemony has ever produced, equipped with the newest, most advanced battle suits and augmented armor that the most technologically advanced nation in the Charted Territories is capable of producing. Instead of fighting as they have been ordered, they are simply standing in the open where they may easily be seen. Many of these would welcome a way to be apart from what they find left for them here."

He was being cautious, not coming right out and saying anything in so many words. This was a delicate situation, but we had no time for subtleties.

"You're looking to defect? Betray your country?"

Keital bristled at my words. "Is it treason to leave behind that which is wrong, Colonel? Is it treason to want to end life under a tyrant? What do you think must happen to motivate my people to simply stand there while your units layer them with half a dozen lock-ons each? Let me ask you, after watching a hundred of your grandfathers and a hundred of your children sent to needless deaths in the Chancellor's name, who is the one who has been betrayed?"

I had nothing to say in response to that, so I switched away from him and thought about it. "Alpha, where the hell are you? They say they're looking to defect. I'll feel a whole lot more secure having this conversation if all of Alpha gets back here right now."

"We're working our way back carefully, sir. I've got my guys watching these back stabbers close enough to count the pores on their foreheads. You know what kind of tricks they're capable of. I don't want to give them our backs, no matter what he's saying. In a minute we'll turn and then let you…hold on!" His transmission was cut short.

My troops were very scared, very nervous, and feeling very vulnerable; Keital's likely felt the same, standing out there in the open. Both sides stood at close range to their ostensible mortal enemies, each with enough firepower to quickly level this entire city, or what remained of it anyway.

One group had taken an irrevocable step straight into the heart of the unknown in a bid for finding a better way, a fatal step if their overtures were rejected, for their own government would execute them for sure. True, as a sign of faith they had symbolically laid down their shields and stood vulnerable before us, braving our mercy, but my troops had only recently seen the Hegemony attack them with children. There could be no trust here.

Someone fired.

I don't know what motivated that first shot, it could have been anything from a righteous anger, done in ignorance of the current negotiations, to just a sweaty and nervous hand that tightened a bit too hard on an unsecured trigger. Whatever the reason, a single beam of energy, from one of my warriors, lanced out to tear the rocket pod off of one of the bird Man O'Wars. A thousand more followed in the next few seconds.

The Obertsleutnant hadn't been embellishing when he said his warriors were the finest. They reacted faster than I would have ever thought possible, moving through the withering fire with a grace that only the most elite warriors could ever manage. It didn't matter. The Obertsleutnant's soldiers had basically thrown down their arms and surrendered. He'd been right about something else too, Abate's troops *had* layered each of the Man O'Wars with a half dozen lock-ons.

Once again we slaughtered the enemy. I could only watch helpless, even as I shouted for a general cease fire. It only lasted for a few seconds, but that's all it took. The butchery was quick and brutal. I could claim that we won, but I won't.

I didn't even say a word, not to anyone. I just turned my Cutthroat back toward our evacuation point and resumed walking. It was hard going over all the debris left from the destruction we'd wrought in bringing down the buildings. I didn't care. I only shook my head at the waste, the squander that had happened this day.

But there was still a war to fight, and we still had our duty.

Chapter Twenty-Seven

Evacuation Zone Kilo Five
Alpenschlagg Mountains, Dammerung
Gottenheim
Krupp Hegemony

April 21, 2659

"Command Three, this is Victor One One. Standard security check and FO reporting grid three four six three secure. There's nothing human out here that's still moving. Plenty of buzzards, though."

That last part I could believe all too easily, and they were probably getting fat, too. With all the Krupp troops who had died in the three assaults so far—and our own dead whom we could no longer go out and safely retrieve—the big scavenger birds had enough food to last a lifetime.

"Roger that, Victor," I responded, "but keep them open. Fleet still has plenty of bandits out there, make sure you see them first. The next transport is away in five, so expect some to come about then."

"Victor copies, Command. Will expect company in three-or-four." I could almost hear Hornaday chewing over whether he should ask the next question or not. "What's our support status?"

"Victor, you have priority fire support on one, that is oscar november echo, mortar battery."

That answer obviously didn't make him terribly happy. I couldn't blame him, I was less than thrilled with the situation myself. True, an entire mortar platoon can pump out some serious firepower, but with what we were facing it was like attacking the ocean with a bucket.

Nevertheless, all the engineers left on the ground were too busy with demolition work to set up much more of anything else, and all the other heavy gun crews had been evacuated as soon as they reached our position. There just wasn't anything else that anyone could do about it, and Hornaday understood that. "Copy that, control. Please advise if more assets become available. Victor One One out."

The grand plan was finished, we'd lost. The Coalition of Nations and its grand crusade to smash the 'evil' Krupp Hegemony were both done for. The Chancellor had succeeded in simultaneously ripping the heart out of the alliance and the expedition they'd sent. It was a master stroke of brilliant military and political maneuvering that left us scrambling to retreat safely while everything fell apart at the seams.

The only thing remaining was the last of the dying. Even that was only a matter of time, and we few who had survived to this point knew it well.

The Sunnites were in full retreat along the length of their border, hoping to fall back to a position where they could defend themselves in some manner, but without control of their capitol on Saraset the heart had gone out of them entirely. The loosely federated Associated Stars was no more, civil war and Hegemony backed political intrigue bringing down one of the Charted Territories' finer examples of good government. Both nations, if such they still were, had pulled their troops back from the fighting here months ago. I didn't blame them. However few they were, they were needed more at home.

As for those of us still left on Gottenheim, for almost three weeks now we'd been literally running for our lives, really stopping only long enough to re-supply, catch a catnap, and set up to support the next group as they came bounding past us. Then the cycle would start again as we held our position as long as it was feasible, abandoning it at the last possible moment to bound past those who'd dug in behind us.

The Krupp casualties were horrendous. Even conservative estimates put them at three or four times our losses. That didn't matter, the Chancellor had blasted through our blockade and returned home with at least a dozen times our numbers, each more willing than the next to die for the glory that is Krupp. Most of us were not quite so motivated.

Frankly, the only thing that kept our withdrawal from being a full rout was Krupp. That's not to say that no one tried just dropping their weapons and running for it, some few did, but they hadn't made it far. Only those who kept at least some of our wits and weapons about us as we ran for our lives actually did live. No, it was that rigid Krupp organization that held them back from immediately pursuing an enemy that had broken. It gave us time to regroup somewhat, though the end result surely seemed fated to be the same.

I switched to a group-wide broadcast. "All Victor units, this is Command Three. Next lift is in five, I say again, five minutes. Expect bandits in three to four. Everybody into firing positions, weapons free. Good luck and God bless.

Command out." A host of clicks answered my message, my computer ticking off each affirmation as it came in. Some few of my group leaders gave brief verbal replies, the occasional creak or scrape sounding in the background as battle weary Man O'Wars and warriors moved into their giant-sized foxholes. No long responses came back, my few remaining troops were simply too worn out for anything more.

The Dogs of War were acting as the rear guard for the entire coalition's retreat off world. Marshal Matheson had offered this as the last service we could provide on Gottenheim. The official version of negotiations was that concessions had been made to the Uryists throughout each nation, increasing political and cultural power and prestige for them, even surrendering certain cabinet level positions to their representatives. Ury itself was even granted partial autonomy.

The most popular unofficial version, twisted by rumor and innuendo but nevertheless likely containing some kernel of truth, said there had also been a few threats involved in the short negotiations. One extremist remark hypothesized that the deal had been made with several orbital fleets facing off at gunpoint; some of the nationals demanding the Dogs cover their backs or be left to die all together, and Matheson, backed by the Dominion, demanding changes in leadership or he'd switch sides.

I knew many of the key players in those stories, and none of it sounded in character, especially none of the acts or words attributed to Matheson. However, a Jarvyn destroyer had been reported destroyed in an orbital firefight with Krupp forces that had neither damaged any other ships nor resulted in any additional Hegemony losses. There had been three Dominion missile frigates in that patrol area, though.

It was enough to make one wonder, even more so knowing that many nations would likely welcome any opportunity to eliminate our politically incorrect and inconvenient free agent army. Whatever the actual course the negotiations took, they'd resulted in us watching and covering as every other boat on the planet, from the enormously huge *Jupiter* class ones to the tiny infantry moving *Bailey* class ones, rocketed into the outer atmosphere and away from the hell we'd found unleashed against us on Gottenheim.

I switched over to speak with my roving team leaders a bit more privately. "Give me final ACE reports. Good news will be rewarded with praise, bad news gets the messenger a trip to the front lines." No one laughed at my pathetic attempt at humor, but with our situation so bleak, I was willing to try anything to improve the spirits of my people.

"Alpha team is okay for cannon ammo, a thousand plus rounds for most, but we're down to three dozen heavy missiles total. Two of my wounded armored infantry have refused to medivac since they both have light HEPCs, and two of my Man O'Wars are so shot up they couldn't limp off the line if they had to. The rest report eighty five percent or greater combat effectiveness." There was a brief pause as Link received a report on another channel. "My combat engineering team just dug out another three infantry from Delta." Only their suits could have kept them alive when they got buried in their foxholes. Most of Delta hadn't been prepared and that rockslide had effectively wiped out the entire unit. "They claim they can still fight, so I'm keeping them. That brings us up to 23 infantry that are still combat effective, sir."

"Sounds good, Link. Can anything be done about those two Man O'Wars? Someday we are actually going to get out of here, and I don't plan on leaving anyone behind."

"I've got a couple of techs checking now, sir, but those artillery rounds that hit them had some screwball electronic stuff in them, and it's still interfering with the techs' scanners. If they didn't both have full missile loads, I'd just forget about them."

"Roger that. Bravo?"

"Sheila here." It was a sign of just how strung-out we all were that we no longer made smart remarks about Joseph's name. "Bravo has ten Man O'Wars without missiles, and three below the five hundred mark on cannon rounds, but we're okay on rockets. All my wounded are still okay to fight. All said, I've still got twenty-five of my Man O'Wars and near seventy infantry, all are better than eighty percent effective."

So, there was good news still available on this battlefield, if in small quantities. I would take what I could get, we all would. "Copy that, Bravo. How did you get so lucky?"

"Clean living, sir," his reply came immediately. "That, and God blesses those that don't waste time giving other people grief about their names." He was following my lead and trying to maintain a sense of humor. I hated to quash that.

"Whatever you may say, you've earned your reward. You've got right-of-the-line." An ancient term from days when the best soldier would stand at the right end of the skirmish line so that nothing would encumber his sword arm. In modern days it simply means that a soldier or group is the prime unit, everyone else's activities are bent to supporting them. In either era, the distinction is generally the last honor a soldier receives that isn't posthumous. I was signing Sheila's death warrant, and we both knew it.

"Understood, sir, and thank you." He meant it too, a true warrior to the end.

Everyone else had already left the planet, their transports outbound to the jump points. It was time for the Dogs of War to pack up and go home. Only the Dominion had left anything at all behind to help us, and that consisted mostly of aerospace power. That was why were where we were, in the Alpenschlagg Mountains, the best place we could find to cover our own collective ass. So far it had worked well enough, we'd gotten all the non-combatants and general staff away, only those of us left on security would remain after this one last big boat. Then it would be everyone for themselves as we scrambled aboard the final remaining transports and raced for the sky, hell bent on outrunning any last Hegemony attempts to finish us off.

I didn't want to die anymore, and yet I feared it was all but inevitable this time. I shook that thought away, I still had my duty.

That was ever my excuse, and ever my downfall.

"Brody," I said, "what's your latest?"

"Charlie company is low on rockets and cannon rounds. We've been taking mostly infantry and artillery, so we're nearly full on missiles. I've got a couple of Delta's people who limped in from our aid station after it was evac'ed." She paused in her report, probably checking a real-time update before continuing. "One of them isn't going to make it, and the other is likely to lose her right arm. Fifteen of my twenty-three Man O'Wars have damaged servos, six with leg damage from the infantry, four torso problems, and five with arm trouble. We can handle more infantry or more artillery, but if we get both I'm gonna start losing people in large numbers, and I don't even want to think about what'll happen if we get armor or augmented down here."

I didn't want to think about it either, but that was my job. Erika Brody wasn't going to have much of a unit left soon, even if this next wave was a small one. She was my only senior infantry officer, though, I couldn't afford to lose her.

"Erika, if things get tight, you bug out."

"We can't abandon position, sir," she protested loudly. "We'll leave the whole flank open."

"If Gamma does their job, that won't be a problem for now, and then I'm going to need you to run the infantry while we beat it back to the boats." I was already checking our deployment positions. They were woefully weak no matter how we positioned ourselves. It didn't matter, we didn't need to win, we just needed to delay.

"I hear you, sir, but I don't like it."

"Protest noted," I nodded to myself. "How are your infantry doing?"

"I've got sixty-two left in fighting condition. If anyone can spare a few, and some ammo, I'd appreciate it."

"I'll see what I can do, Erika, but don't hold your breath. Command out."

As much as I wanted to give her some reinforcements, I couldn't; I didn't have any left. The attacks she'd been repulsing on her part of the line hadn't been any heavier than anyone else's, and everyone had significant losses and problems, some even worse than the ones we were experiencing on the ground.

Our orbital forces, though still holding secure in their areas of control, were seeing greater and greater numbers of enemy vessels jumping into the system and moving into attack positions; the aviators were running the most risky of sorties, blazing in between the huge battleships and carriers to harass and spy on the enemy. Even after we left the planet our departure might not be uncontested.

One more minor adjustment to my communications, this time to talk to someone much closer to me, but still someone that didn't need to know how desperate our defenders were getting. "Gamma, you ready again?" I asked.

"As always, sir," Parting's voice came back, serious as ever. I could see him, dressed in the lighter protective armor of the non-infantry, squatting beside the huge cannon battery that was Firebase Three. The myriad mortars, howitzer units, triple A guns, anti-artillery batteries, and missile and rocket launchers surrounding our entire position atop this spike were all dwarfed by the power of these main Widow Maker cannons. Each of the four barrels measured over a meter in diameter, fully capable of throwing shells weighing as much as a small Man O'War for ranges well beyond the horizon, making it the only reason we were still alive and breathing on this planet.

Three times Hegemony forces had assaulted our positions, hoping to catch us and at least a few dropships still on the ground and loaded with valuable information. Three times these cannons, and the others like it at the remaining four firebase installations, had destroyed armor, augmented armor, and infantry at a level only rivaled by orbital bombardment. Each time they had returned, pushing harder and farther than the last. Each time we had less units to defend with as we lost them through casualties and evacuations both.

We'd hardened these firebases as much as possible, and we still controlled the sky above, at least for a little while longer, meaning the Chancellor had to chop his troops up in our grinder if he hoped to get to us. He didn't seem to mind that, at least not too badly, and eventually he would win through. When we'd planned this out, our best case scenario had said we could withstand five assaults, our worst said two. We were expecting number four at any moment.

"Everything checks out green," Parting reported. "Even orbital reports a conditional clear that they might be able to help us out in a tight spot or two."

Well, some more welcome news. Maybe God's hand really was somewhere in all of this. I allowed myself the luxury of a brief, tight smile. "When thou art in tribulation, and all these things are come upon thee, even in the latter days," I quoted to myself from the scriptures, not even needing to read the verses I'd pasted up inside my cockpit, "if thou turn to the Lord thy God, He will not forsake thee, neither destroy thee."

I took comfort in the verses, holding out that small bit of hope in my heart. My prayer, uttered with my pickups turned off and willed to heaven with ever fiber and sinew of my being, was heartfelt and sincere, if perhaps not eloquently worded.

"Help me." I was about to say that I didn't want to die, but a strangely peaceful feeling washed over me and the words changed of their own volition as they came out of my mouth. "Help me to not be afraid, and to fight with honor. Have mercy on the souls of those who fall today." As a closing I simply added, "Be with me."

The screens went crazy as if cued by my words. The smaller artillery pieces started firing off in every direction, explosions and plumes of smoke sprouting around us thick as forest trees as their salvos found their targets. The anti-artillery batteries were twisting every which way possible, detonating missiles, shells, and rockets high above our heads; shrapnel and debris rained down around those of us still outside of the shelters. A glance to my displays confirmed that the electronic jamming and counter-jamming war had also been renewed as our techs, buttoned up tight inside the bunker, and their computers went insane trying to stay one step ahead of the opposition.

"Alpha has contacts at two one and two three."

"Charlie is engaged at four niner!"

"Bravo in sweep, stand by Charlie."

The whole mountaintop seemed to vibrate and hum as the big guns turned into position, seeking their first target. My Man O'War stumbled forward despite its tether and my preparation when the cannon fired and the shells sucked all the air along behind them in a giant whoosh. A huge fireball bloomed on the top of another spike, even taller than this one, if not quite so substantial. The entire column collapsed, presumably on top of a fairly large number of Krupp soldiers. Unconsciously I counted the seconds. After three I heard the blast of the explosion and the rumble of the slide.

"Charlie pulling back to Tango Romeo Papa three. Where are you Sheila?"

"Foxtrot Oscar is gone. Alpha has heavy armor! We need some support over here."

"Bravo's here, hold tight Charlie."

A flight of Dominion attack planes zipped overhead, barely fifty meters over my head. I could clearly make out their full ordnance loads, just waiting to kill enemy targets. They were heading the wrong way though, apparently bent on helping someone else out. I couldn't complain, everyone else needed the aid at least as much as my people did, but that didn't keep me from wishing.

"Alpha, status on the armor," I said.

"Bullying through, Command. Suggest detonate mines in golf niner."

"Can do," I said. I also triggered the mines we'd had enough time to replace farther down that approach.

"That slowed them down, Command, but we need something more."

"I'll see what I can find, Link. Keep your heads down and…" I stopped short as another voice buzzed in my ear.

"Omega Command Three, this is Tactical Eye on the *Prometheus*. We are in position for support, suggest you go to ground."

I didn't hesitate for even a moment. "All Victors! Ground now!"

Fire washed down from the sky as if the aurora borealis had gone psychotic and sought to write her further glory in the blood of our enemies. The massive amounts of energy released by the naval bombardment boiled away rock and dirt, weapons and armor, machine and man, metal and flesh. It superheated the air to such an extent that I was hurled backward even harder than I'd been sucked forward by the Widow Maker's shot. My tether snapped and for a moment I thought I'd be thrown over the edge of the cliff, reinforcing my units below in a rather abrupt, implausible way.

Fortunately I managed to clamp a tight hold on the corner of the bunker I'd been tied to, and held on as wave after wave of shimmering explosive energy saturated the entire area in front of us. The whole planet seemed to shake, I could almost swear that the entire column (the one our engineers had assured us was perfectly stable and quite suitable for mounting a Widow Maker on) swayed back and forth like a branch in the wind. Then the energy cascades stopped, the world returned (more or less) to its original color and motion, and I was able to return to my command position near the bunker. The Hegemony troops recovered at least as quickly as my own.

"Hope that helped, Three. *Prometheus* is now out of position. We're picking up boats."

"Copy, Eye, and thanks." Back to tactical communications. "Talk to me people."

"Charlie falling back to Tango Romeo Papa two. Augmented armor inbound, bombardment only bought us some time."

"It worked over here! Krupp armor is stalled, Alpha requesting permission to engage."

"Negative, Alpha, sweep through to Charlie," I said. The days of making Krupp pay, of punishing them, were long behind us. Now I just wanted to get every one of my people off the planet alive.

"We have targets, Colonel," the Dominion Major said. His patrol of Snipers were spread along the rim of our spike, prone and scanning the terrain for kilometers. A handful of Javelins stood behind them.

"Engage, Major, try for command units when possible." The Snipers began snapping off shots, at least one every five seconds or so. Far below us, in places of perceived safety, Krupp unit leaders died.

A general broadcast tone sounded across all channels. "The *Blood's Legacy* is away! The *Blood's Legacy* is away!" A ragged cheer went up from the throat of every Dog there, probably a few in orbit as well, even as I turned to confirm the report with my own eyes.

There she was, the last of our *Jupiters*. The boat (almost big enough to be called a ship) looked for all the world like a giant metallic egg. Its own very impressive weapons systems were cutting loose with their full firepower, targeting everything from incoming artillery and missile fire to aircraft and ground units. The massive beast accelerated upwards, breaking free of gravity's bonds on a plume of fire and smoke that tore a brilliant jagged scar across the blue sky.

A glint of sun caught my eye near the *Blood's Legacy*, just a brief flash that could have been any random piece of debris or fighter craft. I knew it wasn't though, and my intuition paid off once again. I rolled to my right at the same moment as my computer announced that someone, somewhere had gained a lock on. Laser blasts flashed through the space where I'd been standing but a second ago.

"Incoming attack craft!" I shouted on my local channel. My computer sent the vector information along to the triple A units, but the ECM war was going against us on this one, none of us could get a solid lock on the plane. A couple of Javelins launched Seeker missiles anyway.

The plane roared in, an oddly shaped angular black plane, with three more like it following in a tight formation. Lumpy shapes detached from each of the craft, good sized bombs diving down on us. Anti-artillery guns brought down most of the bombs, detonating them well away from us, though the blasts still rocked our position. Three still fell on target, two smashing into the far side of the bunker and doing very little damage to the hardened structure.

The third landed on a howitzer and mortar position, sending up a huge explosion as all the ammunition cooked off. Fortunately I'd gone with my gut instinct and, unlike other commanders, had insisted on the engineers wasting their precious time dividing our stores into many separate areas with vented armored shunts designed to minimize the effects of just such an occurrence. Nevertheless, screams echoed briefly through the communication channels and a large section of the mountaintop slid away, dropping at least fifty soldiers and two Snipers to their deaths and destruction below. Though they'd been under my command I couldn't have told you even one of their names.

I lined up a manual shot, knowing full well that I'd never get that lucky, but hoping it might work anyway. A long, sustained burst blasted away from my Cutthroat, hurling death through the air around the attacking Krupp craft. None of it had any effect on the Hegemony planes as they sped away. Their escape was not clean, though. A half dozen Dominion planes whipped by at the same level as the mountaintop, their variable geometry wings swept fully forward for maximum maneuverability, obviously in pursuit of these elusive targets.

The Widow Maker fired again, this time down into one of the twisting valleys sprawling out below us like some monster spider's web. The explosion blew through the narrow passage in both directions, sweeping before it the broken remains of whatever poor fools had been down there. Smoke and dust blasted up in a man made geyser of debris that shifted slightly in the wind.

"Command, this is Alpha. You still there? The armor has pulled back but we're getting a lot of augmented here. Unable to link up with Charlie."

"Copy," I said, tearing my eyes away from my tactical displays to focus on my strategic ones. "Bravo, advise situation."

"Command, this is Bravo Two, Bravo One is down, no ejection. We are under heavy augmented strain."

Again I lacked the opportunity to mourn a fallen comrade. I could only tell myself that I'd have one more haunting face to look forward to when this was all over. I almost looked forward to welcoming Sheila's ghost to the family. "Can you fall back, Bravo?"

"Maybe, but we are pinned pretty tight."

"Get out if you can, hook up with Alpha." Another adjustment. "Charlie, where you at?"

"We are right under you, sir. That avalanche you sent our way almost finished off what little we have left. I've lost all my augmented armor. We're basically holding on the Snipers alone. When are we bugging out?"

Right on cue another general all channels tone sounded. This time I recognized Marshal Matheson's own voice. I should have realized he would intend to be the last Dog off of this miserable rock. "All Dogs, this is Prime, fall back on the boats by the numbers! Command groups, get your people out then follow them in! Let's go now people!"

"Alpha, Bravo, Charlie! Back to the boats!" I shouted. Now things were going to be moving fast indeed. "Move by Tango Romeo Papa zero. Count them through and hit the mines. Pray the boys in engineering did their job right." If they had, enough rock should be falling down to temporarily seal in our entire valley, buying us at least enough time for us to be on our way. If not, then our trip might end up being really, really short; maybe not even reaching the current lofty height I already enjoyed.

Two affirmative answers came in from Bravo and Charlie, then Link's voice came on. "They've brought their armor back up and they're almost getting past us as it is, sir! If we fall back now they'll be at the boats before we are." He grunted with the effort of whatever task he was doing. "You're going to have to leave without us, sir. We'll hold here until you're clear, my word on that."

"I don't need heroics," I chastised him, "I need my people off this planet in one piece! Fall back now!" I redirected my communications. "Gamma, I need you to fire down on TRP one, danger close. Alpha's down there."

I was kind of hoping the Widow Maker was going to take the shot, but that was probably impractical and too dangerous given the close quarters my troops were operating in down there. Instead, what remained of the lesser cannons, mortars, and direct fire MLRS units opened up, all concentrating on holding back the enemy just long enough for our people to successfully disengage. It wasn't as dramatic as the big gun, but the effect was more or less the same.

"Alpha, fall back!"

"Command Three, this is Evac Control. Commands Two and Five are in. It's past time to bring your group in. You're on the *Archaeopteryx*." Good, at least we'd be on a fast boat. I had no love for hanging almost motionless in the air, relying on the aviators to get us away safely. I wanted the trip to be as quick as possible.

"Copy, Control. We'll be there, don't leave without us."

"There are no guarantees, Three. Be here now."

It was taking too long. My people should have been able to fall back by now, we weren't that spread out, or at least we shouldn't have been. My displays showed two of my groups only a bit behind where they should have been, but one wasn't showing clearly at all.

"Charlie is past Tango Romeo Papa zero, Bravo is right behind me, Command." Brody sounded hurt, I hoped it wasn't serious, but there was nothing to be done for it now.

"Where the hell are you, Link?" I demanded.

"This is Alpha Five, we've lost One and Three! We are pinned down, there is no way we're going to get clear, sir! There are too many of them and they're right on top of us, you have to detonate now Command, or they'll get through!"

I selected and informed my people well, I trusted their judgment. When they told me twice that disengagement was impossible and delay fatal, I believed them. I pushed my visor up long enough to wipe my hands across my face, then, with a tear in my eye that could have been from the dust but wasn't, I detonated the mines, collapsing the valley walls just as the engineers had planned.

"Bravo, Charlie, position?"

"We're at the boat, Command," Brody said, breathing heavily. "Charlie's onboard and strapped in, I'm getting Bravo aboard now. We're just waiting for you, the Snipers, and Gamma."

"Command group, Gamma, fire controls and ECM on auto, we are evacuating now. Bring your boys in, Major."

I followed my own instructions, locking down all the systems on my Cutthroat and popping the hatch. I only took enough time to grab a set, then

I was sliding down to the ground below, vaguely upset that, of all things, I was losing yet another Man O'War on this stupid planet.

We had two escape pods still left, we'd lost one in the air attack. It would be enough, if somewhat crowded, but we were motivated to be friendly. I made certain the first pod was stuffed as full as possible with my Gamma team before I let them close the hatches and hurtle over the cliff, trusting that their jump jet and chute system would deploy properly to prevent them from simply drilling a hole in the ground at the bottom, yet still get them down a hundred times faster than the lift systems could.

The last members of my command group were just crushing into the last pod, sharing breathing space with the Dominion warriors. "All units, this is Command Group One, we have a breach! I say again we have a breach! They're coming in right below us!"

Despite the panic starting to wash over the command groups' faces, I left them crushed there and sprinted back over to one of the artillery observation posts. The displays, and my own confirmation through the optical enhancements, reported how dire the situation was. Hundreds of meters below the pinnacle that held Firebase One, the only Dominion controlled firebase, Krupp forces were literally pouring into the valley, racing for the passage into our landing zone. Armor, augmented armor, infantry, and mobile artillery were all coming through.

Even as I watched, some of our bravest aviators made attack runs on the position, but with our own ECM capabilities weakened by the evacuation, they were unprotected from the Krupp weapons that sought them out. A couple of bombs landed successfully, rending Man O'Wars and infantry limb from limb, but the planes themselves were quickly brought down by the triple A fire. Firebase Four was evacuating now, and couldn't have gotten sufficient angle from their position to have much effect anyway.

I ran back to the escape pod. "Anyone here left from Gamma?" A chorus of negative answers, all nervous and tense. They couldn't help out here, and my duty was to get them clear. I slammed the hatch closed from the outside, then backed off and externally triggered the launch system. This pod too blasted over the cliff's edge and out of sight.

I went back to the OP, checking to see if the situation was still as grim. Of course it was, no Homeric deus ex machina rescue was in store for me. I briefly wondered if I shouldn't have just jumped aboard the pod and hoped to make it to the *Archaeopteryx* before the Krupp troops made it far enough to threaten our escape. That was a pipe dream though, there wouldn't have been enough time. None of us were going to make it unless someone found a way to slow them down or significantly reduce their numbers.

The Widow Maker was my first thought. I climbed into the gunner's seat and found myself confronted by a totally alien control system, apparently designed by a madman high on drugs. I fiddled with a few of the controls a bit, but nothing useful was happening. Obviously I wasn't going to be able to decipher it quickly enough to be of any use. I likewise crossed the other artillery pieces off of my list of possibilities, there wasn't time. I needed something familiar.

A wave of Krupp attack planes blasted overhead as I exited the gun. The automated triple A guns had fallen silent, likely jammed. Either they realized that we'd abandoned this position or else they were just gunning for our landing craft because they simply flew past me and toward our LZ. One of them suddenly disintegrated, probably under concentrated laser fire from the ground. With just the eyes I was born with to see, I couldn't tell for certain what weapon had been used, or from where it had been fired.

Heart pounding hard enough that I could probably have seen it if I'd looked down at my chest, I ran with all my might back to my Cutthroat. My hands and feet propelled me back up to the cockpit where I reversed the lock down I'd implemented just moments ago. My screens popped back to life, mostly devoid of any useful information, a testament as to who now had the upper hand in the electronic war.

I paced over to the edge of the cliff, examining the Firebase One pinnacle closely. If we could knock down a portion of it, that would block the Krupp advance, but no one had thought to mine our own firebase positions, likely afraid that Hegemony electronics would be able to detonate them at an inconvenient time of their choosing. I looked over the line of enemy forces advancing down the valley and knew what I needed to do.

Visions of Captain Kay's warning once again appeared to me. Jonny and the aftermath of Madrigal swam before my eyes as well. I closed my eyelids tightly, trying to pinch off the memories. Then I forced them open again and prayed to God for forgiveness. I lined up the shot and launched all of my missiles.

The heavy weapons bucked my Man O'War as they leapt from their launch racks, tearing away in a fury. I could almost see each individual billow of smoke produced as the missiles' rocket engines accelerated them across the intervening kilometers and toward their target. Their IFF transmitters rendered them immune to Firebase One's anti-artillery and missile fire, not that any of that was working very well now with the Krupp jamming getting stronger by the second. The missiles all hit their target exactly, the mighty armor killing warheads detonating deep within the ammunition dump of Firebase One.

The Widow Maker ammunition all touched off at the same time, along with whatever other rounds were stored there. The explosion was enormous, shattering the pinnacle and destabilizing the ones around it. Ever so slowly, as if unsure of whether or not to go, the pinnacle collapsed entirely, sending rock cascading down into all of the surrounding valleys, bouncing through enemy and, if present, friendly formations alike.

I closed my eyes and swallowed hard when the spike that had held Firebase Four also collapsed. I knew it hadn't been fully evacuated yet, its personnel still would have been assembled at the base. I didn't know how many line units would have still been there, but it didn't matter. They were all gone now. Once again, my own people, my own friends and allies, had died by my hand.

I turned my Cutthroat toward the lift assemblies, numbed by my own actions and caring very little about whether I made it down successfully. I'd saved the others, or at least as many as I could, but perhaps the price had been my own soul.

Chapter Twenty-Eight

Dogs of War Battlecarrier *Prometheus*
Jump Point Alpha Two Two
Zwei System
Krupp Hegemony

May 1, 2659

I just stared at the screen, unblinking. It stared back, unblinking. I tried to focus on the words before me, but the fog created by a numbed confusion combined with a lack of sleep, made that task almost impossible. For the third time I pulled the blanket tight around my shoulders to help ward off the chill I felt, knowing that it would soon have me sweltering instead. In a few moments I would abandon it to the floor once again, seeking to cool off. I ran a hand through my hair (was it thinning?) and tried to force some sense upon a chaotic and unforgiving universe.

I leaned back, tilting my chair as far as it would go, and studied the ceiling, hoping to find inspiration somewhere up there. The cold, hard plate gave little hope that I was anything but alone in the universe. I pleaded with God to give me the words I was searching for in my task. I prayed that He give me some sign, some inspiration. I hoped that He had not abandoned me as I'd once abandoned Him. Like the ceiling, He too gave me little hope that I was anything but alone in the universe. I wanted to cry.

Instead, I closed my eyes. I may have actually fallen asleep as nodding off briefly wasn't an uncommon thing for me to do. It didn't matter. Dream or memory, vision or illusion, I watched from a view port of the ill-named dropship *Archaeopteryx* as it rocketed away from Gottenheim. Far below I could still see, receding quickly, the wounded landscape I'd blasted, bringing a mountain down and burying hundreds, maybe thousands of enemy troops; burying hundreds of our own troops. Enemy fire blazed all around us, Krupp ground troops and aircraft taking advantage of this last chance to destroy us. Occasionally we were hit, but I didn't care, I was far beyond that point. My mind and thoughts, my cares and worries, were still far below, wondering what it felt like to die trapped in a cockpit under a hundred million tons of rock. Those who suffocated or were crushed had it easy. At least one or two would probably have to wait for starvation or dehydration to end their lives. Those of the coalition would know they'd died at the hands of one of their own, and I was that one.

I shuddered awake. It must have been a dream, I'd still been in my Man O'War when the *Archaeopteryx,* flightless bird that it was, lifted off of Gottenheim. I'd never looked back or even seen pictures of the rockslide. It seemed so real, though, so vivid, even after awakening. It was this dream and ones like it, these constant flashbacks and guilty thoughts that had prevented me from sleeping much. I suppose I could have asked for something from sickbay, some narcotic to ease the pain of slipping into sleep, but I was so leery of taking even that small step back toward a dependency on drugs that I was willing to suffer instead.

"Happy May Day, Colonel," Marshal Matheson said. He stood in the doorway to my stateroom. It was out of the way, and I was sharing it with one of the naval officers. We were squeezed into a cramped little space, spartan and bare and a long way from anyone else's quarters, but it was exactly what I wanted.

The Marshal's sudden appearance caught me by surprise, I hadn't been paying much attention to my surroundings and had not heard his approach. I had left the door open, not as an invitation to anyone to enter, but because the ship's air circulation wasn't very good in this room, especially since it hadn't originally been intended for use by two officers. I think it had originally been intended as a broom closet.

That open door probably had looked like an open invitation to just walk right on in, an open door policy, if you will. Truthfully though, something as petty as a closed and secured door likely wouldn't have stopped the Marshal. I began to stand, but he waved me back down to my seat. I didn't sink back to where I had been though, I tried to sit on the edge in perfect military posture, giving him my full attention, draping the blanket over the chair's back and out of the way.

"And to you, sir," I replied with a slow nod. Then I confessed, "Though I have to say that I don't much feel capable of experiencing much happiness myself, or of celebrating holidays."

Matheson nodded. Belatedly, I offered him a chair from the desk next to mine. The Lieutenant Commander who used it was on bridge duty currently, and thus had no need of it. He wouldn't have tried to take it away from the

Field Marshal, anyway. Matheson accepted and sank all the way back, making himself very comfortable. He glanced around and took in the hefty stack of papers that were piled on my desk, as well as the screen that currently displayed a list of names; a very long list indeed.

He extended a finger and pointed at the clutter on my desk. "What's all this?" he asked as if truly ignorant. I doubt that was the case, but he made it sound pretty good.

I couldn't dodge the question when he was so blunt about asking it, but I'd have tried anyway if I'd been awake and alert enough to think of a better, equally plausible explanation. Unfortunately, I hadn't slept much at all in the days since we'd left Gottenheim.

Besides the memories and dreams, besides the thoughts and worries, there were just too many faces following me around now, too many questions being asked whenever I closed my eyes. The questions were my own, they echoed every one of my own thoughts, but the voices belonged to many, many others. I had collected a very large number of ghostly visages and their questions over the years, gotten so used to their presence in fact that I hardly even noticed them, or spared them much thought.

This newest group was numerous, and very insistent in their demands for answers that I just didn't have. I knew from far too much personal experience that they would eventually become weaker, though they would never disappear completely. I just didn't know how long it would take for them to fade, or just how far they really would fade.

"These are the names and files for every one of the task force soldiers who were killed in the blast, sir."

"I surmised as much. What are you doing with them?" He tipped his chair back far enough that it rested on the desk behind him, raising two of the chair's legs off of the floor; a very undignified position for a man of such high rank. I think it was merely a calculated tactic, designed to make me open up and lower my guard to his questions. Perhaps if I'd had more sleep it wouldn't have worked so well, but then he might have used a different approach. As it was he appeared so relaxed, so nonchalant, that I envied him and wanted to know what his secret was because, despite the fact that I knew it had to be a show put on for my benefit, I wanted to at least be able to fake it that well. I knew he had to be feeling a great deal of stress, he'd just been one of the key leaders presiding over the biggest, most one-sided defeat in recent human history. No matter though, because he wasn't showing it in the slightest. As for me, my back and neck ached, even my teeth hurt. The stresses of this whole affair were not killing me (or rather, if they were killing me they were doing so very slowly) but they were exacting a fairly high physical toll all the same.

I shrugged in response, unable to frame any sort of believable lie. "I'm drafting letters to their next of kin."

"Why? Won't their own immediate commanders be responsible for doing that?" Of course that was true, it somehow just didn't seem like enough. A form letter saying that your blood relation or love of your life, your reason for living, has fallen in the defense of freedom. *We are ever so grateful for all he or she gave and the cause still goes on. By the way, this person who meant the world to you was killed by one of our own officers who has a past history of this sort of thing, but he did sort of save the day. Oh, by the way, did you know that we still lost anyway? We feel for, and appreciate, your sacrifice very much.*

I told Matheson as much.

"It's understood fairly universally that people sometimes, on occasion, get killed in wars," he said. I raised an eyebrow to hear him sound so trite about it. "Even so, no one has ever found a way to truly soften the blow when we find that the list naming those who have fallen includes one of our own. That hurts in a way that can't be improved, but one of the reasons we leave out any details about the circumstances of their deaths is to avoid additional stresses in situations like this. It's enough that they died, nothing more."

I didn't agree with that. "I don't know what else I can do, sir, but I feel that I have to do something. The truth always comes out eventually, and I'd prefer to set the record straight and take responsibility before any rumors get out of hand. I think they," I gestured toward the list of names scrolled across my display, "all deserve at least that much from me."

He leaned forward, replacing the chair legs to their more stable position and looked at me thoughtfully. "Are you doing this for them and their kin or for you?"

"Both, sir," I answered immediately. "For me, I want to know that I didn't just turn my back and run into the woods again like I did on Madrigal." What I really wanted was to be able to tell this batch of ghosts that at least I'd done something for them, that some of their questions need not be the same as the very first group's. I hoped maybe they could rest better knowing that their families, at least partially, understood the sacrifice that had been made.

"I also want their survivors to know that their loved ones did not die in vain. I want them to understand that their loss saved many other lives and that it was something those soldiers would have understood. I want them to believe that every one of these precious, unique individuals died making a difference."

"What you want is for them to forgive you," he said sharply.

What could I say to that? With that seemingly simple phrase he had struck to the very root of my thoughts and actions. Yes, I wanted forgiveness from the voices, from the faces. I wanted forgiveness from those who still lived and had lost something irreplaceable; I wanted to know that they would not hate me. I wanted forgiveness from myself and my parents.

Most of all, I wanted forgiveness from you, Jonny.

"Yes, sir, I do."

"Do you really think a letter of regret and responsibility from the man who pulled the trigger will make them do that?"

My head snapped up hard and I looked at Matheson incredulously as a chill raced up and down my spine. Tears leapt unbidden to the corners of my eyes, threatening to fall. What I had done I'd done for all of us. Maybe I should not have. Truly, I probably should not have.

"Sir, I had thought that you approved of my actions."

"I did, and still do," he said with a nod. "I name you a hero. Your quick, decisive thinking was the only thing that allowed any of us to get off that world alive. I've recommended you for about a dozen different awards and another promotion. Most of the other general officers have agreed, and I expect all of those recommendations to pass committee without a single hitch. I truly do believe you did what needed to be done, I'm grateful to you for doing it, and I'll gladly welcome you into the ranks of the general officers. But I'm not the one who will be judging you. That duty," he pointed to the computer display, "is a task that is theirs and theirs alone."

One more try to make him understand. From the heart, not the head this time. "Sir, my brother died on Madrigal eight years ago, under circumstances very similar to this, and I can look you straight in the eye and swear by all that I hold holy that there are still nights when I lie in bed and wonder if I can ever forgive the man responsible. Some days I still think the best solution would be to put a gun to his head and pull the trigger." I paused at that confession because it hurt; because it was true. "I don't want anyone else to have to go through that, sir. Besides, you didn't see how the Terran Guard reacted when they found out I was with this task force. Even more than my desertion, they were angry because I'd worried only about my own pain, and not about the others who had lost family because of my actions. I'd not make that mistake again, sir."

Matheson nodded his understanding. "A laudable goal, but do you really think this will make a difference? Each of these victims' next of kin will have received an official letter by now explaining the sacrifice made by their loved ones. If they inquire further, they'll be told exactly what happened; there'll be no white washing or cover up, none of the rumors you're concerned about. That's because we believe that you did the right thing, so we don't need to hide it away. All of that will help, but the knowledge and loss will still hurt those who have been affected. It always will."

I pondered that for a moment. "I can't just sit here and let others deal with the fallout of my actions. I have to do something, sir."

"Good," he said, clapping me on the shoulder. "Because that's why I'm here."

"Excuse me?" Belatedly I added, "Sir?"

"Did you really think I came here just to have a long philosophical debate with you about a subject you won't change your mind about?"

I didn't know how to answer that question safely, so I kept my mouth shut.

He rose up from his seat and gestured that I should vacate mine. When I did so, he sat in it and took control of my computer. He browsed through the list of names rapidly, looking for something or someone in specific.

"I would like you to help out the survivor of a particular soldier."

I was very puzzled. First he didn't want me to write letters to help the survivors, now he wanted me to do something else to help the survivors. I was, to say the least, perplexed. "Who?" I asked.

"This one," he said, stopping with a single name highlighted. "Major Eric Fitzpatrick. He was with the Terran Guard's Eighty-Eighth at Firebase One when...well, when he died."

So. Even the great Field Marshal Jamie Matheson, a legend of our own day on the battlefield, was having difficulty finding the proper terms to use for what had been done. Even though he'd given me this lengthy talking to about his support for me and the rightness of my actions, he still didn't want to label the murder and tragedy for what it truly was. His skirting of a more accurate description made me realize anew the true horror of what I had done. What I had had no other choice but to do.

"He was staff to General Mason," he continued, "so the General knew his family fairly well. Apparently Fitzpatrick's wife is also part of the task force, an officer, and she is not taking this well at all. Those who've talked to her say she is deeply distraught, almost psychotic. Mason asked me, as a personal favor, because he was well acquainted with Fitzpatrick, to send someone over to check on her and see if they can help get through to her. You know, see if there is anything they can do to help her come to grips with the situation or gain a firmer understanding of what and why. He specifically requested one of my people who was directly involved, someone who can relate. If you're feeling up to it, I'd like that person to be you." He lowered his chin and raised his eyebrows. "Can you do that?"

"How can you even ask if I'm up to that, sir? I was directly responsible for the death of her husband. She probably thinks I'm a murderer." I privately wondered if that wasn't an exact and accurate description of what I was. A serial murderer as well as a mass murderer given the length of the crimes I'd committed in my life.

So many dead, so many live ruined, all because I'd been born.

"Just a moment ago you were telling me not to write letters to the families and now you're ordering me to go talk to one face to face? I don't understand, sir."

"It's not an order, Chase, you don't have to go. I can find someone else, but I would like it, I would appreciate it, if you would go."

"Why?" A single word that has been so pivotal throughout all of history. No syllable is more loaded and charged with earth-shattering implications. "I mean, I suppose I can try and help her come to terms with the reality of her loss by letting her know what really happened and why it had to happen, but I don't know what good that'll do. That's a job for a trained counselor or therapist." First I justify contacting the survivors to let them know, then I start making excuses to avoid doing just that. The Marshal and I had exchanged roles rather quickly. Of course, I'd never meant to actually go face-to-face with a survivor. I didn't want to have to look them in the eye when I confessed my role. "I know what it is to lose someone close, and no matter how heroic or logical it can take a good long time before you're able to see that."

That's assuming you ever can, right, Jonny? I doubt that *I* ever can.

"It might not do her any good at all," he confessed. He unfolded his arms and placed them on the desk's edge, leaning his weight into his words. "But it might. And what's more important to me right here and now is that I do think it'll do a world of good to help you see what the worst is like."

He studied me for a moment. I wondered if indeed he measured and weighed me, and found me wanting.

"Do I really think that you can do more for her than the fleet medical and psychiatric staff are able to do? No. Do I think she'll enjoy meeting you? No, though I do believe that it will help her, regardless of whether she enjoys the experience. General Mason seems to think it'll do some good, and after the way he stood by us right to the end, I'd like to honor his requests.

"What I really believe is that you will be forced to confront your own fears, your own limitations, perhaps your own failings. If you can deal with that, looking someone square in the eye and telling them that you're the reason their loved one isn't coming home, you can deal with anything, and you'll know it. You can put away all these lists of the dead and get on with the work of the living. The galaxy has suddenly become a very unstable place, and I'm going to need very stable generals by my side in the years ahead."

He paused while I thought that through. Then he surprised me.

"The faces don't ever go away, Chase, I know. I've been playing this grandest of games for longer than you've been alive, and I've got several legions of ghosts haunting me every night. If you go on, if you come with me and do the things that need to be done, you will only add to their number. What you need to know is that you can live with them. And this, more than anything else, will give you that knowledge."

I blew out a deep, slow breath. "I'll go."

Matheson only nodded.

Was I ready to face the worst? I'd run halfway across the Charted Territories once before to avoid facing the need to answer that question, could I answer it now? I wanted to believe in my ability to face reality, but I was unsure. I wavered for a few moments, trying to decide if I should go see this poor woman or simply flee from the faces once again; run from the ghosts that I carried within me in the futile hope that they couldn't keep up with me. I shuddered in horror at the thought (and memory) of once again dulling sensation in substance abuse, but it wasn't that which truly spurred me on. Nor was it the fear of more endless, sleepless nights tormented by memories, questions, ghosts, and guilt that overcame my fears of confronting

Fitzpatrick's wife. In the end, it was Marshal Matheson's faith in me that gave me the courage to try.

I promised myself that at least one ghost would be put to rest for good today, maybe grateful that I'd told his wife I was sorry. If Matheson was right, a few other ghosts would also go with him when he went. I wanted to believe that, all of it, but my faith there was lacking. I only went because he believed in me.

I caught a fleet shuttle over to the Dominion Terran Guard Carrier *Neptune*. The flight was as agonizing as the wait for any combat mission had ever been. I worried about what I would say, how I would approach and be approached, what the aftermath of our encounter would be. I worried that I would be attacked, that I would be forced to fight back to defend myself, perhaps hurting this woman even more than I already had, If such a thing were possible. I worried that I would be shunned; spurned; turned away and spat upon.

Most of all, I worried that I would be forgiven.

I'd spent so many years believing that I was a callous murderer. For Jonny, for a drunk on Hashama, for Collem, for so many others that I didn't how to handle the idea of a victim or family member telling me they forgave me.

Maybe that's why God never told me He did.

Perhaps the ghosts, terrifying and horrible as they were, had become comfortable companions; ones I would miss if they were to go away. I was so used to defining myself by my pain that I feared I would give up a part of myself if I let even a small part of it go. I wonder how different things could have been. If only.

I wiped my sweaty palms against my trousers and tried to fight down the flock of butterflies that were so rapidly reproducing in my stomach. The mental and physical exercises that I'd learned to reduce stress and fight off panic during tense field situations seemed to have no effect now. Even my disciplined training failed in the light of this unique mission. Regardless, I still sat there rolling my head in circles around my neck, shrugging my shoulders, breathing deeply, and dropping my tongue. At least it kept my mind partially occupied.

The slight shudder of the shuttle signified our successful docking. I hurried to disembark, almost trampling over the other passengers, all of them scrambling to get out of the way of a senior officer. I worked my way through the receiving lounge area quickly enough, and found a crew listing on a display screen in the corridor.

Actually, the first thing I did was find a refresher so that I could empty my bladder, void my bowels, and throw up twice. I was so scared and worried, and felt so very inadequate for the task ahead. I prayed that God would somehow take this cup from me, knowing all the while that it was a job that I, and no other, had to do.

With the help of the ship's directory and crew listing it was a relatively simple job to hunt down the location of the Fitzpatricks' quarters. Even my attempts to delay by walking around aimlessly in an ignorant refusal to look at the corridor maps displayed everywhere were frustrated when a young, helpful yeoman noticed that I looked lost, asked where I was going, and kindly pointed me in the right direction. It was only a short walk and a lift ride before I found myself standing before an officer's quarters' doorway. Apparently I hadn't walked slowly enough to avoid this juncture in my life, apparently God did want me here.

I tried to believe that He knew what He was doing. I had to believe that He did.

I tried to focus my thoughts as I stood there staring blankly at the closed door. How could I approach this woman; me, the man who had killed her husband? Could I get her to see that his sacrifice had not been in vain? That he had known of this possibility and, like her, had accepted the risk as necessary to defend his beliefs? That his death had allowed many, many others to live?

Would she care, or would she simply hate me because I was alive and he was dead? I felt a yawning chasm open up in my stomach, then suddenly collapse with all the fury and power of a singularity. I was more afraid to face one woman in tears than I'd ever been to charge the enemy in combat, no matter how hopeless the situation had seemed.

I couldn't stand in the passageway forever though, no matter how much I wished to deliberate over what I would say. I prayed for this ordeal to end swiftly as I raised my hand, which I noticed was shaking not just visibly but violently, and knocked on the door, far harder than I had intended. The door wasn't latched and fell open part way at my strike. I peered through the visible opening, but could make out nothing other than a sliver of light.

"Hello?" I called out too softly. "Mrs. Fitzpatrick? May I come in?"

I waited a moment, but there was no response. I cleared my throat heavily, wiped my palms once more, and tried calling again. "Mrs. Fitzpatrick? It's

Colonel Aarons. Field Marshal Matheson asked me to come by."

Still nothing.

I pushed the door open about halfway and called yet again. Once again there was no response. Feeling very uncertain of what I should actually do, I pushed the door open all the way. Inside I could see a small living room of a size appropriate for a married pair of officers of this rank. The cozy common area had been tastefully decorated with earth tones on matching furniture and arranged in a way that made the quarters seem larger than they really were.

I probably should have left then, I had no more legal or moral right to be there, but I knew that if I fled now, however justifiable it might be, I would never be able to work up the courage to come back. Instead of standing self-consciously in the corridor or running away rapidly, I stepped inside. I moved clear of the entry and closed the door partially.

Everything was neatly made. The tan couch covering was perfectly tucked in around all three seat pads. The pillows were arranged just so, inviting any visitors to plop down, kick up their feet and make themselves comfortable. The coffee table was polished and clean, the glass almost invisible but for the light glaring off one corner.

There was not a speck of dust or dirt anywhere to be seen. I glanced at the desk in the corner. It too was immaculate, cleared of everything save two sheets of paper. I approached the desk, careful not to disturb the chair that had been pushed in under it, and perused the papers. One looked to be the official Terran Guard letter informing Mrs. Fitzpatrick of her husband's untimely death in the course of his duties. It was actually far better written than I'd expected, making the man out to be a voluntary martyr, sacrificed in the name of freedom. Nothing about being shot up by friendly fire.

The other paper seemed to be a handwritten note from General Mason expressing his deepest sorrow and regrets for her loss. This one brought a tear to my eye as it drove home the fact that this life I'd ended had belonged not just to one man, but to his family, his friends, and his comrades. With one decision and the press of a button I'd taken all of that away forever.

I was almost surprised to see that neither letter mentioned me by name, even though I knew that such a thing would violate standard procedures. For some reason I felt that my crime should be shouted from the rooftops, informing all of civilization that Chase Aarons had once again killed his own allies in pursuit of his own, probably selfish, goals, all because he, better than God or anyone else, knew what needed to be done for the good of all. I wanted to be named the butcher that I felt I was, and I wanted everyone to know of it.

Another thing surprised me. Most people who aren't as emotionally scarred as me decorate their quarters with pictures of their family and loved ones. Hanging from the walls, and standing on one shelf, were several displays of such pictures. The puzzling thing was that they only displayed the man I assumed must have been Fitzpatrick. He was a good looking guy, similar in build and face to Jonny, though he seemed to lack the quick smile that had always graced Jonny's features.

The displays on the wall all showed Fitzpatrick at his duty stations. One appeared to be a commissioning ceremony, another a shakedown, the term by which warriors refer to their first ride in a new Man O'War. The display on the shelf showed Fitzpatrick with some older people I assumed were his parents, and a few shots of him with some children, maybe his own.

I shook my head, not understanding why Mrs. Fitzpatrick would remove her own pictures. I could perhaps understand the faulty logic of removing her husband's pictures, so that she not be reminded of him and his absence, but removing her own pictures was beyond my ken.

I definitely should have left then. Obviously, no one was home, and if I was discovered it wasn't going to help the situation. First I killed the man, then I ransacked his home. Instead, I called out one more time to see if anyone was home. Of course, there was still no answer.

Puzzled, apprehensive, scared beyond belief, I approached the bedroom. As I passed the refresher I noticed that it too was immaculately groomed and tidied. Every towel hung in place, every cleansing item stored properly. Again, not a spot of dust could be seen anywhere. Apparently even in her overwhelming grief this woman was able to clean religiously, maybe even obsessively. Perhaps that was all that was keeping her sane.

I pushed the bedroom door open slightly. Through the crack I could see a perfectly made bed, and a closet opened all the way, with every single thing hanging therein arranged properly and in its place. Each sleeve was creased perfectly, each buckle and clasp shone in the light. The shoes and boots stood perfectly aligned on the racks below, also polished to perfection. I pushed the door open all the way and stepped inside, losing almost a years growth as I came face to face with Fitzpatrick's wife.

It was Rachel.

She still wore her beautiful brown hair long, framing a face that still had the flawless skin I remembered so well. That cute little nose of hers still stood at just the right angle, the one I used to tease here relentlessly about, the one that fit in perfectly with her delicate cheek structure and adorable little ears. She wore her long white dress uniform, now sporting the rank of a major, and that made her even more beautiful, as wearing a uniform had always done. On her left breast I was surprised to see a Medal of Honor, with a cluster yet. On her right she wore an Ace's ribbon with a total of eleven clusters beneath. Scores of other awards and medals decorated her uniform, covering both sides of her chest and telling me she'd been as busy and as effective as ever in the time we'd been apart.

Her figure was still perfect, long limbed and unfailingly athletic. Only the slight mound of her belly betrayed the fact that she was pregnant. Her brilliant green eyes made unblinking contact with mine, reading the very depths of my soul, just like old times. I could see that she'd been crying heavily, the puffiness and streaks still present despite her attempts to cover them up.

I stood there staring in shocked, immovable silence.

Here at long last was my Rachel. Widowed, carrying another man's child, but still my Rachel. As beautiful as the last day I'd seen her, perhaps more so for all the longing I'd had to be with her once again. My Rachel!

I loved her still, of course I did. I'd always loved her, and I'd always wanted to find her again, though I'd lacked the courage to try. I'd been trapped in my own waking nightmare and hadn't wanted to drag her into it. I couldn't count how many sleepless nights I had spent endlessly wondering about her, about how she was doing, fantasizing about one day returning to her and starting the life we were supposed to have had together. I'd missed her so terribly much all these years, and that pain had never diminished, though I'd gotten better at hiding from it.

A thousand times I had meant to just pack up and leave, go out and find her, search this whole galaxy if necessary and at least explain to her what had happened to me and why, to tell her that I loved her still and that that love would never die. A thousand times those plans had been abandoned as impossible dreams, or because I was simply too scared to try and tell her that I loved her still. Even the more realistic goals of sending her a message, of trying to contact her through her parents or the military always ended up sidetracked. Always there had been one more mission, one more important thing to do first.

Now, after six long years of hell and torture, after an uncountable number of prayers and pleas, God had heard my heart's true desire and given me one more chance to make right the one thing in my life that meant more than all others combined. In the time when I most needed support and understanding, when I was once again at my lowest and could only possibly make it through by aid of a miracle, when I needed someone to simply put their arms around me and tell me they loved me no matter what, He had done it. My Lord, my God, in his infinite wisdom, glory, and grace, had seen fit, at long last, to finally, miraculously, return Rachel to my life.

And she'd hanged herself.

Epilogue

Navanh Mental Hospital
Vientiane, Asia
Terra
Sons of Terra Control Zone

December 25, 2661

It's been over two years.

After that, nothing seemed of any importance. I don't care to remember what happened after. I'd guess that I was shuttled around to a few different places. I have brief, almost subliminal memories of needles in a ship's hospital, and what I think was a hospital on Islamabad, but that's all. I'm told that after a year the Sons of Terra agreed to allow any who were suffering, and so wished, to return to Earth and this particular facility. Not too uncivilized for a nation I'd always been taught was just one short step up from rock throwing cavemen.

I asked to go home, and this was the only home that anyone knew I'd ever really had.

It is, somehow, strangely comforting to be home again, as if I've come full circle, finally returning to that which I'd left so long ago. I'm routinely assured that this hospital is simply one of the finest facilities in the Charted Territories for dealing with mentally damaged soldiers. Even before I'd joined COTC I'd heard of Navanh and the cutting edge therapy provided there, though back then it was usually used as the butt end of jokes made at each other's expense and never discussed otherwise.

During my stay here I've seen a few other vets from Gottenheim, vets from several nations and militaries. I try not to spend any time around them, I think they all look at me with the same accusing and unforgiving eyes that I use to look at myself. They all know what I've done; what I've caused. They know the depths of the pain and suffering I've invoked, and they hold me responsible for every last part of it.

What is even worse—in so many ways worse—is that sometimes it seems that they think that I look at them the same way they look at themselves. Most of them look at their reflections with the same mix of disgust and loathing as I have when I glance in the mirror. Perhaps Krupp's way truly is better. They just shoot their broken soldiers in the head and bury the bodies in unmarked graves. A quick and painless end to a miserable and pointless existence, an end I now believe I envy.

I sent a message to Liz, but her former roommate sent me a note back saying that she had moved to Aurora with her new husband after their wedding three years ago. He was some sort of top notch computer consultant, and he moved around every couple of years. No, she hadn't stayed in touch and didn't know of any current address, sorry.

I called Jonny's family, but when a little girl with her daddy's eyes answered the phone I broke down crying and had to disconnect before I even got a single word out. She was too beautiful, too full of life and smiles for me to talk to her. My tears choked me for hours afterwards, and all I'd done was make eye contact. If her mother checked the phone log and recognized my image, or the location I'd called from, she didn't return my call. I never worked up the courage to try again.

Is this really the great adventure I once believed myself destined for? What kind of cruel joke has God played to make me believe so strongly in my own mission in life, then give me this? Has His infallible plan been served; has the grand cause of creation been advanced; has the universe been made a better place because I lived?

I doubt that very much.

I miss Jonny more than I can say. My twin brother—half of me, almost literally. He died, like so many others, not to advance the cause of righteousness, but because my own callous cruelty reached out and ended his existence. I miss everything he meant to me, his easy laugh, his concern for me, his support and faith.

Why, God? Why him and not me? I thought I did everything right, everything that made sense, everything that seemed the right thing, and yet I murdered my own twin.

Many of the patients in this hospital are missing limbs or organs. Without a second's hesitation I would trade every one of them any loss just to have

Jonny tell me he believed I could get through this one more time.

I miss Liz. I miss not knowing her, not finding out what kind of a woman she finally grew into, what kind of a husband she found, and what she thought of all of this. What happened in all those years that I was away? Why didn't I ever call her to find out?

Because I couldn't. My own weaknesses, my personal character flaws, couldn't get past my own shallow suffering and pain and reach out to anyone else.

I miss Rachel more than I can begin to say, and I killed her too, as surely as if I'd hung the noose around her neck myself. I wonder if she ever knew what happened to me, what suffering I'd gone through, and that I missed her always. Did she still know and believe that I truly had loved her? That I still do? What did she think, as she made her plans to grow old without me, raise children that weren't mine? Was I any more than a footnote in her life story? I hope that she is happy now, finally at peace. Please, God, if ever you answer one prayer, let it be that one.

I miss my mother. She really was my best friend. I miss seeing her smile and tell me she was proud. I miss having her listen to my ideas and fret over my safety.

I miss…

In the end, it seems the doctors were right. I *have* put it all in perspective and found the pattern that links everything together; I just needed a better vantage point to recognize it. I now know how this story must end. Just one more loose thread to tie off here, and then it will be finished.

It's probably not the result they expected from this exercise, but it's still a cure, nonetheless.

And when I see God, I will ask him why.

Merry Christmas, Mom, I'll see you soon.

Glossary

AAA (triple A) - anti-aircraft artillery; missile, energy and projectile weapons designed to shoot down aircraft

ACE - ammunition, casualties, equipment; a brief report on a small unit's combat status.

AGM - air-to-ground missile

AIL - anti-infantry lasers

Alting - roughly translates as 'a common assembly;' the name used by the NPJF for their cells

Arty - artillery

AO - area of operations

ASAP - as soon as possible

ASDF - Associated Stars Defense Force

AWOL - absent without leave

BLA - Banin Liberation Army; ostensibly a peaceful reformation organization, they have been growing increasingly active in violent resistance to the Protectorate government; apparently receiving heavy materiel support from a foreign nation

CCC (triple C, C^3) - command, control, and communication

CO - commanding officer

COTC - collegiate officer training corps

DZ - drop zone

E and P - evaluation and placement

ECM - electronic counter measures

Eltee - lieutenant, from the abbreviation Lt.

EMP - electro-magnetic pulse; a side effect of nuclear blasts; will disable all but the most heavily shielded electronics

ETA - estimated time of arrival

EV - extravehicular

EW - electronic warfare

FNG - (expletive) new guy

FO - forward observer

FTX - field training exercise

Furball - battle involving a large number of planes
GPA - grade point average
GPS - global positioning satellite
HEPC - high energy particle cannon
HQ - headquarters
HWS - Human Wasting Syndrome
I-tool - intrenching tool; a fancy term for a folding shovel
ID - identification
IFF - identify friend or foe; a transmission identifying the targeted unit as a friendly force to prevent so called "friendly fire" casualties
IQ - intelligence quotient
Kay/Klick - kilometer (slang); 1000 meters, or 0.629 miles
KIA - killed in action
LD/SD - look down/shoot down
LAPES - low altitude parachute extraction system; system of offloading cargo from a plane by using parachutes to pull the cargo out the rear loading doors while the plane flies just above the runway
LBE - load bearing equipment; a belt/suspenders/vest system to which a wide variety of pouches, equipment, and supplies can be attached
LZ - landing zone
Medivac - medical evacuation
MIA - missing in action
MLRS - multiple launch rocket system; fires unguided rockets as a form of artillery
NCO - non-commissioned officer
NPJF - New Popular Jarvyn Front; a terrorist organization ostensibly fighting for the liberation of all New Paris Protectorate worlds that have been seized from Jarvyn during the internecine wars of the last century; fanatical and resourceful, they appear to have sponsorship from some of the larger nations in the Charted Territories
OBT - officer basic training
OP - observation post
OPFOR - opposing force
PA - public address
PBI - poor bloody infantry
PFC - private first class
SAM - surface-to-air missile
Sit-rep - situation report

Sjambok - tough, short whip; traditionally made out of rhino leather or similar synthetic material; will easily cut through even the heaviest of protective clothing and the skin beneath

SOG - surface-to-orbit gun

SWAT - special weapons and tactics

SWOT - strengths, weaknesses, opportunities, and threats

TO&E - table of ordnance and equipment; a military unit's organizational plan

TRP - tactical reference point

XO - executive officer

Phonetic Alphabet:	Phonetic Numbers:
Alpha	One
Bravo	Two
Charlie	Tree
Delta	Four
Echo	Five
Foxtrot	Six
Golf	Seven
Hotel	Eight
India	Niner
Juliet	Zero
Kilo	
Mike	
November	
Oscar	
Papa	
Quebec	
Romeo	
Sierra	
Tango	
Uniform	
Victor	
X-ray	
Yankee	
Zulu	

Printed in the United States
1156200003B/1-21